THE NEW NATURALIST
A SURVEY OF BRITISH NATURAL HISTORY

THE WORLD OF SPIDERS

The aim of this series is to interest the general reader in the wild life of
Britain by recapturing the inquiring spirit of the old naturalists. The
Editors believe that the natural pride of the British public in the native
fauna and flora, to which must be added concern for their conservation,
is best fostered by maintaining a high standard of accuracy combined
with clarity of exposition in presenting the results of modern scientific
research. The plants and animals are described in relation to their
homes and habitats and are portrayed in the full beauty of their
natural surroundings

THE NEW NATURALIST

THE
WORLD OF
SPIDERS

by

W. S. BRISTOWE

M.A., SC.D.

WITH 14 PLATES OF PHOTOGRAPHS
4 IN COLOUR
AND DRAWINGS BY ARTHUR SMITH
COMPRISING 22 HALF TONE PLATES
AND 116 TEXT FIGURES

COLLINS
ST JAMES'S PLACE, LONDON

First published 1958
Revised Edition 1971
Reprinted 1971

TO HELEN, BELINDA
GINIE AND RICHENDA

SBN 00 213256 7
© *W. S. Bristowe, 1958*

Printed in Great Britain
Collins Clear-Type Press, London and Glasgow

CONTENTS

v

PLATES IN COLOUR

PLATES IN BLACK AND WHITE

PLATES IN BLACK AND WHITE

It should be noted that throughout this book Plate numbers in Arabic figures refer to the Colour Plates, while Roman numerals are used for Black-and-White Plates

EDITORS' PREFACE

IN 1736 it seems under one hundred and fifty British spiders were known. By the 1860s the score was just over three hundred, by 1881 over five hundred, by 1939 556 and at present about 580.

These statistical facts prove, if proof be needed, that the study of British spiders has had its major development much later than that of more popular natural history groups such as birds, butterflies and moths and flowering plants. Indeed, as W. S. Bristowe shows excellently in the interesting historical sections of this book, our science of spiders has always been the province of a small group of devoted specialists, generally, in close communication one with another. Few members of the devoted clan of spider investigators of the last hundred years have been professionally trained zoologists — and most of them have been amateurs, in the strict sense of the word. It would also appear to have been more frequent for an amateur than for a professional zoologist to make original discoveries and rise to eminence in the subject.

W. S. Bristowe is an amateur in the true tradition of British scientific natural history. Though a scientist by training he did not pursue science as a profession and he now occupies a high administrative post in Imperial Chemical Industries.

There have been, in the course of years, some learned and a few popular books on the British spiders; but in offering *The World of Spiders* we believe that the *New Naturalist* is contributing something quite new and of outstanding importance. No *New Naturalist* book sets out to become a purely systematic and identificatory guide to the plants or animals with which it deals; and in this book, Bristowe makes no attempt to duplicate, for instance, the excellent textbook on British spiders by Locket & Millidge, published by the Ray Society in 1952–53. Bristowe's book is a broad one, pursuing the British spiders generally and describing how they are related with the world around them.

We suspect that the secret of Dr. Bristowe's compelling and fluent style is his enthusiasm. We are certain that this enthusiasm will prove infectious and that *The World of Spiders* will breed a new generation of spider-watchers. We write the words 'spider-watchers' deliberately;

though Bristowe is a great collector and a great deal of our future knowledge of British spiders must rest on the fruits of collection, yet he is a master spider-watcher. Of all the redoubtable naturalists who have made the British spiders their field he is the one who has paid most attention to their behaviour.

It is from his observation of living spiders that Dr. Bristowe has been able so felicitously to describe the suitability of the basic plan of construction and behaviour of spiders for life on land. Spiders, indeed, are the only group of invertebrates, apart from insects, to have made a real success of life on land. Bristowe describes, in a masterly way, just how, in each family, the basic plan has been modified to fit its members for their various ways of life; and in the course of this description he dwells, in a most interesting and compelling manner, upon their most striking characteristics — their peculiar eyes, their elaborate courtship, the different (and often extraordinary) ways in which they construct their webs and snares. He is also at pains to mention, in interesting detail, the many superstitions that have been gathered around them.

In commending *The World of Spiders* to our New Naturalist readers we are bound to say that, in our opinion, the 232 drawings in line and wash, by Arthur Smith, must rank as some of the most beautiful and accurate pictures of spiders ever to have been published.

THE EDITORS

AUTHOR'S PREFACE

My fifty-sixth birthday is an appropriate day on which to write this preface because it just about marks my half century of spider watching. Casting my mind back to early beginnings, I remember so well my aunts and uncles — all graded in my affections according to their willingness to share my interest in watching spiders fight or feed and build their webs. Later, when I could read and had made the acquaintance of all the English books dealing with spiders I was left with a feeling of great puzzlement, because the greater experts seemed to leave off where I wanted to begin. They had described with precision the appearance of the corpses, in words often unfamiliar to me, and had left to other people the task of writing about their habits — which was accomplished with meagre observations, often in contradiction of what I felt certain I had seen myself. When I had recovered from the shock of discovering that not everything in books was true, it dawned on me that nobody in Britain had ever taken any deep interest in living spiders, and that I was already adventuring in an almost unexplored field. I began to think of myself as an expert on British spiders by the time I was seventeen, whereas now, many years later, I know myself to be little more than a student at the threshold of another world.

In my quest for understanding this other world I have often tried to imagine myself half an inch high walking through jungles of grass, as though I had drunk from the bottle labelled 'Drink Me' which caused Alice to dwindle. The first result is a series of nightmare encounters with monsters like centipedes, hunting wasps and ants, far more terrible than our crocodiles, snakes or packs of wolves. Later on, however, one can scarcely avoid being fascinated by this cruel but amazingly interesting Lilliputian world at our feet.

Discovery of the unusual and the unknown have provided the principal spur to sustain my enthusiasm through the years; and I can say with truth that, short of the major emotions, spiders have provided me with greater delight than any of my other varied interests whose frontiers they have often crossed in marriage. Thus they have enriched

xi

and been enriched by my separate pursuit of small islands, more than a hundred of which I have visited, and of mountain summits where I love to be. They have accompanied me on my incursions into sport and superstition, folklore and even antique shops from which I have emerged with many spider curios in china and bronze. When untempted by weather to roam abroad, I have sometimes arisen from examining forgotten books in libraries or even from cathedrals with additions to spider lore. Thrills of a different kind have been associated with a search for spiders themselves in places of historic interest, ranging from the gardens of Buckingham Palace to the mythical home of Odysseus on the island of Ithaca; and I confess to feelings of sentimental awe when watching spiders in the Garden of Gethsemane or in the cave on Patmos where St. John wrote his Epistles.

It is unfortunate that spiders should have a prominent long-legged ambassador who creates prejudice against his race by invading the privacy of our bathrooms, because he makes it harder for me to convince people who already accept the wonders of bee and ant life that spiders are even more worthy of admiration. Bees and ants have had the advantage of skilful chroniclers — how I wish I could match their art of description. In my attempt to convey some of my pleasures and excitements to others I have had to avoid compiling an anthology and to make this book a personal one in which my own gleanings absorb most of the space.

Intimacy with our British species is not helped by the absence of familiar English names. The principal task I have set myself is to write about spiders in general, and of the particular ways of some species belonging to each of our twenty-four families. All our known species are listed in an appendix; but those who seek means of identifying them must consult the excellent book called *British Spiders* written by my friends G. H. Locket and A. F. Millidge (1951–3).

The finding of words to describe the habits of spiders, their senses and mental processes, without implying similarity to our own, is always a difficulty. Remarks on instinct and intelligence in chapter 19 on 'The Orb Web Builders' will show where I stand in fundamental belief and, if I depart from this in my choice of words elsewhere in the book, I have done so in order to avoid the dulling effect of circumlocutions. How easy it is to fall from grace can be illustrated by a past error to which my friend, T. Savory (1935), called attention:

"Some biologists", he wrote, "confidently endow the animals

observed by them with conative or with emotional or with conscious states for which there is no justification. For example, Bristowe writes of a spider [*Ciniflo*] attracted to a vibrating tuning fork — 'The owner of the web immediately rushed forth, and with considerable excitement seized upon the fork and walked up it, biting it continually and trying to find a tender spot.' . . . It may be said in defence that the writer means only that the spider behaved *as if* it were excitedly seeking a tender spot; to which the obvious reply is that, since words have meanings, it is well to choose those which express what the writer wishes to convey."

My affection for Savory was increased by a postcard from him bearing the one word 'touché' after I had gently called his attention to the gross indecency of a seemingly perverted spider which he accused of being a 'flower-lover' in one of his books !

It is not my intention to dwell on the difficulties which beset a writer, and particularly one who has only his limited spare time in which to watch, think and write about spiders; so I should like to conclude by paying a special tribute to my artist, Mr. Arthur Smith. At our first meeting he ended the afternoon standing on a chair perched on a table with a torch under one armpit whilst he busied himself with pencil and paper sketching a *Pholcus* on the ceiling. His enthusiasm has never waned; and I shall always remember him slowly sinking deeper and deeper into a New Forest bog as he made drawings of the *Dolomedes* poses which are included in this book. Apart from his skill as an artist, his keen perception has led to interesting discoveries which I had overlooked, including the use of the third leg by the water spider in entrapping an air-bubble, and the precise postures adopted by the male *Pisaura* during courtship.

For photographs I am indebted to the kindness and cooperation of J. Markham, J. Sankey, W. H. T. Tams, Walter Murray, E. A. Robins, W. H. Spreadbury, H. J. Sargent, B. C. Hardman, S. M. Ballance and J. Clegg.

My only contribution to the illustrations is fig. 103 which had previously appeared in *The Comity of Spiders*. I have to thank the Ray Society for permission to reprint this and to the editors of *Endeavour* for allowing me to reproduce figs. 45 and 48.

W. S. B.

ADDENDUM

DURING the eleven years which have elapsed since *The World of Spiders* was published the vigorous and excellent work of such specialists as G. H. Locket, A. F. Millidge, J. A. L. Cooke, E. Duffey, P. Merrett, J. R. Parker, D. J. Clark, A. A. D. La Touche, A. M. Wilde and others has added species to the British list and considerably to the knowledge of county distribution. Work at home and abroad has also revealed synonyms and necessary changes in nomenclature.

A need to reprint the book without revising the text, save for a few minor corrections, has caused the publishers to seek a brief addendum.

On page 14 reference is made to Eleazar Albin's book on spiders published in 1736. In two papers (*Entomologist's Gazette*, April and October 1967) I have tried to make amends for the complete omission of references to a forgotten naturalist, famous in his day, called Joseph Dandridge (1664-1747) whose manuscript notes and paintings in the British Museum (Sloane 3999) prove complete plagiarism of both by Albin. Dandridge never published anything himself but for the last quarter of a century of his life he was our leading all-round British naturalist.

One particularly interesting development in the past ten years is the discovery that some of the Surrey heaths shelter rarities previously known only from the New Forest or Dorset like *Oxyopes heterophthalmus* Latr. and *Tarentula fabrilis* (Clerck). Another rarity, *Dictyna viridissima* (Walck.) is turning up in several places in or not far from London including Buckingham Palace garden and the compound beside the British Museum (Natural History).

Many names are undergoing change but the time is not ripe to introduce them all. It seems inevitable that *Pardosa* will replace *Lycosa* and that some *Tarentula* species will become *Lycosa*. *Ciniflo* is likely to revert to *Amaurobius* and *Amaurobius* to *Coelotes*. Our common House Spider, *Tegenaria atrica* C.L.K., will probably be altered to *T. saeva* Blackwall.

Work by various authorities has revealed several synonyms making the following changes necessary:

Heliophanus expers O.P.-Camb. to *H. melinus* L. Koch.
Silometopus interjecta (O.P.-Camb.) to *S. reussi* (Thor).
Silometopus curtus (Sim.) to *S. ambiguus* (O.P.-Camb.)
Cornicularia karpinskii (O.P.-Camb.) to *C. clavicornis* Emerton.
Entelecara errata (O.P.-Camb.) to *E. media* Kulcz.
Mecopisthes pusillus (Menge) to *M. silus* (O.P.-Camb.)
Diplocephalus adjacens O.P.-Camb. to *D. connatus* Bertkau.
Gongylidiellum calcariferum (Sim.) is moved to the genus *Wiehlea* and various species of *Lophocarenum* to the genus *Pelecopsis*. Cooke has recently shown that our *Lophocarenum nemorale* Bl. should be called *Pelecopsis mediocris* Kulcz. and that our *L. stramineum* (Menge) is a new species, *P. locketi* Cooke.

We must brace ourselves for many more changes before long, however aggravating this may be. Excellent studies by P. Merrett on Linyphiid epigynes has corrected earlier ideas of relationships between species and this will entail the regrouping of some species into fresh genera. Work on the Theridiidae by Dr. Levi in America will shortly necessitate changes in our genera within that family. Apart from this a comparison of specimens often shows that the same species has been described under two or more names, in which case the earliest name should, in my opinion, always be adopted out of loyalty to the original author and no plea of convenience and common usage should prevail where identification is certain. In other cases identification of the 'type' is uncertain and this leads to differences of opinion which should be resolved by the International Commission of Zoological Nomenclature once and for all.

Species new to science or to the British list discovered since *The World of Spiders* was printed in 1958 include the following:

Clubionidae
  Clubiona similis L. Koch.   J. F. Peake. Norfolk.
Salticidae
  Salticus mutabilis Lucas. Dorset.
  Epiblemum affinatum O.P.-Camb. D. J. Clark discovered this in O. Pickard-Cambridge's collection labelled *Salticus zebraneus* C.L.K.

Heliophanus auratus C. L. Koch   J. A. L. Cooke. Essex.
Theridiidae
   Achaearanea veruculata (Urquhart) A New Zealand species in the
                                          Scilly Isles.   P. Merrett and Miss Rowe.
Linyphiidae
   Gonatium corallipes (O.P.-Camb.) G. H. Locket and A. F. Millidge.
                                          Kent.
   Centromerus albidus E. Sim. G. H. Locket and A. F. Millidge.
   Centromerus parkeri Cooke.   J. A. L. Cooke. Scotland.
   Centromerus tantalus Parker.   C. Parker and J. A. L. Cooke.
                                          Warwickshire.
   Wideria stylifrons (O.P.-Camb.)   E. Duffey. Norfolk.
   Lessertiella saxetorum Hull.   J. A. L. Cooke and P. Merrett.
                                          Allendale.
   Lasiargus gowerensis Locket.   G. H. Locket. S. Wales.
   Trichopterna cito (O.P.-Camb.)   G. H. Locket, A. F. Millidge
                                          and A. A. D. La Touche. Sussex.
   Typhocrestus simoni Lessert.   J. A. L. Cooke. N. Wales.
   Carorita limnea (Crosby and Bishop)   E. Duffey and P. Merrett.
                                          Cheshire.
   Trichoncus hackmani Millidge.   J. A. L. Cooke. Essex.
   Rhaebothorax paetulus (O.P.-Camb.) J. A. L. Cooke. Scotland.
   Meioneta simplicitarsis (Simon)   G. H. Locket and A. F. Millidge.
                                          Dorset, Surrey, Hants.
   Trematocephalus cristatus (Wid)   P. Merrett. Surrey.
   Maro lepidus Casemir.   C. Parker. Yorkshire.
   Erigone psychrophila Thor.   J. A. L. Cooke. Scotland.

Apart from these 21 additions, G. H. Locket has described a subspecies, *Dicymbium nigrum brevisetosum*, and Mrs. J. O. I. Spoczynska
has collected several specimens of an American species, *Coleosoma
floridanum* Banks (Theridiidae) in a hot-house at Kew.

July, 1968.   W. S. B.

CHAPTER I

SPIDERS IN LITERATURE
& SUPERSTITION

S PIDERS may be liked or disliked but nowhere are they ignored. Indeed they might be called the Jekylls and Hydes of the animal world, so deeply and in such different ways have their individualities impressed themselves on man. The fantasies of folklore, in which animals act and think like man himself, combine to portray the fox as a cunning rascal and the owl as the possessor of great wisdom: but the spider emerges as a far more complex being. Sometimes she is the admired heroine deserving of reverence, at times the recipient of men's souls after death, and at other times the villain who induces fear, abhorrence and sinister forebodings. The contrasting parts she plays in folk-tales, in nursery rhymes and even in our imaginations today, can be traced back to the admiration inspired by the superb beauty and effective skill of her weaving and to fear instilled by her venom or cunning cruelty and general creepiness—especially at night.

Outside the realms of folk-tales it must also be noted that man in various stages of cultural development has believed spiders to have some practical uses in ridding him of noxious insects, in being able to foretell and even influence the weather, and in possessing medicinal properties, all of which have added to his respect for them.

The really remarkable feature of all these diverse thoughts and beliefs, of multiple origin throughout the world, is that in every continent and in nearly every country they seem to have yielded one common idea—that it is unlucky or unwise for man to kill a spider unnecessarily.

The evolution of this *protective mythology* starts with thoughts and beliefs such as I have mentioned, and leads to the sparing of spiders' lives by Europeans and Mohammedans, by the Hausa tribes of West Africa who make them folk-tale heroes on account of their superior wisdom, by the Bhils and Mats of India who worship them as the recipients of ancestral spirits, by the Chibchas of Central America because rafts of spiders' webs are needed by dead souls to cross a river on the way to the centre of the earth, and by the Teton Indians of North America lest they are avenged by the spiders that they fear.* Should a Teton Indian chance to kill a spider he says "O, Grandfather Spider the Thunder-Beings killed you", so that its spirit will tell the other spiders that the Thunder-Beings were responsible for its death.

Our poets such as Chaucer, Spenser, Coleridge, Shakespeare, Shelley, Southey, Dryden, Thomson, Henry More, Blackmore, Tennyson, Empson and others have all noticed spiders; but they are divided in their emphasis on the Jekyll and Hyde element in the spider's individuality.

> The window . . . . where gloomily retir'd,
> the villain lives cunning and fierce, mixture abhorr'd.

Here Thomson (1727–1746) imputes cunning and ferocity, whilst Shakespeare in the *Merchant of Venice* emphasises their sinister machinations:

> Here in her haires the Painter plaies the spider,
> and hath woven a golden mesh t'intrap the hearts of men.

The old Anglo-Saxon name of attercop for a spider, which survived in Forfar and Lancashire within living memory (like the Danish word eddercop), meant 'poison-head'; and the exaggerated poisonous properties of spiders frequently appear in literature. The English proverb quoted by Bishop Latimer as "Where the bee gathereth honey, even there the spinner gathereth venome", is reflected by Wyatt (1538–1603) in the following verse:

> Nature, that gave the bee so feate a grace
> To finde hony of so wondrous fashion,
> Hath taught the Spider out of the same place
> To fetch Poyson by strange alteracion.

These and other unfavourable references can be balanced by others displaying admiration and affection. The name 'spider' in itself signifies recognition of her skill as a spinner; whilst the gaelic name of Mamhan allaidh used in Ireland and Scotland has the pleasant meaning of a

* For sources of information, see Bristowe (1945).

little wild deer. Companionship is claimed in the *Anthologia Borealis et Australis:*

> *In this wild, groping, dank, and drearie cove,*
> *Of wife, of children, and of health bereft,*
> *I hailed thee, friendly, spider! who hadst wove*
> *Thy mazy net on yonder mouldering raft;*
> *Would that the cleanlie housemaid's foot had left*
> *Thee tarrying here, nor took thy life away;*
> *For thou, from out this seare old ceiling's cleft*
> *Came down each morn to hede my plaintive lay,*
> *Joying, like me, to heare sweete musick play,*
> *Wherewith I'd fain beguile the dull, dark, lingering day.*

References to spiders' love of music are frequent: but I am afraid it is 'cupboard love'. A tuning fork touching a spider's threads can cause excitement similar to that of the vibrations set up by a bluebottle in the web of an *Araneus* or a *Ciniflo;* and a violinist can bring about the same response.

The Miss Muffet of our nursery rhyme, whom I have revealed as Patience, daughter of the celebrated naturalist Dr. Thomas Muffet (1553–1604), showed her feelings for a spider when she fled from a large one which "Sat down beside her" despite, or more probably because of, her upbringing in rooms where her father said the House Spider "doth beautifie them with her tapestry and hangings", and where he dosed her with spiders to cure many ailments. Incidentally I notice that a modern "Miss Muffet" met with no sympathy from Judge Carey Evans at Norwich in February 1948 when he ruled that a spider or two on the bedroom ceiling was no reason for walking out of the hotel without paying her bill.

Literature contains references to many people besides Dr. Muffet who genuinely admired and liked the companionship of spiders—not to mention his friend "a great Lady yet living who will not leave off eating them"; and I can give three quaint examples from my personal experience, in each of which the powers of spiders to influence man's destiny led to a respectful association. The first was of a gambler whom I met in Monte Carlo in 1924. He carried a glass-topped box, half red and half black, in which a spider was shaken to decide on which colour his money should be staked. The second was of a famous London tattooist who told me in 1935 that he had been employed on several occasions to tattoo a small lucky spider on the backs of young women.

The third was of a burglar with whom I came in contact in 1933. He had had several small spiders tattooed on his forehead in the belief that they would bring him success in his profession.

Most people, myself included, hate large House Spiders (*Tegenaria*) in their homes but welcome tiny Money Spiders (*Linyphiidae*) on their clothes in the country. 'Twice a week', writes a correspondent in the *Daily Express* (1956), 'I call on an old lady (in Worthing) and thoroughly search her house for spiders. If I find any, I have to pick them up without harming them and deposit them in a field, some distance from her house. I am paid five shillings a visit'. I am convinced by many enquiries that the majority of country-dwellers in Britain would avoid killing even the large spiders they detest, and that some people still throw the Money Spider gently over the left shoulder or even dangle it on a thread three times round their heads. Neither they, nor my gambler, tattooist or burglar acquaintances, can do much more than speak of the gifts which a Money Spider's presence betokens, or the ill-luck which the killing of a spider will bring. Sometimes they are able to quote the old rhyme which is widespread in the United States as well as in Britain where it originated:

> *If you wish to live and thrive*
> *Let a spider run alive.*

Did this threat or promise arise from a belief in the usefulness of spiders or from some folk-tale ? I have searched far and wide both at home and abroad for an explanation and will start by speaking of the beliefs in the usefulness of spiders.

In South Wales and bordering English counties I have heard that spiders should be cherished in houses because of the good luck they bring. This could have arisen from the knowledge that they killed insects, and is interesting to compare with the information I collected in India, Malaya and Brazil that a large Crab Spider (*Heteropoda*) is left undisturbed because it kills cockroaches. In this sense a rhyme has often been quoted to me in the northern counties of England:

> *Kill a spider, bad luck yours will be*
> *Until of flies you've swatted fifty-three.*

Southey's way of saying this in his poem on 'The Spider' is as follows:

Spider thou need'st not run in fear about
To shun my curious eyes,
I won't humanely crush thy bowels out,
Lest thou should'st eat the flies.

Some tolerance is indicated here on account of their use in killing insects. We meet with it again when we come to the use of spiders and their webs for medicinal purposes.

One of Ben Johnson's characters says he "sweeps no cobwebs here, but sells 'em for cut fingers" and Shakespeare, in *A Midsummer Night's Dream*, makes Bottom say, "I shall desire you of more acquaintance good master cobweb. If I cut my finger I shall make bold of you". These quotations introduce us to the use of spiders' webs in staunching the flow of blood, which was advocated as early as the first century A.D. by Dioscorides. The use of web for this purpose was widespread in Britain and elsewhere in Europe during past centuries and friends tell me that it still lingers on in country districts in Cheshire, Hampshire, Hertfordshire and Sussex as well as in Italy and elsewhere on the Continent. The staunching effect is due to physical and not chemical properties.

Eleazar Albin (1736) seems to have introduced an unusual refinement when he beat web up with frogs' spawn and allowed the mixture to dry on a pewter plate before applying it; and, he says, "with this remedy I saved a gentleman of worth in Lincoln Inn Fields who had bled at the nose several hours, when all applications failed which were used by two eminent surgeons".

The belief that spiders in a bag or nutshell hung round the neck would ward off or cure fevers and other diseases was current in the days of Dioscorides and Pliny, and was upheld fifteen centuries later by such sages as Matthiolus and Aldrovandus. Some doctors thought that the fever was drawn out of the patient; and in the seventeenth century, when lapidaries were fashionable, even spurious spider stones alleged to have been extracted from the sacred bodies of the Diadem or Garden Spider were put on the market.

As a next step to amulets, perhaps, the temptation arose to swallow the charm so as to gain the concentrated benefits infused by the spider's body. Anyhow, from the sixteenth century onwards I have found dozens of references to spiders being swallowed by those suffering from fevers, and the practice, though on the wane, continued in Britain until malaria itself was stamped out in the nineteenth century. The species generally recommended was a House Spider (*Tegenaria*). Dr. Mead, quoted by Sarah Harrison (1764) had the following prescription:

"Take a spider alive, cover it with the new soft crummy Bread without bruising it; let the Patient swallow it fasting. This is an effectual cure, but many are set against it."

Dr. Watson (1760) was not so fussy about the bruising and paid a little more attention to disguising the nature of his medicine:

"A spider gently bruised and wrapped up in a raisin or spread upon bread and butter."

His patients who benefited where Cinchona had failed included sixty fever-stricken prisoners in the Isle of Man.

Dr. Muffet seems to have regarded spiders as a household remedy for most ills. In particular he wrote "for the most part I find those people to be free from Gowt of hands or feet in whose houses the spiders breed much". If his readers or patients agreed with him, and if they thought spiders had the power to ward off fevers or provide a cure for most ills, it is not improbable that they hesitated before ridding their homes of them.

Coming now to the belief that spiders can foretell the weather, we find that this was current in Pliny's day and still survives in Europe and America amongst some farmers and mariners. "Spynners ben tokens of divynation, and of knowing what weather shall fal" says one old writer, but I am inclined to agree with H. McCook that the "prognostication is after the facts instead of before them". It has to be admitted, however, that the subject has never been thoroughly tested.

Omens of good weather include an orb-weaver in the centre of its web, the appearance of a sheet-builder at the mouth of her retreat, the building of orb-webs immediately after rain has stopped, and the descent of gossamer on fields or ships at sea. The approach of a severe spell was said to be foretold by the entry into houses of spiders from outside and a shortening of the orb-weavers' lines.

The Linyphiid spiders chiefly responsible for gossamer spin their threads for the most part on sunny autumnal mornings following a cool night and are wafted upwards on the rising air currents which these conditions provide. Thus gossamer can rightly be associated with fine weather in autumn and early winter. The earliest known reference to the gossamer flecks is made by Pliny when he wrote "in the year that L. Paulus and C. Marcellus were consuls it rained wool", but one has to go back no further than three centuries to find that gossamer puzzled the minds of countrymen, poets, and even scientists in Britain. Chaucer wrote:

> *Sore wondren some on cause of thonder,*
> *On ebb and floud, on gossomer, and on mist.*

Thomson spoke of gossamer as "filmy threads of dew evaporate" and Quarles wrote:

> *And now autumnal dews are seen*
> *To cobweb every green.*

Spenser described "a vele of silk and silver thin", than which

> *More subtle web Arachne cannot spin,*
> *Nor the fine nets which oft we woven see*
> *Of scorched deaw do not in th'ayre more lightly flee;*

The belief linking gossamer, weather and dew is clearly shown in these quotations but one is nevertheless amazed to find that so celebrated a scientist as Robert Hooke made the suggestion to the Royal Society in 1664 that it "is not unlikely that those great white clouds which appear all the summertime may be of the same substance" as gossamer.

Dr. Hooke's ideas help to make sense of the nursery rhyme which describes the old woman who was tossed up in a basket:

> *"Old woman, old woman, old woman" said I,*
> *"Oh whither, oh whither, oh whither so high ?*
> *To sweep the cobwebs out of the sky"*

Perhaps we ought not to feel too smug at our greater enlightenment today when we recall that both in the 1914–18 and the 1939–45 wars floating gossamer flecks gave rise to scares of some new form of chemical warfare, even supported in 1941 by the alleged evidence of a Kentish golfer's blistered wrists ! My advice to the War Office was to cancel warning circulars issued to the Observer Corps.

In contrast to Pliny's description of gossamer flecks as wool we find that English countrymen sometimes used to refer to the flecks as 'feathers'. These 'feathers' looked not unlike goose-down; they were seen only on fine days and frequently during the fine spell in November known as St. Martin's Summer when a goose festival was held. The origin of the word gossamer has given rise to much dispute and at least nine different explanations have been put forward. I prefer 'Goose-summer' because of the combination of the 'feathers', fine weather spell and season for geese. Goose was sometimes spelt 'gose' and 'goss' and summer also occurs as 'sumer' and 'somer' so the gap between 'goose-summer' and 'gossamer' is easily bridged (Bristowe, 1945).

Be that as it may, the association of spiders with the weather and the belief that they could even influence weather was given as a reason why spiders should not be killed lest bad weather should result.

Local events have sometimes left their mark, as in the story of Robert Bruce and the persistent spider which inspired him to rally his courage and his men in one more attempt to defeat the English which proved successful. The actual cave in which he watched the spider is in doubt, but in one reputed to be his in Arran I watched with interest the faltering footsteps of *Zygiella x-notata* on the roof at the cave mouth. This species builds her orb-webs across the windows of millions of Englishmen's windows and if this were to remind us of the discomfiture she caused our ancestors many years ago, we may console ourselves by reflecting that she now obliges us by trapping numerous flies intent on entering our homes.

It is said that the story of Bruce's spider has influenced Scotsmen not to kill spiders.

An older legend which is interwoven into the folk-lore of many countries is of a local hero who escaped his pursuers through a spider building her web across the mouth of his hiding place: this persuaded his pursuers that no one could be concealed beyond it. According to the Jews, it was David who escaped from Saul in this way. In Mohammedan countries it was Mohammed who avoided the Coreishites through a spider spinning her web across the mouth of his cave. In Italy St. Felix of Nola and in Japan a twelfth century hero named Yoritomo escaped in a similar manner. In Bulgaria and in Cornwall the story is told of Christ being saved from Herod. The details with which the stories are embroidered make it clear that all have a common origin and, as it is best known to Mohammedans wherever they live (including such outlying areas as Siam and Java where the story was repeated to me), it is probable that it originated with them.

The story is probably a folk-tale inspired by admiration for the spinning powers of a spider but it is interesting to hear that a similar incident occurred in England in the nineteenth century when, according to the late Dr. A. R. Jackson, the police failed to break down a locked door behind which a fugitive murderer was hiding because a spider's web in the keyhole convinced them that the lock had not been used for a considerable time.

This widespread folk tale of the hero saved from his pursuers has had little or no influence in Britain but has been cited to me personally as well as in literature as the reason why Mohammedans should never kill a spider.

The story of Arachne, the Grecian maiden, who was changed into a spider for daring to challenge the Goddess of Wisdom to a spinning contest and doomed to spin and weave for ever afterwards has, however, had a profound effect in Europe and elsewhere. Long after the story had been forgotten the superstition persisted, like a flower without stem or roots, that a spider found running over one's clothes had come to spin new ones. This superstition has often been recorded, both in Europe and America, but once the idea had become divorced from its context it was natural that variations would occur. In Maryland it used to be said "If you kill a spider upon your clothing you destroy the presents it is weaving for you". It is no large step from new clothes to a present, a legacy, money, good fortune or even the arrival of a stranger which might portend good fortune or a gift. All these variations are known but I have been unable to trace that relating to money before the seventeenth century.

The 'Money Spinner' or 'Money Spider' is identified in the Oxford Dictionary as our Zebra Spider (*Salticus scenicus*) but this is quite out of keeping with present ideas and inappropriate because it spins no snare. Nowadays opinions are divided between small scarlet mites and small shiny-bodied black Linyphiid spiders: as the mites are neither spiders nor spinners of silk the palm must be handed to the small black Linyphiidae whose claims are strengthened by the silver canopies with which they cloak our fields in autumn. This 'smother of spiders', as I have called it elsewhere, is a striking sight which gave rise to the idea of silver being manufactured by these spiders.

Although the Money Spider is said to bring money or some other gift, it is widely supposed in Britain to be unlucky to kill any spider and this I ascribe with little doubt mainly to the Arachne myth which taught our ancestors to expect good fortune of some kind from this industrious and skilful maiden who had been transformed into spider shape.

With spiders in general being regarded as lucky, it is not surprising to learn that in some parts of England the appearance of a spider in the path of the bride or bridegroom on their way to church was heralded as a sign of future happiness and prosperity. Hindus in eastern Bengal think much the same of a particular spider (*Marpissa melanocephala*) if it has a fly in its mouth, so they collect a supply to release at the wedding. In Egypt nothing is left to chance: there I learned that it is a common practice to place a spider in the bed of a married couple on their wedding night!

How remarkable it seems that superstitions should be so carefully observed in civilised countries, but let us remember that we are brought up on fairy stories as children and that the premium we pay for an outside chance of some rich reward is negligible.

FIG. 1. The earliest known drawing of a spider and flies by a prehistoric artist on a cave wall in Gasulla Gorge, Castellón

CHAPTER 2

THE DISCOVERY
OF BRITISH SPIDERS

ONE SPIDER (*Lycosa pullata*) saves Wigtown from being the only
county in England, Wales, Scotland and Ireland from which
none has been recorded. At the other extreme we have Hampshire
and Dorset with over four hundred species known to inhabit them.
I myself believe that knowledge of our species and their distribution
rivals that of any other country in the world and this despite the fact
that practically all this knowledge has been accumulated by the work
of a series of clergymen, schoolmasters, doctors and businessmen in
their spare time.

Although this book is filled so largely with my own personal observations, I am fully conscious of my dependence on the work of earlier
and contemporary writers for basic knowledge which it is easy to take
for granted, so I should like to pay greater tribute to them than merely
to list their papers in a bibliography. As this is a book on British Spiders,
I confine myself to tracing the growth in knowledge of our own spider
fauna by speaking about the men who have contributed most to this,
although I also owe much to such great contemporaries and personal
friends abroad as P. Bonnet, A. Petrunkevitch, L. Berland, J. Millot,
W. J. Gertsch, B. J. Kaston, H. Wiehle, H. Peters, the late U. Gerhardt,
the late E. Neilsen and Jocelyn Crane.

If we start in the sixteenth or early seventeenth century, we can
scarcely fail to think it remarkable how scholars like Dr. T. Muffet
and the Rev. E. Topsel preferred the influence of tradition and superstition to the evidence of their own eyes and accepted freely the fantastic
statements of Gesner or even of the Ancients like Aristotle and Pliny.
The manuscript of Muffet's 'Theatrum Insectorum' preserved in the
British Museum was completed in 1589 and this has a small copper-
plate engraving of its author on the title page which conveys an
impression of a pleasant man with a sense of humour which is fleetingly

reflected in his literary style. His original drawings are in colour which make identification of *Araneus cucurbitinus, A. diadematus, A. quadratus* and *A. marmoreus pyramidatus* etc. far easier than in the published work.

After graduating in 1572 at the age of nineteen, he moved from Trinity, Cambridge, to Caius where he occupied rooms beside those in which I lived exactly three hundred and fifty years later. Although he taught me nothing except the entertaining errors of his time and the discipline of not smoking for nearly a year whilst I paid for his book, I am grateful to him for disclosing to me the probable identity of the Miss Muffet of nursery rhyme fame. My reasoning is along the following lines: 'tuffet' is an unusual word, therefore it was introduced to rhyme with Muffet; Dr. Thomas Muffet is the only Muffet of sufficient fame to be included in the Dictionary of National Biography; he was an ardent admirer of spiders; he had only one daughter, named Patience, who might well be expected to have grown up with a horror of spiders because he prescribed them as pills and ointments in the treatment of most ailments. Unlike Dr. Muffet I do not bow to authority (in this case to I. and P. Opie, 1951) which rejects my conclusion, without suggesting another, on the slender grounds that the rhyme is unknown in print earlier than 1805 and that there were *later* imitations in which other names were substituted for Muffet. Only in 1955 did my friend, Mrs. Campbell of Canna, record in print for the first time the words and music of Hebridean songs which are believed to be thousands of years old. As for later substitutions, many a friend or enemy has been lampooned by substituting his name for that of another in rhymes or poems.

There is neither science nor reliable natural history before the time of Dr. Martin Lister. His 'Historiae Animalium Angliae' contains a tract with illustrations of thirty-four different but unnamed species of spider, and in it he says 'I do not want anyone to think that I have described absolutely all the species but I make bold to say that no one can find casually in this country any new species not described by me'. I forgive him for this classic overstatement because of his beautiful simplicity of wording on a tablet in the cloisters of Westminster Abbey which I had admired for many years before associating it with him: 'Jane Lister dear childe died October 7th, 1688'. Neither Jane nor her brother Michael, on the same tablet, are listed with his other children in the Dictionary of National Biography but the burial records confirm their parentage.

During Martin Lister's time there were some interesting developments which did not seem to influence him or later araneologists for many years to come. The Minutes of the Royal Society for April 29th, 1663 refer to a drawing of a six-eyed spider by the versatile Dr. Robert Hooke. This is the earliest record of a spider drawn under a microscope, but the exciting possibility exists that Sir Christopher Wren made earlier drawings which may be lying unrecognised in some museum or library. Wren 'was the first Inventor of drawing Pictures by Microscopical Glasses', according to T. Sprat (1667) and Hooke himself admits to 'coming after Dr. Wren'.

Wren's drawings of invertebrates attracted great attention at the Royal Society and on May 17th, 1661, Sir Robert Moray wrote that 'The King has commanded to . . . Charge upon you in his Name . . . to delineate by the Help of the Microscope the Figures of all the Insects, and small living creatures you can light upon, as you have done those you have presented to His Majesty' (see M. E. Power, 1945). Wren soon wearied of this task and arranged for Hooke to satisfy Charles II's demands.

Later it was announced (H. Power, 1664) that Wren and Hooke would write a book together in which their illustrations would appear, but ultimately Wren left Hooke to complete this task. Bearing in mind the friendship of these two men, the original plan for joint authorship, the knowledge that Wren had made several drawings, and the existence of two distinct styles of drawing reproduced in the 'Micrographia', it seems highly probable that several of the drawings were made by Wren. Several of Hooke's drawings can be identified from the Minutes of the Royal Society where he used to display them. Those believed to be by Wren were completed in a much bolder style and included a Harvestman and a Louse. Surely we get confirmation for this belief from the reply by John Harrington to an attack by Mathew Wren (Sir Christopher's cousin) on his political Utopia in 1659. Sneeringly Harrington referred to Mathew Wren as 'one of those virtuosi who had an excellent facility of magnifying a louse and diminishing a commonwealth', thereby associating him with his cousin whose drawings had attracted such wide attention (M. E. Power, 1945).

For my part, I would rather discover a Wren drawing of a spider than a spider new to Britain; but my searches at Windsor, the British Museum, the Natural History Museum and the Royal Society have not brought to light any of his invertebrate drawings. Although we cannot be sure that he drew a spider, we can feel certain that his pioneer work and his influence on Hooke in the same art combined to influence

others to make more careful examination of the anatomy of invertebrates.

Although spiders formed the subject of two books during the
eighteenth century there are no grounds for pride in our scientific
advancement during this period. Eleazar Albin figured about a
hundred and fifty spiders — several of them colour forms of the same
species — in his book entitled 'A Natural History of Spiders and Other
Curious Insects' (1736), but he does not attempt to describe or name
them. This was followed in 1793 by Thomas Martyn's 'Aranei or a
Natural History of Spiders' with better illustrations but with the same
defects although, strangely enough, he appends a translation of Clerck's
excellent pioneer work on Swedish spiders published in 1757 with the
binomial system of nomenclature employed for the first time.

It is not until we come to the article on spiders in the 1816 edition
of the Encyclopoaedia Britannica by the twenty-six year old Dr. W. E.
Leach that we gain an impression of a scientific study of our fauna
with careful identifications, descriptions and thoughts about relationships. In this article he mentions about thirty species to illustrate the
scheme of classification he adopts. These include such rare and locally
distributed species as *Atypus affinis*, *Segestria florentina*, *Scytodes thoracica*,
Eresus niger and *Myrmarachne formicarius*, none of which had been recorded in Britain before. Here we had a man of great promise making
important contributions over a wide field of zoology so it was a tragedy
when he was forced by mental illness to give up his work at the British
Museum at the early age of thirty-one. We had to wait a hundred and
twenty-eight years before another member of the British Museum staff,
Mr. E. Browning, added a spider to the British list.

Although so little work depicting or classifying British spiders found
its way into the literature before the time of Leach, we may suppose
that amateur naturalists could recognise many species without being
able to name them. I have found, for instance, in the British Museum
(Great Russell Street) an extensive album of beautiful insect and spider
paintings made by a Miss Kemp of Reading between 1807 and 1816.
Amongst these we can recognise nearly twenty species, including *A.
marmoreus pyramidatus*, whose appearance in all the older books suggests
greater abundance then than now, before swampy ground had been
drained so extensively.

In the course of his mission to convert the Irish, St. Patrick is
credited with having destroyed all vermin and it used to be said that
this included spiders:

Happy Ierne, whose most wholesome air
Poisons envenomed spiders, and forbids
The baleful toad and viper from her shore.

Spiders were also thought to be affected by Irish timber and Irish earth. Meredith Hanmer tells us in 1633 that William Rufus imported oak frames from Dublin in 1095 for the roof of Westminster Hall 'where no English spider webbeth or breedeth to this day'. And we learn from Sprat's History of the Royal Society of an experiment in the seventeenth century 'of a Spider not being inchanted by a Circle of Unicorn's horn, or Irish Earth, laid about it'.

The myth of Ireland's freedom from spiders could not be sustained after 1834 when Dr. R. T. Templeton published a paper giving excellent descriptions of some spiders from Belfast with the best anatomical illustrations which had been published up to that date. He founded the genera *Oonops* and *Harpactes*.* This paper was followed by a manuscript book on the 'Arachnida of the North of Ireland' containing descriptions of forty-three species largely grouped in new genera but, after prolonged delays, this manuscript was rejected in favour of the more comprehensive work in preparation by John Blackwall who had also started to publish papers in the eighteen thirties. At first it was planned that these two pioneers should write a book jointly but, perhaps because of Blackwall's predominant share of the work, Blackwall's 'History of the Spiders of Great Britain and Ireland' ultimately appeared in 1861–4. This included some of Templeton's drawings and descriptions but did not adopt his proposed genera which, by modern standards, may well have been justified and might have survived.

This comment on Blackwall's caution is the nearest approach to criticism I can allow myself to make. Blackwall's book was superb with good descriptions of 304 species and illustrations in colour of unsurpassed beauty and accuracy. A great many of his species were new to science at the time the manuscript was completed but a delay of ten years before publication allowed continental workers to gain priority for specific names they had given to several of these new species during that period.

R. H. Meade of Bradford was a friend of Blackwall who should be remembered less for his minor contributions to spider knowledge than

---

* The international laws of nomenclature do not allow a bird and a spider both to bear the same name. Ornithologists had priority by a matter of months, so I changed *Harpactes* to *Harpactea* (Bristowe, 1939).

for his part in arousing in Blackwall's successor, the Rev. O. Pickard-Cambridge, an interest in spiders and in introducing these two great men to each other. These were acts of incalculable importance because O. Pickard-Cambridge spanned three generations and had a great influence on each. He helped the ageing Blackwall to bring his manuscript book to completion; he brought about a huge advance in knowledge during his own working life; he encouraged and trained a band of younger enthusiasts to carry on with the work after he had left the scene. O. Pickard-Cambridge only wrote one book, which gave excellent descriptions of all the known British spiders despite its modest title of 'The Spiders of Dorset' (1879–81). The illustrations were few and inferior but he published papers almost annually between 1853 and 1914 with good illustrations which seemed to improve progressively the older he got. With the help of a band of devoted friends and collectors, Blackwall's list of 304 species had been increased to 457 by 1874, 518 by 1881 and 532 by 1903. This was Pickard-Cambridge's last list but he continued to add and describe further species until he finally retired from work in 1914 when he was eighty-six.

The Rev. O. Pickard-Cambridge's most noteworthy disciples were Cecil Warburton, his nephew F. O. Pickard-Cambridge, Dr. A. R. Jackson, W. Falconer, the Rev. J. E. Hull and G. H. Carpenter.

Warburton's main period of activity lay between 1885 and 1900 during which time he collected four species new to Britain. Although his interest wandered to other invertebrates at the close of this period, he published an attractive little book called 'Spiders' in 1912. At the time of writing he is in his 105th year and when he was a hundred it was noted in the Sunday Times that his name appeared that week amongst the winners of their crossword puzzle competition.

F. O. Pickard-Cambridge's papers were published between 1889 and 1905 (three years after his untimely death). His work was of a high order. For the most part it comprised the re-examination and re-grouping of the numerous species which had been described by his uncle during the previous half century. He soon discovered that some species had been described more than once under different names whilst in other cases, as in the genus *Tetragnatha,* he found several different species lurking under one specific name. His work led to the formation of new genera (*Hillhousia, Mengea*) and to the addition of sixteen species to the British list. Finally it should be mentioned that he added to our knowledge of distribution by preparing several county lists for the Victoria History of the Counties of England.

Our extensive knowledge of the spiders in the northern counties is due mainly to Dr. A. Randell Jackson, W. Falconer and the Rev. J. E. Hull. Each published his first paper in the eighteen nineties but their main work belongs to the twentieth century. During the thirty years which followed O. Pickard-Cambridge's retirement most collectors turned for assistance in identifying their captures to one of these three, and especially to Jackson who had taken O. Pickard-Cambridge's position as leading authority. Jackson was a potential 'giant' in the Blackwall and O. Pickard-Cambridge mould but his time and energy were sapped by the duties of a busy medical practice in Chester which left him no opportunity to complete the magnum opus which had become so badly needed.

An analysis of his papers published between 1899 and 1944 shows that he added forty-seven species to the British list and cleared up many synonymic problems by comparing British with Continental specimens.

As with O. Pickard-Cambridge, Jackson's influence has extended far beyond his death in 1944 through the help and encouragement he gave to the next generation of enthusiasts. His generosity, at a time when the absence of any up-to-date book made comparisons with specimens almost necessary for the identification of obscure species, can best be illustrated by his repeated remark to visitors like myself: 'Do some collecting from my collection whilst I am out on my rounds'.

Yorkshire was Falconer's main hunting ground but he also paid special attention to Wicken Fen, the Isle of Wight, and Lancashire, with incursions into Wales, after retiring from his job as a schoolmaster. In the course of his period of activity between 1896 and 1939 he found ten species new to Britain.

Hull's best work was done in Northumberland and Durham where he found at least two species new to science. He specialised on the Linyphiidae and re-grouped many of them into new genera of which six have received general acceptance (*Halorates, Diplocentria, Ostearius, Agyneta, Rhabdoria, Meioneta*). Hull's latest paper on Essex spiders was published in his ninety-fourth year and this may not be his last as his keen interest still remains although his former meticulous care in diagnosis has diminished.

In 1899 F. P. Smith, a self-taught young Londoner of humble origin, began publishing papers at the age of nineteen. The papers showed considerable originality and skill. His work on the Linyphiidae led to the creation of three new genera (*Erigonidium, Monocephalus* and *Lessertia*) and that on the Lycosidae to the addition of *Xerolycosa nemoralis* to the British list. In 1912 he forsook spiders as abruptly as he had appeared on the scene. When I eventually traced him, shortly before his death in 1946, it was found that the mystery of his abrupt disappearance from the spider world was explained by the need after he had married to earn more than the thirty shillings a week he was earning as a clerk at the Board of Education. Thereafter he became the first pioneer in the development of nature films.

Another interesting character of a different type was a Lichfield shop-keeper called L. A. Carr who made no pretentions to expert knowledge but was a remarkably fine collector. By sheer hard work he amassed a collection from his area of over three hundred and twenty species. 'Go out and get 'em' was his motto and away he strode day after day on this quest for many years up to about 1922 by which time, presumably, he had 'got 'em'.

In Ireland T. Workman brought R. T. Templeton's list of 43 species up to 125 in 1881, which the Rev. Dr. G. H. Carpenter increased to 225 in 1895. In a series of papers between 1907 and 1938, D. R. Pack Beresford was chiefly responsible for this total mounting to the present total of 318 and for providing extensive knowledge of their distribution in the various counties.

Wales got off to a good start through Blackwall living in Denbighshire after retiring from business in Manchester at an early age, but their list has mounted to 334 only as a result of collecting done by visitors such as Jackson, Falconer, Savory, Wild and myself.

James Hardy was the first extensive collector in Scotland and his results were combined with those of others in a list of 215 species published by O. Pickard-Cambridge in 1877, to which extensive additions were made by W. Evans between 1894 and 1918 after he had retired from an insurance office. Evans was an all-round field naturalist and he sent his captures to G. H. Carpenter for identification, who in turn forwarded critical species to O. Pickard-Cambridge. Eight species new to Britain were discovered in this way as well as many more new to Scotland. The next big advance was made by Jackson in the course of two brief expeditions to Scotland in 1913 and 1914 when he added twenty species, half of which were new to Britain. A few later additions by myself and others bring the total to 337.

Work by Jackson and others since O. Pickard-Cambridge's list of 532 British species had been published in 1900 had not only added many species but had also made it necessary to remove several species from that list. The result of these additions and subtractions was to enable me to publish a list of 556 species for the British Isles in 1939 to which I added one further species in 1941, bringing the total by that date to 557. Incidentally, the greater mobility of collectors of my generation due to the advent of motorcars is illustrated both by the fact that I had been able to collect in fifty-seven counties by that date (since increased to sixty-four) and that six of the seven species new to the British Isles which I had collected were found in different counties, with an eighth in the Channel Islands which has since been found on our mainland.

Long before Jackson died a great need had arisen for an up-to-date book showing how all our species could be identified. Indeed I had started pestering him to write such a book almost as soon as I knew him in 1917 and his answer was always the same — that he would write one when he retired. Within a short time of his death in 1944 I initiated a plan to write such a book jointly with G. H. Locket and A. F. Millidge, although my own pleasure had lain more with living than with dead spiders. By the time I had completed an introductory chapter and sections dealing with the Atypidae, Oonopidae, Dysderidae and Scytodidae, it had become apparent to me that the time at my disposal after an exacting day's work in a London office with frequent visits to other parts of Britain would not allow me to do my full share, so I reluctantly withdrew from this happy partnership of friends. My regrets were lessened by the knowledge that their completed work would be worthy of the highest praise and so it proved to be. 'British Spiders' by Locket and Millidge appeared in two volumes in 1951 and 1953 respectively. We are indeed fortunate in having this schoolmaster and industrial chemist as successors in the Blackwall, O. Pickard-Cambridge, Jackson series.

At the present time there are, I believe, more active contributors to our knowledge of spiders than ever before who deserve mention for their past achievements or high promise. Those who have described spiders new to the British list include G. H. Locket and A. M. Millidge, E. Browning of the British Museum, Dr. A. A. D. La Touche whose skill as a collector is rivalled by his powers of diagnosis, E. Duffey, A. D. Blest and A. M. Wild.

Others who have added to our knowledge of the distribution of British species include Theodore Savory, J. H. Murgatroyd, J. L. Cloudsley-Thompson, A. E. Le Gros, J. A. L. Cooke, G. P. Lampel, M. H. Williamson and D. J. Clark.

The present list of British and Irish species now stands at 584 species and others will be added as the years go by.

It has always surprised me how little the great taxonomists of whom I have been writing seemed to care about the living spiders. To nearly all of them the listing and describing of the specimens was the final objective with some knowledge of the habits being stored up only as an aid to more effective collecting. Early spider-watching by Blackwall was soon abandoned for specialisation on taxonomy, and the writings of O. Pickard-Cambridge, Jackson, Falconer, Hull, Carpenter, Pack Beresford and the others with minor exceptions followed the same pattern of narrow specialisation. Refreshing exceptions during the nineteenth century were F. Enock who made an excellent study of the life-history of one spider, *Atypus affinis,* and Maule Campbell who published papers on stridulating organs, glands and sexual organs. Neither of these men were authorities on spiders in general and if one wanted to read about the habits of British spiders it was necessary during that century to read books by general naturalists like Kirby and Spence or J. G. Wood whose range was limited and whose accuracy was variable.

Later, during what I might roughly call Jackson's generation, we can find minor excursions from taxonomy by R. I. Pocock, F. P. Smith and C. Warburton, but little else of a biological nature will be found in the literature until early in the nineteen-twenties when a younger generation appeared on the scene with papers by Savory, Locket and myself. In Savory's case a useful series of books were published including 'The Biology of Spiders' (1928) and 'The Spider's Web' (1952). These were largely commentated summaries of biological studies made by naturalists anywhere in the world with additions from his own experience in Britain. Locket's papers dealt chiefly with mating habits and allometric growth. My own covered a wider range and in 1939/41 'The Comity of Spiders' was published in two volumes which was followed by a slim book in the King Penguin series entitled 'Spiders'.

It is encouraging to notice that there is a distinct movement away from the former attitude which regarded the collection and preparation of lists as the ultimate objective. M. J. and B. J. Marples wrote an interesting paper on the habits of *Hyptiotes* and *Cyclosa conica* in 1937 and N. J. Clarke is making an excellent study of the life history of *Scytodes* comparable with that of Enock on *Atypus.* D. A. Parry is engaged on physiological research, T. H. Savory has made experiments on the mental equipment of spiders and their tropisms and E. Duffey has made some masterly ecological investigations. Studies in ecology and the varying environmental requirements of different species in explanation of their distributions are also the subjects for enquiry by J. L. Cloudsley-Thompson, A. E. Le Gros, J. A. L. Cooke, C. P. Lampel and M. H. Williamson.

After many years of neglect a fresh interest in spiders is awakening with the emphasis spread more widely between taxonomy, biology, ecology and physiology.

CHAPTER 3

STRUCTURE & CLASSIFICATION

UNLIKE INSECTS, spiders have only two parts to their bodies, simple eyes, no antennae and four instead of three pairs of walking legs. Nor do they go through a larval or pupal stage in their development.

In contrast to their relations in the Class Arachnida like the Harvest-men, Mites and Pseudoscorpions, the two parts of their body, the cephalothorax and abdomen, are joined by a very narrow neck or pedicel. The spiders also differ from their relations in having abdominal spinnerets and palpal organs used by the male in mating.

Viewing a spider from above we see that the cephalothorax is covered by a chitinous layer or plate which is called the carapace. The cephalothorax represents a fusion of the head with the thorax and the original junction of the two parts is often clearly marked.

The head bears eight eyes, except in the Oonopidae, Dysderidae and Scytodidae, where there are six due to the disappearance of the anterior median pair originally derived from the first cephalic somite or segment. This pair, when present, have a direct retina and are usually dark in colour. The other six were derived from the second cephalic somite and have an indirect retina. These may have a pearly lustre or be dark in colour. Dark eyes are often called 'diurnal' and pale eyes 'nocturnal' but there is probably no real significance in these names.

The jaws with which spiders bite are known as the chelicerae. Each chelicera consists of a stout basal segment from the apex of which a needle- or thorn-like fang is articulated. Near the tip of this is a tiny opening from which poison is squeezed along a duct from a sac con-tained in the basal segment or extending into the cephalothorax. The chemical composition of the poison is complex and varied. It may affect the nervous system or the blood or both, but nobody need fear spider bites in Britain.

UNDER AND UPPER SIDES OF ARANEUS

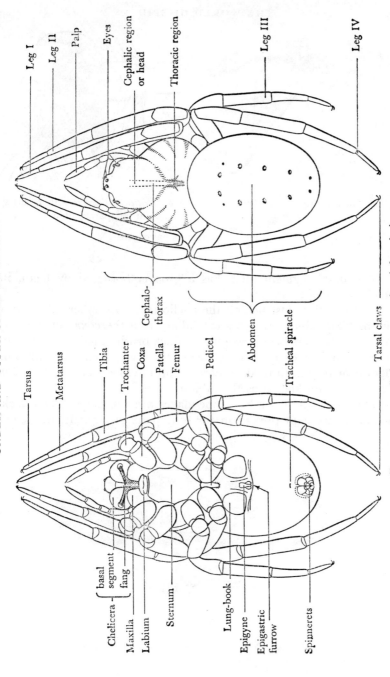

FIG. 2. *Araneus diadematus*—ventral and dorsal views

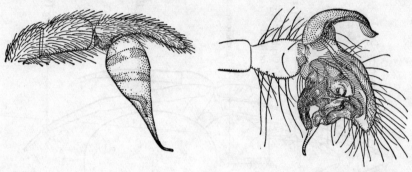

a. Segestria florentina, simple type   *b. Nesticus cellulanus* with tarsus split
                                              and jutting paracymbium

FIG. 3.   Male palpal organs

The basal segment often has a groove, bordered by teeth, into which the fang folds.

The mouth is just behind the chelicerae. On either side of it are the maxillae which are lobes extending from the coxae of the palps. The inner borders bear a scopula or thick brush of hairs which help in sifting food and cleaning or greasing the legs. Sometimes the inner edges bear tiny teeth used in mashing up the food. Behind the mouth is a small plate known as the labium.

The first pair of leg-like appendages are the palps. These lack a metatarsal segment present in the four pairs of legs. In the females

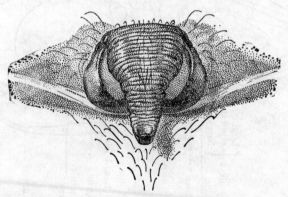

FIG. 4.   Epigyne of female *Araneus diadematus*

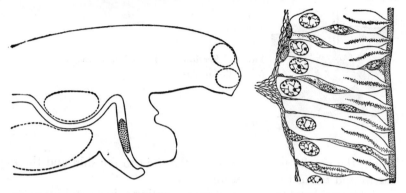

a. Longitudinal section showing area in the.
gullet

b. Section of cells
(after J. Millot)

FIG. 5.   Taste glands

there is often a terminal claw. In the adult males the terminal segment or tarsus is swollen and has no claw. The swelling is due to the presence of the palpal organ which is unique in storing sperm derived from the body and in being inserted in the female's body during mating.

In its simplest form this roughly resembles a fountain-pen filler with a flexible bulb or haematodocha inside which is a reservoir for the sperm and a coiled tube leading to a stiff spur known as the embolus (see fig. 3a).

The hollow in which the palpal organ rests is called the alveolus. In primitive forms this is small and circular. In some families this has spread backwards and finally split off part of the tarsus known as the paracymbium (see fig. 3b).

The palpal organ can be incredibly complicated with the embolus associated with a variety of apophyses which help to guide, protect and ease the process of mating.

The next segment, the tibia, is provided in the males of several families with a spur, called the fixator, which fits into a chitinous pouch in the female's abdomen to hold the palp firmly in position during the mating process (see fig. 66, p. 135).

The four pairs of legs arise between the carapace and the sternum. They all have a coxa, trochanter, femur, patella, tibia, metatarsus and tarsus. The first two are very short. The femur is analogous to our

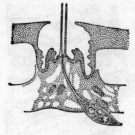

FIG. 6.   Section of Trichobothrium
(after P. Gossel)

thigh, the patella to the knee-cap, the tibia to the shin and the metatarsus and tarsus to the foot and toes.

The tarsi have two claws in most hunting spiders and three in most
web-builders. A primitive feature in some families is a distinct cushion
or onychium on which the claws are placed (cf. Scytodidae).

The abdomen is of variable shape and form. At the front of its
lower surface can be seen two oval light patches (four in *Atypus*,) which
represent the book-lungs. Here we have what amount to blood-filled
chambers with an air vestibule behind them communicating with the
outside through a slit. From the forward walls of the vestibules many
parallel narrow air-pockets have been invaginated and pushed forward
into the blood-filled chambers.

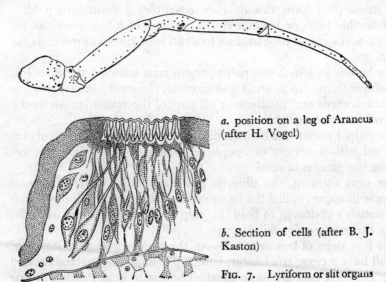

a. position on a leg of Araneus
(after H. Vogel)

b. Section of cells (after B. J.
Kaston)

FIG. 7.   Lyriform or slit organs

Behind the book-lungs are exposed the female's genital organs, after her last moult. These are of great value in identifying species (see figs. 4 and 66). Internally the two ovaries come off oviducts that join to form a single tube. This opens in the centre of a long groove called the epigastric furrow extending across the abdomen. Quite separate are two other orifices which receive the male's palpal emboli and lead by a duct to the spermathecae where the sperm is stored until egg-laying when it is discharged into the egg-mass.

In British spiders (except *Atypus*) the second pair of book-lungs have been replaced by two spiracles leading to tracheal tubes just behind the epigastric furrow (Oonopidae, Dysderidae) which later have merged in all other British spiders into one spiracle usually situated just in front of the spinnerets. In some families the tubes extend internally into the cephalothorax; in others they are confined to the abdomen.

In the Asian Liphistiidae, the spider equivalent of the Coelacanth fishes, there are four pairs of spinnerets in a central position (Bristowe, 1933). In all British spiders these have migrated close to the abdominal tip and are represented by three pairs and a cribellum or a colulus, or neither. The cribellum is a small flat plate, divided in some spiders, just in front of the spinnerets, from which silk is combed by a neat comb of bristles on the spider's hind pair of metatarsi. The colulus is a small functionless lump in the same position which may be the remnant of the fourth pair of spinnerets.

Five or six different types of silk-glands, producing silk for different purposes, may open at the spinnerets through many small spigots.

Behind the spinnerets lies the anal tubercle.

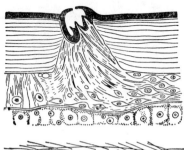

a. Section

FIG. 8.   Tarsal organ

b. Position on tarsus
(after H. Blumenthal)

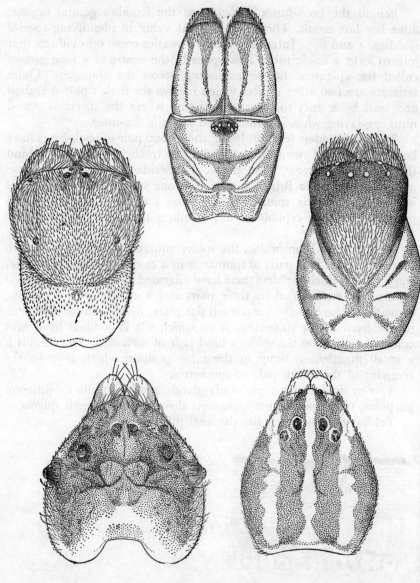

a. *Atypus* (Atypidae)

b. *Eresus* (Eresidae)

c. *Ciniflo* (Dictynidae)

d. *Hyptiotes* (Uloboridae)

e. *Uloborus* (Uloboridae)

FIG. 9.   Carapaces

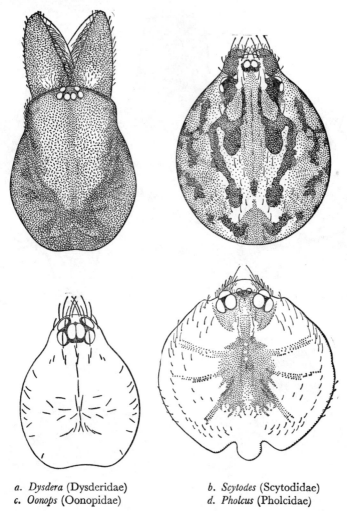

a. *Dysdera* (Dysderidae)
b. *Scytodes* (Scytodidae)
c. *Oonops* (Oonopidae)
d. *Pholcus* (Pholcidae)

FIG. 10. Carapaces

The senses of spiders and the organs through which they operate are not yet fully understood. The eyes have been mentioned. Millot has discovered taste-glands in the gullet (see fig. 5). The spider's keen sense of touch may be associated with hairs on their tarsi connected with their nervous and muscular system.

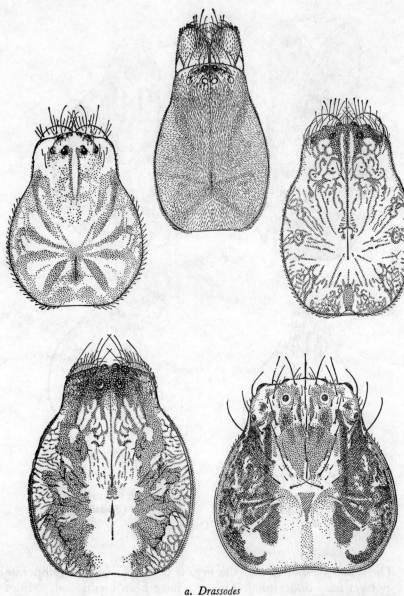

a. Drassodes

b. Micrommata (Sparassidae) *c. Clubiona* (Clubionidae)
d. Anyphaena (Anyphaenidae) *e. Xysticus* (Thomisidae)

FIG. 11. Carapaces

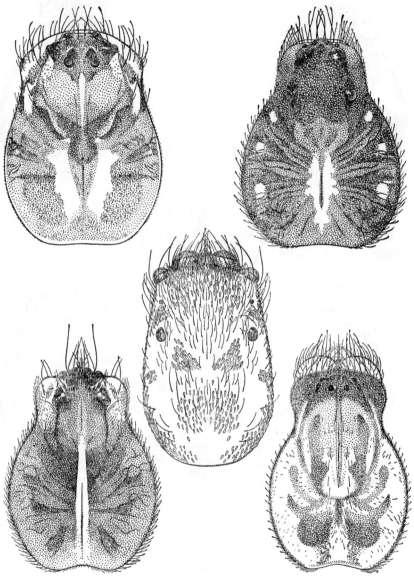

a. *Oxyopes* (Oxyopidae)

c. *Salticus* (Salticidae)

d. *Pisaura* (Pisauridae)

b. *Lycosa* (Lycosidae)

e. *Tegenaria* (Agelenidae)

Fig. 12.   Carapaces

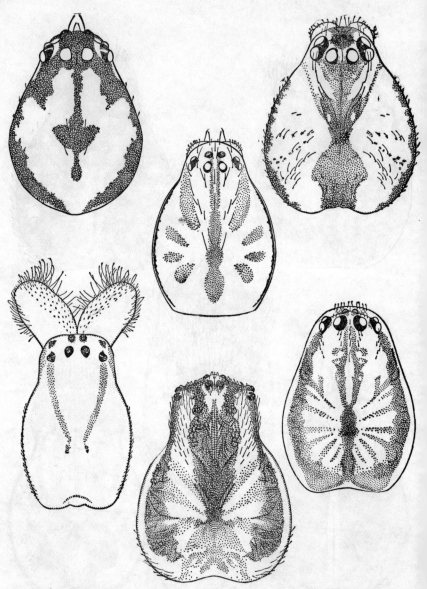

a. *Ero* (Mimetidae)
    c. *Theridion* (Theridiidae)
b. *Nesticus* (Nesticidae)
d. *Tetragnatha* (Tetragnathidae)
e. *Linyphia* (Linyphiidae)
    f. *Araneus* (Argiopidae)

FIG. 13. Carapaces

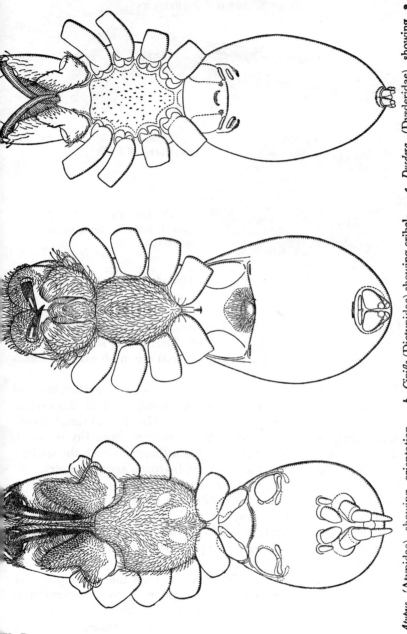

a. *Atypus* (Atypidae) showing orientation of fangs, labium fused to sternum, 2 pairs of book lungs, no epigyne, 3-segmented posterior spinnerets

b. *Ciniflo* (Dictynidae) showing cribellum between the spinnerets and single tracheal slit

c. *Dysdera* (Dysderidae) showing a pair of tracheal slits behind the book lungs, and no epigyne

FIG. 14.   Ventral surface

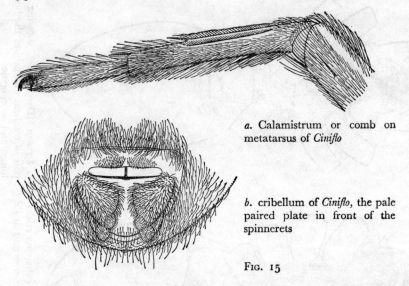

a. Calamistrum or comb on metatarsus of *Ciniflo*

b. cribellum of *Ciniflo*, the pale paired plate in front of the spinnerets

FIG. 15

Other sensory organs include fine erect hairs on the legs known as trichobothria (see fig. 6), widely distributed lyriform or slit organs found especially on the legs (see fig. 7), and a tarsal organ on each leg tarsus (see fig. 8).

The trichobothria may provide perception of air currents and orientation in the web as Palmgren (1936) suggests and also certain types of vibration which we detect as sound. The slit and tarsal organs are more likely to be receptors of heat, pressure, humidity or smell, but neither satisfies me as being the organs through which the spider's strongly developed chemotactic or taste-by-touch sense operates.

Illustrations of the carapace and arrangement of the eyes in a species selected from each family will help to assign spiders to their correct families (see figs. 9 to 13).

If we look at the underside of *Atypus* (fig. 14a), our only representative of the Atypidae, we can notice the following characters found in no other British family. Huge chelicerae with an upward and downward movement, two pairs of book-lungs and long posterior spinnerets with three segments. A labium fused to the sternum is shared with the Scytodidae and Pholcidae; the absence of a genital plate or epigyne is shared with the Oonopidae, Dysderidae, Scytodidae, Pholcidae and Tetragnathidae.

The underside of *Dysdera* (Dysderidae) shows a pair of tracheal slits just behind the epigastric furrow instead of the second pair of book-lungs (fig. 14c). These will not be seen in *Oonops* (Oonopidae), although they are conspicuous in other members of the family, whilst *Scytodes* (Scytodidae), the only other member of a six-eyed family, has a single tracheal slit like all other British spiders.

Fig. 15 shows the calamistrum on the metatarsus of the fourth leg of a *Ciniflo* (Dictynidae) and a cribellum, whose position just in front

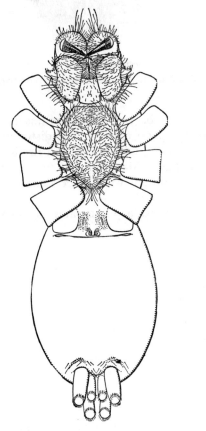 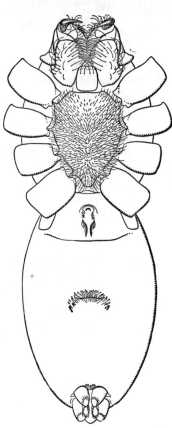

a. Drassodes (Gnaphosidae) showing long tubular spinnerets and wide separation of the anterior pair

b. Anyphaena (Anyphaenidae) with tracheal slit halfway between spinnerets and epigastric furrow

FIG. 16.   Ventral surface

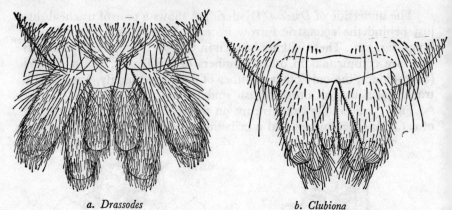

a. Drassodes   *b. Clubiona*

FIG. 17.   Spinnerets of *Drassodes* (Gnaphosidae) and *Clubiona* (Clubionidae) compared

of the spinnerets can also be seen in fig. 14b. Just in front of this again
is the tracheal slit. The drawings of carapaces and eyes will distinguish
this family from the other cribellate families, Uloboridae and Eresidae.

Drawings of our six-eyed *Scytodes* (Scytodidae) and our two species
of eight-eyed Pholcidae make their confusion with other spiders unnecessary (figs. 10, 48 etc.).

The underside of a *Drassodes* (Gnaphosidae) illustrates the single

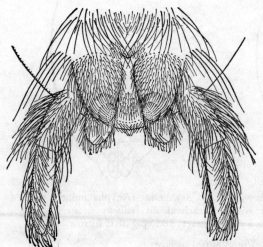

FIG. 18. Spinnerets of *Tegenaria* (Agelenidae) showing
long two-segmented pair

FIG. 19.   Part of first leg of Ero (Mimetidae) showing the row of typical bristles

tracheal slit and the characteristic spinnerets (fig. 16a). This family is best distinguished from the Clubionidae by the wider separation of the anterior pair, which are also more cylindrical (fig. 17). *Anyphaena* (Anyphaenidae) is distinguished by the unique central position of the tracheal spiracle (fig. 16b).

Our vivid green *Micromatta* (Sparassidae) has a slightly crab-like stance which is still more marked in many of the Thomisidae. This latter family have no cheliceral teeth.

The Salticidae and Oxyopidae can be recognised by their eyes (see fig. 12).

Eyes distinguish the Lycosidae from the Pisauridae (fig. 12) and in the latter, as well as in the Agelenidae, the males have a tibial spur. Both have notched trochanters in contrast to the Agelenidae whose long two-segmented posterior spinnerets also serve to distinguish them (fig. 18).

Although nearly all the species in the six families of my last group are easily assigned to their families by their habits, the families tend to merge into one another with the result that reliable characters without exceptions are difficult to give. The front legs of the Mimetidae have their tibiae and metatarsi with a series of long curved spines alternating with short ones (fig. 19). The labium is rebordered in the Nesticidae, Argiopidae, Tetragnathidae and Linyphiidae but not in the Theridiidae (fig. 20). The male palp of the Nesticidae has a distinct paracymbium

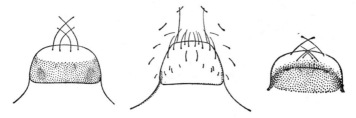

FIG. 20.   Labium. *a. Left. Nesticus* (Nesticidae) and *c. Right. Linyphia* (Linyphiidae) are rebordered in contrast to *b. Centre. Theridion* (Theridiidae)

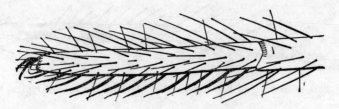

FIG. 21. Comb-footed *Theridion*

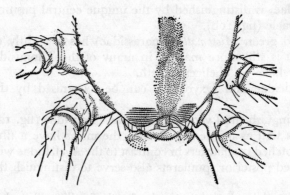

FIG. 22. Stridulatory apparatus of *Theridion* with teeth on the abdomen opposing files on the cephalothorax

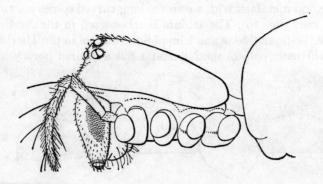

FIG. 23. Stridulatory apparatus of *Linyphia* with a file on the chelicera which is opposed by a small tooth near the base of the palp

(fig. 3b) which is never present in the Theridiidae. The Theridiidae have a characteristic comb of serrated bristles on the tarsi of their fourth pair of legs (fig. 21) and several have no cheliceral teeth. They also have a stridulatory apparatus between the abdomen and cephalo-thorax (fig. 22) whereas in the Linyphiidae it is situated between the chelicera and the coxa of the palps (fig. 23) and absent from either position in the other families. The very large chelicerae of the Tetra-gnathidae and their simple sex organs with no epigyne in the female distinguish them from the other families. Like the Argiopidae most of the Tetragnathidae build orb webs.

The scheme of classification I favour covering our British spiders is broadly similar to one I proposed in 1938:

<pre>
                    Order ARANEAE
              Sub-Order MYGALOMORPHAE
                  Family Atypidae
              Sub-Order ARANEOMORPHAE
                Division CRIBELLATAE
Group 1   Family Uloboridae
  „   2   Families Dictynidae, Eresidae
                Division ECRIBELLATAE
Group 1   Families Oonopidae, Dysderidae
  „   2   Families Scytodidae, Pholcidae
  „   3   Families Gnaphosidae, Clubionidae, Anyphaenidae,
                          Sparassidae, Thomisidae
  „   4   Family Salticidae
  „   5   Family Oxyopidae
  „   6   Families Lycosidae, Pisauridae, Agelenidae
  „   7   Families Theridiidae, Nesticidae, Mimetidae,
                          Argiopidae, Tetragnathidae, Linyphiidae
</pre>

The species known to inhabit the British Isles are listed in an Appendix p. 282.

CHAPTER 4

THE ANCESTRY OF SPIDERS

THE half million years or more during which man has inhabited
the world may sound like eternity to us and yet this is as a winter's
night to a year when compared with the antiquity of spiders, whose
history stretches back to the Devonian period some 300 million years
ago. It is the Rhynie chert beds of Aberdeen which have yielded the
indistinct outlines of the earliest known spider, *Palaeocteniza crassipes*
Hirst, and it is one of my disappointments that considerable search
has failed to reveal to me another specimen which might provide a
closer knowledge of its structure and appearance.

The immense antiquity of spiders is rivalled by that of their relations. The Devonian chert beds of Aberdeen, for instance, also
contain mites and extinct Trigonotarbi, whilst these and spiders are
all antedated by scorpions preserved in Silurian rocks laid down up
to 350 million years ago in Lanarkshire, western Europe and North
America.

If we could travel back in time to a somewhat later period 250
million years ago and roam in our imagination amongst the lowland
forests of club-mosses, horsetails and ferns of the Upper Carboniferous
period, we should find representatives of nearly all the arachnid Orders
with which we are familiar today. Our search would reveal scorpions
(Scorpiones), spiders (Araneae), mites (Acari), harvestmen (Phalangida), Solifugae, Ricinulei, pedipalps (Uropygi and Amblygi) and
also several extinct Orders.

Although arachnids were already so well differentiated at this early
date, mammals and birds had not even appeared on the scene, whilst
insects were still in their infancy. None of the insects were capable of
flight except for a few clumsy neuropterous and orthopterous forms.
There were no beetles, bees, ants or earwigs, and spiders had to wait
another 100 million years before flies arrived in the Jurassic period !

The arachnid Orders are so ancient that palaeontology has as yet been incapable of revealing their origin. The rocks in many parts of the world have not yet disclosed their wealth of information, but although we can hope for new evidence we must never expect fossils to represent more than a tiny proportion of the forms of life inhabiting particular localities, let alone the world, at any one time. What proportion, I wonder, of our present fauna is in process of being filed away for fossilisation now? And in what condition will the soft-bodied forms be when the process is completed? I ask these two questions because it is easy to expect too much from palaeontology, both as to the preservation of terrestial forms in full evolutionary series and as to the detailed structure of those occasional clues which invariably tantalise us with the incomplete preservation of their structural details. No wonder should be felt at the differences of opinion which still exist as to the origin of the Class Arachnida and the relationships of the Orders it contains. There is not even agreement as to which Orders should be included despite the tremendous advances in our knowledge made by Prof. A. Petrunkevitch, on whose valuable publications I largely depend for information in the course of this chapter.

Depending on their different interpretations of the structure of fossil forms and of their evolutionary history some authors would include the Trilobita, Copura, Xiphosura, Eurypterida, Pycnogonida, Tardigrada and Pentastomida in the Class Arachnida whilst others would exclude the whole lot. The latter course is adopted by such modern authorities as Prof. A. Petrunkevitch (1949) and the team of French experts responsible for the Traité de Zoologie (1949), who both include only terrestrial forms. Where experts differ it is necessary to make one's own attempt at reconstructing the history of events.*

Life began in the pre-Cambrian waters more than 1,000 million years ago; and in the course of time some aquatic worm-like creatures developed in which the body somites (segments) became grouped into a prosoma and an abdomen. From these forms, I suggest, came the earliest trilobites, or their immediate ancestors, from which developed the antennae-bearing Cambrian Trilobita, Copura and Crustacea in one direction and the Cambrian Xiphosura and Ordovician Eurypterida without antennae in another. The divergence had started along two different streams and these led to the Crustacea and Arachnida

---

*I am heartened by seeing that several of my conclusions closely resemble those in an important paper by F. Raw (1957) received after my manuscript was in print.

respectively; but, being cousins as it were, it is only to be expected that these early aquatic crustacean and arachnid forms, or some of them, had a close resemblance to one another.

Both the Xiphosura and Eurypterida are clearly related to the terrestrial arachnids as well as to each other but, whereas the Silurian scorpions are likely to have sprung from Eurypterid stock, it seems probable that spiders and the other air-breathing arachnids developed along a different route from a primitive or ancestral xiphosuran form from which the Eurypterida may also have stemmed. This earliest arachnid may not have been far different in general appearance from the xiphosuran Aglaspida (see fig. 24, p. 47).

Whether we include the Xiphosura and Eurypterida in the Arachnida or place them in a different class depends, as I see the problem, on what we decide to do with the scorpions. The Silurian scorpions had squat legs suggesting semi-aquatic habits or more probably recent emergence from the aquatic life of their forbears. They were amongst the earliest colonists of dry land and yet they were already so specialised in structure as to make it unthinkable that they were the ancestors of the other terrestrial arachnids. The latter, therefore, must have sprung from one or more other aquatic forms which independently adapted themselves to aerial respiration.

This suggests that scorpions are not quite so closely related to the other terrestrial arachnids as has often been supposed, and that they ought not to be grouped with them in the Arachnida *unless* the aquatic forbears of both are also included. To do otherwise would be equivalent to grouping 'cousins' together whilst excluding their 'fathers' and their common 'grandfather'. One possible course would be to erect a separate Class for the Xiphosura, Eurypterida and Scorpiones, all of which have abdomens with a tail spine, but my own conclusion is that all three should be included in the Class Arachnida.

Before pursuing the evolutionary story any further it will help later discussion to list the Orders which I include and to group them according to my ideas of their relationships.

Class ARACHNIDA

Sub-Class I   MEROSTOMATA

Order 1 Aglaspida (extinct)
" 2 Synziphosura (extinct)
" 3 Xiphosurida (King Crabs)
" 4 Eurypterida (extinct)

Xiphosura (aquatic)

Sub-Class II	PECTINIFERA	
Order 5	Scorpiones (Scorpions)	(terrestrial)
Sub-Class III	EPECTINATA	
Order 6	Anthracomarti (extinct)	
,, 7	Haptopoda (extinct)	
,, 8	Acari (Mites)	Latigastra
,, 9	Architarbi (extinct)	(terrestrial)
,, 10	Phalangida (Harvestmen)	
,, 11	Pseudoscorpiones (False Scorpions)	
,, 12	Solifugae	
,, 13	Ricinulei	
,, 14	Kustarachnae (extinct)	
,, 15	Palpigradi	Caulogastra
,, 16	Uropygi (Whip Scorpions)	(terrestrial)
,, 17	Amblypygi	
,, 18	Araneae (Spiders)	
,, 19	Trigonotarbi (extinct)	

Having listed the sub-Classes and Orders which I include in the Arachnida the story can be resumed at the point where the sub-Classes Pectinifera and Epectinata arose from primitive forms of Merostomata. These developments started during the Silurian period, with the periodic alternation of land and sea levels and the slow emergence of new land areas—which offered the chance, that some succeeded in taking, of changing from aquatic to aerial respiration. This important alteration in habitat was inevitably accompanied and followed by structural changes. Some of these changes represented similar macro-evolutionary trends independently pursued along different lines of descent. Others were peculiar to each line of descent and led to differentiation into the various Orders in my list.

A macro-evolutionary trend towards simplification had started amongst the aquatic ancestors and this persisted amongst most of the terrestrial descendants sometimes with similar results. This simplification involved loss of abdominal appendages or their adaptation into organs of respiration or spinning, and loss of abdominal somites (segments) accompanied by progressive simplification of the internal anatomy.

Evolutionary changes leading to differentiation included the fusion of the cephalothorax and abdomen in some forms (Acari etc.) and the narrowing of the junction between cephalothorax and abdomen into a pedicel in others (Araneae etc.); the development of leg-like palps in some (Solifugae etc.) and palps terminated by pincers or chelae in others (Pseudoscorpiones etc.); the adaptation of the pygidium into a terminal whip-like structure with sensory functions by means of secondary segmentation (Uropygi etc.) or the tail-spine of the last somite into an important weapon (Scorpiones). These and many other changes had, as we have already shown, practically completed the differentiation into separate Orders by the Carboniferous period some 250 million years ago.

It is a long step from the early Cambrian pre-aglaspid type which founded the Arachnida to the arrival of the first spider some 250 million years later. The evolutionary route is unfound; but even in our present state of knowledge it may be possible to discover a few sign-posts by making some comparison of the living with the dead. I have suggested that the Pectinifera (scorpions) came from Eurypterid stock and I am now anxious to reconstruct the appearance of the ancestor of the other branch, the Epectinata, from an analysis of the structural features common to many of its descendants. Here is the result.

Cephalothorax broadly joined to the abdomen (as in the Xiphosura, Eurypterida, Pseudoscorpiones, Phalangida, Acari, Architarbi, Haptopoda, Anthracomarti and some Trigonotarbi).

Chelicerae chelate (as in all Orders except the Araneae, Uropygi, Amblypygi and Trigonotarbi) and possessing a coxal segment (as in the Xiphosura, Eurypterida, Phalangida, Palpigradi and the extinct Orders except the Trigonotarbi). Cheliceral coxae squeezed in the same plane as the coxae of the palps and legs (as in the Xiphosura, Eurypterida, Haptopoda and Anthracomarti) instead of lying dorsally as in all the other Orders.

Eyes comprising a median and two lateral groups (as in Eurypterida, Xiphosura, Uropygi, Amblypygi and some Araneae).*

Palps leg-like (as in the Eurypterida, the extinct Orders and the Phalangida, Araneae etc.) and with the coxa expanded into a gnathocoxa (as in Xiphosura, Eurypterida, Pseudoscorpiones, Phalangida etc.).

Legs with two tarsal claws (as in all extinct Orders where they can be seen and in most living Orders).

* Median eyes have been detected in the Haptopoda, Kustarachnae and Architarbi; lateral eyes in some Trigonotarbi; none in the Anthracomarti. Amongst living forms there are lateral eyes in Pseudoscorpiones, median eyes in Solifugae and Phalangida, and none in the Palpigradi and Ricinulei.

Abdomen with twelve or more somites visible (as in Eurypterida, Pseudoscorpiones, Uropygi, Amblypygi and some Liphistiid spiders).

Book-Lungs on the 2nd and 3rd somites at least (if it had adopted a terrestrial life at this stage).

Superficial appearance probably somewhat compact with short stout legs and not unlike the Haptopoda and Anthracomarti.

No known fossil specimens conform exactly with all the requirements necessary for the ancestor of the Sub-Class Epectinata but the specification beckons us towards the Haptopoda and Anthracomarti, or a near ancestor with more post-cephalic somites.

In departing from the type of mouthparts shared by the Haptopoda, Anthracomarti, Eurypterida and Xiphosura, certain later Orders had more room for their chelicerae to develop in size and strength and to become formidable weapons like those found in the Solifugae, Pseudoscorpiones, Phalangida etc. This stem flourished whereas the Haptopoda and Anthracomarti with their feeble chelicerae became extinct.

Search must next be directed to the finding of an ancestor nearer to spiders than this founder of the Sub-Class Epectinata.

One noteworthy trend in the evolution of some of the Orders was towards the formation of a waist at the point of the cephalothorax and abdomen. The living Orders in which this is conspicuous include the Solifugae, Ricinulei, Palpigradi, Uropygi, Amblypygi and Araneae. The Ricinulei and Palpigradi have many features which link them fairly closely to the Uropygi and Amblypygi whilst these last two Orders are generally believed to be the closest living relations of the Araneae, so the formation of the waist has resulted in all these Orders, and the Solifugae which is less distinctly related, being placed in a group called Caulogastra. This also includes the extinct Kustarachnae and the Trigonotarbi.

At this point the evidence of relationships provided by the mouthparts comes to our aid, as it did when considering the position of the Haptopoda and Anthracomarti in the evolutionary pattern and as it will do again when we begin to arrange Araneae into Sub-Orders. Three of the waisted arachnids, the Uropygi, Amblypygi and Araneae, have not got chelate chelicerae. The explanation which seems likely to me is that an arachnid arose either in late Silurian or early Devonian times in which the cheliceral coxa had disappeared and in which the immovable finger of the 'pincer' had degenerated into a large tooth-like process on the basal segment leaving the movable finger as a hinged fang (Bristowe, 1954). Turning our attention to the extinct Trigonotarbi (found in the Rhynie chert and elsewhere) which Prof. A. Petrunkevitch separated from the Anthracomarti in 1949 and placed in a Sub-Class of their own, we find that they possess chelicerae of the same design. What is more, the connection of the cephalothorax and abdomen is narrow in some of these. Petrunkevitch rightly points out that the Devonian Trigonotarbi were in a labile state with a variable number of abdominal somites so in this Order we might have the ancestor of the Araneae, Amblypygi and Uropygi (see fig. 24). However, I must not shirk the problem of spiders' spinnerets and book-lungs.

Petrunkevitch writes (1942): "The spinnerets are modified abdominal appendages of the fourth and fifth abdominal somites. Like all abdominal appendages of Arthropods they are true pleopods, biramous in structure". This generally accepted view is supported by the survival of four pairs of spinnerets in spiders of the genus *Liphistius* situated just behind the book-lungs and occupying the second and third somites.

Another generally accepted view is that abdominal appendages on the second and third somites, just in front of the somites bearing spinnerets, became modified into the two pairs of book-lungs.

If both these beliefs are right as is usually assumed, the ancestral spider had book-lungs on the second and third somites with spinnerets on the fourth and fifth which had developed from biramous appendages before these appendages disappeared. This line of argument leads to the supposition that spiders arose from some arachnid which had recently adopted a terrestrial life and that they were not descended from any forms in which the appendages had vanished or been modified into book-lungs on the fourth and fifth as well as the second and third somites.

If this is right the common ancestor of the Araneae, Trigonotarbi, Amblypygi and Uropygi had freshly emerged from the waters and still had biramous appendages or flaps on the fourth and fifth somites which developed into spinnerets (Araneae), or disappeared (Amblypygi, Uropygi) or were modified into book-lungs in some Trigonotarbi—provided Petrunkevitch is right in thinking he has detected the faint outlines of book-lungs on these somites. Perhaps, however, these faint outlines were the bases of badly preserved rudimentary abdominal appendages. Or were they spinnerets or unprojecting structures of the cribellum type ?

I admit to experiencing some difficulty in accepting the classic theory that spiders' spinnerets arose directly from the projecting biramous appendages of some arachnid freshly adapting itself to a

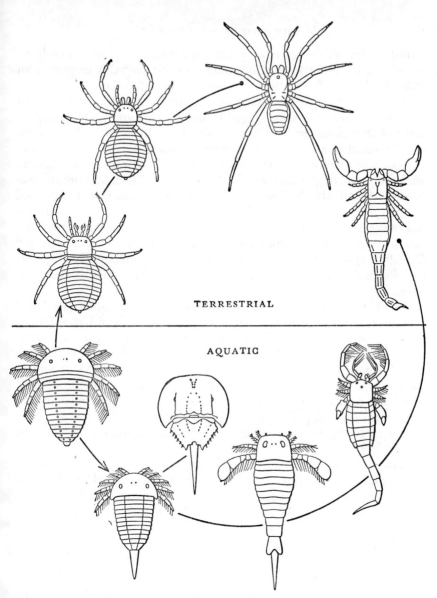

TERRESTRIAL

AQUATIC

Fig. 24. Reconstruction of the evolution of spiders and scorpions from a hypothetical ancestor which gave rise to all arachnid Orders. An aquatic pre-Aglaspid
form giving rise (1) to an early undiscovered terrestrial Anthracomart and thence
to an early undiscoverd Trigonotarb from which spiders arose, and (2) to an early
Aglaspid form from which King Crabs and Eurypterids arose, an early form of the
latter leading to the terrestrial scorpions

terrestrial life. Although it is possible, it seems to suggest too early an origin and too great a use of silk when this was probably employed for little else besides fabricating a protective cover for the eggs.

Departure from orthodoxy is apt to provoke a storm, but is it not also possible that the appendage-like appearance and paired arrangement of the spinnerets may have misled us as to their origin ? Might not the small quantity of silk originally needed have been emitted as excretory matter from abdominal orifices, the outlets of coxal glands, after the projecting appendages had vanished ? Then, as more silk was needed, the silk glands developed and the simple orifices were modified into projecting spinnerets with the advantages of movement. In one line of descent a pair of the orifices might never have become projecting but they could have expanded into a sieve-like plate — the cribellum.* Cribellate spiders undoubtedly arose very early in the history of spiders and Petrunkevitch himself thinks that they existed in Carboniferous times.

Whichever view of the origin of spinnerets is accepted, my belief remains that the Trigonotarbi, Araneae, Amblypygi and Uropygi form one little group, the Caulogastra, and that an early trigonotarb form may have given rise to the other three Orders. This early trigonotarb would have had a cephalothorax narrowly joined to the abdomen, chelicerae comprising a basal segment and fang with no coxal segment and lying dorsal to the palpal coxae, eyes comprising a median and two lateral groups, palps leg-like, legs with two tarsal claws, an abdomen with twelve visible somites and with book-lungs on the 2nd and 3rd somites (see fig. 24).

The macro-evolutionary trend towards simplification led to the loss of abdominal somites (although twelve, the original number, are still discernible in some Liphistiids). Besides the acquisition of abdominal spinnerets, spiders developed poison glands early in their existence (which are not present in some and are small in other Liphistiids), and their unique palpal organs.

In some Acari and Solifugae the chelicerae, and in the Ricinulei a pair of legs, are used in the fertilisation of the female, so it is not difficult to picture some ancestral spider picking up its sperm drop in its palps and placing this in the female's vulva. The next step was for a small cup-like depression to be formed below the tarsal claw and later for this to develop into a closed sac whilst the claw became an intromittent

---

* The freshly hatched *Heptathela* (Liphistiidae) have only two pairs of spinnerets and acquire four pairs after the first moult (M. Yoshikura, 1954).

organ with a small aperture at its tip. The great advantage of this was that the male did not have to risk losing the female whilst he ejaculated sperm as he was now ready for mating before he had found her. The pouch or receptaculum seminis is provided with transverse striated muscles like those of a trachea which supports the idea of an invagination of the body-wall. The absence of a claw on adult male tarsi, even where this was present before they were adult, seems to support the idea of it being homologous with the embolus. Embryological studies show that the embolus tip is formed immediately behind the tarsal claw in *Segestria* (Harm, 1931).

In some of the more primitive spiders the palpal organs are nearly terminal, both palps are inserted simultaneously, as they were originally when holding the sperm, and the organs are as simple as a fountain pen filler with a sharp embolus, and a tube leading into a pouch or receptaculum seminis in the bulb.

At last there was a true spider and I believe I can roughly describe it:

A cephalothorax connected by a narrow neck or pedical to an abdomen, as well as a pair of palps and four pairs of legs as in all living spiders. The body was somewhat squat, the legs short and the palps not much shorter than the legs. Eight eyes (two in a median position and two lateral groups of three); an abdomen with twelve segmentations, if we include the anal tubercle and pedicel; two pairs of book-lungs; chelicerae with an upward and downward movement of the fang which was opposed by a large tooth giving the chelicerae a chelate appearance; small poison glands confined to the basal segment of the chelicerae; maxillary lobes undeveloped; narrow sternum; simple sexual organs (no female epigyne; male palpal organ almost terminal and consisting of a piriform bulb terminated by a short curved embolus); leg tarsi terminated by two claws on an onychium; eight spinnerets (or six and a paired cribellum) situated centrally on the ventral surface of the abdomen just behind the second pair of book lungs; five pairs of cardiac ostia; not less than four pairs of dorso-ventral abdominal muscles; complex intestinal diverticula.

Every one of these characters has survived but not all of them in any one spider.

Very early in their history, probably in Carboniferous times, a
WS E

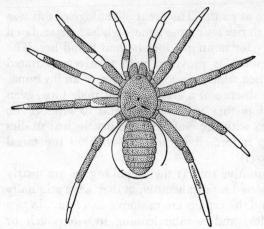

FIG. 25. *Arthrolycosa antiqua*
Harg. from N. American coal
measures. The white portions
are reconstructions, the shaded
areas are taken from a drawing
by Petrunkevitch of the fossil
remains. This spider closely
resembles the primitive Liphistiidae of Asia

torsion of the basal segment of the chelicerae took place in some spiders
so that the fangs moved laterally, inwards and towards one another.
These spiders were the founders of our Sub-Order Araneomorphae, to
which all British spiders belong except the Atypidae in which the fangs
strike downwards in a roughly vertical direction. The Atypidae belong
to the Sub-Order Mygalomorphae.

Perhaps this change in the chelicerae was correlated with a departure from a ground-living habit after insects had started to hop and fly,
with the consequent evolution of silk snares on which the pick-axe blows
from their chelicerae would be less effective than on the solid ground.

The Mygalomorphae have retained their two pairs of book-lungs
(but amongst Araneomorphs, only the Hypochilidae, have done so).
The posterior pair have been replaced in other spiders, first by a pair
and later by a single spiracle leading to a network of tracheal tubes.
As this change must have taken place very early in the history of the
Araneomorphae, it is interesting to find that the primitive foreign
Hypochilidae are cribellate spiders.

Since spiders probably first roamed the countryside in the Devonian
period there may have been about as many generations of spiders as
there are seconds in ten years separating the varied descendants of
today from their earliest spider ancestor. Thus time and the astro-
nomical numbers of individual spiders born in each generation to the
numerous species inhabiting the world, now probably far more than
100,000, have both been on the side of evolution whether the changes
in structure and habits have been gradual or more sudden. They have

PLATE I. *Thomisus onustus* (8 mm.) on heather.

experienced many alterations in climate in the course of their long history, and gradual changes from tropical to arctic and from humid to dry conditions have undoubtedly accelerated and encouraged changes. Those which have suffered extinction have been replaced by others which were able to adapt their habits and structure.

Whereas our two sub-Orders were already in existence in the Carboniferous period 220 to 275 million years ago, it is likely that all or nearly all our twenty-four families and several of our modern genera had been founded by the Oligocene period 35 to 45 million years ago. The researches of A. Petrunkevitch have already revealed representatives of sixteen families in the Baltic Amber of that period: Dictynidae, Oonopidae, Dysderidae, Pholcidae, Gnaphosidae, Clubionidae, Anyphaenidae, Thomisidae, Sparassidae, Salticidae, Pisauridae, Agelenidae, Mimetidae, Theridiidae, Argiopidae and Linyphiidae.

My own view is that the divergence of our twenty-four families from the ancestral spider may have been roughly along the lines of fig. 26.

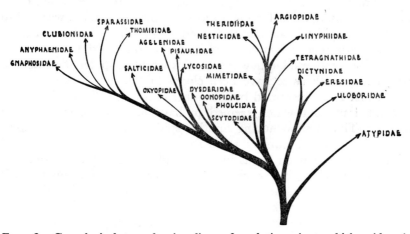

Fig. 26. Genealogical tree showing lines of evolution along which spiders in British families may have passed

CHAPTER 5

THE INFLUENCE OF NUMBERS

I N Holinshed's delightful sixteenth century *Chronicles* we read that "Domitian sometime and an other prince yet living, delited so much to see the iollie combats betwixt a stout Flie and an old Spider". I must confess that as a child I shared this delight. A war against flies had been declared. Gummy flypapers had been posted in the kitchen and I had been armed with a 'swatter', in whose use I was far from adept, so I watched with fascination the greater dexterity and skill of the Garden Spider in catching and disposing of the flies which came her way. Later, when I grew up to find how much there was still to learn about spiders' food and their methods of gaining it, I pursued the subject with renewed enthusiasm and was rewarded by gaining a glimpse of a remarkable new world, this world of spiders and insects, which might otherwise have been closed to me.

At first I was rewarded by a number of isolated discoveries which fascinated me but which seemed to have no connection with one another. That a slow-moving hunting spider called *Scytodes* captured insects by squirting gum at them from a distance; that wherever I found a rare specimen I was likely to find others in plenty; that *Ero* is a specialist which feeds exclusively on other spiders; that many small black Money Spiders are unpalatable to other spiders; that the taste of many insects will make spiders retire to be sick. Then, all of a sudden, these and other isolated incidents began to form a pattern round one central theme, the theme of numbers. I had found that in one Sussex field which had remained undisturbed for several years there were at certain seasons more than 2,000,000 spiders to the acre. The existence of this staggering spider population not only made me contemplate afresh their importance to man in controlling insect hordes, but to realise the keenness of competition amongst spiders themselves for the available food supply and to reckon the effect of their menace on the evolution of protective devices by insects.

First let us think for a moment about the number of insects they destroy. Even if we were so cautious as to attribute a hundred victims in the year to each spider, I calculate with a very conservative estimate of the spider population for the country as a whole that the weight of insects consumed annually in Britain exceeds that of the human inhabitants. I feel certain this is a safe claim to make. As a matter of fact, some spiders can eat their own weight of insects in a day when the opportunity is provided, and, although this is not typical, I have counted more than 500 small insects caught during one day in the gummy threads of a single *Araneus quadratus*. To give spiders full credit for the part they play in controlling the insect population it should also be known that in seasons of insect abundance spiders wax fat on their exceptional harvest and lay more eggs than in lean years, thus helping before long to restore the balance. What all this really amounts to is that spiders rank easily first as the enemies of insects, with birds and other insectivorous creatures trailing along far behind.

Perhaps it may be wondered what 2,000,000 spiders in an acre field can find to eat? Small springtails (Collembola) would come first in the list and flies would come second. The competition, which our population figures suggest, has led to specialisation and what might be likened to a form of rationing so that the maximum amount of spiders can survive with the minimum amount of competition. We find, for instance, that several species are restricted to the rigorous climate of our mountain tops whilst others are confined to the warmth of greenhouses. Some species are marshland specialists, which die within a few hours in dry surroundings, whereas those species which are adapted to life in houses can survive for months in a dry box without water. Some spiders hunt insects which are active in sunlight whilst others, the night shift, emerge when darkness falls to feed on the fresh set of insects which are then active.

These are examples of adaptation to cold and heat, to wet and dry conditions and to light and darkness. If we confine ourselves to one small area we will find that some spiders by reason of their size capture large insects whilst others destroy only small insects, that the web-builders capture mainly flying insects whilst the hunters attack those which run on the ground. Another thing which helps to reduce competition amongst our 584 species is that some reach maturity and lay eggs in the spring whilst others do not reach their adult state until the late summer months.

Perhaps the best example I can give of the ever-present competition amongst spiders for the available food-supply is provided by a group of islands like the Scillies. Here on the largest island there are about 100 species but this number diminishes progressively as we pass to smaller islands. Some of the very tiny islands are reduced to six species of spider and these all belong to different families or are, at least, of different size or habit, because an island of this area can only support one of each type of specialist.

Wherever competition amongst island spiders becomes really acute the extinction of a species in that island of small area need not be caused, or at least clinched, by cannibalism or starvation but by the numbers falling below the minimum necessary to ensure the males and females coming together. Numbers are again involved, numbers and area. If we take a tiny Money Spider to illustrate the danger and assume there is one of each sex on an island with an area of an acre, calculation will show that the chances of their ever meeting are remote. If a female has a sheet web spanning 2.5 cms. which a male has to touch in the course of random wandering before he can detect her presence, and if his legs span half a centimetre, he would have to walk no less than 82.5 miles on the average before finding her. The distance would be increased to 194 miles if she were also a wanderer with no fixed base. Even if there were two hundred specimens of the species on this tiny island, half male and half female, he would have to walk 1,452 yds., if she had a web, and 3,421 yds. if she was also on the move. The males of many species are short-lived in the adult state and these distances would probably be beyond their capacity unless they were grouped closely together, as is often the case, before his march began.

When we make similar calculations for a larger spider like *Agelena*, assuming web and leg-span respectively of 1 ft. and 2 ins., we find that the lone male would have to travel on average 7.1 miles to find the only female. With a hundred of each sex to the acre the distance would be reduced to 124 yds. If we take hunting spiders with a similar leg span, like *Pisaura*, the solitary male would have to walk 19.4 miles or, with a hundred of each sex, the average distance required of a male would be 342 yds.

The smaller the species the more abundant it must be to escape extinction. Even the spiders which are thought to be rare must be common somewhere and will be found in plenty once we find the right place and understand their habits.

In considering the effect of the spider menace on the evolution of protective devices by insects we must try to picture a small defenceless insect in an acre field surrounded by 2,000,000 pairs of spiders' jaws. What chance of survival would it have ? If it could hop out of danger when threatened, its chances would be improved; and it would be safer still if it could fly from one place to another instead of having to walk. When spiders first appeared during the Devonian period about three hundred million years ago there were no flies. The spiders fed on crawling invertebrates. Is it unreasonable to suggest that the spider menace represented a principal factor in the evolution of the hopping and flying powers which innumerable insects now possess ?

We all remember the riddle: "Why did the fly fly ?". The answer: "Because the spider spied her" takes on a new significance if we accept the idea that flies might never have acquired the ability to fly at all had the spiders not existed !

Evolution, whether unconscious as in the development of insect structure and behaviour or conscious as in man's development of new methods of attack or defence, is never solely on the side of the defender. So, in this case, the diversion of substantial insect traffic to the air led through competition for food-supply amongst the spiders to the development of new methods of attack. Gummy orb webs like those of the Garden Spider were slung in the air to entrap insects in flight. Another method, reminiscent of barrage balloon technique in the last war, is employed by *Agelena* and other spiders, where taut cables arrest the flight of an insect and cause it to fall on to a concave sheet. Here ground staff in the form of an agile spider is waiting to pounce on a victim whose escape is impeded by trip-wires.

We try to avoid being bitten by insects by smearing fluids on our skins. Someday we may discover what causes insects to have preferences for some people over others; and then it may be possible to achieve immunity by injecting ourselves with a substance which will dissuade insects from wanting to suck our blood. Many insects have achieved this kind of protection from spiders without the need for injections. Besides having a sense of taste in their mouths spiders have what is known as a chemotactic, or taste-by-touch sense, in their palps and legs which frequently enables them to reject an insect without inflicting a bite. This benefits both the spider and the insect. The distasteful insect may escape a wound and the less impulsive spider may avoid sickness, for it is a common occurrence to see a spider stagger clumsily to a nearby leaf to wipe away drops of liquid vomited from its mouth after biting an unpalatable insect.

Several unpalatable insects, including the Burnet, the Cinnabar and the Magpie moths, show one very interesting feature when caught by a spider. They lie quite still and allow themselves to be bitten. Were they to struggle, the spider's reactions to movement are so strong that it would probably inflict a series of bites despite the flavour and this would lead to the insect's death. By remaining motionless they are usually bitten once and then carried on to the edge of the web and dropped to safety. I say 'safety' because these insects which lie still appear to be none the worse for one bite and I am inclined to think that they may have developed some partial chemical immunity to spider poison.

It is true to say that insects like the Burnet and Cinnabar moths which are distasteful to vertebrate animals are also unpalatable to spiders, but by far the largest number of those rejected by spiders on account of their flavour are readily accepted by birds, toads and other insectivorous vertebrates. These include many plant-bugs, ants, sawflies, ichneumons, beetles, mites, woodlice, certain flies and certain spiders. When we find that many of them, including some plant-bugs, aphids, beetles, ants and harvestmen, exude a fluid unpalatable to spiders only when they are attacked, the defensive nature of the distastefulness is obvious. Further, the fact that in many cases this defence is of no avail against vertebrate animals makes it clear that spiders, their greatest potential enemies, can be held chiefly responsible for the evolution of these defensive fluids.

I have just mentioned that many plant-bugs, beetles and mites are rejected on account of their flavour. Those which are not have often adopted another means of defence. Some have developed armour-plating which is impenetrable to most spiders; the interesting thing to notice is that here again, as with the strongly distasteful insects, the heavily armour-plated ones draw in their legs out of harm's way and lie still, secure in their armour, until they are discarded.

Those who know Kipling's Second Jungle Book will remember Baloo's recitation of the Laws of the Jungle. Strangely enough he forgot to mention one very important law. This is that you should take care if you encounter any creature which is coloured black and red or black and yellow. Such creatures are to be avoided for their bite, sting or flavour. These warning colours are respected by vertebrate animals but neither spiders nor, I believe, other invertebrate creatures have learned to take heed of them. Although red and black Burnet and Cinnabar moths are rejected by spiders they have first to be tasted or touched. Thus the reason for rejection lies in their flavour rather than

their colour. Having discovered that the message of warning colouration is understood only by vertebrate animals we can understand why
it is that this colour code has not been developed by insects much below
say a fifth of an inch in length. On smaller insects it would never be
noticed by mammals, birds or toads.

It is well known that spider-hunting wasps of the family Pompilidae
induce panic in spiders, which often prevents them using their jaws in
self-defence when cornered. These wasps are often black and red, but
this does not provide the explanation as others which are grey and
white produce the same effect. Attract the attention of a Garden Spider
to a freshly killed Pompilid in its web and after one touch it will beat
a retreat more hasty than that from any unpalatable insect. This is not
due to flavour, as I shall show presently, and it seems evident that these
wasps have something in the nature of Warning Scent of which spiders
have an inherited dread. Besides this the wasps also contribute to the
fear they inspire by Warning Movements. The waving of their legs and
the jerking of their bodies serve as a threat which is understood by
insects and spiders. If the female spider jerks her body in an unaccus-
tomed manner when she is not receptive to the courtship of a male he
will either retreat or remain at a safe distance. The hunting Pompilid
vigorously and continuously jerks her body and vibrates her wings and
antennae. Thus she induces fear and therefore gains safety from injury
by Warning Movements before they make contact and by Warning
Scent directly the spider touches her.

There is one interesting exception to this which helps to support my
conclusions. There is a spider known as *Ciniflo* which is never attacked
by these wasps because it weaves a certain type of web like adhesive lace,
which the wasp cannot negotiate. If a Pompilid is placed in one of these
webs the *Ciniflo*, which has had no reason to inherit any fear of these
wasps, attacks and kills it without hesitation. The fact that it eats the
wasp shows that it is not unpalatable.

Some conclusions to be drawn from an awakening to the importance
of numbers are:

First, that spiders can be placed top of the list of potential enemies
of insects.

Secondly, that the vast spider population can only survive as a
result of divergent specialisation which has produced the maximum
population with the minimum amount of competition.

Thirdly, that many individuals of each species must be concentrated
in an area or else the sexes will not meet and the species will not survive.

Fourthly, that the spider menace has led to the evolution amongst insects of protective devices, including flavours distasteful to spiders and armour-plating which spiders' fangs cannot penetrate. The menace may even have been a principal factor in the evolution of hopping and flight.

Lastly, that new defences and forms of aggression are constantly in process of being evolved and of vieing with one another for supremacy.

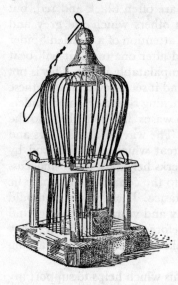

FIG. 27.   A Chinese spider-fighting cage in the author's possession

CHAPTER 6

THE LIFE OF A SPIDER

THE biographer cannot fail to find vast differences in the life-histories of spiders as he passes from one family to another, but an outline of their general features will save some explanation and repetition later.

The point in the spider's life-cycle at which to start my story was decided after reading an essay by Dr. William Kirby (1835) to which my friend Dr. F. A. Freeth had called my attention. Besides being a splendid naturalist, Dr. Kirby was a deeply religious man who tormented himself with the implications he drew from the first chapter of Genesis. Here he learned that all creeping things were already created in the lifetime of Adam and Eve, so what could this mean but that lice, ticks, bugs, fleas and other noxious pests were all dependent on them? As a result of long and anxious meditation he convinced himself that some of these creeping things were lying dormant in the egg stage until there were more human beings to share the burden!

Whether or not Dr. Kirby solved the age-old question of the priority of the chicken or the egg, I find it convenient to start with the development of the egg.

Gradually the embryo spider begins to take form on the outside of the egg yolk just below the chorion or 'shell'. Buds appear on the cephalothorax and become differentiated into the chelicerae, palps and legs whilst other buds are at first associated with 8 to 12 segments of the abdomen recognisable at this early stage. In the course of its development the embryo spider is recalling its aquatic ancestry from a segmented creature with abdominal appendages, but before long these buds all disappear except for those on the second to the fifth somites or segments. Buds on the second and third somites are transformed into book-lungs and those on the fourth and fifth into spinnerets.

When the embryo, ventral surface outwards, has nearly encircled the yolk, the chorion or outer covering is burst open by the pressure of the expanding embryo helped in some species by a little egg-tooth close to the base of each palp, which is shed later.

In most spiders the freshly hatched baby has no hair, spines, pigmentation or tarsal claws, nor can it feed or spin. There is no parallel here with the larval stage of an insect but we see before us an incompletely developed spider.

In the course of a few days this spiderling has absorbed most of the remaining yolk, and has increased its size considerably since escaping from the confines of the encircling egg covering. Now it sheds its skin for the first time; and a true spider emerges with hair, spines, claws, sight, and powers of feeding and spinning. With some exceptions it is still inside the egg-sac, and here it will remain for a matter of days or months according to the season and the weather. Then the young spiders cut their way out of the egg-sac and emerge. We are still watching stages in the evolutionary history of the spiders themselves so the young of different species and of different families resemble one another more closely now than they will later in their lives.

At first they may show little inclination to feed as they are still obtaining their food-requirements from yolk material in their abdomens. They may cluster together in the sunlight in a tight ball (*Araneus diadematus*), or climb on to their mother's back (*Lycosa*); they may remain in their mother's burrow (*Segestria*) or in the special tent she builds for them (*Pisaura*). Before long, however, the time arrives when they need food; and here again there is considerable variation in the amount of parental care they receive. In some species of *Theridion* the babies can be seen sharing a fly with their mother, but still more touching and remarkable is the female of *T. sisyphium* who hangs down in her web and allows the young to feed from her mouth. The young of *Amaurobius* stay feeding in their mother's burrow longer than any other young spiders I know, and finally they may even make use of her corpse as food when the end of her life arrives (see fig. 93, p. 197).

So long as the young are provided with food they usually show little sign of attacking one another; but most mothers do not provide food for their young and an early scattering is necessary if substantial cannibalism is to be avoided. This scattering can either be gradual or else sudden and complete. The young of *Pholcus*, for instance, start by hanging motionless in their mother's web, but gradually, as the days go by, begin to migrate inch by inch along the walls where they live, spinning little webs in which to catch small insects for themselves. The more sudden type of emigration takes the form of aeronautic flights on sunny days. The young spiders climb to the top of grass or other herbage where they stand with abdomen tilted upward and squeeze out silk which is drawn upwards by the air-currents until the pull is sufficient for the young spider to float into the air. It is not yet fully established as to how many families scatter in this way; but my own experience suggests that several families, including those which are primitive in many respects, like the Atypidae, Oonopidae, Dysderidae, Scytodidae and Pholcidae, do not take part in these flights. They may be able to bridge short distances by hanging down on a thread, as I have seen a young *Segestria* doing, and being blown laterally on it,

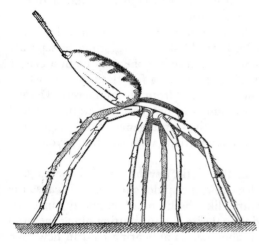

FIG. 28. The aeronaut about to embark

or else letting out another thread which makes contact with a neighbouring object, but they will not be met with high in the air or far from land like other spiders.

Casualties are high in the egg-stage but they are likely to be higher still amongst very young spiders, of which many are gobbled up by swallows and swifts during their aeronautic excursions, or descend on water or other unsuitable environments. Those which survive these hazards will find a host of enemies waiting for them at ground level, and also extremely keen competition for the tiny insects which their limited stamina demands they should have without delay if death from starvation is to be avoided. Some undoubtedly die from starvation, — I have seen this happen to the babies of a *Pholcus* in the room where I am writing. But I suspect that the abundance of small insects in

Britain, in contrast to the tropics, is adequate for more spiders than food supply will support later in their lives.

Growth makes further moults necessary when expansion is prevented by the skeleton of cuticle in which the body is enclosed, and this process may be stimulated by hormones produced by an internal organ discovered by A. Schneider (1892). Immediately after the old skin has been shed the fresh cuticle is soft; and it is only at this time that internal pressure enables the cephalothorax to expand and the legs to lengthen, whereas the more elastic abdomen can grow progressively larger in between the moults. This means that there is a steady increase in the length of a growing spider, with sudden spurts at each moult due to the increased size of the cephalothorax.

Before each moult a spider loses interest in food for a few days and then hangs immobile whilst its old skin is beginning to separate from the new. According to her normal habits she may be in a cell or in the open, but even the Wolf Spider spins a few threads from which to hang by her legs and by another thread from her spinnerets. Despite her utter helplessness whilst a moult is in progress it is strange to find so little evidence of special protective stratagems. Some Agelenids block the entrance to their tubular retreats with silk but beyond this I know of nothing.

Presently a distinct split in the chitin develops round the edge of the carapace just above the legs, and the spider's movements cause the entire carapace to pivot upwards like the lid of a box lightly hinged at the pedicel. By now the abdominal skin is also splitting along the sides and the upper surface of the abdomen is appearing clad in new pale skin. Then by slow stages the spider has to haul her legs out of the old cuticle like fingers from a glove. This is done by rhythmic contractions and extensions of the legs and is eased by a lubricating fluid which lies between the two layers of chitin. At first the spider's body may be inverted in a horizontal position, but by the time the legs are freed she may have pivoted through an angle of 90° and be hanging with body vertically downwards on the thread from her spinnerets (see fig 29).

The freshly moulted spider is pale and soft, and she remains hanging until the chitin hardens. During this time of waiting the legs are repeatedly flexed and Bonnet (1930) has shown that these exercises are necessary to ensure supple joints. Prevention causes the legs to be permanently stiff and distorted.

The difficulty with which the legs are extracted makes it all the

John Markham

PLATE 2. *Micrommata virescens* (13 mm.)

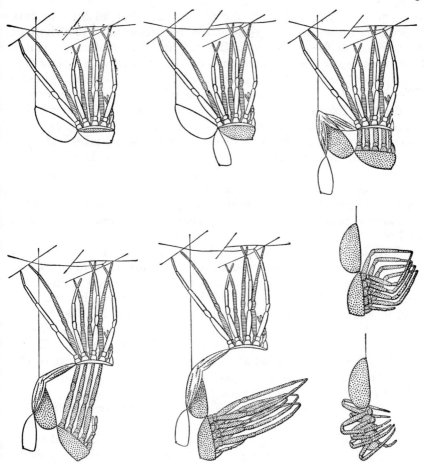

FIG. 29. A *Dolomedes* moulting. Stages in the process (after P. Bonnet)

more remarkable that the bulky palpal organs of an adult male should have succeeded in passing through the narrow inelastic palpal segments. The conjuring trick is achieved by trailing this pliable mass behind the tarsal tip in an extruded position (Bonnet, 1930). It is only at the final moult that the male and female genital organs are exposed and that the male adopts his full colours in species where he differs from his mate.

In a very young spider the moult may take only a few minutes but as it grows older and larger the process may last an hour or two. Sometimes it dies during leg-extraction due, apparently, to a shortage of lubricant or to some climatic factor. The number of moults varies, with size being the principal determining factor. A very tiny spider may have to moult only three times compared with ten in our largest species (*Dolomedes*). Following the same general rule fewer moults are needed by the male than by the larger female, and he usually matures before she does. This is a distinct advantage in some species like *Drassodes* where the male's mating with his fierce spouse often takes place just after her last moult when she is in no state to harm him !

Since moults take place in order to allow growth the reason for fewer moults in small spiders is not surprising. A freshly hatched *Erigone*, for instance, is already one third the length of its parent whereas the comparable proportion for a large spider may be more like one twelfth or less.

Rate of growth is affected by the amount of food consumed in a given period, which is related both to its availability in quantity and the amount of suitable hunting weather. Scarcity of food or inclement weather will retard moults. Retarded development will, in turn, often lead to more moults than is normal for the species. Thus Bonnet has found that the normal ten for *Dolomedes* can be varied from nine to thirteen according to the conditions provided in his laboratory. Before leaving this subject it should also be mentioned that large spiders, like *Atypus* and *Tegenaria*, which survive for a year or two in the adult state, often have one further moult each year.

It seems to have been characteristic of primitive invertebrates that lost limbs were renewed during subsequent moults, and this phenomenon has been inherited by spiders. If a spider's leg is seized by an enemy, a slight tug results in it being left in the enemy's grasp whilst the spider makes an escape. The leg snaps at the weakest point which is between the coxa and the trochanter. Thereafter a new leg begins developing within the coxa, complete but in miniature form, which uncoils at the next moult. It takes three or four moults to catch up in size with that of its pair. Bonnet's experiments have shown that severed maxillae, chelicerae and spinnerets can also be renewed. This helps to show that regeneration is inherited from primitive ancestors rather than being a process specially evolved by spiders to escape their enemies.

The young spider's independent existence usually starts after the second moult. In general terms it conforms to the habits of its mother

PLATE I. Madonna and Child, painted on spider's web by Joann Burgman of Innsbruck early in the nineteenth century, is framed between two sheets of glass in Chester Cathedral.

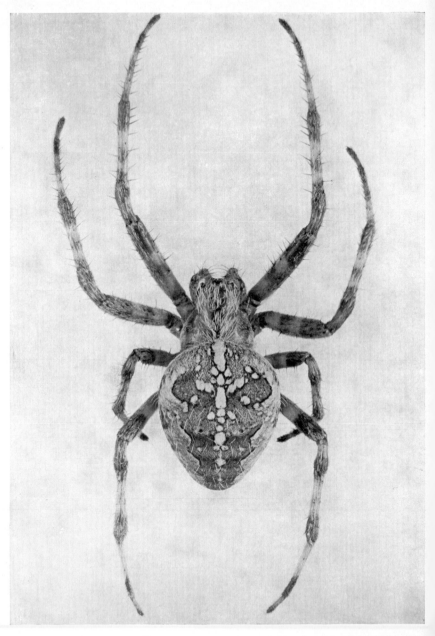

PLATE 11. The Garden Spider, *Araneus diadematus* (12 mm.)

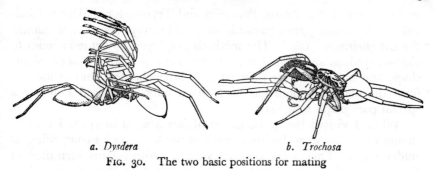

a. Dysdera   *b. Trochosa*
FIG. 30.   The two basic positions for mating

in the method used to capture prey; though in some cases these habits resemble more closely the less specialised methods of some earlier ancestor. From this time onwards it may never again be out of touch with silk threads of its own manufacture.

Survival is menaced at all stages in a spider's life by the direct and indirect effects of climate, to which spiders have partly adapted themselves by their choice of habitat and their behaviour. Floods and droughts are both obvious killers; but the absence of enough feeding days in an excessively bad spring or summer can cause a host of spiders to fail to mature and lay eggs before the season has passed.

If climate, in its widest sense, is the principal enemy, there are many other enemies waiting to eat or parasitise spiders. Ranging through the animal kingdom the largest known individual consumer amongst fish is a trout, amongst amphibia a toad, amongst reptiles a lizard, amongst birds a starling, and amongst mammals a shrew; but the principal menace really comes from the invertebrate world on account of its huge population (Bristowe, 1941). Just as man's worst enemy can at times be man, I believe spiders destroy more spiders than any other enemy. These may be followed by hymenopterous insects (Pimpline

FIG. 31.   Two sperm webs, the platform in each case measuring about 3 **mm.**
WS—F

and Cryptine Ichneumons, Pompilid and Trypoxylonid Wasps, Chalcids, etc.). Beetles, ants, parasitic flies, and centipedes, do not exhaust the list (Bristowe, 1941). The methods employed by some enemies to capture spiders, and of spiders to escape them by adaptations of colour, shape and behaviour, are referred to in later chapters; but as menace from the plant kingdom has never been fully recognised I devote a special paragraph to it here.

When I visited the arctic island of Jan Mayen in 1921, I noticed thousands of the dead bodies of each of the four species comprising its spider fauna. They were covered with a white fungus identified as *Cordiceps*. At that time I was told it developed on their dead bodies. Now I believe it kills the spiders and is almost the only enemy these spiders have in this cold damp island. Recently Mr. E. A. Ellis has introduced me to the fungus *Torrubiella albolanata* Petch, in Wheatfen. Here I saw countless Linyphiids and frequent specimens of a small Agelenid (*Antistea elegans*) killed by this Hypocreaceid fungus. It appears first as a faint whitish bloom on the living spider, which soon becomes sluggish and dies. The white bloom becomes powdery and bears conidia at which stage it is known as *Cylindrophora aranearum*. After a further week or two the perithecia erupt from the now floccose conidial layer and these look like yellowish tipped painted nipples emerging from the tomentum when they are ripe. So far as it is known this fungus is restricted to the Norfolk Broads where it attacks spiders' eggs as well as spiders, but there are several other species with a similar habit recorded from Yorkshire to Sussex. (T. Petch, 1948).

Having survived the threats of starvation, climate and enemies the male spider, if he is a web-builder, abandons his web, and spends his time searching for females and courting them, often with little effort devoted in between whiles to feeding himself. His remaining span of life is usually short, and post-mortem investigations would show that death was in most cases due to exhaustion and under-nourishment rather than to slaughter by the females as is commonly supposed. Such tragedies do occur but are comparatively rare.

The mating habits are unique in some respects and highly remarkable in others. They are widely variable and very important in the study of evolution and of relationships, as well as in helping to understand the functions and nature of puzzling structures and senses.

In simple outline what happens is this. Within a few days of his final moult the male builds a tiny triangle or band of web, usually measuring only a few millimetres in length, on which he deposits a drop of sperm after tapping his genital opening against it. His palpal organs absorb this and he goes in search of a female. On finding one he may seize her to prevent escape and then stimulate her by fondling her with his legs; but more generally there is a form of courtship before he attempts to take possession. In web-building spiders this is tactile and in the nature of morse code, since it is carried out by tweaks of the web and vibrations set up (in some families) by stridulating organs. In long-sighted hunting spiders the courtship is visual and more in the nature of semaphore, in that the legs and palps may be raised or waved in droll antics which display plumes or other decorations developed only in the males. Courtship by either method avoids him being mistaken for prey and stimulates the female. The male adopts one of two basic mating positions which have many variations. Either he creeps under her from in front and inserts both palps, or one at a time, into twin orifices leading to her spermathecae, or he climbs on to her back and leans over to insert one palp at a time. Muscular contractions cause the body fluid to surge along the legs and palps, and to exert pressure on the elastic walls of the sperm reservoir. This pressure ejects the sperm.

Soon after mating is completed he recharges his palps, which is a process called sperm induction, and usually travels in search of another female.

The sperm is stored in the female's spermathecae, for long periods if necessary, and is discharged into the egg mass when this is extruded from an orifice in the epigastric furrow. The fluid egg mass is usually deposited on to a saucer of silk prepared by the mother and is then covered with more silk. Many mothers stay on guard until the young emerge but those who abandon them often camouflage the egg-sacs with mud (*Agroeca*) or debris (*Araneus*), give them an outer covering of tough papery silk (*Zelotes*), suspend them from a thread (*Ero*) or provide some other means of protection.

In general terms the number of eggs in a sac varies with the bulk of the species (and of the individual belonging to a single species) owing to the eggs of smaller spiders being bigger relative to body size than those of large species. At the extremes we have the tiny *Oonops* laying only two eggs, compared with up to a thousand by *Araneus quadratus*. But this is not the complete story; because most spiders lay more than one batch of eggs and there is a tendency for those which lay very few eggs at a time to lay many batches.

The maximum number of batches a species can lay — and this number varies considerably in different species — is perhaps seldom achieved in nature because it is dependent on ideal climatic conditions over a prolonged period and an abundance of food. Thus in our climate the oncome of autumn prevents, I think, both *Araneus quadratus* and *A. diadematus* laying more than one batch, whereas the latter is said to have laid no less than six batches in captivity under conditions where summer warmth continued.

Where several batches are laid by a spider, there is usually a downward trend in the number of eggs in successive batches; but it is surprising how one mating will enable a female to lay fertile eggs over a long period, even if this is extended from the autumn of one year to the spring of the next.

Making allowances for the number of batches laid by different species, I would estimate that the total number of eggs varies for different species from about twenty-five to a thousand, the average for all our species being brought down to a hundred or less by the large number of small Linyphiids in our fauna.

Before leaving the subject of eggs I should like to repeat three general 'laws' of special interest. Small spiders lay fewer and relatively larger eggs in each batch than large spiders. Small spiders, with relatively larger eggs, need fewer moults to attain their full size. Well fed spiders lay more eggs than half-starved ones.

In closing this outline of the life-cycle it is appropriate to speak briefly about the natural span of a spider's life.

Some Argiopids may pass the winter as eggs or as young still nestling together in the egg-sac. These may die in the following autumn when they are about one year old or slightly less.

Many Lycosids, Salticids and other spiders hatch in spring or early summer and die during the summer or autumn of the following year when they are about one and a half years old.

Some spiders like *Tegenaria* and *Pholcus* may live two or three years by surviving a year or two after they are grown up. Others like *Scytodes* and *Atypus* take more than a year to mature and then survive a few more years after that.

I notice a tendency for the more primitive spiders to grow up more slowly and to live longer than the more modern types, and also for larger forms to reach their full growth more slowly than their smaller relatives, but this is not invariably the case.

In captivity Bonnet (1935) has shown that life can be prolonged by shielding spiders from extremes of climate, by retarding their growth with a scanty food supply and by denying them mates. All three factors

combined to give me an *Atypus* with perhaps nine years of life in a
cool greenhouse.

FIG. 32.   Pompilid wasp stinging a spider

CHAPTER 7

THE ATYPIDAE
Purse Web Spiders

SOME years ago I passed in stages from the enchantment of hope to blank disillusionment when a naturalist told me that he had seen spiders at New Milton in Hampshire some twelve years previously which built genuine hinged trap-doors similar to those familiar to him from Jamaica. He produced a witness and the two observers were both so confident in their account of what they had seen, and were so sure of the exact spot, that I found my initial scepticism giving way to feverish excitement. Two strenuous week-ends were spent in intense search

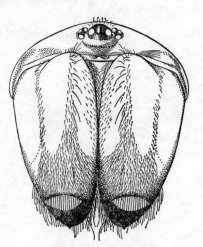

FIG. 33. *Atypus* face

for confirmation of this thrilling discovery, during one of which I was accompanied by both my informants. Alas, it had been a myth — a faded imprint on the mind whose outlines became distorted when the effort was made to delineate the details.

Why had he delayed twelve years before announcing such a spectacular discovery? Because our *Atypus affinis* has been incorrectly called the British Trap-door Spider and he had only just learned that no known British spider really made a trap-door. Although tubular bag-like purses are no longer fashionable amongst men, the name Purse-web Spider applied to *Atypus* in America is more appropriate.

Atypus is a spider of distinction and mystery which has aroused widespread interest ever since she was first recorded in Britain by by W. E. Leach in 1816. This is our sole representative of the sub-Order Mygalomorphae to which the Trapdoor Spiders and so-called Bird Eating Spiders of tropical countries belong. She has huge chelicerae which largely contribute to an appearance so strange that we must expect something unusual from her; and she does not disappoint us.

Long before sealed room mysteries were invented by detective story writers, naturalists were puzzling over the methods employed by *Atypus* to keep herself alive whilst living in a long silk tube sealed at both ends. Two excellent studies by F. Enock (1885, 1892) largely provided the solution to this problem.

Atypus affinis is now known to inhabit a number of places in Herts, Cambridge, Essex, Middlesex, Kent, Sussex, Surrey, Hampshire, Dorset, Cornwall, Somerset, Pembroke, Glamorgan and Offaly. I have also found her in the Channel Islands, Isle of Wight, Scillies and Lundy. On the continent she extends from Denmark to Algeria and eastwards to Hungary.

Neither *Atypus* nor her handiwork can be confused with any other British spider. The female is a clumsy short-legged light brown spider whose body reaches about 12 mm. in length (see Plate IV, p. 81). The cephalothorax and stout legs tend to have a greenish tinge and the almost translucent appearance of a cave-dweller. The slim male, which reaches 8 or 9 mm., is very dark brown, or almost black, as befits a night wanderer. Conspicuous features shared by no other British spider are the massive forward-projecting chelicerae with an upward and downward movement of the fangs, two pairs of pale almost circular book-lungs on the lower surface of the abdomen and long three-segmented posterior spinnerets (see figs. 9, 14, pp. 28, 33).

Atypus lives in a sealed silken tube with no visible entrance or exit. This tube is usually eight or nine inches in length, although one has been found exceeding fifteen inches. All but two to three inches pass steeply down into the ground whilst the portion above ground resembles the inflated finger of a glove (see Plate IIIa, p. 80). The two end portions of the tube, where the spider needs room to turn, are the most spacious. The tubes can be found at all seasons of the year; but during the winter when the spiders are in a state of hibernation the aerial portion is collapsed. At other times they may easily be mistaken for roots projecting from the soil. The silk is intermixed with earth or sand grains implanted by the spider which helps to make them inconspicuous. They are most easily seen during a sunny period shortly after rain has fallen because the tubes dry more quickly to a lighter tone than the moisture-laden soil beside them. Banks and slopes with a southerly aspect composed of sandy, chalky or friable soil are preferred. Such soils are easy to excavate and do not get waterlogged. Many seemingly suitable places can be searched in vain but once an *Atypus* tube is discovered others will be near at hand. I once counted thirty-two in nine minutes along a road-side bank at Cooden Beach. Here they were on almost bare ground, but usually they are concealed under heather or grass. In some parts of Cornwall they occupy cliff chinks. Normally the exposed "finger" points up the bank or stands erect amongst the foliage, but sometimes the threads which originally directed the "finger" upwards have been broken and it has been swept in a downward direction.

Some early naturalists thought *Atypus* must emerge at night to hunt prey, whilst others were convinced that she subsisted on earthworms which blundered into the subterranean portions of the tube. Sometimes the tube was found to have more than one side-branch and this it was thought might help to increase the hunting field — or did it represent a separate abode for the male ? The mysteries of her habits stimulated F. Enock to make the only detailed study of any spider's life in Britain carried out during the nineteenth century (1885, 1892) and so excellent was his work that later naturalists have been able to add comparatively little to what he learned. These two papers were unillustrated so I was interested when Mr. H. Sargent drew my attention to some drawings by Enock for an article by Grant Allen in the Strand Magazine (Vol. XVI, 1898).

An *Atypus* starts living in a closed tube directly she has wandered from her mother's home. The first simple tube may not be the last, but in a short time she has settled in a place which suits her and only disaster will then cause her to move during the rest of her life. The framework of the aerial 'finger' is first spun round the spider with its tip attached by threads in an upward direction. Some earth at its base is then excavated with the spider's fangs and a load is carried between the chelicerae and is pressed into and through the scaffolding, where cement from her mouth causes some of the grains to adhere. Each fang is used like a delicate tool to place and space the grains of earth evenly in and on the outside wall of the silken covering. By twisting the abdomen up, over, and from side to side further layers of silk are added. More earth is excavated and more layers of silk are added until the first tube is completed. Thereafter the spider's growth is matched by extensions and enlargements of the tube, the earth always being brought to the top in the manner already described.

Although the silken tube is thick, elastic and unattached to the walls of the burrow it is seldom possible to collect the spider by pulling up the tube. After hauling it a short distance, sudden firm resistance is encountered due to the spider driving her fangs like an anchor into one side of the burrow and pressing her abdomen firmly against the other. If the tug-of-war is continued the tube breaks and the spider is lost.

There are two effective ways of capturing *Atypus*. One is to coax her into the aerial portion by means of a grass or insect and then to cut off her retreat; the other is to dig out the entire tube.

The inflation of the 'finger' is brought about simply by the passage of the spider's body along it, as can be seen by pressing it flat and then coaxing the spider to the surface. The earthy reinforcement to its elastic sides helps to stiffen the walls.

During the winter months from about November to early February, *Atypus* is in a state of hibernation at the bottom of the tube, and the aerial portion remains in a collapsed condition. The combined effect of rain and frost causes the walls to lose their elasticity and become cemented together. This forces the spider to build a fresh sector or fork above and occasionally below the ground when activity is resumed in the spring, but the old sector is then out of use.

The idea that *Atypus* feeds largely on earthworms gains no support from examination or tests. The larger remnants of her meals ejected from the top of the tube and the smaller fragments at the bottom show that her main food comprises beetles, bees, flies, earwigs and woodlice, all of which would have been caught above the ground. Soft creatures, like worms, would not leave such permanent evidence, and experiment with worms placed on the surface 'finger' has shown that they get torn in the encounter, leaving at most a part of their bodies in the spider's possession which cannot readily be hauled into the tube. Although *Atypus* may suck the worm's juices for a time, she does not appear to finish the meal.

At one time it was believed that *Atypus* emerged into the open at night and prowled abroad in search of food, but in fact she is a hermit, living like an anchorite in his cell, and waits for insects to crawl over the exposed 'finger' which is the normal extent of her hunting field.

The way in which an insect is seized can be watched by tickling the tube with a grass stem. Quite suddenly two shining curved fangs are violently protuded through the web; and it can be seen from their position that the spider strikes in shark-like manner with lower side uppermost. If a buzzing fly is held against the tube the fangs pierce its body and hold it like fish-hooks. The fangs are, of course, hinged to the massive basal segment of the chelicerae and a clenching movement now pulls and presses the insect against the tube wall beneath which this basal segment lies. After a certain amount of tugging and jerking, in the course of which one fang at a time may be withdrawn from its victim to assist in the next operation, a slit appears in the tube wall through which the insect is pulled.

Although this procedure has been seen by many observers since Enock first described it, there is one very interesting mechanical detail which I have been able to add (Bristowe, 1954). Each basal segment of the chelicerae has a neat line of 11 or 12 sharp teeth resembling a saw, and when the violent clenching movement takes place the struggling insect is of course crushed against them. Quite apart from their function

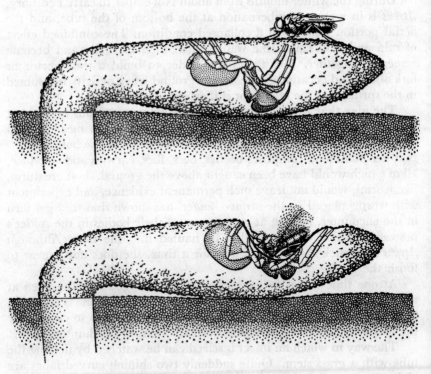

FIG. 34. *Atypus* catching a fly by transfixing it with her long fangs and slitting the tube wall through which it is hauled

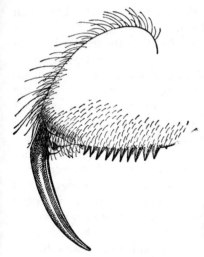

Fig. 35. Teeth on basic segment of an *Atypus* chelicera which perforate the tube wall and saw a slit in it

in wounding and mangling the victims, these teeth perforate the tube in two narrowly separated lines so that a neat slit is easily made in the tube wall by the tugging and sawing movements which follow (see figs. 34, 35).

From what I have written it will be seen that the huge conspicuous chelicerae fulfil a number of important functions in the life of *Atypus*. The exceptionally long fangs excavate and help to carry the earth, implant the sand grains on the outside of the tube, and pierce, poison and hold the victims. The basal segments play their part in carrying the earth to the surface, in pulping the food and in tearing open the tube.

Once the insect is inside the tube, *Atypus* carries it down to the chamber at the bottom and then usually fastens it to one side whilst a return journey is made to the surface. Here the fangs are employed to pull the gaping edges of the slit together before it is patched by a number of zig-zag lateral sweeps of the spinnerets across it.

Surprise is sometimes expressed at the apparent rarity of males: but the explanation is really quite simple. Right up to the time of their final moult the males resemble slender females except for a slight swelling of the palps after the penultimate moult. Then, after their last moult, they emerge in their true colours from the somewhat shorter tubes in which they have been living up to that time and go in search of females. This usually occurs in late September or in October when naturalists may not be in search of them.

When the male finds a female's tube he stops momentarily, as if petrified, and then taps rapidly with vibrating palps and legs. There is no visible response. He pauses and then continues. Still there is no sign of movement from within. Presently he tears an entrance in the tube and enters. Simple though these preliminaries may be they are of the utmost importance. They have prevented the female from transfixing him with her fangs. His code signals have had this immediate effect, and their repetition makes closer approach still safer as by that time her preying instincts have given place to her sexual instincts. She has inherited the instinct to react in this way to his particular signals and he the instinct to signal with this code in response to contact with the webbing of the tube. His is a chemotactic or taste-by-touch sense and hers a tactile one. Should they meet face to face in the unnatural surroundings of a cage she will do her best to kill him because he has been unable to give the right code signal.

If the female is immature or pregnant his advances from outside the tube are repulsed by another signal — a sharp tug or series of tugs at the tube. Her warning signal usually causes him to withdraw discreetly.

So much I have seen. His retirement into her opaque tube has concealed the rest of the proceedings; but Prof. U. Gerhardt (1929) has watched the mating of an allied species, *A. muralis* Bertk., by persuading the female to spin an earth-free tube in captivity. He noticed that the continuation of the male's serenade had a visible effect on the female's vulva which rolled outwards and open. Before tearing a hole in the tube wall the male exuded a large drop of saliva on to it which may, Gerhardt thinks, have had a softening effect. Once he was inside he ran rapidly up and down, and then came to rest facing her. Then with his front legs and partially opened chelicerae he pressed her flat against one wall with her ventral surface directed inwards. Holding her thus by rearing his cephalothorax, and still facing in the opposite direction to her, he inserted his palps alternately. When in repose, the male palpal organs lie along the ventral surface of the tarsus: but now the whole tarsus is twisted round and that part known as the conductor is introduced into the female vulva as well as the embolus, which suggests that it is not homologous with the conductor of the Araneomorph spiders. Also unlike the proceedings in most of the Araneomorph spiders, the right palp enters the female's right genital opening.

After each palp had been inserted two or three times for periods ranging from twenty seconds to twenty minutes there was a rest period of half an hour before a second series started of much the same kind. Rhythmic swellings of the bulb were noticed during copulation and when it was completed the male extracted his palp with a violent wrench and beat a retreat. He did not leave the tube however and, although males may eventually pay the penalty, husband and wife often appear to live together in amity or indifference for several months. Some males may die a natural death, others may be killed, but some survive the winter and escape. It is these last ones which are sometimes met with in the open in spring and early summer months.

FIG. 36. *Atypus* egg-sac slung inside the tube

The eggs, numbering about 100 to 150, are enclosed in an elongated silken sac which is slung by the ends like a hammock from the upper wall of the terminal chamber where the mother spends most of her time. The eggs are laid as early as June in the Scilly Islands but elsewhere July and August are the usual months. The young may hatch in August or September, but they remain quietly in their mother's tube until the following spring, usually March or April, when on sunny days they can be seen emerging by a small hole in the tube and clambering up the vegetation trailing a fine band of silk. I have never seen them floating in the air but I have noticed them running along bridges formed by threads wafted from one plant to another. Then, before night falls, they build their first little tubes and either enlarge them on succeeding days or else move on to more favourable sites.

Unless this account of *Atypus* life is seriously at fault, the remarkable fact emerges that eighteen months normally elapses between mating and the emergence of the young from their mother's nest. This exceptionally long period prepares us for the slow rate of growth and longevity of the spider.

Maturity is not reached, I believe, until the spiders are about four years old. A mating in September is followed by egg-laying in July and the departure of the young in the following March, eighteen months after the mating. Thereafter the mother may cling to life, and perhaps have another brood, during another two or three years, making a total life of seven or even eight years. I have little doubt that this period is sometimes exceeded as I once kept a female for five years after she was fully grown. Evidence from other families suggests that longevity is a primitive feature (Liphistiidae, Scytodidae etc.)

CHAPTER 8

THE CRIBELLATES

Lace-Web Spiders

THREE families of British spiders have a cribellum and a calamistrum. These families are the Eresidae, Uloboridae and Dictynidae. The cribellum is a small inconspicuous flat elongate plate immediately in front of the spinnerets. The calamistrum is an even comb, resembling a hair comb, on the metatarsus of the fourth pair of legs (see fig. 15, p. 34). The cribellum is a sieve-like plate from which a viscid substance is extruded through minute pores, combed out by the calamistrum and combined with ordinary threads from the spinnerets to provide a composite lace-like strand of a faintly bluish colour.

THE ERESIDAE

Only one species has been found in Britain; and so gorgeous is the male *Eresus niger* that it is every collector's dream to find one. Six males and one female were found between 1816 and 1906, and none since that date: so it is generally feared to be extinct as a result of the building which has taken place in the Poole, Bournemouth and Parley Heath localities from which all the specimens came.

The female is about 12 mm. in length and of a sombre velvety black. The smaller male has a

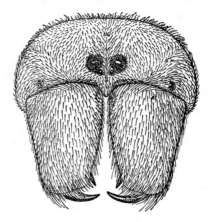

FIG. 37. *Eresus* face

velvety black cephalothorax with touches of scarlet at the edges. He
has stout black legs with white rings and an abdomen of vivid scarlet
with three pairs of round black spots edged with white hairs.

The male is unmistakable (see Plate IV, p. 81). The female's eye
pattern on her massive head distinguishes her from any other spider
(see fig. 9b, p. 28).

Let me say at once that I do not despair of *Eresus* being found in
Britain again, and that I hope clues may help some lucky person to
experience the thrill of feasting his eyes on the brilliant beauty of the
wandering male.

Let me start with an episode in Cornwall. When staying in Penzance
in July 1934 a shop-keeper gave me a graphic description of a bright
scarlet-bodied spider with black spots and black legs which he, his wife
and daughter had all watched in amazement at Kynance Cove in 1932
during the early part of the summer. It was standing beside some thick
matted web and it had struck them as being so remarkable that they
had watched it for several minutes and had often described it to their
friends — even referring to such details as the iridescent white rings on
its black legs. Their description was so clearly that of an *Eresus* male
that I persuaded them to lead me to the exact spot on the heathery
hill-slope some hundreds of yards above Kynance Cove. Although we
found no *Eresus* they utterly rejected such spiders as *Agelena* and *Pisaura*
saying that these were not only the wrong colour but also the wrong
shape. When I got home I sent them a preserved specimen from
southern Europe asking them to say if they thought or if they were
absolutely sure that this was the same or a different spider. They were
all positive it was the same spider.

Although caution will not allow me to accept this as proof it must
surely raise our hopes; and the fact that I met with no success myself
does not destroy this hope, because early July is not the season for males.

The chances of finding *Eresus* can be greatly improved by a knowledge of its habits. The description which follows is based partly on
my experience on the Continent but mainly on accounts given by
E. Norgaard (1941) in Denmark.

Eresus is to be found on heathery slopes with a southern aspect, and
the females build their nests alongside heather at the north edge of
sandy spaces where they are in full sunlight and protected from wind.
The female excavates a vertical burrow up to three inches in length
which is lined with tough silk. One side of the burrow lip is extended
upwards and over, forming, as it were, a roof. Extending from the

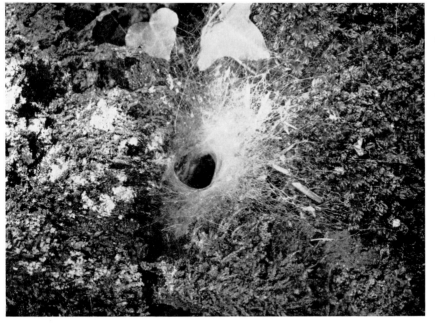

b. Collar of silk built by *Amaurobius terrestris* on a bank. (*H. Sargent*)

a. Aerial portion of closed tube built by *Atypus affinis* in a bank. (*H. Sargent*)

PLATE III

b. Eresus cinnabarinus male (8 mm.) (*W. H. T. Tams*)

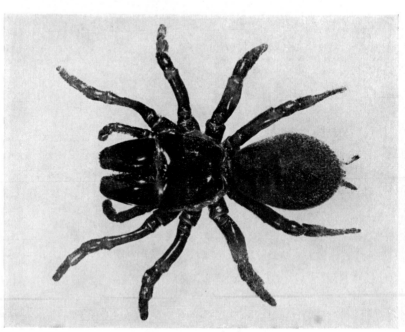

a. Atypus affinis (12 mm.) (*W. H. T. Tams*)

PLATE IV

edge of this roof are a number of criss-cross threads attached to the heather which take the form of a small, or sometimes even quite a large, sheet connected to the adjoining heather. This sheet represents the capture threads of the snare. The individual threads are all very strong and a microscope reveals that they comprise two straight threads and four crinkly ones combed through the calamistrum.

The female lurks beneath her roof. Remnants of her victims, attached to the outside walls of the tube, suggest that her principle diet comprises beetles and grasshoppers. She invariably attacks the leg of a victim which she pulls firmly into the capture threads. Not until the struggle ceases does she pull her prey down into her burrow if it is a formidable insect.

The male resembles the female in colour until his final moult in August or September. In our climate it seems probable that he hibernates soon afterwards and has to wait until April or May before he mates with a female, because, as the summer proceeds, the females of his generation close their burrows until the following spring. When he comes to a female's web in the spring, he starts walking about on it with stiff jerky steps and trembling body. Presently he approaches her and pushes his way under from in front, usually without resistance or even with the assistance of her third and fourth pairs of legs. Although mating may last for hours, only one palp is used but this is inserted again and again. (Gerhardt 1928).

In May she lays about eighty pale yellow eggs in an agglutinated mass which she covers with two layers of silk. The outer layer is woolly and composed of cribellate web camouflaged with food remnants or vegetable matter. The finished egg-sac is lenticular, about 9 mm. in diameter and 3 mm. in thickness. This is stored in the burrow at night, but she pushes it up and fixes it under the roof during the day where the eggs will get greater warmth. Gradually, as the weeks pass, the roof surface is extended and a closed chamber packed with silk is completed above the ground where the young hatch sometime in June. Here she dies in July or August and the babies hibernate in cells around her corpse. It seems likely that the normal life cycle is one month over three years.

If *Eresus* still lives in Britain, the males are most likely to be found wandering in the open in April or May on southern tracts of heather near the sea. The nests of the females, which have been likened to a cornucopia, would be most conspicuous between April and June, and should be sought at the edge of heather. My own inclinations would

WS–G

be to search in April any surviving terrains answering this description near the original neighbourhood close to the Dorset — Hampshire borders, as well as at Kynance Cove and the Isle of Wight. If anybody finds *Eresus* before I do, I shall feel no resentment !

THE ULOBORIDAE

Our two species are easily distinguished from all other British spiders and from each other both by the unusual arrangement of their eight diurnal eyes (see fig. 9, p. 28) and by their habits. Both are rare species inhabiting, so far as is known, only three or four localities.

Let us start with *Uloborus walckenaerius*. She reaches a length of about 6 mm. and has a whitish body with grey stripes down the centre and sides of the abdomen. Her first pair of legs are much longer and stronger than the others and their slightly swollen tibiae are armed with six or seven tooth-like spines.

Uloborus is known from various parts of the New Forest, from Bloxworth Heath and Wellington College. As a schoolboy I once found her on the Ranges at this third locality, where she had previously been recorded by one of the masters, but the exact spot is now overgrown with trees, so I have had to visit Beaulieu Road in the New Forest in order to acquaint myself with her habits. *

Here, as elsewhere, she spins her horizontal orb web on heather in open but sheltered situations. Her web, its mode of construction and her mating habits are all so similar to those of the Argiopidae that it seems almost unbelievable that they have been evolved independently and yet she is a cribellate spider. The hub, the free zone, the radii (about 30 to 40 in number) and the spirals are all present in the web, and temporary spirals are spun during construction as in the Argiopidae. Indeed the only marked difference is in the texture of the spirals and in the manner in which they are laid down. During this operation she circles in a sideways position with her front legs stretched out laterally whilst combing out the cribellate threads and attaching them from radius to radius.

The finished web has a stabilimentum or ribbon of silk, not unlike that of the Argiopid *Cyclosa* except that it is white, which extends across the web and is interrupted only by the central area of the strengthening zone. When constructing the stabilimentum, Wiehle (1927) tells us that she moves outwards from the hub laying a broad strip of silk along a radius and then turns round to swing her body rapidly from side to side

* Note: Now known also from Surrey heaths.

whilst using her hind pair of legs to press the freshly spun silk on to the initial strip.

Uloborus has no retreat. She sits in the centre of her web with the long front legs stretched out close together. When she is aroused from this position of rest by the struggles of an insect, the legs separate in order to aid her detection of its direction. She shakes the web and then moves straight towards the insect, turning as she approaches to throw some silk over it with her hind legs.

So far as we know the Uloboridae are unique amongst our spiders in having no poison glands and unlike the Argiopidae they do not bite their victims until they start to eat them. After a first wrapping *Uloborus* cuts the insect free from the snare and carries it to the hub where she holds her bundle in her second and third pairs of legs and revolves it, whilst drawing threads from her spinnerets with the fourth pair. Only when this second wrapping process is finished does she bite the insect for the first time.

The spiders become adult in May or June and the slim male goes in search of a female. After finding an inhabited web he lays down a special mating thread in the same way as the Argiopid spiders and dances up and down on this. She swings her body up and down in response and then by degrees moves towards him on to this mating thread. Presently she hangs downwards and he makes a jab at her epigyne with one of his palps. The first jab may be unsuccessful, but directly the palp is inserted he grasps her with his legs and a swelling of the palpal bulb can be seen. Each palp is inserted once for about five minutes before they part.

After constructing a small silk platform between forked threads and depositing a sperm droplet, the male changes his position to the lower surface as in the *Mimetidae* and Linyphiinae and reaches round its edge with each palp in turn to insert the embolus into it. Absorption takes about a quarter of an hour.

When the time for egg-laying arrives in June the female makes a rudimentary web nearby comprising a hub, a few radii and perhaps a few spirals. Here she constructs and hangs an irregular elongate lightish brown egg-sac of papery silk containing about 70 to 100 eggs. This she guards for a few days, before abandoning it in order to make a fresh web.

The young spiders emerge, after moulting for the first time within the egg-sac, and build small rudimentary webs without spirals. The fact is that at this stage they have no calamistrum or cribellum and it

is only after their second moult that these
appear and that they can complete the kind
of web normal for their species.

Our other Uloborid is a peculiar looking
spider with very remarkable habits. The full
grown *Hyptiotes paradoxus* female may reach
6 mm. in length and has a lumpy awkward
appearance not out of keeping with her
frequent pose as an excrescence of a twig on
which she sits. The legs, especially the hind
three pairs, are short, and the cephalothorax
small in relation to the humpy abdomen
which varies in colour from ginger to dark
brown. The smaller male is remarkable for

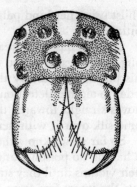

FIG. 38. *Uloborus* face

the immense size of the palpal organs, each of which is about as
voluminous as the entire cephalothorax ! It would be an advantage
to adopt the remarkable habit of an American Theridiid (*Tidarren*)
which amputates one of his palps before he is fully grown.

Hyptiotes is found in the New Forest, at Box Hill and at Glengariff
(Cork). It was also recorded from the Lake District nearly a hundred
years ago, but has not been rediscovered there. In my experience, the
female lives in shade on the twigs of box and yew or other conifers
where she builds a triangular web representing one seventh of an orb
web. It has four radii and ten or more spirals which have been combed
from the cribellum. The cribellate spirals have a zig-zag appearance
owing to the spider drawing them a short distance along the radial
thread before crossing the next inter-radial space.

Hyptiotes is unique in building a triangular snare, and the way in
which it is built is so complicated (H. Wiehle, 1927; M. J. and B. J.
Marples, 1937) that I shall dwell only on the operation of the completed
snare. The spider sits inconspicuously, with her body touching a twig
and with her front legs outstretched, holding a thread attached to the
apex of the triangle. The first surprise is to discover that there is not
a single thread stretching from the web to the twig. The spider herself
forms a bridge between one thread, passing from the twig to her
spinnerets, and another from the web which she is holding taut. This
latter thread she has hauled so tight that there is usually a loop of slack
which is held by the third pair of legs. In other words she is suspended
in mid-air between two unconnected threads.

Complete stillness is maintained in this strained position until an

PLATE V. *Ciniflo similis* (11 mm.) combing threads with her calamistrum.

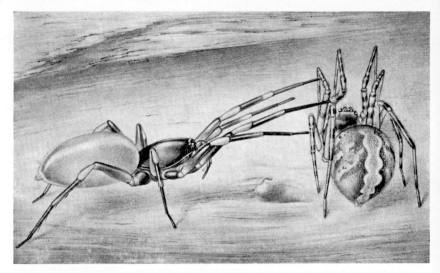

a. Harpactea hombergi (6 mm.) measuring *Theridon melanurum* (3.75 mm.) before attacking.

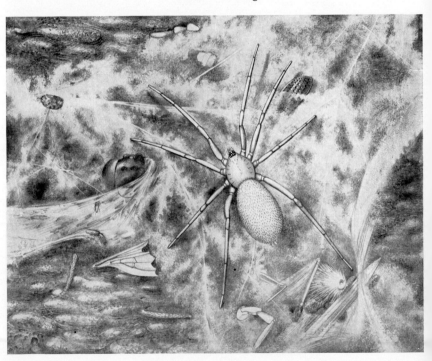

b. Oonops pulcher (2 mm.) scavenging under bark in the web of a *Ciniflo*.

PLATE VI

insect touches the snare. The trap — for so it may be termed — is sprung once, twice and perhaps three times by the spider, whilst she simultaneously releases the coil of slack held by the third pair of legs, lets out more silk from her spinnerets and gathers up the trap line with her front legs. Each time the trap is sprung, she is projected forwards closer to the snare and on reaching the insect, now firmly enswathed in the folds of the slackened spirals, she further envelops it in silk drawn from her spinnerets by her hind legs.

Cutting the bundle free and carrying it in her palps, she travels back towards the twig and pauses before reaching it to wrap the insect still more securely. With front legs stretched out at right angles along the single thread, and with abdomen hanging vertically downwards, she revolves the insect with her third pair of legs whilst the fourth pair draws silk from her spinnerets.

The watcher is amazed at the variety of different tasks allotted simultaneously to her different pairs of legs whilst she is poised precariously in the gap between the threads which link her base to the snare.

The wrapping of the insect is a lengthy process which may take

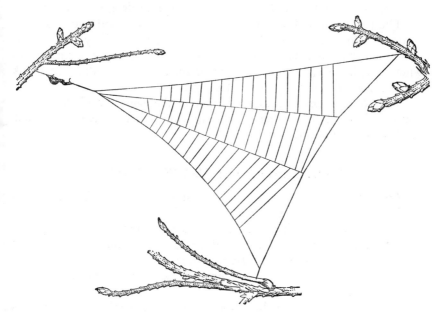

Fig. 39. *Hyptiotes* (6 mm.) in her trap snare

nearly half an hour, so thickly is it festooned with silk. When this is at last finished she backs towards the twig, with her parcel in her palps, drawing in the bridge threads as she goes. On reaching her destination she bites the insect for the first time and pumps digestive fluid into it. She is a slow eater and a meal may take twenty-four hours according to Marples.

Hyptiotes reaches maturity in late summer and mating does not take place until early spring. The male spins a mating thread and dances on it until the female comes to him and hangs down from it. Then he bounds forward and inserts one palp while the other is held vertically upwards. Exactly how the very long embolus is fully inserted in her body is still a mystery, even to U. Gerhardt who has watched this happen under a microscope, but it implies the existence of a long and complicated passage in her abdomen. The bulb swells during the mating and the full act of mating may comprise the insertion of each palp three times without fresh courtship in between.

The separation is peaceful and during sperm induction the male applies his emboli direct into the sperm drop in turns of about half a minute until it is all absorbed. Unlike *Uloborus*, however, he does not move his position below the web after the sperm drop is in place.

The female lays about 10 to 25 eggs in a batch and encloses these in dense white silk covered with an outer layer of dirty olive green parchment-like silk. The shape can be narrow or squat according to whether it is fastened along a twig or on the bark of the tree trunk but it always has some pimply elevations.

The young seem to pass the winter in the egg-sac and they reach maturity in the late summer of the following year two years after their mother became adult.

THE DICTYNIDAE: *Mesh-Webbed Spiders*

Anyone wanting to make the acquaintance of a *Ciniflo* should go to the nearest wall or wooden fence and look for her characteristic meshed web on its surface surrounding a circular retreat leading into a crevice. The fabric is not a uniform sheet like that of its frequent neighbour, the House Spider (*Tegenaria*), nor is it slung like a hammock. When freshly spun the threads have a lace-like appearance and a bluish tinge.

The territories of the three species of *Ciniflo* overlap but the webs in the walls of a dry shed are likely to belong to *C. similis*, those found on the trunk of an old tree to *C. fenestralis* and those in shady and damper situations in walls or at the entrances to caves or tunnels to *C. ferox*. Cloudsley-Thompson has shown that all three lose water very rapidly above a critical temperature of 35°C, but *C. similis* less rapidly than the other two, which explains her colonisation of drier situations. This species is not an uncommon wanderer in our homes in autumn. All three have a wide distribution but *C. ferox* becomes rare in the north.

They have a raised and shining head which is in contrast to the paler thoracic portion of the cephalothorax. The most characteristic marking on the abdomens of *C. similis* and *C. fenestralis* is a wide dark bar extending backwards to a midway point. This tends to be lighter in *C. similis* than in *C. fenestralis* whose markings are usually brighter and more clear-cut. The larger *C. ferox* has an almost black abdomen bearing what vaguely reminds me of a pale skull and crossbones marking. This gives her a sinister appearance and she is certainly a formidable monster in her own territory. Indeed, the webs of all three species are singularly adhesive when fresh and the spider's venom takes effect on an insect quite quickly.

The prey are for the most part crawling forms but it is noticeable that the spider responds more quickly to the vibrations of a buzzing fly than to the slower ones set up by a struggling earwig. She also responds rapidly to the vibrations of a tuning fork touching one of her threads and can often be lifted right out of her web whilst she is clambering over it, biting at its hard surface.

These spiders always bite a leg of their victim and then, moving backwards, start to haul the insect back to their retreats. When dragging a large insect across adhesive threads a considerable pull has to be exerted and this is effected by the spider hauling with her hind legs and pushing forwards against the web with her front legs. If the burden is a heavy one her progress will be in a series of jerks and the hind legs will be seen to bend whilst the front legs straighten as each jerk is made.

Some insects, including the spider-hunting Pompilid wasps, seem to have oiled legs which prevent them from sticking securely to the gum-studded spirals of a Garden Spider's web, but the lace threads of a *Ciniflo* are more successful and an attack on them is launched without the slightest hesitation or appearance of fear. This is a fact of great interest because my experiments on other spiders show them to have inherited a response to Pompilid wasps which sends them rushing away as though they were in a panic or else produces a state of semi-cataleptic paralysis when cornered which often prevents their using their fangs

in self-defence. The inference we can draw is
that *Ciniflo's* ancestors have had no reason to fear
these wasps so their descendants have naturally
acquired no responses to the wasps different
from those normally aroused by other insects.

The freshly spun threads of the Dictynidae
have a distinctly bluish tinge. This colouring is
largely due to the texture of the threads and
the way in which they are spun. *Ciniflo's* spinning operations take place soon after dark and
as the spider usually stops spinning soon after
the light of an electric torch is shone on her it
may take a little time before her exact methods
are accurately worked out. The abdomen is
tilted slightly upwards and the femurs of the
hind legs stand out laterally, almost at right

FIG. 40. *Ciniflo* face

angles. The remaining segments of one hind leg are directed backwards
and inclined somewhat inwards, whilst those of the other leg are bent
inwards at the tibia nearly at right angles in such a way as to allow
the tarsal claws to clasp the other hind leg at the base of its metatarsus.
In this position the calamistrum, or comb, on the metatarsus of one
leg is situated just behind the spinnerets. The spider remains stationary
with the anterior pair of spinnerets stretched outwards and the posterior
pair erected vertically from the body. The two threads spun by the
anterior pair are untouched by the metatarsal comb so they remain
straight whilst those spun by the posterior pair are combed out by a
rapid oscillation of the legs into loops and flounces. At the same time
a bluish viscid substance is teased out from the cribellum and pressed
into these loops in two narrow winding ribbons. At intervals she moves
in such a way as to stretch out the ribbon she has spun (see Plate V,
p. 84).

This seems to be a very slow method of building a snare compared
with the rapid circling of an *Araneus* round her web, but *Ciniflo* only lays
down a few fresh threads each night and does not build a fresh
snare.

Eggs are laid chiefly in June and July and the males of *Ciniflo similis*
mostly reach maturity towards the end of August or September in the
following year. Courtship takes place after dark and I have seen males
serenading the females in nearly every web as late as October 5th.
The male taps the web vigorously with his abdomen and palps and

continues to do this as he advances towards her retreat. She emerges and drives him away. After a period of courtship, which may be lengthy, the actual mating lasts only a few seconds during which each palp is inserted once. U. Gerhardt thinks that the female mates only once and that the male dies soon afterwards but I should be surprised if either of these beliefs is correct.

The eggs are not laid until the following June or July so it will be seen that in this species a new generation is born every two years. The mother deposits her cluster of eggs in a specially prepared cell in her retreat under bark, under a stone or in a crevice, where she remains on guard until after they hatch. The number of eggs is related to the size of the species and of the individual, as is usual amongst spiders, and a typical *C. similis* may lay about fifty eggs in a batch compared with eighty or more by the larger *C. ferox*. Cloudsley-Thompson has recently illustrated these general rules more precisely by comparing the weight of the mothers with that of the eggs they had laid. Thus a very small *C. similis* weighing 47 mg. had laid eggs weighing 43 mg., whilst an unusually large female weighing 202 mg. had laid eggs weighing 164 mg. Compared with these figures, *C. ferox* females of 119 and 383 mg. had laid eggs weighing 116 mg. and 178 mg. respectively.

The other principal genus in this family is *Dictyna* with eight species, most of which are only 3.5 mm. in length or even less. *Dictyna arundinacea* is our commonest species and is widespread in England, Scotland and Ireland, so it is difficult to explain why it has seldom been found in Wales. The brown cephalothorax has white longitudinal lines of white hairs on it and the abdomen has a wide irregular dark band down the front half followed by a series of cross bars with light grey areas on either side. Like that of most of the other species the snare is a small inconspicuous meshed veil of threads radiating downwards from a heather shoot or grass head which it surrounds. On and across these straight radial threads the lace-like cribellate threads are then drawn which catch the legs of insects, often much larger than the spider herself, whose remnants remain as evidence of past victories. As usual in this family it is the insect's leg which is always bitten until it is dead; and the prey's size never deters the spider from launching an attack.

As the summer progresses the veil becomes more dense and form-less, owing to new threads being added without the old ones being removed, and inside this cluster can be seen six or more lens-shaped egg-sacs each with a protective outer covering of cribellate threads. They may contain about eight to eighteen eggs (see fig. 41.)

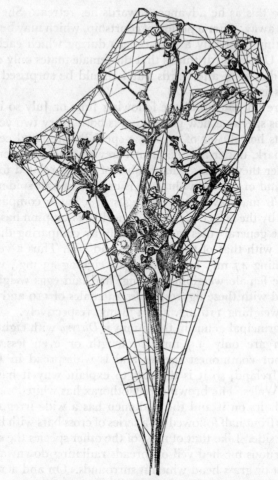

FIG. 41. *Dictyna arundinacea* (3 mm.) beside her egg-sacs in her snare

In June, when the male seems to stay for a month or more in the female's web, a rough chamber with several openings is spun in which they both live. This seems to be the work of the male soon after he first arrives. He starts by making his presence known by walking about with vibrating legs and touching her with these whenever he meets her, whilst she responds in a similar manner but then turns away, leaving him to bustle about biting threads, weaving new ones and gradually

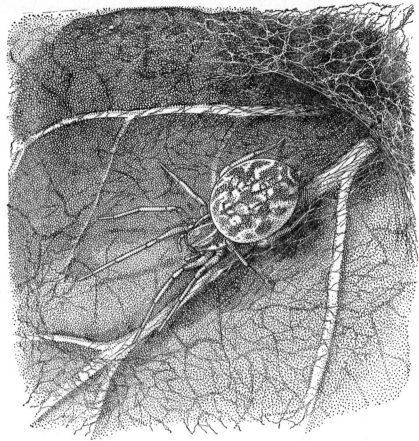

FIG. 42. *Dictyna viridissima* (4 mm.) in her snare beneath a leaf

forming his rough mating canopy. Vibratory salutations are exchanged whenever they meet and eventually she enters his canopy and he gently squeezes himself under her from in front with trembling legs and twitching abdomen. On the only occasion that I have watched the mating the male left the female after using one palp.

In places similar to those where *D. arundinacea* is found are the slightly smaller *D. uncinata* and the darker almost black *D. latens,* but neither seem to extend northwards into Scotland. In both species the males move about in their females' webs with vibrating legs and occasional pulsations of the abdomen in a similar manner to that of the male *D. arundinacea.* In Locket's description of the mating in *D. latens* (1926), one palp was inserted three times and the other four during a total period of about a quarter of an hour, whereas in *D. uncinata* Gerhardt has seen the male insert each palp once for a period of half an hour to an hour. Although there may be variations in the number of insertions comprising an act of mating, the procedure is otherwise very similar in these species, including the swelling and collapse of the bulb every twelve to fifteen seconds.

Sperm induction in this genus usually takes place within an hour of the male leaving the female. For this purpose he weaves a small band which is held taut by the third pair of legs and may be inclined at an angle or be even vertical. The palps are used alternately to absorb the sperm, which takes a quarter to half an hour.

There is another group of species within the genus *Dictyna* with somewhat different appearance and habits. *D. viridissima,* for instance, is a vivid green spider, with some traces of rust on the male cephalo-thorax and legs; and very appropriately she spins her snare across broad green leaves like those of apple and lime. She is known only from five localities in Surrey, for three of which D. J. Clark is responsible — Box Hill, Kew, Kingston, Tooting and Wimbledon — so she must be re-garded as a rare prize. Berland's observations on the Continent have shown that the excavated inner margins of the male's enlarged chelicerae are used to grip and hold closed the female's chelicerae. She seems to become adult in late summer whereas the pale whitish or light greenish-yellow *D. puella,* with a carmine dot or stripe on her abdomen, may be found in the mature state as early as June. She also builds her little snare across the surface of leaves like those of lilac and other broad-leaved trees or bushes. There is often a little platform of white silk across the hollow of the leaf below which she sits and from which a few incon-spicuous cribellate threads stretch outwards.

Before leaving this genus I should like to emphasise the unusual friendship which seems to exist between the males and females. I have mentioned the special canopy built by the male *D. arundinacea* in which they live together for prolonged periods, but I can add to this that it is not uncommon for the males and females to share in the capture and eating of a fly.

a. Scytodes thoracica (6 mm.)
(*W. H. T. Tams*)

b. A victim at which she has squirted gum from her chelicerae. (*W. H. T. Tams*)

P L A T E V I I

W. H. Spreadbury

PLATE VIII. *Pisaura mirabilis* (14 mm.) guarding her nursery.

CHAPTER 9

THE DYSDEROIDEA

Six-Eyed Spiders

THE six-eyed Oonopidae and Dysderidae are linked together in one Group, the Dysderoidea (Bristowe, 1938); but I ought to mention that we have one other six-eyed spider belonging to the family Scytodidae which is of very different appearance, and which is dealt with in the next chapter along with the eight-eyed Pholcidae to which it is related more closely.

THE OONOPIDAE

Our two species of *Oonops* are about 2 mm. in length and flesh pink in colour. Everything about them is pink, the abdomen, cephalothorax, legs and even the eggs. These are our only genuine Oonopids although three other species of *Diblemma, Ischnothyreus* and *Triaeris,* have arrived in plants from tropical countries and succeeded in surviving in hot-houses at Kew and elsewhere. Like *Oonops* they are tiny, but in contrast they are light yellow-brown in colour and have hard chitinous plates, or scuta, covering part of the upper and lower surfaces of the abdomen. *Diblemma donisthorpei* is remarkable in having only two eyes.

FIG. 43. *Oonops* face

Superficially our two species of *Oonops* are exactly alike and it was not until I took notice of their difference in habits that it was realised we had two species in Britain. *Oonops pulcher* lives under stones and bark, or amongst dry clumps of herbage (including birds' nests) whilst *O. domesticus* lives in houses. Both have long paired spines below the tibiae of their front pair of legs, but whereas there are four pairs in

O. pulcher, there are five in *O. domesticus.* The males can also be distinguished by the palpal embolus which is long and thread-like in *O. pulcher* and short and squat in *O. domesticus.*

It is not entirely surprising that these tiny spiders should have received little attention because they live in silk cells during the day and only emerge in search of prey at night. Their walk is so characteristic that the slow smooth groping progress of *O. domesticus* across the ceiling, without pause or change of direction, can be recognised by a keen-sighted person at least six feet away in spite of the spider being only 2 mm. in length. When need arises an *Oonops* can dart forward or backward like lightning, but when she catches an insect she may not use this reserve of speed. Despite her large eyes she is short-sighted and depends chiefly on touching an insect in the course of her groping perambulations. Strangely enough, she may then stroke it gently before moving forward quite smoothly to deliver a bite and the insect may make no attempt to escape as though it was soothed by the gentle stroking. It can be supposed that the real purpose of these motions is exploratory and that the insect is being measured for size and tested for palatability by her taste-by-touch or chemotactic senses. If the insect proves to be too large the *Oonops* will dart backwards. If it is a distasteful fly like *Sciara* or *Cecidomyia* she will withdraw.

Another interesting thing to notice is that if an insect struggles to escape it may either be pounced on or else firmly restrained by the tarsal claws of the spider's front legs. No other spider except *Scytodes* makes so much use of the tarsal claws for holding, so we can correlate this with the possession, by these two genera only, of tarsal claws armed with two rows of teeth.

In Cornwall, I noticed some years ago that *Oonops pulcher* frequented the lower surface of stones harbouring such large spiders as *Ciniflo ferox* and *Tegenaria atrica* and that she behaved as though she were a tolerated guest. She moved with her customary stealth amongst the matted threads of their retreats feeding on the remnants of their meals. Later on I found a similar association in Surrey with *Ciniflo fenestralis* under the bark of Plane trees (see Plate VIb, p. 85). This is the nearest approach amongst British spiders to the specialised habit of an entire genus of tropical Theridiid spiders (*Argyrodes*) which spend all their lives in the web of large *Argiopids.*

There is no one season in which to find grown up specimens of *Oonops* because many batches of eggs are laid throughout the summer months. Both the pink eggs — there are only two in each batch — can be seen through the white silk of the egg-sac which is constructed in their mother's cell.

I have watched the mating of *Oonops pulcher* as early as March and of *O. domesticus* as late as December. The mating habits of the two species of *Oonops* with their primitive type of sexual organ are similar. When a male and female come into contact they stroke each other's legs and a snapping of the chelicerae may take place. If she is not willing to receive him she runs away, otherwise she stands her ground whilst he holds her legs with his tarsal claws and gently pulls her towards him. Then, with small convulsive jerks, he creeps underneath her from in front and tilts her cephalothorax upwards over his own. The tarsi of his two front pairs of legs hold the tips of her front pairs of legs.

Nothing was known about the mating habits of the Oonopidae when I first watched the procedure in *Oonops* and the exciting moment had now arrived. Would he insert both palps at once, as in other families with primitive sexual organs like the Dysderidae, Scytodidae and Pholcidae, or would the palps be inserted alternately as in all our other species ? Having attained the mating position he tapped her vulva lightly with both his palps and then seemed to insert both simultaneously — or was only one inserted and the other held in readiness just beside it ? Owing to their small size it was necessary to repeat the observations and arrange that the mating took place in a position which allowed me to watch through a microscope. Eventually I was able to establish that the palps were inserted *alternately* after all, but later observations by U. Gerhardt and myself on foreign species confirmed nevertheless that simultaneous insertion is typical for the family.

The palps of the *Oonops* male were held so close to the female's vulva that, even in six matings by *O. pulcher*, I was uncertain how many times each palp was inserted during the one to two minutes that copulation lasted. During this time the only movements were a rhythmic jerking of the palps and the rise and fall of the leg spines.

Sperm induction by the male is a quick process lasting only a few minutes and this usually takes place within a quarter of an hour of the female leaving him. After drawing his palpal organs through his chelicerae for a short time he weaves a narrow band on which he deposits a drop of sperm after tapping his body against it. He inserts his emboli into the drop simultaneously for less than a minute and his palps are then recharged.

The Dysderidae

The attractive name of
Dysdera is borne by two
fierce and rather sinister
spiders which have a
knock-kneed appearance
as they walk smoothly
forward with groping gait
due to the defective vision
of their six pale eyes. On
making contact with their
prey or foe, their jutting
chelicerae will unbare a
huge pair of fangs with
which to do battle.

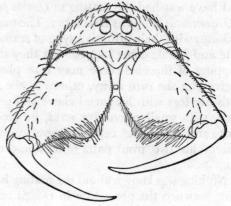

Fig. 44. *Dysdera* face

Our two species are
similar in general appear-
ance and habits. The carapace and legs are brick red, the smooth
tubular abdomen is light grey or white; and they usually reach between
10 to 15 mm. in length (see Plate 3, p. 209).

The males can be distinguished by their palpal organs but the
absence of an epigynal plate prevents our separating the females by
this means or being sure that they are adult. However, the leg spines
provide a reasonably constant character for use in distinguishing the
two species. *D. crocata* has two very tiny black spines on the dorsal
surface of the femurs of the first pair of legs close to the basal end which
are not present in *D. erythrina*. On the other hand *D. erythrina* usually
has two spines side by side on the basal half of the ventral surface of
the tibiae of the first pair of legs (in addition to lateral and apical
spines) compared with one in *D. crocata*.

During the day they are usually to be found in silk cells under
stones or amongst thick clumps of vegetation on light sandy or chalky
soils but they emerge at night to prowl in search of their prey. They are
most abundant close to the sea coast in South and South-West England
but *D. crocata* extends into Scotland whereas *D. erythrina* is scarce even
in northern England.

When a spider has some unusual structural feature, like the huge
chelicerae of a *Dysdera*, I become inquisitive and wonder if it serves
some special function. What kind of prey does a slow-moving short-

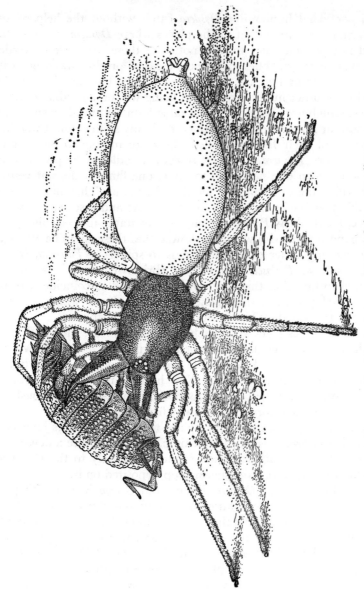

Fig. 45. *Dysdera crocata* (10 mm.) transfixing a woodlouse

sighted nocturnal hunter like *Dysdera* catch without the help of any snare? Snails are abundant in the places where *Dysdera* is found, but I could not persuade her to take notice of these. Ants were avoided and so were earwigs. Flies and moths escaped or else cowed her with the vigour of their flapping wings. Eventually I found that *Dysdera* differed from other hunting spiders in being willing and able to attack woodlice, which are abundant in the same habitats and slow enough in movement for *Dysdera* to catch with ease. Many spiders reject woodlice on account of their flavour whilst others are unable to pierce their dorsal armour. *Dysdera*, however, seizes a woodlouse by pivoting her cephalothorax on one side so as to insert one fang in the soft ventral surface whilst the other pierces the dorsal armour. This manoeuvre is only made possible by the size of her chelicerae and it seems likely that woodlice, particularly *Philoscia*, comprise her staple diet (see fig. 45).

My experiments with woodlice showed that these could be arranged in a descending order of distastefulness to spiders — *Porcellio, Oniscus* and *Armadillium, Philoscia, Platyarthrus* (Bristowe, 1941) — so it was interesting to find that this order was later found to coincide with the relative development in these genera of lobed glands which secrete a fluid when the woodlice are attacked (Gorvett, 1956).

When the sexes meet and touch each other's legs, they both open their chelicerae and gently move their legs up and down. Slowly the male creeps forward and the female raises her body to enable him to squeeze under her from in front. Now he may nip the lower surface of her abdomen and then he inserts both his palps simultaneously for about half an hour before leaping away from her.

Sperm induction seems to take place three to five hours later after the male has chewed his palps for a time. He spins quite a dense wide band and the palps are stretched round alternately to the underside of this in order to absorb the sperm drop deposited on it.

It will be seen that *Dysdera* differs from *Oonops* in using his palps simultaneously during copulation and alternately during sperm induction. Presently we shall find that *Segestria* differs from both in using his palps simultaneously on both occasions and this can be regarded as having been the normal procedure in the ancestral Dysderoidea.

Dysdera's egg-laying takes place in June and July. The female lays about sixty yellow eggs and wraps them in white silk inside her own dense white cell.

All the Dysderidae are inclined to have tubular bodies but in none is this more marked than in our slim longish-legged *Harpactea* which serves as a link between *Dysdera* and *Segestria*. *Harpactea hombergi* reaches up to 7 mm. and has a dark brown cephalothorax and legs with a pale to dark grey abdomen. Like *Dysdera* she belongs to the night shift and lives in cells during the day under bark or stones, or in dry matted vegetation including birds' nests. When she is on the prowl her front legs are waved in front of her like sensory feelers and she quickly measures the height and breadth of any invertebrate she encounters as well as its palatability (see Plate VIa, p. 85). If it is too formidable she will withdraw like a flash or hold it at bay by stiffening her legs. If an attack is to be made, this is almost instantaneous and fierce. She has not got the large chelicerae of a *Dysdera* but she will attack other spiders of similar bulk to that of her own, her long lithe body and ferocity reminding me of a ferret.

Harpactea's mating in the spring differs only in detail from that of *Dysdera* and lasts three to five minutes. Batches of about twenty pink eggs are laid from May to July and these are guarded by the mother in her cell.

Our only other Dysderid genus is that of *Segestria* which has three species, with general appearance and habits different from those of *Dysdera* and *Harpactea*.

The six eyes are in groups of two, not far distant from each other, and there is a dark abdominal band comprising a series of lobes connected by narrower necks which is reminiscent of the pattern on an adder's back. In *Segestria senoculata* this marking is clear and uniform in colour, in *S. bavarica* the centre of the lobes is pale and in the adults of *S. florentina* it may not be visible at all because the rest of the abdomen is equally dark in the adults. Size alone is a help to identification since *S. senoculata* is usually about 9 mm., *S. bavarica* about 12 mm. and *S. florentina* is a monster which may even reach as much as 23 mm. Apart from differences in the male sexual organs, *S. senoculata* has only one pair of ventro-lateral spines on the metatarsus of the first pair of legs compared with three in the other two species (apart from two unpaired spines in all three species), *S. bavarica* has a broad black band on the pale lower surface of the abdomen and the generally darker *S. florentina* has shining metallic chelicerae which flash green in the sunlight.

The *Segestriae* live in silk tubes in wall crevices or under stones and bark, from the open entrance to which a dozen stout straight threads stretch open the rim and act as 'fishing lines' (see Plate IX, p. 112).

The only widespread species is *S. senoculata*. This is now known from every English county and it extends to the North of Scotland. She lives in sheltered situations but also thrives on small exposed islands including the Scillies, the Skelligs, the Farne Islands and the Outer Hebrides.

Segestria bavarica is known from isolated spots near our southern coast including Portland and Ringstead; and I have found colonies on Lundy and the Channel Islands in walls as well as in the rocky hill-sides close to King Arthur's castle at Tintagel. To complete the list of localities I must mention one specimen from under the bark of a tree in the Scillies and an old record from Berkshire which need confirmation.

John Blackwall's illustration of the huge green-jawed *S. florentina* (=*S. perfida*) used to fill me with a strong desire to find one, but, as the only four known specimens had been found in Plymouth, Exeter, Bristol and Grange-over-Sands, it seemed likely that these were stray importations from the warmer countries where she lives. Grange-over-Sands was the only site of capture this century so a special visit was made which confirmed that it was not established there, and that the specimen had been collected close to a fruiterer's shop. Then, quite suddenly in 1934, my luck turned. Mr. Savory gave me the address of a man in Exeter who had just found one in his house. Without delay or warning to the collector I rushed down to Exeter, woke him from an afternoon nap and had found the webs of at least fifty specimens in his garden wall by the time he had dressed. I was too excited to give him the well-earned pleasure of showing me the spot on his drawing-room carpet where his discovery had been made !

Having got my eye in I soon found thriving colonies at Tiverton, Bristol, Bridport, Exmouth and Fowey, but if I ever find myself boasting I must try to remember that I also found an extensive colony in Westminster on walls which I had passed every day during the previous nine years !

Segestria florentina is only established in southern towns with near access to the sea. I have failed to find her in Bath (from which she was wrongly recorded), Dorchester, Weymouth, Folkestone, and Dover, so it would seem likely that the colonies are derived from chance importations which can establish themselves only in the warmer southern ports.

Once the tube entrance of a *Segestria* has been seen it cannot be confused with the matted web of a *Ciniflo* on account of the long straight 'fishing lines'. To catch one of the spiders it should be necessary only to brush one of these lines very gently with the fine tip of a grass and then to block the spider's retreat with a blunt instrument, but the theory has to be put into practice. When tried on a full grown *S. florentina*, on a warm summer's day when she is active, it is unusual for the beginner's nerves to stand the strain of this huge spider, with her flashing green jaws, darting out with the speed of lightning, biting fiercely and then backing into her tube once more all in the space of about two seconds. She is very fierce and will bite violently at a pencil blocking her retreat.

Spiders of this genus are adapted to a life in narrow tunnels by having a tubular body and by having three pairs of legs directed forwards. Before the spider actually pounces on a passing insect she pauses

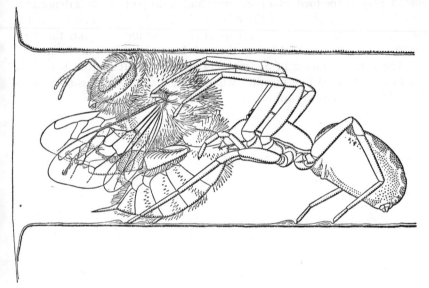

Fig. 46.   *Segestria* hauling a bee along her tube so that sting and jaws cannot harm her

for an instant in her doorway to identify the direction by touching eight of the 'fishing' lines with the tips of six legs and her palps. Her sight is of little use to her but her sense of touch is of the utmost importance.

One interesting feature of *Segestria's* life in a tube is that a formidable insect armed with a bite at one end or a sting at the other is jerked further down the tube every time it starts to bend one end towards the spider. The jerk causes the abdomen and head both to trail behind if the insect is clasped somewhere near the middle, as is usual, and very soon the spider's poison will quieten all resistance (see fig. 46).

So far as my limited experience goes, the male *S. florentina* reaches maturity in July or August and then goes in search of a female. He gives warning of his approach by shaking her threads. Then he darts underneath her with chelicerae bared and seizes the base of her abdomen with his fangs whilst both palps are inserted at once. She remains quite still and he thrusts her upwards at an angle while the tips of his first two pairs of legs hold the tips of her front legs. The palpal organ is revolved intermittently through an angle of about 90° for about ten minutes and then he leaps clear.

Several hours later he begins chewing his palps and then spins a few threads in the form of a band on which a drop of sperm is deposited. The palps reach out round the edge of the band and absorb the sperm simultaneously. The whole process of sperm induction from the time he starts to spin until he leaves the web lasts about half an hour.

The spring mating of *S. senoculata* is similar but in that species it lasts only three to five minutes whereas in *S. bavarica* it usually takes from fifteen to twenty minutes.

CHAPTER 10

THE SCYTODOIDEA

Spitting and Daddy-Long-Legs Spiders

AUTHORITIES have not been in agreement as to the relationships of the two families *Scytodidae* and *Pholcidae* but I reached the conclusion some years ago that their structure and habits favoured their inclusion in one group (Bristowe, 1938). Judged solely on our British species this relationship is not so apparent as it is when we compare some of the foreign species. Three simple examples are provided by the eyes, the webs and the sexual organs. Our *Scytodes* differs from our Pholcidae in having six eyes, no webs and simpler palpal organs. Some foreign Pholcids have six eyes and simple palpal organs, whilst some foreign species of *Scytodes* build webs similar to those of our *Physocyclus* (Pholcidae).

THE SCYTODIDAE : *Spitting Spiders*

Fortunately our only species of this interesting family is no longer the extreme rarity it used to be. *Scytodes thoracica* was first recorded in Britain by W. E. Leach in 1816 and during the next hundred and twenty years only about six specimens were found in five southern counties — Dorset, Wiltshire, Sussex, Kent and Oxford. Since about 1936, however, she has been rediscovered in all these counties, often in several places and in abundance, and has also been found in the Isle of Wight, Hampshire, Somerset, Gloucestershire, Berkshire, London and Cambridge. *Scytodes* is a domestic species belonging to

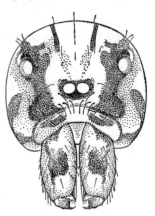

FIG. 47. *Scytodes* face

a family which does not indulge in aeronautic dispersal so we must attribute the spread to the increased movement of people from place to place during recent decades, with *Scytodes* in their furniture.

Although I have found as many as twelve specimens during an evening's search in a single house in Litton Cheney, Dorset, I had to make her acquaintance first during a visit to Majorca in 1930 where she lives under stones. My first introduction to the genus was in a year when I also met and studied the habits of four other species in Malaya with interesting results.

Some of the tropical species build small sheet webs but most, like *Scytodes thoracica,* are slow-moving short-sighted nocturnal hunters with little apparent means of livelihood. Slowly they promenade the walls with thin groping front legs incapable of breaking into a sprint or spring. How vividly I remember the thrill of discovering the answer to this puzzle of their food supply. This lay in their remarkable habit of squirting gum from their chelicerae when a quarter of an inch still separated them from their prey. The insect was stuck firmly to the ground so the spider could now deal with it at leisure without any need for quickened steps.

On my way home from Malaya after seeing four species behaving in this way, I called on my friend, Lucien Berland, in Paris to give him the news only to learn from him that M. Monterosso (1928) of Italy had made this same discovery two years earlier! Also, J. Millot (1929) had already investigated the internal structure of a *Scytodes* with his customary skill and had found that its characteristic high-domed cephalothorax contained huge glands divided into portions containing gum and poison connected with the fangs.

It was in trying to understand the mechanism shortly after this that I made a further interesting discovery. All that one sees is one jerk, and the insect is immobilised — but not as might be expected with one splodge of gum. To my amazement I found the insect was enmeshed by two sets of ten to twenty viscous threads, one set squirted from each fang and the two sets meeting in the middle. The action is too rapid to follow under a lens or microscope but the inevitable inference is that the chelicerae are oscillated from side to side at the moment of discharge too rapidly for the eye to see (see Plate VII, p. 92 and fig. 48).*

I have watched this process operated hundreds of times by *Scytodes thoracica* and have then seen her advance with caution on her victim. If there is any struggle she bites a leg and draws back. After a succession of pecks, with pauses in between each, the insect dies from the effects of

*Or up and down? I am told the gum pattern conforms with such movements and not as in fig. 48.

FIG. 48. A fly fastened by gummy threads squirted from the chelicerae of a *Scytodes* (6 mm.)

FIG. 49. *Scytodes* egg-sac attached by threads to the spinnerets and held by the palps

the poison and *Scytodes* then drags it free from its sticky bonds. The meal then begins a short distance from the area of sticky threads. There is no chewing. Digestive fluid is pumped into the insect through the small punctures which have been made by the fangs and the partly digested body fluid is then sucked until nothing but the empty and almost undamaged shell of the insect remains.

The squirting of gum is also used effectively as a protective device against spiders larger than herself; and this, combined with the stealth of her movements, allows her to move without disaster amongst the threads of a *Pholcus* web slung between wall and ceiling.

Although I have kept *Scytodes* in captivity for prolonged periods, my knowledge of their development is greatly enriched by the careful observations of Noel Clarke who has made a study of their life history at Folkestone, and I am grateful to him for allowing me to draw on his observations in the account which follows.

Although mating has been seen in all months from March to October, egg-laying seems to be confined to July and August. At this time the female only lays one batch of eggs, which can be followed by another batch at the same season in the following year, and even a third batch if she survives yet another year as is sometimes the case in captivity. The first batch comprises about 20 to 35 eggs; there are fewer eggs in the subsequent batches. The eggs each have a diameter of about 0.75 mm. and the batch is enclosed in a pale cream egg-sac with a diameter of 3.5 to 3.75 mm. Her own body length ranges from 5 to 6 mm. Clarke has pointed out to me that the egg-sac is held beneath her body by her palps and by threads from her spinnerets — not by her chelicerae as in the Pholcidae. This leaves her free to squirt gum in attack or defence and, when she captures an insect, she suspends the egg-sac beside her until the meal is finished.

The eggs hatch after about two weeks, but a further two weeks elapse before the young spiders emerge with the assistance of their mother who has loosened the threads of the casing. Their first moult takes place after they have hung motionless for about ten days on a network of threads in which the mother has suspended the egg-sac. In this respect they resemble the Pholcidae and differ from most other spiders, where it is customary for the first moult to take place within the egg-sac.

When the young spiders first emerge the eyes and the tarsal claws are well-defined. There are even two rows of teeth on one of the paired claws of the first and second pair of legs as in the adult spiders. By contrast the chelicerae are ill-defined and no feeding takes place until after the first moult. Directly they have recovered from this delicate operation they disperse.

From this time onwards the periods between moults and the length of time before the spider becomes adult are influenced both by the season and by the amount of food they eat. No moults take place between mid-October and March. The young spiders hatched from eggs laid early in July usually succeed in moulting a second time in late September or early October before further development is arrested by the oncome of winter, unless food has been scarce — in which case the second moult is delayed until the following spring or early summer. Young which have hatched from eggs laid in August or even late July usually pass the winter after only one moult.

Development is slow in this family, and a second winter is passed in an immature state. By this time they have usually had four or five moults, or sometimes only three, out of the six which bring the female to her mature state. A male only needs five moults so he may become adult when he is just over a year old, but when this does not happen the retarded development often results in six moults being necessary before he is fully mature.

There is considerable variation in the time it takes for *Scytodes* to become adult but two to three years is probably normal for a female with no very clear season for reaching maturity. Adults and young can be found at all times of the year though they are mainly concealed in crevices during the winter months.

Mating is a listless affair. When a male finds a female he touches her with his legs and then climbs over her without any preliminary courtship and creeps under her, belly uppermost, from behind. She responds by raising her body high on her legs like an umbrella above him and then allows him to tilt her somewhat backwards. Meanwhile he is feeling the lower surface of her abdomen with his chelicerae until he finds two small chitinised pockets just behind her genital openings into which the fangs are sunk. Holding her thus he inserts both palps simultaneously.

Two phases are noticeable in the mating of *Scytodes*, the first comparatively short and active and the second longer during which little seems to be happening. Sometimes the second phase is dispensed with and, in consequence of this variation in procedure, copulation usually lasts either about 4 to 9 minutes or else 25 to 50 minutes. During the first phase the palps may be withdrawn every 5 to 10 seconds and then reinserted after a brief pause. During the second phase both spiders may remain quite motionless with the palps inserted until he suddenly withdraws them and leaves her.

Males do not show any marked hostility to one another and they may even court each other for a time. Sometimes a male will repel another male, in the same way as an immature female who is courted, by squirting a small quantity of gum at him; but this is not developed into an attack.

Sperm induction is not easy to see because it seems to take place at no fixed time after the palps have been emptied. However, Gerhardt (1930) succeeded on one occasion in seeing it during a morning following an act of copulation on the previous day and his account is particularly interesting in providing fresh biological evidence in support of the structural evidence for grouping the Scytodidae with the Pholcidae.

After chewing the palps and drawing them through the chelicerae the male spun a few criss-cross threads and then stretched one of these across the underside of his abdomen with his third pair of legs as in *Pholcus*. Then he tapped his genital aperture against this thread and presently seminal fluid began to adhere to the thread until finally this had merged into a single drop. The spider then drew back a little and inserted the tips of the crossed emboli into it where they remained for twenty minutes until the drop had been absorbed.

When a *Scytodes* is approaching the end of her life she becomes less active, her abdomen shrinks and her colour darkens. She may still squirt gum but this is chiefly defensive as she is no longer feeding. Having taken two to three years to become adult she may survive another year or two in natural conditions and attain a ripe old age of five in captivity.

THE PHOLCIDAE: *Daddy-Long-Legs Spiders*

Pholcus phalangioides must be well-known to people who live in the South of England, Wales and Eire. She sits unobtrusively in corners of rooms between ceilings and walls hanging motionless from a scaffolding of fine invisible threads. Her presence is not resented because she seldom moves and is regarded as an innocuous creature which may be useful in catching mosquitoes or clothes-moths. *Pholcus* did not live in my childhood home at Stoke d'Abernon,

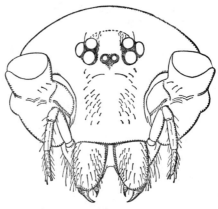

FIG. 50. *Pholcus* face

Surrey, although she thrived elsewhere only about ten miles further south, so the quest of an explanation inspired me to trace her distribution. This had to await the acquisition of a motor-bicycle and then, with the impudence of youth, I zig-zagged across England ostensibly seeking rooms in hotels or lodgings whose ceilings I viewed with nonchalant interest. My apologies are no doubt due to a host of hoteliers for gaining entry under false pretences, but in the result their unwitting co-operation enabled me to draw a map which showed that *Pholcus* inhabited houses coinciding with the narrow southern strip where the average temperature throughout the year exceeds 50°F. North of this strip she is normally confined to cellars where temperature varies little with the seasons and is usually about 50° to 52°. Probably it is the absence of certain extremes of cold over a period which determines whether *Pholcus* can survive.

Pholcus can go for long periods without water like most domestic

FIG. 51. *Pholcus* (10 mm.) wrapping an insect

species, but occasionally she descends from her web in search of it and drinks greedily when she finds it. She cannot survive life in rooms where there is constant central heating and it would seem that her eggs will not hatch in this very dry atmosphere.

Several kinds of spider become restless in autumn and enter houses from outside. *Pholcus* takes a heavy toll of these and, with ungainly strides, ambles towards any which touch her threads fastened to the wall or ceiling. It is at a moment like this that we can see the advantage of long legs, because she can draw threads from her spinnerets and fling them over the intruder from a distance, whilst keeping herself well out of range of serious danger. The prey is securely trussed in silk before she delivers a first tentative bite.

If she becomes alarmed by the invasions of too bulky a flapping insect she holds firmly to her scaffolding with all her legs, flexes her muscles and rapidly oscillates in a circular motion. The spider's outlines becomes blurred and she is almost invisible. The snare vibrates vigorously and the unwelcome intruder retreats or breaks loose.

In my present home near Tunbridge Wells I have every opportunity of watching *Pholcus* throughout the year. She is a slim spider with extremely long fine legs but at times she is visited by an even slimmer longer legged male. He advances cautiously with some gentle vibration of the body and eventually succeeds in embracing her. He hangs below her, facing in the same direction, and after one or two quick jerks with his palps succeeds in inserting both simultaneously. After this, very little movement is noticeable until he breaks away, sometimes as long as three hours later. He does not remain with her much longer and has usually left her web not later than the following day.

The habit of simultaneous insertion is a primitive one shared by the Pholcids with the Oonopidae, Dysderidae and Scytodidae; but the way in which the male *Pholcus* and *Scytodes* recharge their palps takes us still further back in the history of spiders. A drop of sperm is deposited on a thread held taut across his genital opening and from here it is picked up in his chelicerae and absorbed by alternate applications of his palps in the case of *Pholcus* and simultaneously by both palps in *Scytodes*. I have shown elsewhere (p. 44) that arachnid ancestors of spiders had pincer-like or chelate chelicerae whose design has been retained to a greater extent in the Pholcidae and Scytodidae than in other families, and that in two other arachnid Orders (the Solifugae and certain of the Acari) the transfer of sperm is effected with the help of

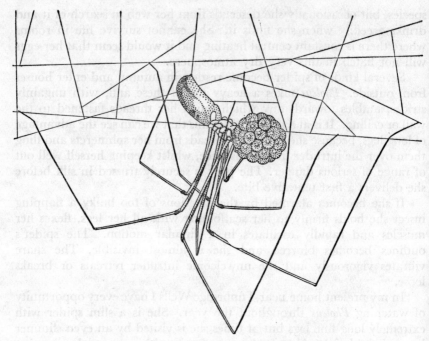

FIG. 52.   *Pholcus* with egg-sac held in her chelicerae

chelate chelicerae. Here then we may be witnessing a practice forsaken long ago by all other spiders.

Normally, the female lays her first batch of eggs in June or even earlier, followed by a second and third batch in July and in August after the young from the previous batches have dispersed. A female can lay fertile eggs in May or June after a mating in the previous summer and I have seen a mating take place as late as the end of September.

The eggs, in a circular bundle, are held together by a few threads and the female carries this bundle about in her chelicerae although she may temporarily sling it in her web in order to capture an insect or even to mate with an insistent male (see fig. 52). The eggs may hatch in two or three weeks' time and the young then hang motionless like washing on clothes-lines for the next week or fortnight during which time they take no notice of any disturbances such as those caused

PLATE IX. *Segestria florentina* (22 mm.) at her entrance in a wall.

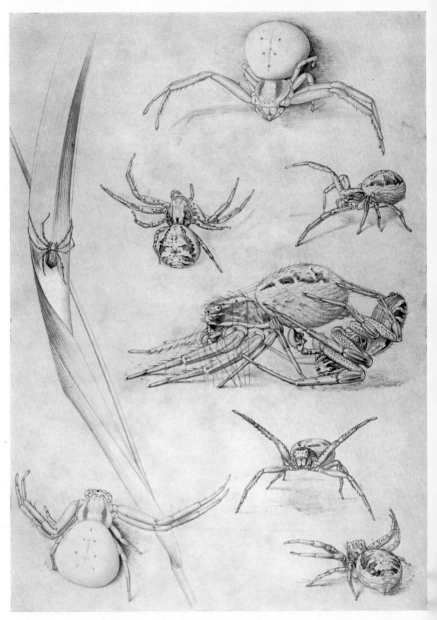

PLATE X. Crab spiders. Two sketches of *Misumena vatia* (10 mm.) waiting to seize prey, one of *Philodromus dispar* (5 mm.) beside her egg-sac on a curled leaf and five of *Xysticus cristatus* (7 mm.). In one, the *Xysticus* male is mating with a female he has fastened with silk. Below this, a female in a threatening posture.

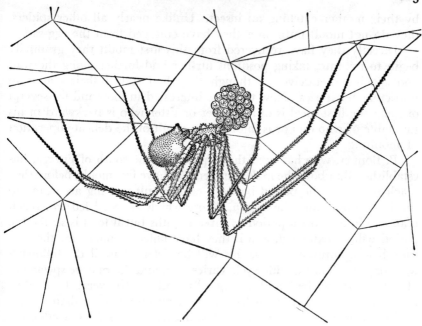

FIG. 53.   *Physocyclus* (2·5 mm.) with egg-sac

FIG. 54.   *Pholcus* in winter position

WS—I

by their mother catching an insect. Unlike nearly all other spiders, they do not moult until after they have emerged from the egg-sac.

Directly they have recovered from this first moult they gradually begin to migrate, taking positions further and further along the wall and spacing themselves as though they had staked their claims to particular territories. Now they are interested in food and for several of them the first meal is of a brother or sister who is backward in his timetable or who dies or is injured as a result of the delicate operation of moulting.

P. Bonnet, who has bred these spiders in the south of France, has established that both the males and females have five moults before they reach maturity, the period between each moult varying according to the food supply and the season. Those which are well fed can reach maturity in as short a period as three months but if food is scarce the period will be extended, and if they have failed to moult for the fifth time before autumn arrives, this will be deferred until the following May or June. Thus the life cycle varies a lot and the mature specimens of both sexes can be found during all months of the year. Once they have reached maturity their lives may linger on for more than a year.

When frosts appear in autumn and early winter *Pholcus* adopts a strangely rigid posture pressed tight against the wall with legs bent back in an unnatural position, and in this position she remains motionless until warmer weather returns (see fig. 54).

We have only one other Pholcid in Britain and her globular abdomen slightly tinged with blue need never be confused with the cylindrical body of *Pholcus*. Apart from shape, *Physocyclus simoni* Berl. does not exceed 2.5 mm. compared with 10 mm. in the case of *Pholcus*.

Since my first discovery of *Physocyclus* in a cellar at Bury St. Edmunds, I have found her in dry wine cellars in a dozen other English counties ranging from Cornwall to Durham; and it seems clear enough that she has been imported with wine from France where she has also been found in cellars.

Although she also makes a scaffolding snare, in my experience this usually develops into a flimsy sheet beneath which she hangs until an insect arrives. The prey is wrapped, sucked and finally dropped to the ground as in *Pholcus* when only the dry carcase remains.

The male advances towards the female with body trembling, lunges forward at the last moment and inserts both palps. For the first few minutes some movement may be noticed but after that there is immobility for a further twenty minutes except for a slight rhythmic movement caused by the ejection of sperm. After they have separated, he sometimes attempts further courtship but P. Bonnet believes that in this species the female never mates more than once.

About twenty eggs are laid during the night a month or two after the mating and these are only strung together with the minimum number of threads with the result that the egg-sac looks rather like a bundle of tennis balls in a string bag. The mother carries the eggs in her chelicerae until they hatch a month or more later. As in the case of *Pholcus* the first moult takes place outside the egg-sac after the young spiders have remained motionless for about ten days. The spiders moult five times before reaching maturity six to seven months after hatching, but Bonnet has shown that the males live for two years and the females even three to four years.

Batches of eggs may be laid at intervals of about ten weeks and the females usually lay three batches, all of which are fertile, from the one act of mating. This means that each female may lay 60 to 70 eggs in her lifetime.

It will have been noticed that our Scytodid and our two Pholcids are restricted to man's houses and cellars in Britain. In warmer countries I have found *Scytodes* under stones and *Pholcus* in sheltered situations away from houses.

THE CLUBIONOIDEA

Gnaphosidae, Clubionidae and Anyphaenidae

NOBODY seems to have worked up much enthusiasm for these families. Generally speaking they are dull in appearance and seem to be dull in their habits: but I should like to show that there are at least a few exceptions. Drab most of them look in their uniform grey (*Herpyllus*), black (*Zelotes*), fawn (*Drassodes, Clubiona*) or brown (*Gnaphosa*) with no pattern to break the monotony, but at least we have the ant-like *Micaria* whose scales scintillate with all colours of the rainbow in the sun and *Cheiracanthium* with her sage-green abdomen lightened by yellowish-green patches and a carmine stripe down the centre. For the most part these spiders are night-hunters and are the panthers or pumas of the invertebrate world—with *Drassodes* as the queen of their plant forests, ready to contest her supremacy in mortal combat with any other spider.

THE GNAPHOSIDAE: *Drassidae*

These are short-sighted hunters which belong to the night shift and spend their days in silk cells under stones or other secluded places.

If an English name were needed for our only domestic species, which is found rarely away from man's buildings in hollow trees, it would be appropriate to call her the Mouse Spider on account of her glossy grey abdomen. But she can be a very fierce mouse. She reaches 11 mm. and has short brown legs and a rather narrow head. For many years she has been known as *Scotophaeus* but we ought to call her *Herpyllus blackwalli*.

FIG. 55. *Drassodes* face

Her ability to survive without water for months if necessary suits her for a domestic environment and here she prowls at night on walls and ceilings in search of prey, retiring behind pictures or to crevices in walls during the hours of daylight. Trailing a thread as she walks, she pounces with speed and ferocity on flies, mosquitoes or clothes moths and usually buries her fangs at the junction of the legs on one side of the insect. If she is confronted by too formidable an adversary she turns rapidly away with her abdomen waving almost vertically in the air, trailing a wide band of silk from laterally extended spinnerets as a shield against pursuit (Bristowe, 1941). She will chew dead or dying insects and I know of several cases where lepidopterists have suffered from *Herpyllus* discovering their specimens on setting boards during the night.

The lithe flexibility of the abdomen and long spinnerets of *Herpyllus* will be noticed in captivity when she starts to enclose herself in a cell by sweeping her abdomen up, down and to the sides trailing bands of silk from her spinnerets.

The males have small inconspicuous palpal organs and are nearly as large as the females which they closely resemble. Some fierce sparring takes place when they meet, accompanied by violent jerks of the body, but there is no genuine courtship and I have seen this result in the death of a male or even a female. If the female is ready to receive him she merely stops sparring and lets him creep over her. Standing above her and embracing her with his second and third pair of feet he turns her abdomen slightly to one side and inserts a palp without any delay. His leg spines rise and fall about every two seconds in time with the expansion and collapse of the palpal bulb for about five to seven minutes and then he quickly tilts her abdomen in the opposite direction to enable him to insert his other palp for about twelve minutes. On the two occasions I have watched the mating in July the first palp has then been inserted for a second time for five to eight minutes before he left her. In one case the mating lasted twenty two and in the other twenty seven minutes. The female's preying instincts are never deeply subjugated and a fierce rearguard action marks his retirement if he tarries.

Drassodes lapidosus is the largest and fiercest of the six species belonging to her genus in Britain. Like the others she is of a uniform fawn colour with a distinct pinkish tinge. She is lithe in movement and sleek in appearance. Normally she reaches 10 to 15 mm. so it was exciting to find a race of giants measuring up to 22 mm. on Skellig St. Michael off the coast of Kerry.

Commonly she lives amongst dry clumps of grass etc. or under stones and emerges from silk cells at night to prowl like a panther in search of food. *Drassodes lapidosus* is widespread from the South of England to the North of Scotland but is nowhere more abundant than in the Scilly Islands where she vies for dominance with *Textrix* and *Dysdera*. It is unusual to find more than one of the three species in a single space under a stone, but, fortunately for *Textrix,* there are innumerable stones and rock crevices in these islands.

Her ferocity and skill in fighting have been known to me for many years but, in order to enable Mr. Arthur Smith to make a series of sketches illustrating her technique, I staged fights with opponents as large or larger than herself. For this purpose I started with a *Ciniflo ferox.* The arena was a low-roofed glass-topped cardboard box approximately six inches square.

Before the fights started Mr. Smith was convinced that the sleek *Drassodes* would scarcely stand a chance against the sinister-looking *Ciniflo ferox* whose black abdomen significantly bore paler markings resembling a skull and cross-bones.

Presently the two gladiators face one another a short distance apart. *Ciniflo* raises her front pair of legs and lunges forward aggressively with fangs stretched outwards to inflict a bite. Evading this onslaught, with stiffened front legs to avoid being rushed, the *Drassodes* makes her counter attack in the next instant. Like lightning she outflanks her opponent. Half on her side, with body arched out of harm's way and with her nearside legs touching the *Ciniflo,* she swings round and over the *Ciniflo* in a semi-circle so that she is now poised over her adversary and facing in much the same direction. As part of the same movement her fangs are buried in the further side of the *Ciniflo's* cephalothorax and as part of her technique she had put all *Ciniflo's* legs on the nearside out of action with a band of silk trailed over them as she completed her rotating movement. This band was anchored to the ground before the attack then launched, passed over the legs, over the tip of *Ciniflo's* abdomen and then anchored to the ground beyond, often over the hind leg of the far side.

Drassodes now has a grip from which she cannot be dislodged by her shackled victim. *Ciniflo* heaves and snaps but *Drassodes* keeps her legs well out of danger and before long all is quiet. The battle is over (see Plates XI, XII, pp. 128, 129).

The action is so rapid that it had to be repeated many times before the artist, bent on recording exact detail, was able to complete his series of drawings. Within two days one *Drassodes* female had defeated no less than fifteen formidable opponents belonging to five different species — *Ciniflo ferox, C. similis, Pisaura mirabilis*, an immature *Tegenaria atrica* and *Araneus umbraticus*.

In nature the male is to some extent safeguarded by reaching maturity in April, before the female has reached her full size or strength, and it is customary for him to stake a claim to an immature female either by building a cell adjoining hers or even sharing one with her until she undergoes her last moult. Directly she reaches maturity he takes full advantage of her temporarily weak state after the moult to mate with her.

Although mating may take place in April, both sexes can be found several months later and mating can be attempted and achieved, though with greater danger to the male, as late as July. If he finds her in a cell his approach is heralded by his swaying up and down on the silk wall with trembling legs and body. Here he is in comparative safety with the cell wall separating him from disaster and he only makes an entry if she does not rattle her body and snap at him from inside the cell. If, on the other hand, he encounters her in the open, he leaps backwards to avoid the fierce attack she always makes after the first contact. During later contacts he draws back less abruptly and cringes with his legs somewhat drawn in, except for the first pair whose femora are inclined backwards, and the rest of the segments raised in a defensive attitude. Provided he is not driven away he then cautiously stretches out his front legs to touch her, if she still makes no hostile movement, he smoothly moves towards her and tries to creep on top of her. His balance of safety is still narrow and she may continue to drive him away but he usually becomes bolder and she less hostile. Sometimes he will even stand firm to spar with her and on such occasions she may be the one to retreat. Finally she submits to his advances and he mounts her back with quivering front legs which embrace her. Quite suddenly she becomes limp and he leans over one side, turns her abdomen slightly towards him and taps her epigyne with one palp. This tapping precedes each insertion of the palp.

During the mating the spiders face in opposite directions, with the male, who is above, holding the female with the second and third pair of legs. He lies somewhat obliquely across her body and uses his right palp when he is leaning over her left side.

On one occasion, late in April, when a male was mating with a female which had only just moulted, one palp was inserted for 26 minutes and the other for 42 minutes, but in two instances where males mated with females in June the total time has been less and the palps were alternated several times at intervals of about ½ to 3 minutes. In one case the operation lasted 6 minutes during which each palp was inserted four times and in the other 18 minutes during which one palp was inserted 9 times and the other 6. The first and principal phase, however, seemed to last about 8½ minutes.

During the mating the bulb swells out and collapses with the discharge of sperm and it was noticeable that whereas early in the proceedings the swellings took place about every second they later became less frequent.

Adults can be found at most seasons but I have no evidence as to how many broods each female has. The eggs are contained in thick white egg-sacs and enclosed in a spacious silken chamber shared with the female. A count taken of eggs in 7 sacs opened late in June showed a variation between 81 and 115 eggs.

Zelotes is a genus of lithe glistening black spiders usually to be found under stones, especially in coastal and chalky areas. The collector will find them to be elusive when he tries to catch them. Their egg-sacs, fastened to the underside of stones, are nipple-shaped and often pink. The outer covering is smooth like paper, for the female incorporates excrement and saliva in the silk and polishes the surface by rubbing it with her chelicerae (E. Nielsen, 1932). Sometimes the mothers are found sitting beside their egg-sacs, but more often they forsake them when the strength of the horny covering protects them against attacks by mites and other insects which devour spiders' eggs. *Z. latreillei,* which reaches a length of 8 mm., is our commonest species on chalk, whilst the smaller *Z. electus* is a specialist on sandhills.

Coming now to the genus *Micaria,* of which much the commonest species is *M. pulicaria,* we find beautiful little spiders with scale-like hairs reflecting green and red lights. The fact that their movements, size and general appearance are antlike and that they are often to be found running close to ants has led to the belief that they are associated with ants in some manner. Although this is not the case, they can easily be mistaken for ants such as *Acanthomyrmex niger,* especially as their front legs are not unlike the antennae of ants in the way they are held out in front and made to quiver. Conflicting views as to what advantages, if any, were gained by the many antlike spiders of the world had never been tested so I decided to carry out some experiments with *Micaria.* Here we had a spider which resembled an ant less than most of the

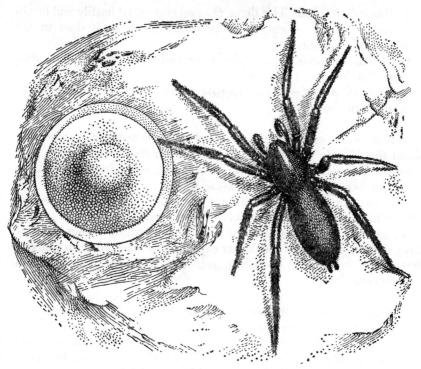

FIG. 56. *Zelotes* (8 mm.) with egg-sac under a stone

other ant mimics, so proof of advantage would suggest that even greater benefit was gained by the more antlike species. I have said elsewhere that other spiders constitute an individual spider's worst enemy, so I offered a *Micaria* to six different kinds of spider with the following results:

1. *Zelotes latreillei.* In the course of its wanderings *Micaria* approached and touched *Zelotes,* which immediately turned aside and ran away. Another *Zelotes* met a *Micaria,* sprung on it, drew back, and retreated.
2. *Trochosa terricola.* A *Micaria* approached a stationary *Trochosa* and the latter raised its body and allowed the *Micaria* to run underneath it. This happened on several occasions and it behaved in the same way with an ant.
3. *Xysticus erraticus.* This Crab-spider sat quite still and took no notice of the *Micaria.* A second *Xysticus* behaved likewise.

4. *Drassodes lapidosus*. This fierce *Drassodes* retreated hastily and began spinning itself a retreat in self-protection, just as it does in the presence of an ant.

5. *Clubiona terrestris*. The *Clubiona* jumped at a *Micaria*, but then immediately turned and fled.

6. *Tegenaria domestica*. The *Tegenaria* pounced and then followed the example of the *Clubiona*.

These results seemed to show conclusively that there is something about the *Micaria* which helps to preserve her from attack by at least some other spiders with which she is likely to come in contact in the course of her wanderings. The same spiders were found to react in exactly the same manner to the ant, *Acanthomyrmex niger,* but we are still left in doubt as to whether *Micaria's* immunity is due to appearance, taste, scent or feel. Several of the spiders which shunned her are very short-sighted, so in these particular experiments it would seem unlikely that either appearance or taste played a part. I tried a new set of experiments:

1. Two *Micariae* of different sizes were left in a box together. The larger ate the smaller specimen.

2. A dead *Micaria* was thrown in the web of *Tegenaria domestica* and the *Tegenaria's* attention was drawn to it with the aid of a fine grass stem. The *Micaria* was devoured without hesitation.

3. A dead *Micaria,* and also a very sluggish specimen which was apparently unwell and making no movement, were seized without hesitation by *Agroeca proxima*.

4. A dead *Micaria* was accepted by *Araneus diadematus* and subsequently the same spider wrapped in silk and ate a living one.

These experiments eliminate appearance, taste, scent and also, it would seem, feel as well. However, if we watch *Micaria's* movements with care we will see that she *walks with rapid steps and with front legs quivering sensitively like the antennae of an ant.* Now in the first set of experiments the various spiders took to flight *after being touched with these front legs,* whilst in the second set of experiments the *Micariae* were either dead, motionless or enswathed in such a manner that their movements could not come into play. Thus it seems evident that the antlike movements associated with antlike spiders play an important part where short-sighted enemies are concerned (the vibrations of the

FIG. 57. *Micaria pulicaria* (3 mm.) beside a cell containing her egg-sac

front legs in particular), and also against attack from longer-sighted enemies on account of the contribution these movements make in increasing their likeness to ants.

When *Micaria* meets an ant she retreats immediately although it would seem that she has learned the 'ant-language' sufficiently to deceive other spiders. She certainly does not prey on ants, so any association which appears to exist arises from her habit of running in the sun like ants. When she is not in movement, and therefore in greater danger from enemies, she encloses herself in a silk cell under a stone or bark.

Micaria's eggs are enclosed in a stiff sac which resembles a rimmed pot and I have found as many as three inside a single cell. Although the mother does not usually remain with them until the eggs hatch, she often returns to the same cell after a hunting excursion.

THE CLUBIONIDAE

The spiders of this family are closely related to the Gnaphosidae and those belonging to the principal genus of *Clubiona* look very like *Drassodes* with the spinnerets providing the easiest distinguishing feature (see figs. 11, 17, pp. 30 and 36). Like the Gnaphosidae they mostly weave silk cells in which to harbour themselves during the day but, whereas some *Clubiona* species live on the ground amongst clumps of grass or under stones, several mount higher than is usual for *Drassodes* and live amongst the foliage of trees (*C. brevipes*). April and May are the chief months for reaching maturity; and with few exceptions the females guard their egg-sacs inside thick white cells from June or sometimes July onwards.

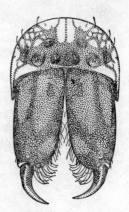

FIG. 58. *Clubiona* face

One of the commonest of our nineteen species of *Clubiona* is *C. reclusa*. This is a dark brown spider which lives amongst grass or herbs and reaches a length of up to 8.5 mm. In common with other members of the genus these short-sighted hunters have no marked courtship, and what there is can involve rough seizure by the male who must not lose contact once he has found his mate. Sometimes he may find her in her cell, and he will then make his presence known before they come to grips; but, when this is not their method of introduction, the male *C. reclusa* uses his chelicerae to seize and hold her, if necessary by the abdomen. After a momentary struggle she remains quiet and he climbs on to her back. Facing in the opposite direction he pinches the front of her abdomen several times with his chelicerae before leaning over one side and tilting her abdomen so that he can insert his palp. During the next hour one palp may be inserted for about twenty minutes, the other for about half an hour and then the first palp again for about ten minutes before he leaves her. At each change from one side to the other he pauses to pinch her abdomen with his chelicerae. The bulb starts by swelling and collapsing every fifteen seconds during the mating accompanied by a rise and fall of the leg spines, but later in the proceedings this rhythm is slowed down.

Half an hour after leaving her I have seen him begin to spin a tubular shelter open at both ends across which he has then constructed a small ribbon of silk at an angle of 45°. At intervals he pauses to chew his palps and also the tips of his hind legs as though to moisten them before passing the latter across his genital opening. When the ribbon of silk is finished he taps his abdomen against it until a small drop of sperm is deposited on it. Then, without changing his position, he alternately reaches his palps round the edge to the lower surface of the ribbon and absorbs the sperm. The induction process lasts five minutes during which each palp is inserted in the sperm a dozen times.

When eggs are going to be laid the female usually selects the broad leaf of a bramble or other plant, curls it over and encloses herself inside a strong white silk-lined chamber. In this snug retreat she deposits a compact mass of thirty to sixty yellow eggs and here she may be found guarding them from June or July onwards.

Clubiona terrestris is a slim pale yellowish spider reaching 6 mm. in length and is perhaps even commoner than *C. reclusa*. She lives on trees and bushes as well as amongst herbs and under stones. Town life does not suit most of the *Clubionae* but both this species and *C. corticalis* are exceptions which I have collected in the garden of Buckingham Palace and elsewhere in London.

The male *C. terrestris* mounts the female's back without using his chelicerae to bite her. Then he taps her with his palps and scrapes the base of the cephalothorax by means of a rapid opening and shutting of the basal segments of his chelicerae without exposing his fangs. The mating follows similar lines to that I have described for *C. reclusa* although it may last two hours. On one occasion the alternate insertion of each palp lasted an hour and a quarter, and then they were each inserted two or three times more for shorter periods during the next three-quarters of an hour. Each time he changed sides he paused to scrape the base of her cephalothorax with his chelicerae in the same way that *C. reclusa* paused to pinch his female's abdomen; and I expect we should regard these actions as a repetition of courtship with a stimulating effect on the female. The bulb-swelling and spine-rising movements are also noticeable in this species.

Nearly all the *Clubionae* are of a uniform yellow-brown to dark brown colour but there are three species with a distinct body pattern of pale or pale and dark chevrons. The largest of these, *C. corticalis*, ranges up to 10 mm. in length. She lives mostly under the loose bark of trees during the day where she also guards her bundle of yellow eggs in a thick-walled cell. Sometimes she makes her way into houses and is then seen promenading the walls at night in search of insects. *C. compta* and *C. genevensis* L. K. are both smaller and paler in colour and live respectively amongst the foliage of trees or bushes and under

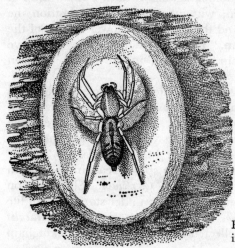

FIG. 59.   *Clubiona corticalis* (8 mm.) in a cell with her egg-sac under bark

stones near the coast. *C. compta* is quite common and widespread in Britain whereas *C. genevensis* had only been recorded from Lulworth and Ringstead until my own discovery of her in the islands of Scilly, Ramsey, Skokholm and Guernsey.

The genus *Cheiracanthium* can be distinguished from that of *Clubiona* in many ways, including the colouration of its species, their longer and slimmer front legs with no spines on the upper surface of the femurs and the narrowing forward-slanting chelicerae.

Cheiracanthium erraticum is the commonest of our three species and also our most handsome Clubionid. She reaches 7.5 mm. and has a carmine dorsal stripe flanked by narrow greenish yellow patches on a background of dull green. Other touches of carmine near the spinnerets brighten the back quarters.

Cheiracanthium pennyi is similar in general appearance but is known in Britain only through the capture of a single male in 1872 by a master at Wellington College, Berks, after whom it was named. The species is known on the Continent and will almost certainly be found again in the Wokingham area. The male is needed for identification and this should be searched for in April. The curved tapering tarsal spur of his palp differs from that of *C. erraticum* in not coming to a fine point.

The third species *C. virescens* is of much the same size and build as the other two but her plain grey-green abdomen without any pattern makes confusion unnecessary. She tends to live in drier situations and to guard her eggs in cells built under stones; this is another distinguishing feature, because *C. erraticum* constructs her cell in grass heads bent over in a characteristic fashion or inside curled leaves of plants.

The genera *Zora* and *Agroeca* both seem to sit uneasily in this family and there are some authorities who move *Zora* to a family of its own whilst my own incomplete knowledge of *Agroeca* habits points to a substantial departure from what is typical for the Clubionidae.

Taking *Zora* first, the eye pattern on her characteristically narrow head is very much like that of the Lycosidae although the eyes themselves are smaller. Basically the spiders are pale yellowish or light grey in colour with two dark bands down the cephalothorax and with series of dark spots on the abdomen. The four species are all about 6 mm. in length and they live on the ground amongst heather, grass or moss. *Z. spinimana* is the only common and widespread species in Britain and I am nearly as guilty as other naturalists in having largely neglected the study of her habits, a study which is fully deserved by the doubts which are held about her relationships with other spiders.

Zora spinimana walks smoothly and slowly with her front legs stretched out in a groping manner in front of her. A May mating which I once watched was a simple affair. Waving his front legs up and down the male moved towards her without hesitation and was allowed to climb over her head on to her back. Then he reached under her abdomen with one of his front legs and pulled her almost on to her side. Copulation lasted six minutes during which one palp was inserted for two and a half minutes and the other palp three and a half minutes after a change of sides.

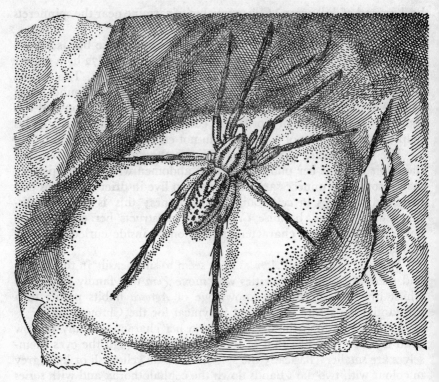

FIG. 60. *Zora spinimana* (6 mm.) on her egg-sac under crumpled paper

I have found the females sitting on their egg-sacs both early in June and also in mid-August — so they probably lay two or three batches of eggs in the course of the summer. In one case I counted twenty-four eggs in a loose bundle, which had been surrounded with a small quantity of loose-meshed silk and then covered over with a white sheet through which the yellow eggs could still be seen indistinctly. This sheet extended well beyond the egg bundle, so the egg-sac had a flattened appearance. The shape may be roughly an oval with smooth edges or else irregular — according to whether it is slung under a flat stone or across the uneven foliage of a heather shoot. Unlike typical Clubionids *Z. spinimana* builds no cell.

Although *Agroeca* has a different eye-pattern with two curved rows of four eyes in a compact group, some of the species look rather like a

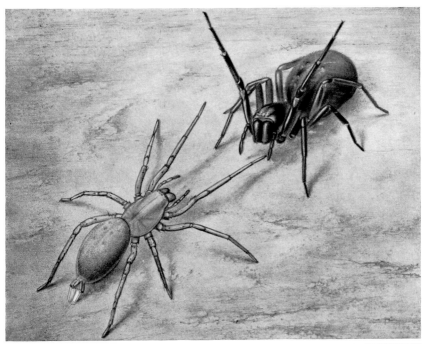

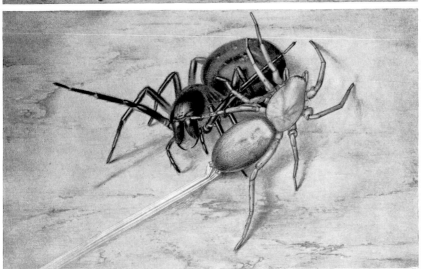

PLATE XI. *Drassodes lapidosus* (14 mm.) is a fighter. In this plate and the next her methods can be seen in a contest with *Ciniflo ferox* (14 mm.)

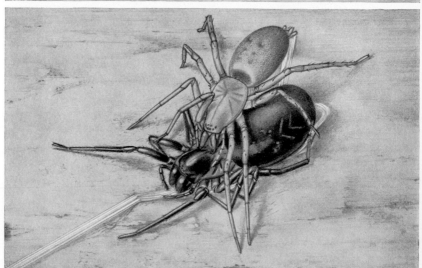

PLATE XII. *Drassodes lapidosus* fighting *Ciniflo ferox* (*contd. from* PLATE XI)

Zora. Abdominal spots tend to be joined into bars and the background to be darker; in fact *Agroeca brunnea* reminds me superficially of a young Lycosid of the genus *Trochosa*. This species is commonly found under heather or in grass clumps, but her exciting egg-sacs have attracted more attention than the light brown spider herself. The mother climbs up a heather twig or a grass stem and there suspends her egg-sac on a wide-based silk stalk. The eggs are enclosed in a cone-shaped covering of silk with an outer covering of white silk in the shape of a bell or Japanese lantern. The cone has a circular opening at the bottom through which the young can escape into the small space below it inside the bell. The white bell is an object of interest and beauty which can often be seen from June onwards despite the fact that this is not really the completed work of the spider. It is next covered with a thick layer of earth carried by the spider from the ground beneath; and the spider's work of art is transformed into a more or less circular bauble of mud (see fig. 61). This may afford protection against some enemies after she abandons it, but after all this toil the camouflage is penetrated by several species of Cryptine ichneumon whose larvae feed on the eggs (Bristowe, 1941).

One point of interest about my incomplete observations on the mating habits of this genus is that they were made at Sandwich early in April 1929; and that it was not until after I had made a further visit there in 1938 that it was found the specimens belonged to a species which was new to the British list (*A. lusatica*). This may provide an example of the greater interest I have always shown in living than in dead spiders but it also exposes a lack of thoroughness in putting every spider through a post-mortem examination under the microscope!

The courtship had points of great interest in being unlike anything recorded in this family but in having a distinct relationship with the procedure of the *Anyphaena* male which is described later.

The male *Agroeca lusatica* raises his first two pairs of legs, or sometimes only the first pair, and wags them up and down at regular intervals of a quarter to half a second. After he has done this several times in front of her, these legs are suddenly vibrated so rapidly for two or three seconds that only a blurred image of them was visible. Thereafter the wagging and the vibrating phases were alternated; he reminded me of a drummer beating time eight to sixteen times and then giving a roll on his drums for about three seconds. I feel sure that this form of courtship conveys vibrations to the female, perhaps along the surface of a plant, rather than having visual significance but unfortunately my

WS—K

females were not prepared to mate and chased the serenading males away.

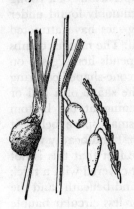

FIG. 61. *Agroeca* egg-sacs *a.* covered in mud, *b. A. brunnea* and *c. A. proxima* before being cased in mud

ANYPHAENIDAE : *The Buzzing Spider*

Our only species, *Anyphaena accentuata,* is closely related to the Clubionidae but is easily distinguished by the conspicuous tracheal spiracle uniquely situated in the centre of the lower abdominal surface (figs. 11, 16, pp. 30, 35). Her better developed claw tufts of clavate hair enable her to cling to the leaves and twigs of the trees and shrubs amongst which she lives, and her two black arrow tip markings on the light cream or grey background of her abdomen give her a distinctive appearance (see Plate XIIIb, p. 148). Her movements and rapid pounce on insects are somewhat reminiscent of a *Philodromus,* but she is not quite so crab-like in her stance and can be distinguished by her eye pattern as well as by the features I have just mentioned.

FIG. 62. *Anyphaena* face

A new discovery which I shall describe here for the first time has led me to suggest that *Anyphaena* deserves to be called the Buzzing Spider.

She is easily found by beating the lower branches of conifers and oak trees. She sometimes weaves a flimsy silk shelter amongst the leaves; but for the most part her shelter during the summer months is provided by the leaves themselves and here amongst the foliage she pounces on small flies and leaf hoppers.

Adults of both sexes can be found early in May, but so can quite young specimens from what I suppose are a later brood of eggs. The males die soon after the mating season and only a small proportion survive far into June.

I have watched the courtship on many occasions from mid-May onwards but have not yet succeeded in seeing them mate; which leads me to think that the female may accept a male only once or during a short period after her final moult.

If a male wanders on to a leaf over which a female has passed a gentle tremor of the abdomen may start. Presently this gets more pronounced and is accompanied by upward and downward as well as inward and outward jerks of his outstretched palps. This may continue for several minutes and then he starts walking about with jerky steps looking for the female. Having found one and having been repulsed, he takes up a position in front of her with the femurs of the first pair of legs bent steeply backwards and with the other segments raised defensively in the air. For a time he sits flat on the leaf with his abdomen wagging up and down and his palps vibrating inwards and upwards. Then, quite suddenly, he becomes galvanised into vigorous courtship of a kind which I had not seen in any other spider.

Slightly raising his body he takes a jerky step or two forward with the abdomen tapping so violently against the leaf for about two seconds that the sound of its impacts is clearly audible. Now the front legs are reached out in front of him and he remains apparently quite still for about three seconds with his body pressed downwards against the leaf. Advancing towards her, or else circling round to find her again if she has fled, he alternates these short advances with the short pauses. When, as in my first observations, the male was courting on the sides of a box, I was amazed to hear a high buzzing sound, not entirely unlike the shrill buzzing of a fly, during the periods of his apparent immobility.

At first I was completely mystified. Viewing the spider from above I could detect no explanation; until at last my wife noticed from a position to one side of me that the outline of his abdomen was blurred by vibrations far too rapid for the eye to follow and that the tarsi of the outstretched front legs were equally blurred in outline by the same vibrations. The vibrations of the spider's abdomen reminded me of those of a tuning fork and the sound of a tuning fork touching a hard

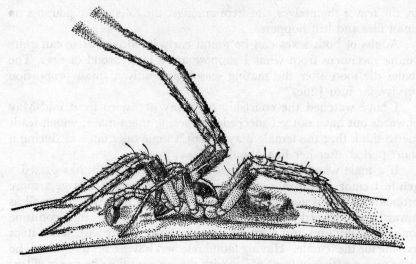

FIG. 63.   *Anyphaena* (6 mm.) male vibrating abdomen during courtship

surface like cardboard or glass as had been the case with my captive spiders.

In alternating series I had been hearing tap-tap-tap-tap-tap-tap buz-z-z-z-z-z-z-z and I soon noticed that these signals brought a female from below a leaf to the upper surface on which he was performing. The message is probably conveyed to the female through her tactile senses, although it is possible the vibrations set up oscillations of the fine hairs or trichobothria standing up like wireless masts on the female's legs.

I have often noticed that captive specimens of this and other species in need of water will rapidly find their way to drops placed on the lid or wall of their box.   The slit organs or the tarsal organs (see p. 34) probably enable the spider to detect the water.

In mid-June the females lay their eggs. These are enclosed in a flattened white egg-sac over which the mother stands on guard in a silk cell which is often inside the curled edge of a leaf. From the time she lays her eggs *Anyphaena* changes in colour from cream to grey.

CHAPTER 12

THE SPARASSIDAE & THOMISIDAE
Crab Spiders

THESE two families also belong to the Clubionoidea. They earn their name of 'Crab Spiders' from the lateral curvature of their legs, combined with an ability to move sideways in a crab-like fashion. Although they build no snares, they depend on their prey coming to them instead of going out to chase it like many of the other hunting spiders. Some will spring at an insect with agility when it comes quite close, but others, more portly in build, remain in ambush until their stout front legs can clasp it in firm embrace whilst the chelicerae are buried in its neck.

THE SPARASSIDAE

Various large spiders with crab-like stance are commonly imported in hands of bananas. *Heteropoda venatoria* Linn. has travelled the world in this way and is a well known inhabitant of houses in most tropical countries. There she catches cockroaches and carries a flat dingy white egg-sac in her chelicerae at the appropriate season. In about 1948 it was suddenly noticed that *Heteropoda's* place at Covent Garden had been taken by two relations with dark markings on their abdomens and with conspicuous black spots and rings on their legs. These proved to belong to the genus *Torania* and called attention to a switch to West Africa for banana imports.

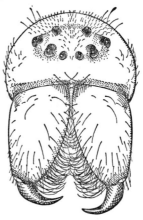

FIG. 64. *Micrommata* face

Perhaps it is fortunate that the young of these large sinister Sparassids cannot survive in our climate.

Our only resident Sparassid is one of our most attractive spiders and her beauty vies with the grandeur of *Dolomedes* for first place in my affections (see Plate 2, p. 62 and XIII, p. 148). The first encounter with *Micrommata virescens* is a memorable occasion. Although she can exceed half an inch in length, she is seldom noticed even in the drives and open spaces in woods where she can be abundant, and this is because her vivid green colouring blends so perfectly with the blades of Purple Moor-grass (*Molinia caerulea*) on which she is poised head downwards to spring on passing insects. Her claw-tufts and scopulae, or clumps of special hair on the tarsi, make movement on vertical surfaces secure.

It is interesting to find that in extreme youth the young are hay-coloured; because the clumps of *Molinia* are also hay-coloured at that season before the fresh shoots emerge. At this stage their slim bodies make confusion possible with young *Tibelli*, but, whereas a *Tibellus* gets more elongate as she grows older the reverse happens to a female

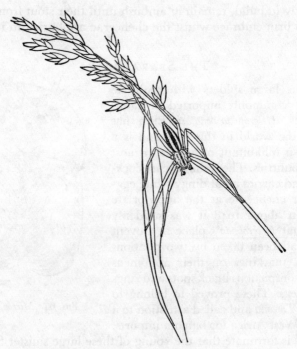

FIG. 65.   *Micrommata virescens* male (8 mm.)

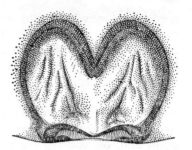

b. Female epigyne, showing chitinised pockets at the base into which the tibial spurs fit and hold the palp during mating

a. Male palp showing tibial spur

FIG. 66. *Micrommata virescens*

Micrommata, who can become quite portly. The male resembles the female until shortly before his final moult, after which he is revealed in all his splendour. The slender build of youth is maintained but his abdomen is bright scarlet and yellow with green flanks, the scarlet markings being arranged on a yellow background in three narrow bands down the entire length of the abdomen.

Micrommata lives mainly in the South but the species is locally distributed and has been recorded from Yorkshire and Northumberland. June seems to be the main month for the final moult, but for this to be accomplished the spider has to grow very rapidly from the youngster stage in which the winter is spent. In consequence of this I have noticed that the final skin is sometimes not cast until well into July in exceptional years when cold and wet spring weather has seriously limited the number of days during which the spider could feed and grow.

When a male encounters a female he avoids the risk of losing her by springing straight at her without any introductory courtship and roughly seizing her abdomen or a leg with his chelicerae. Strangely enough the fierce female makes no serious resistance to this sudden attack and without further delay he caresses her with his legs and climbs on to her back. From this position he leans over one side to tilt her abdomen and insert one of his palps. Mating is a long affair in this species and may last six or seven hours with each palp being inserted once only for about half that time. At the end he leaps away with agility as though this were a moment of danger for him. Nevertheless his disappearance within a few weeks is more likely to be due to natural causes than to cannibalism.

Two interesting points of detail emerged from my watching *Micrommata,* which helped to explain mating technique in other spiders. The males of several families have a stiff spur on the tibial segment of their palps and, on noticing some abortive attempts by a freshly moulted male to mate with a female, I watched him under a powerful lens in order to discover the cause. It transpired from this that the male inserts his tibial spur into one of two chitinous pockets in the female's body just behind her epigyne and that this locks the palp to resist the pressure set up by the expansion and torsion of the palpal organ (see fig. 66). In this particular case the spur was still soft and flexible, so it bent and came unfixed whenever the bulb expanded with the result that mating was impossible. This disclosed the use and importance of the tibial spur.

The swelling of the palpal bulb is a common occurrence in many spiders but it was whilst watching the long mating of *Micrommata* that I had ample opportunity to link this up with an explanation for the rise and fall of the leg spines in many spiders to which I had drawn attention for the first time in 1922 (Bristowe, 1922). In *Micrommata* the swelling of the bulb and the erection of the spines took place regularly every twenty-four seconds at the start but less frequently as the mating proceeded. It seemed to me probable that the swelling of the bulb was caused by a mounting pressure of body fluid along the legs and palps, brought about by muscular contraction, until the pressure was high enough to discharge sperm into the female's body and to cause the spines to rise and fall at the same time.

When the egg-laying season starts in July it is easiest to find *Micrommata* by examining any small oak sapling growing amongst the grass with leaves a foot or two from the ground; because *Micrommata* usually fastens three or four leaves firmly together so as to form a large silk-lined chamber in which to guard her bundle of green eggs. The chamber is sealed and the emaciated female takes no food until the young have left this sanctuary. I have no evidence for suggesting that she lays a second batch of eggs later in the summer, except that one has occasionally done so in captivity.

I think I must plant some clumps of Purple Moorgrass in my garden

beside a small pool and then introduce *Micrommata* and *Dolomedes* —
my two favourite spiders. After all, I have found them together at
Broadmoor Criminal Lunatic Asylum — just outside the walls of that
establishment !

FIG. 67. *Micrommata* on grass

THE THOMISIDAE

I cannot pretend that many of our
thirty-eight species are gay or beautiful,
and yet there is something very attractive about even the plainest ones,
similar in some respects to the plainness
of a toad, of which *Oxyptila* specially
reminds me. Many have short squat
bodies and in the sub-family, *Misumeninae,* the hind pairs of legs often look
almost atrophied beside the front pairs
which are well-developed to seize un-
wary insects within their grasp. These
walk slowly and little. They lie in ambush for their prey on the ground or on

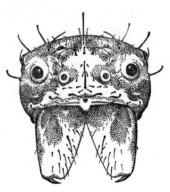

FIG. 68. *Xysticus* face

plants, so it is not surprising to find that many are marked and coloured
in a way which makes them very inconspicuous. Bars and spots form

the usual pattern but there are others with bright colours which nestle in flowers of similar colour to themselves. The more active climbers are found in the sub-family *Philodrominae*, where the back legs are nearly as well-developed as the front pairs.

The principal season for mating and laying eggs is the spring and early summer, and the young which hatch from these eggs are the parents of broods at the same season in the following year. Although they show their ability to see moving insects at a distance of a few inches by pivoting their bodies and outstretched legs round to face them, their sight is very limited and the males resort to no visual courtship. They are distinctly smaller than the females, and in the extreme cases of *Thomisus* and *Misumena* the male is a slim dwarf of 3 to 4 mm., compared with 10 mm. in the paunchy females. Despite a disparity in size the shortsighted male crab spiders must not lose their females once they have been found; and we shall see that they invariably try to mount the females without any preliminaries, even if this means seizing a leg with their chelicerae. The male's taste-by-touch or chemo-tactic sense enables him to detect her identity instantaneously and even in her absence he is stimulated by silk she has spun. Nevertheless his sight can play some small but useful part in general recognition when he is close to her, as he can see when she has passed her season for mating. At this stage in her life she is fierce with him; and at the very first contact, or even before he touches her, she will raise her legs in an attitude of menace and jerk her body up and down as a warning against further approach. The message is not lost on the male who discreetly withdraws.

When a male has succeeded in mounting a female's back he moves about clutching her with vibrating legs before taking up his mating position. This position varies within the family according to the shape of the spiders. A *Tibellus,* for instance, will lean slightly over one side in much the same way as a Clubionid, but the broader abdomen of a female *Philodromus* or *Diaea* makes the male lean further over until he is almost standing on his head. In *Xysticus* and *Oxyptila* the male does stand on his head and over the back of her truncated abdomen in order to reach her epigyne, whilst the dwarf male *Misumena* has to go still further and climb right under her belly.

The mating is a short process in the Philodrominae, and may comprise the insertion of only one palp for half a minute in the extreme case of some *Philodromus* species, whereas in some of the Misumeninae it may last more than an hour during which time the palps are in

FIG. 69. The toad-like *Oxyptila* (5 mm.) sits on her eggs

alternate use many times. The tiny sperm web is in the shape of a
band and the sperm is absorbed into the palps through the web.

When the time comes for egg-laying, the female Thomisid builds a
silk saucer into which the egg mass is poured and covered over with
more silk to form a lenticular egg-sac. An outer protective covering may
then be spun on which the mother stands on guard under a stone, on a
curled leaf or on a heather shoot. She herself remains exposed, in contrast to *Micrommata*, although *Philodromus aureolus* is exceptional in spinning a thin protecting canopy above herself. Thirty to forty-five eggs are
perhaps the commonest number to be laid in a batch by such genera
as *Oxyptila*, *Philodromus* and *Diaea;* but the larger species, including some
Xystici, lay more than a hundred.

The Philodrominae, with their legs of similar length and strength
and their pads of hair, actively climb about on plants and shrubs,
except for *Philodromus fallax* which lives on sandhills (see fig. 70). Here
her grey mottling blends very effectively with her surroundings when
she moves away from clumps of Marram Grass. At the beginning of
June I have watched the males chasing the females and tickling them

with their legs until they can climb on their backs. They then lean over
the side and insert a palp for two minutes before changing to the other
side to insert the other for a similar period. Later in the month the
females lay their eggs in a silk saucer in the sand at the base of some
plant which is then covered in with white silk and finally with threads
of silk carefully coated with sand grains.

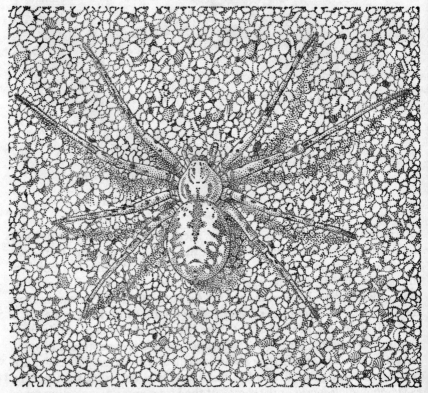

FIG. 70.   *Philodromus fallax* (6 mm.) blends with the sand

All species of *Philodromus* blend well with their surroundings and
the handsome *P. histrio* on heather provides an example (see fig. 71).
Our two very common species on gorse and other shrubs or plants
are *P. aureolus* and *P. dispar* (see Plate X, p.113). The patterns on
the females' abdomens are variable but *P. aureolus* is yellowish-brown

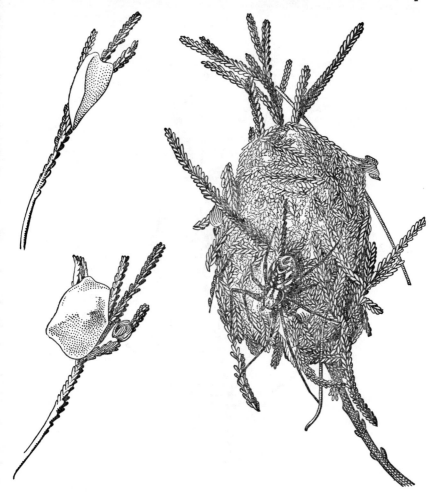

FIG. 71.   *Philodromus histrio* (7 mm.) encloses her egg-sac in a bulky covering of silk and interwoven heather shoots

with a series of reddish-brown spots and chevrons whereas *P. dispar* is often pale buff with indistinct or no chevrons. The males would not easily be recognised as belonging to the same species. They are very slim with long slender legs and the abdomen of *P. aureolus* is much darker with metallic colours reflecting from iridescent hairs whilst that of *P. dispar* is a shiny black.

FIG. 72. *Tibellus oblongus* (9 mm.) guarding her egg-sac

In both these species a mating usually comprises the insertion of only one palp for a brief period of half a minute. On one occasion I have seen a male *P. dispar* chase a female almost immediately after they had parted and insert his other palp for a similar period, but this is unusual, though it was fortunate for me because his palps now needed re-charging with sperm. A narrow 5 mm. ribbon was spun about half an hour later round which he reached his palps from above to absorb the sperm droplet through the web.

Tibellus remains nearer the ground than the *Philodromi* and is usually to be found amongst thick grass clumps. Our two species depart from the usual shape in having long narrow bodies. Both reach up to 10 mm. and are hay-coloured. Although they are agile, they wait in ambush for insects to approach before springing on them, and their custom of sitting head downwards stretched along a stem of similar colour to themselves helps to make them inconspicuous.

A number of large dark spots on the abdomen of *T. maritimus* helps to distinguish her from the commoner *T. oblongus*. Like *Micrommata* the male shows roughness when he meets the female. In late May and early June I have seen a male *T. maritimus* seize her by a leg and drag her on to one side so that he can insert one of his palps. At intervals he changes sides and inserts each palp twice or three times before leaving her after twenty-five to thirty-five minutes.

Passing on now to the more static sub-family Misumeninae in which the front pair of legs are much longer and stronger than the hind pairs, *Xysticus* is the genus we are most likely to meet.

Xysticus cristatus is the commonest of the twelve species and, like the others, her squat body is wider behind than in front. She reaches 7 mm. in length and is mostly pale fawn in colour with markings typical for the genus. These comprise a pale dentated band of some width down the centre of the abdomen flanked on either side by a darker band which may be broken by the indentations of the central band. She lurks amongst grass and low herbage either at ground level or on its foliage and is not so averse to eating an ant from time to time as are most other spiders.

The male of this species allowed me to make a fascinating discovery about his mating technique which was so remarkable as to tempt a northern clergyman to publish such expressions as 'impossible, especially as I have seen the act performed in a different way' and 'there is a fishy odour about his assertion'. I could afford to make no rejoinder, biblical or otherwise, by the time I read his paper; because my observations had already been confirmed in several other species of *Xysticus* by workers in Germany and U.S.A., as well as by myself in Britain and in the Far East. Indeed I only refer to it now, after the lapse of more than a quarter of a century, because of the lesson it taught me never to reject without investigation even the most unlikely tales about spiders. They do the most fantastic things and therein lies part of their fascination.

Directly a male *Xysticus cristatus* came in contact with a female he seized her by the femur of one of her front legs. Having withstood the short scuffle which this provoked he climbed on to her back and circled round with fondling legs. No doubt these movements help to stimulate the female, and they are typical of all Thomisids; but with *Xysticus* they were more prolonged. Suddenly I formed an exciting suspicion. Surely

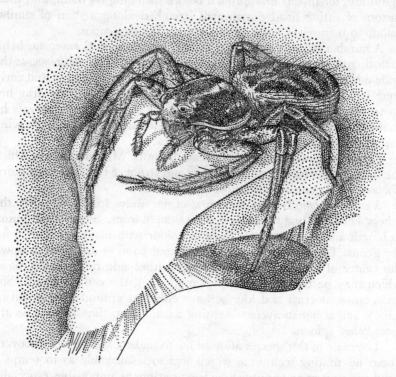

FIG. 73.   *Xysticus kochi* (7 mm.) on her eggs under a stone

he was tying her to the ground with silk threads ! A microscope confirmed that threads were being drawn delicately but with precision over her head and legs and fastened to the ground. Not until this bridal veil had been completed did he tilt her abdomen slightly upwards from behind and crawl head foremost slightly under it from the rear. From this position he stroked her epigyne until his tibial spur anchored a palp in the right position for mating. About an hour and a half later he left her and I watched her disentangle her legs from the protective veil with some difficulty. This veil of silk not only prevented her from seizing him at the dangerous moment of departure but assisted him, perhaps, in anchoring her head whilst he pivoted her body upwards from behind (see Plate X, p. 113).

The number of palpal alternations are numerous and variable during the long mating of a *Xysticus*. On one occasion a male *X. lanio* changed the palps thirteen times during a mating of just under two hours, but on another occasion the mating of the same male lasted with pauses about three and a half hours during which there were considerably more than twenty alternations, some of very short duration and possibly abortive. This provides an interesting contrast to the procedure amongst the *Philodromi*.

Four and a half hours after a male *Xysticus cristatus* had mated I saw him waving his palps in the air and chewing them. Presently he spun a little ribbon of silk about 4 mm. in length on a frame formed by four thick threads. Pressing his body up and down against the lower surface he deposited a drop of sperm which he absorbed through the web by the alternate application of each palp about twenty-five times.

The nine species of *Oxyptila* are smaller and, although they range up to 6 mm., their average size is about 3 to 4 mm. They look rather like a *Xysticus* at first glance but they have narrower heads and less distinct body patterns. They are sluggish spiders and most of them live amongst moss, detritus and low vegetation like diminutive toads. The pale yellow *O. simplex,* however, is commonest on sandhills and I have twice captured *O. sanctuaria* entering houses. This reminds me that the Rev. O. Pickard-Cambridge christened her '*sanctuaria*' in 1871 because he found her for the first time in his church at Bloxworth whilst rebuilding the chancel in memory of his father. One of the surprises of night collecting by torch light is to find that some of the *Oxyptilae* associated with moss and detritus climb up the low herbs at night, from which I suspect that they may feed more by night than by day.

Mating follows much the same course as in *Xysticus* without the rough play at the start or the precaution of fastening the female down.

The vivid green cephalothorax and legs and the light brown leaf markings of *Diaea dorsata* make her quite unmistakable when she is beaten in abundance from such trees as oak, box and yew; but the young are only faintly green with almost white abdomens. She is a southern spider scarcely known in Wales and unrecorded from Scotland and

WS–L

Ireland. In *D. dorsata* mating starts early in May and here again the male mounts the female without introduction or resistance. After tickling her with his legs he leans over one side and changes sides at intervals during the five minutes that mating lasts. Egg-laying takes place from the latter part of June onwards and the eggs, covered over with a thick layer of stiff silk, are partially enclosed in a bent leaf. Here the mother sits on guard until the young emerge towards the end of July. She will eat small insects during this time and chase the larger ones away, or else give the warning signal of outstretched legs and violent thumps of the body up and down (see fig. 76).

When I was sixteen I discovered a bulky bright pink Crab Spider with two conical humps on her body. I rushed to the only authoritative books dealing with British spiders, which then comprised 'Blackwall', 'Staveley' and 'Pickard-Cambridge', and found that the only species with the right shape was yellow, so for a time I was filled with the ecstasy of discovery known to explorers and naturalists. Surely this lovely spider must be new to science or at the very least a new and exciting variety? She proved to be the pink form of *Thomisus onustus;* and it is a strange chance, coupled no doubt with my own methods of search, that whenever I have since found this uncommon species in Britain she is almost invariably bright pink, although even Locket and Millidge describe her in their recent book as being 'whitish-yellow, sometimes suffused with pink'. I have found her in orchids but especially in Bell Heather, where her colouration provides splendid camouflage and her eager outflung pink legs give the appearance of some wisp of the flowers themselves (see Plate 1, p. 49).

Thomisus is one of our most static spiders and she depends on complete stillness for her success. The approach of an insect to the flower on which she is sitting will cause adjustments in her position so smoothly carried out that they are barely noticeable. The insect lowers its head in search of nectar and in a flash it is seized and the spider's chelicerae are buried in its head or thorax. Bees and other insects of greater bulk than the spider herself fall victims to her surprise attacks.

If by any chance a miscalculation is made and the insect is bitten in the abdomen, the *Thomisus* will use her legs to trim it to the approved position with her chelicerae inserted between the head and thorax. From that time onwards there is no further motion until the insect is sucked dry and dropped to the ground. The Thomisids have no cheliceral teeth so they do not mash their food and a consequence of

FIG. 74.   *Thomisus onustus* (8 mm.) with her egg-sac in a heather shoot

this is that the spider retains her advantage of protective colouration
whilst the apparently undamaged insect continues to sit in a natural
position on the flower. My first acquaintance with the yellow form of
this species came as a result of a trip to Spain during which a professor
stalked and netted a Swallowtail Butterfly which was sitting on a flower.
Its failure to move caused him great astonishment; but we both gained
from his manoeuvres, because he had a butterfly in perfect condition
for his cabinet whilst I had the spider !

In July she may be sought on the tips of heather shoots where she sits on a thick egg-sac partially concealed by the leaves which are drawn over it. Now she is wrinkled and thin with her conical humps protruding conspicuously. Although she will gamely protect her eggs from any intruder regardless of size, a cryptine ichneumon manages to outwither and I have twice bred a *Goniocryptus* from her egg-sacs.

Misumena vatia is a much commoner flower species (see Plate X, p. 113). Like *Thomisus* she ranges up to about 10 mm. in length and is southern in her distribution with the midlands as her northern limit compared with Oxford for *Thomisus*. Sometimes her smooth abdomen has small chocolate markings on the shoulders, but usually she is either yellow or white from top to toe. A count of fifty specimens showed me some years ago that 80% were sitting in flowers which matched their colour, despite the fact that the young specimens are, I think, always white. The adults can change from white or yellow, or vice versa, in the space of two or three days; so the principal points to consider are whether she rejects flowers which are neither white nor yellow, whether she has some way of selecting gorse, broom, mullein, ragwort and um-belliferous plants, or whether the result is achieved simply as a matter of chance. I cannot provide the answer but I think that it is largely chance — combined with the occurrence of a high proportion of yellow or white flowers in the sunny meadows and hedgerows particularly frequented by *Misumena*. Some scents may repel her and plants with flimsy stalks would bend and sway too much.

As regards the colour change, Gabritschevsky (1927) says the white-ness of *Misumena* is due to transparency of the hypodermis which exposes to view the guanin crystals in the cells below, whilst yellow colouration is caused by a fluid accumulated in the superficial cells.

Although the ability to change colour has long been an accepted fact, I found that there was no positive evidence of advantage to the spider. A lot of theorising had taken place as to whether there was an advantage of a protective nature against enemies, or in catching their prey, or, as some thought, none at all so I decided to carry out a simple test. Sixteen Dandelion heads were arranged on a grass lawn in rows of four, each flower one foot from its neighbour, and the whole forming one large square. In the centre of alternate flowers I placed a small black pebble of about the same size as *Misumena's* body, and in the centre of the remaining eight flowers a yellow pebble of the same size carefully selected to match the Dandelion's colour. The insects which

a. The vivid green *Micrommata virescens* (13 mm.)

b. Anyphaena accentuata on yew (7 mm.)

PLATE XIII

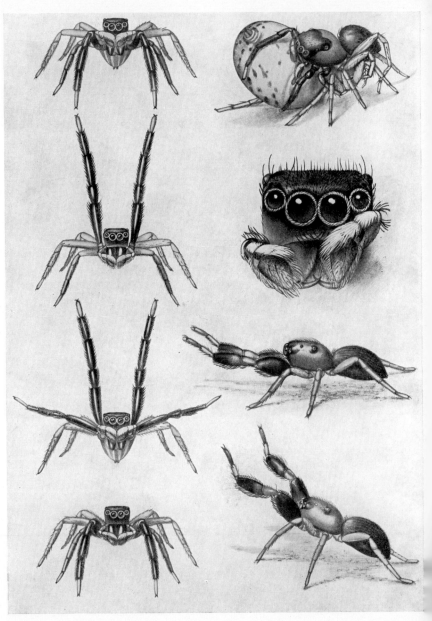

PLATE XIV. Male Jumping Spiders in courting attitudes. *Left:* courting attitudes of *Euophrys frontalis* (3 mm.). *Top right:* His mating position with the female's abdomen tilted. *Centre right:* His face with waving palps. *Bottom right:* Two attitudes of *Bianor aenescens* (3.5 mm.) displaying front legs.

FIG. 75. *Misumena vatia* (10 mm.) on Black Mullein

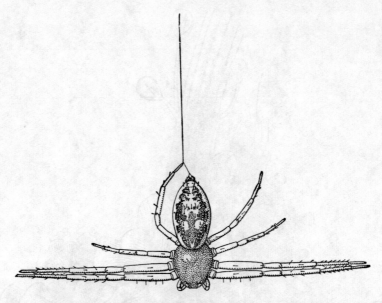

FIG. 76. *Diaea dorsata's* attitude when dropping

visited each flower in the course of the next half an hour were then
counted. The result is summarised below:

INSECT VISITORS	TO FLOWERS WITH A YELLOW PEBBLE	TO FLOWERS WITH A BLACK PEBBLE
Honey bees	10	1
Other bees (*Halictus*)	2	1
Syrphid flies	42	4
Other flies	2	1
TOTAL	56	7

That chance did not account for this result was clearly shown by
the behaviour of the Honey Bees and Syrphid flies which repeatedly
drew back from a flower containing a black pebble whilst they settled
without hesitation on any of those containing a yellow pebble. Indeed,
the only Honey Bee to alight on a Dandelion with a black pebble did
so by crawling up from the side after having misjudged its distance and
come to earth amongst the surrounding grass.

This experiment satisfied me that *Misumena* does gain aggressive advantage from her colour resembling that of the flower on which she sits, but it is harder to prove that she also escapes the attention of birds or other enemies. I can say that I have accumulated records of many spiders eaten by birds in this country and that *Misumena* is not included; but four were amongst the 10,000 spiders listed for me by the U.S. Biological Survey as having been extracted from the stomachs of birds in America. Considering the exposed situations in which *Misumena* always sits and the fact that some do not match their surroundings, this proportion does not seem high. Proof of their partial invisibility to prey provides strong support for the belief that they also gain advantage in escaping enemies. At least they are capable of deceiving a professor !

CHAPTER 13

THE SALTICIDAE

Jumping Spiders

THE Salticidae are the most vivid
and gay of all spiders in the
tropics, where their iridescent flattened hairs or scales glitter brightly
in the sun. Although none of our
British species have the vivid colours
of these tropical relatives their more
subdued patterns are often very
attractive and we inevitably associate
them with sunshine and gaiety as they
walk, skip or dance in the sunlight
of a spring day. Added to this there
is something endearing about the
way they really seem to take notice
of us by swivelling their heads upwards or to the side in order to
watch us.

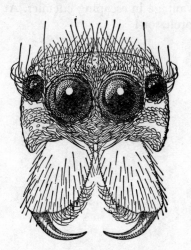

FIG. 77. *Salticus* face

The Salticidae are hunting spiders. They walk in a series of jerks,
pausing to move their cephalothorax, and with it their battery of eyes,
when a moving insect comes within range. Then they stalk it as
stealthily as a cat until it is within jumping distance. The more sluggish
species may make the final jump from a distance of only about twice
their own body-length, but our champion jumper, *Attulus saltator*, can
span a distance greater than twenty times its own length when it is
threatened with capture. Strangely enough their smooth creeping
movements are often accompanied by a fluttering of the palps and a
mysterious flickering of the eyes as though they were hypnotising their
prey or at least riveting its attention whilst they draw nearer.

The flickering of the eyes with a change in colour from green to brown has been the subject of speculation, but whereas some sceptics have put it down to faulty observation — due to slight movements of the spider itself accompanied by an alteration in the direction in which the light is reflected — others have suggested more convincingly that the effect is produced by the posterior tips of the conical eye cavities being drawn together or forced apart by muscular action with a resulting increase in the spider's field of vision. One thing which is certain is that in some species a rapid flickering accompanied by change in colour does occur and when I have watched this under a microscope it has left me with a strong impression of movement of the retina *up and down* the conical eye-cavity, which would suggest a change in focus rather than in lateral range of vision. Even if the spider can swivel its eyes into a squint I do not think I have been mistaken in seeing what I have described.

In the Salticidae the first pair of legs are usually more powerfully built than the others; and this led me to think that they played a principal part in the spider's jumping feats. The removal of one front leg under an anaesthetic, however, made no difference. When I removed one hindleg, however, the spider alighted nearly at right angles to its starting position, thus showing that it is really the hind legs on which the spider depends. Close observation reveals that the front legs are often raised before a jump is made, that they are stretched forwards whilst in mid-air and that they are used to hold the insect on alighting.

The spider trails a thread all the time she is walking and never fails to fasten this before she jumps. This prevents her falling to the ground below the plant or wall on which she may be hunting and swings her back on to a vertical surface from which she has leaped at a fly. A further aid to life on smooth vertical surfaces or swaying vegetation is to be found in the equipment of pads of special adhesive hairs on the tips of their legs.

The four pairs of eyes can all play a part in the capture of prey but their functions and powers of vision vary considerably. The movement of a fly coming from behind the spider will be noticed at a distance of several inches by the small eyes directed upwards from the cephalothorax. The spider then turns quickly to face the insect with the four eyes which are directed forwards along the front of her head. The pair at the sides have a wide field and help in the assessment of distance. The large central pair have the best powers of vision and provide a clear enlarged image of the insect which she is stalking. Identification may occur in some species, according to H. Homann (1928), at a distance of 8 cm. but the leap will still be delayed until the gap between spider and prey has been narrowed.

At night and on other occasions when the sun is not shining, the Salticidae remain in silk cells spun mostly under bark or stones. Here in these cells they lay their eggs and remain on guard although they may sometimes emerge to watch for a passing insect on which to feed. Generalisations usually have exceptions where spiders are concerned; and, after *Ballus* has nestled her eggs in a covering of white silk on an oak branch, she spins a sheet just above it which is drawn taut by a series of eight or ten silk struts and a second sheet above this with openings allowing her to take up a position between these two covering sheets.

I started by implying that the Salticidae have their headquarters in tropical countries: even in our own small country there is a marked falling off in the number of species as we pass from southern England to northern Scotland. All our thirty-two species live in the southern counties of England, but several do not even extend to the midland or northern counties whilst only twelve have been recorded from Scotland (apart from one found only in hot-houses). In Scotland they are usually scarce and I found none at all in Orkney or Shetland. Temperature undoubtedly plays a part. Extreme temperatures in winter may be intolerable to some species; but more important may be the number of hot sunny days in spring and summer that enable them to hunt, prosper and complete their life-cycle.

April and May are the principal months for courtship and late May or June for the first batch of eggs to be laid. By June many of the males have died or become scarce and later in the summer the females also die leaving their half-grown young to pass the winter in cells under bark and stones or underground. *Marpissa muscosa* is one of the exceptions to the rule and she may be found at any season.

Our two species of *Marpissa* are the largest and amongst the more handsome of our Salticids. There is nothing gaudy about them, but their attraction lies in an admixture of greys and browns with some black and white arranged in bands or chevrons. Both species can reach about 10 mm. but, whereas *M. muscosa* makes herself inconspicuous on the bark or lichen of fences, poles and trees, mostly in the southern counties, *M. pomatia* is an inhabitant of fens in East Anglia and south west England where she can be sought in the heads of reeds (*Phragmites*).

Both stalk their prey with the stealth of a cat, leaping on them from a distance of about half an inch; and one characteristic shared by other members of the family is that they can retreat backwards almost as rapidly as forwards. The somewhat flat body of *M. muscosa* is in keeping with her habit of squeezing into narrow crevices under bark where she weaves her cell.

I have been fortunate in having the locally distributed *M. muscosa* in each of the gardens where I have lived in Surrey, Sussex and Kent; and I owe to this species my first insight into the courtship of spiders. When I was a boy I read the vivid descriptions by Mr. and Mrs. Peckham of American male Salticids dancing in front of the females; but there was absolutely nothing in the British literature to suggest that our species did anything similar, so I spent my first day of the Easter holidays with *Marpissa*. To my delight I found that his antics were just as alluring as those of his American relations.

In the presence of a female he watches her closely. Then he stretches his thick front pair of legs high in the air and somewhat outwards, raises his abdomen steeply upwards behind and zig-zags rapidly from side to side, taking three or four steps first to one side and then the other. Gradually he draws closer until he can touch her (see Plate XVI, p. 157).

As befitting a close relation, *M. pomatia's* May courtship is not greatly different. His front legs are raised almost vertically with the tarsi and metatarsi curving backwards and he rapidly swings from side to side as he draws nearer without any appreciable side-stepping or the raising of his abdomen. If she does not drive him away he then stretches his front legs outwards and rapidly beats them up and down over hers like the flapping of an insect's wings. Slowly he creeps over her, leans over one side and inserts a palp.

What form of courtship would I find in the other genera? Having once been captivated by *Marpissa's* lively antics I became eager to enquire and I have now seen the males of all the seventeen genera in action except *Neon* and *Pellenes* (which was probably a chance importation to Folkestone in 1888).

Our southern sandhills are happy hunting-grounds for several species like *Hyctia nivoyi*, *Phlegra fasciata*, *Attulus saltator* and *Synageles venator*, and I will start with these.

Hyctia nivoyi is a slim spider with a narrow tubular body, which runs up and down the stems of Marram Grass. The female reaches 6 mm. in length and has a pale yellowish body with three longitudinal rows of dark spots. The male is still narrower and has dark chevrons on the hind part of his abdomen. In both sexes the first pair of legs are massive and his are dark brown with a metallic sheen except for the tarsi and metatarsi which are yellow. When confronting a female these legs are prominently displayed. He stretches them out sideways at an angle of 45° and walks rapidly from side to side in front of her, raising and lowering them. Throughout these gyrations he faces her all the time; and sometimes he poses with his abdomen bent sharply sideways in a position which will display the dark chevrons on his abdomen.

On one occasion in mid-April she allowed him to approach her after a courtship lasting nearly half an hour. He touched her with his front legs and crept over her with his body and legs twitching. Now he turned round on her back, clutching her with vibrating legs, until they were once more facing in opposite directions, and then he leaned over one side and inserted a palp. Mating lasted 47 minutes during which one palp was inserted five times and the other four.

By contrast *Phlegra fasciata's* courtship is sluggish; though this could partly have been due to the lateness of the season in the second half of May. Jerkily he zig-zagged in front of the female with his palps wagging and with his *three* pairs of front legs all curved forward in an unusual way without being raised. After a short display of this kind he raised his front pair of legs and moved forward to touch her.

Attulus saltator is an extremely lively and much smaller spider (3.5 mm.) whose attractive spotted body harmonises with the surroundings of sand and low vegetation on the sandhills. The male's courtship reminds me of the movements of a ballet dancer. Poised on three pairs of legs he scampers rapidly sideways with his first pair raised steeply and swaying gracefully from side to side. He pauses with the outer leg nearly vertical and the inner leg inclined slightly away from it over his cephalothorax. Then he scampers in the other direction, swaying legs until he stops to pose again with his outer leg vertical and the inner leg bent slightly towards it. This alternation of movement and postures can continue many times when the female is unwilling to accept him.

The fourth spider is not so restricted to our southern sandhills as the others and she is greatly different in appearance and behaviour. *Synageles venator* is a slim ant-like species whose narrow body is inconspicuous as she runs up and down the stalks of the Marram Grass. In mid-June I collected several males and females at Braunton Burrows and put them together on my return home. The males stretched their enlarged front pair of legs stiffly forward and, holding them in this position, they jigged from side to side in the short arc of a circle just

PLATE XV. Male of *Evarcha arcuata* courting a female (7 mm.) guarding her egg-sac.

PLATE XVI. *Marpissa muscosa* courtship (8 mm.)

in front of the females. During these lateral steps the abdomen was
wriggled sinuously from side to side and sometimes raised in the air.
Gradually he drew nearer or further away, without interrupting his
dance, according to whether she remained still or moved towards him.
The male of our other rare ant-like spider, *Myrmarachne formicaria,* also
wriggles and raises his abdomen during courtship (see fig. 80).

   Salticus scenicus is the first member of this family which most people
notice; because its principal hunting ground is the outer walls of our
houses and fences. Her dark body with its white stripes has earned the
name of Zebra Spider. The male is very similar in appearance except
for gigantic unwieldy chelicerae which must be a positive hindrance
to him either in attack or defence, so I waited with expectancy to see
if they served some purpose in his courting displays. In the presence

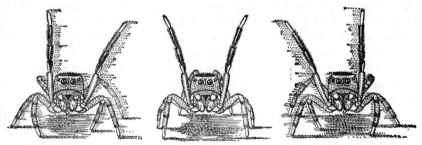

FIG. 78.   The *Attulus saltator* male (3 mm.) pirouettes from side to side during
courtship

of a female he zig-zagged to and fro in front of her with the first pair
of legs raised slightly and stretched out stiffly to the side. The long basal
segments of the chelicerae were also pressed outwards without the fangs
being bared.

   When confronted by another male the use he makes of the chelicerae
is more striking. Both males adopt their courting attitude and draw
closer and closer until the front legs and opened fangs are pressed firmly
outwards against those of their rival whilst the palps are bent back out
of harm's way. This apparently hostile onslaught is really a bloodless
battle, the explanation for which lies, I believe, in mistaken identity
accompanied by enough stimulation of the sexual instincts to dominate
the predatory instincts. Confirmation of the stimulation of one male
Salticid by another is confirmed in an interesting way by placing a

looking-glass in front of a long-sighted *Aelurillus* male. After examining himself in the glass he takes up his courting attitude !

A dark grey speckly Salticid with a squat body which is also to be found on the outer walls of houses and sheds, *Sitticus pubescens,* has a courtship similar to that of *Salticus;* and this is not greatly different from what is found in the genera *Evarcha, Hasarius* and *Heliophanus,* except that in these spiders the front pair of legs is raised and stretched outwards at an angle of 45°. Their courtship is often accompanied by some waving of these legs together with tremors of the body and palps as they move jerkily in front of the female (see Plate XV, p. 156).

Variety we find once more when we come to *Aelurillus v-insignitus.* The female is a plump grey spider with annulated legs and two rows of light spots down her abdomen. Her colouring makes her inconspicuous in pine-wood clearings and on the grey rocks of Lundy where I have also found her. The male is gay by comparison and quite different. His abdomen is black above, with a white stripe down the middle, and pale below. The cephalothorax is also black except for some conspicuous light V markings on his head. His front pair of legs are enlarged and have yellow femurs in contrast to the rest of the segments which are black.

Although this is a very active species the male depends chiefly on poses which may be started when he is as much as six inches away from the female. He stands quite still with his cephalothorax raised high on his second pair of legs, and with his abdomen depressed and touching the ground — while first one and then the other leg, or both together, are raised high in the air. In this pose he displays to the female in front of him his striking front legs, the V markings on the front of his head and the white under surface of his abdomen.

After a short pause his front legs and palps quiver violently. Now he alternates between complete stillness and quiverings of the legs and palps. Sometimes one of the front legs is lowered and the other sways inwards over his head. Mounting excitement is accompanied by his raising himself higher and higher on his legs; and then, at last, he starts to advance with jerky steps and with his front legs thrust forwards towards her.

The female has been watching him attentively and sometimes will leap at him. He can move so quickly himself that he is somewhere else by the time she alights where he had been standing. If she moves out of view behind a leaf, it is amusing to watch him standing on tiptoe in an effort to look over it or peep round the side before he goes in pursuit.

The males of *Bianor aenescens* and *Ballus depressus* both have enormously stout front legs, so it is interesting to see the different ways in which these enter into their displays. Having returned home with a few males and females of the rare shiny black *Bianor* found amongst the short grass clumps on Banstead Downs in mid-May, I placed them together and awaited events. He raised his massive front legs and stretched them both outwards at an angle of 30°. The tibiae are the most striking feature of the male because their great size is exaggerated by a thick tuft of coarse black hair on the lower surface and this is clearly displayed to the female by tilting the tarsi and metatarsi more steeply upwards than the tibiae. In this strange attitude he remained quite still for a short time and then gave periodic twitches of his palps and abdomen. Presently he lowered his front legs and advanced towards her with these legs stretched out stiffly in front of him with the tarsal segments curved slightly upwards (see Plate XIV, p. 149).

Ballus depressus is a small squat spider reaching up to 5 mm. in length, which lives on the twigs and foliage of young oak trees in sheltered sunny positions. The female's abdomen is yellowish with broad red-brown markings whereas the male's abdomen is dark reddish brown without any pattern. His front pair of legs are swollen and almost black except for the tarsi and metatarsi which are yellow. As usual the male's special features are displayed during courtship and in this species his poses are distinctly quaint. Instead of holding up his front legs in the air, he draws them inwards towards him and then sways from side to side, moving a few steps from one side to the other whilst he is doing so. Whereas *Attulus* made me think of a ballet dancer, the movements of *Ballus* reminded me of the sideways staggering of a drunken man.

Lastly I come to one of my favourites. This is *Euophrys frontalis* which is common amongst low herbage and under stones. The female is 4 mm. and cream-coloured with rows of small V-shaped dark markings on her abdomen. These markings are usually absent or inconspicuous in the darker male who has thick dark front legs and a fringe of white hairs on his palps. When placed with a female he raises his handsome front legs with a jerk to an almost vertical position. At first these legs may be waved about but with mounting excitement he stands higher on his other legs and the courtship enters a vigorous phase. Up snap the front legs accompanied by a jerk of the body and

then they are slowly lowered to the ground. Up they snap again with
the same jerk of the body and with a distinct sound as the tarsal claws
hit the ground before their upward ascent is started. Meanwhile he
usually moves one step forward between each upward movement of the
front legs and all the time the white-fringed palps, bent horizontally
inwards tip to tip, are vibrating up and down below his large bright
eyes set amongst the rust-red pubescence on his face. Sometimes in
his excitement the second pair of legs are also raised and stretched out
laterally (see Plate XIV, p. 149).

The female is much affected by this vigorous display of mesmeric
movements and seems to find it difficult to remove her gaze even when
she is unwilling to accept him. On these occasions she jerks her body
up and down as a sign of rejection when he comes too close, whereas
on other occasions she will often raise her front legs in faint imitation
of his own more vigorous movements. Then he touches her with his
front legs, creeps smoothly over her head and leans over one side to
insert a palp. On one occasion I noticed that each palp was inserted
twice before he left her after three quarters of an hour.

In this family the mating often lasts about three quarters of an hour
but in *Marpissa muscosa* it may be completed in about twenty minutes
and in *Evarcha falcata* in three to four hours. Some species including
Evarcha may insert each palp once whereas the palps may be alternated
four or five times in *Hyctia*.

Turning back now to my observations on the courtship of the
Salticidae, it is quite clear to me that the male can be stimulated to
start his displays by the sight of the female alone; but that an awareness
of the female is also effected through his taste-by-touch or chemotactic
senses when he touches ground over which she has passed or web she
has spun. The fact that an *Aelurillus* male will start courting his own
image in a looking-glass confirms that sight alone is enough. On the
other hand, if his eyes are covered with paraffin wax before being
placed in a box with a female, his walk soon takes on a fresh aspect
and he begins pawing the ground with the tips of his palps and feeling
the ground with his legs with every appearance of growing excitement.
The males of *Salticus*, *Heliophanus* and other species will show the same
signs of awareness when they touch the occupied or unoccupied cells
built by females of their own species, so it seems clear that the chemotactic senses are also involved although a sight of the female is necessary
before the males are stimulated sufficiently to adopt their full courting
postures.

As usual amongst spiders there is some relationship between the number of eggs laid in each batch and the size of the spider. *Marpissa,* as our largest species, leads with an average perhaps of about forty-five eggs although sometimes she lays more than sixty. The average for *Heliophanus* and *Salticus* seems to be about twenty-five to thirty compared with the smaller *Euophrys* where an examination of six egg-sacs provided an average of twenty eggs.

Those who have a real affection for the spiders of this family will have to travel far and work hard in order to find all the thirty-three British species, because several are retiring in their habits and others, though abundant in their strongholds, are known only from one or two localities. *Neon reticulatus,* for instance, is widely spread but has to be sought by grubbing amongst the detritus of woods or amongst damp heather. *Hasarius adansoni* has a respectable distribution in England, Scotland and Ireland but has come to us from warmer climates and must be sought only in hothouses. *Neon valentulus* is known only from ground level in the Cambridgeshire fens and *Sitticus floricola* from the heads of Cotton Grass in Delamere Forest. *Euophrys lanigera* may prove to be commoner than the present strange distribution from Budleigh Salterton, Southsea, Slough, South Kensington, Woolwich, Oxford and Northampton would suggest, now that we are beginning to realise that she is a specialist on roofs of houses. If we have to add a ladder to our other equipment in order to catch *E. lanigera* we can at least relax on the beach at Shingle Street in Suffolk whilst we look for *E. browningi* in empty whelk shells !

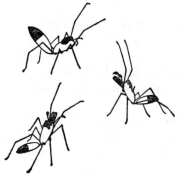

Fig. 79.   *Myrmarachne's* attitudes (5 mm.)

CHAPTER 14

THE OXYOPIDAE

Lynx Spiders

THE Oxyopidae are lithe keen-eyed hunters which sit, leap and run amongst the flowers and foliage of shrubs and herbs. Here they catch their prey and lay their eggs. They flourish in the tropics and only one species, *Oxyopes heterophthalmus*, lives in Britain. She has been found on heather in warm situations sheltered by trees between Brockenhurst, Lyndhurst and Mark Ash in the New Forest but not, I believe, by any naturalist now living. I feel sure she is still there.

FIG. 80. *Oxyopes* face

The body pattern, the pale V marking on the thoracic region, the greater agility, and the stance with the front femora drawn back, should distinguish her easily enough from a young *Pisaura*, but there might be some risk of her being confused at first glance with *Philodromus histrio*. Both live on heather and guard their egg-sacs spun in the heather shoots. In contrast to the bulkier and camouflaged egg-sacs of the *Philodromus*, those built by *Oxyopes* of cream-coloured silk are flat-topped with the faint outline of the eggs showing through the cover.

Oxyopes reaches maturity late in May or early in June after wintering in a half-grown condition. The male goes in search of the female at this time and behaves as though he recognised her by sight at a distance of up to four inches. Gerhardt (1933) tells us that he immediately raises and lowers his palps like some of the Lycosids and then vibrates his abdomen and finally raises vibrating front legs steeply in the air. This sequence of movements is repeated as he draws nearer to her. He mounts the female's back from in front and inserts one palp from the side for a period of about 20 seconds. The bulb swells once and then collapses as he detaches himself. The one insertion completes the act of mating.

During sperm induction the male hangs under the rectangular sperm web and absorbs the drop through the web by the alternate application of each palp several times for periods of about 20 seconds.

The eggs are laid in June and according to Nielsen a sac contains 31 to 78 eggs.

Postscript

A new locality was found by Mr. Hammond in 1959 above Gracians Pond on Chobham Common, Surrey, to which he guided D. J. Clark, A. Smith and myself in 1960. Three immature specimens were swept from heather with a heavy net on 30th April.

CHAPTER 15

THE LYCOSIDAE & PISAURIDAE
Wolf Spiders

Most of our Wolf Spiders lead a wandering existence with no settled homes even after they lay their eggs which are fastened to their spinnerets (Lycosidae) or carried in their chelicerae (Pisauridae). The exceptions include *Trochosa* which retires into a silk-lined hole in the ground and the Pisauridae which build a special tent amongst plants for the young just before they hatch. Beyond this there are a few Lycosidae which spend a large part of their time in burrows (*Arctosa*) or silk-tubes (*Pirata piscatorius*) from which they pounce on passing insects. It is not a great step from this to the spinning of a sheet web round the edge of the burrow, as in the Agelenidae, or to close the

Fig. 81. *Lycosa* face

entrance to the burrow with a hinged door, as in the foreign Mygalomorphae. Both these developments have occurred in the Lycosidae found in other parts of the world but in such cases the females still testify to their wandering heritage by carrying their egg-sacs attached to their spinnerets.

THE LYCOSIDAE

The most famous Lycosid since ancient times has been the dreaded Tarantula of southern Italy; but now her name has been purloined for any of the large hairy Mygalomorph spiders of tropical countries to which she is not even closely related. The Tarantula acquired her name from the town of Taranto and, in turn, bequeathed it to the wild

Tarantella dances which were regarded as symptoms of her poisonous bite for which they also provided the remedy. The victims, according to Topsel in 1658, started 'dancing, swinging and shaking themselves . . . , as though they had spent all their life in some dancing school', and this they continued night and day with the assistance of fiddlers and pipers until they collapsed exhausted but cured.

The current belief is that the main blame should have fallen on quite a different spider, a Theridiid relation of the American Black Widow, *Latrodectus tredecimguttatus,* which lives in the harvest fields. Nevertheless the large Tarantulas have got a venomous bite and during a visit to Patmos in 1933 I was told that a man who is bitten by the closely related *Tarentula praegrandis* is taken to the baker's shop where he is placed in the oven and baked over a bundle of faggots for as long as he can stand the heat. This cure can be compared with Mustaufi's advice in his book on Arabian medical practice written in 1320 (Muzhatu-l-Qulub) which can be translated as follows: 'Let him smell human excrement, fasting, and sit in a hot oven till he sweats and is cured.' Dancing may be more fun but both cures induced heat.

The fame of another large Tarantula in southern France is due to the beautiful descriptions of Henri Fabre but, although our Wolf Spiders are small by comparison, the pen of an Henri Fabre is lacking to show that they are just as interesting.

The leafy woodland floor, the short turf of a hillside or meadow, the open spaces on heaths and marshland, these and many other places are all disturbed in the spring and early summer by the restless movement of active ground-living hunters whose dull brown or grey bodies make them tolerably inconspicuous until they move at our approach. The spring sunshine lures these adolescent Wolf Spiders from their winter shelters to bask in watchful stillness, to chase and spring on small insects, or to indulge in gay courtship after casting their skins for the last time in April or May. These nomads whose pattering footsteps on dry leaves can often be heard in the stillness of a woodland glade, will later pursue their prey with their speed unimpaired by the addition of a massive egg-sac attached to their spinnerets (see Plate XVII, p. 176), or later still by the load of forty babies clinging to their backs.

For the most part these belong to the genus *Lycosa* and, as there are seventeen species all much of the same size and employing similar means to capture their prey, I should like to pause, before speaking of their less conspicuous relations in other genera, to consider the question of competition between them. How do they all manage to survive?

Nearly all of them grow up at about the same time in April and May and are roughly 5 to 6 mm. in length. I think that this similarity in season and size limits the amount of actual destruction by one species of another to reasonably small proportions. In other words I doubt if this is a major influence in their lives and it is interesting to notice that, whereas the largest and most aggressive species (*L. paludicola*) is extremely rare, one of the smallest (*L. pullata*) is undoubtedly the most abundant.

Before looking for explanations the first things to notice are that their geographical distribution and their specialisation on particular habitats both serve to limit the number of species in any one place. Six species are limited to the southern counties and two species (*L. trailli* and *L. agricola*) to the North. As to habitat, *L. trailli* keeps herself entirely to mountain screes, *L. agricola* to river or lake verges, *L. rubrofasciata* to fens, *L. purbeckensis* to mud-flats and the seashore, and *L. lugubris* to woods. It must be rare for any of these species to meet. Apart from this, several other kinds have particular preferences or strongholds, even though they may stray outside them. *L. arenicola*, for instance, is mainly associated with shingle beaches, *L. monticola* thrives on downland slopes and other exposed situations, *L. amentata* lives wherever sun and shelter at ground level are combined, *L. proxima* prefers damp and marshy places and *L. paludicola* seems to favour wood clearings.

Although competition may have played a part in arriving at some semblance of territories, the fact is that the micro-climate required by each species varies slightly although there is considerable over-lapping. Clues to their differing requirements can be gained by noticing where they are or are not found. None live in caves or thickly shaded places. Is their scarcity in cities due to the smoky atmosphere affecting the light rays which penetrate to ground level or to some other cause such as the chemical effect of smoke on the soil? *L. pullata* is the only species in the parks or gardens of inner London and Hull, with *L. amentata* appearing as we come nearer to their outskirts.

Temperature must surely be a factor in limiting some species to the North and others to the South, but whether this restriction is due to extremes of heat or cold at certain seasons, the number of days above the particular temperature at which they feed and complete their life cycle successfully or some seasonal difference at a critical stage in their lives is not fully known.

Apart from *Lycosa trailli* which is a specialist on mountain screes, few *Lycosae* extend far up our mountain slopes. *L. pullata* is in fact the only species I have found above 2,000 feet on mountains in all four countries of England, Scotland, Wales and Ireland. This could represent a temperature tolerance beyond the range of some species but as *L. pullata* is also the species I can rely most on meeting on the scores of islands off our coast from Shetland down to tiny exposed islets in the Scillies, I feel sure that an exposure factor is mainly involved. This gains support from the fact that the other habitual inhabitants of the tiny islets are *L. monticola* and *L. nigriceps*. The former is a dominant species on wind-swept downs. The latter is unique for the genus in leaving the shelter at ground level to climb up amongst the foliage of gorse and even low trees.

The need for water and for humidity are other important factors which help to decide which species can survive in particular habitats. The rate of evaporation of water from the bodies of different species undoubtedly varies as Cloudsley-Thompson, M. E. Davies and E. B. Edney have shown in preliminary work in other families. D. A. Parry has found that some spiders can drink soil capillary water without the need for standing water, and that their ability to do this varies with the size of the spider and of the soil particles, so the nature of the soil itself may make a difference in the species which will thrive on it. Despite this ability to drink from soil capillary water, it is probable that a few species like *L. rubrofasciata* need standing water both for themselves and for their eggs which are dipped in it.

The conclusion to be reached from this survey of facts and speculations is that climatic and micro-climatic factors see to it that territories are roughly rationed so that only a few species are likely to be in direct competition on the same plot of land. It must be realised, however, that there are often damp and dry, exposed and sheltered patches within even a small area. Amongst the most tolerant and ubiquitous species are *Lycosa pullata, L. monticola, L. tarsalis, L. prativaga, L. amentata* and *L. nigriceps;* but shades of difference in their ideal requirements can be detected although some or all may be found close together within one small area. Perhaps it is only on some tiny island with its limited area and food supply that the small differences result through competition in the survival of only one species. Here in this limited area enough must survive to ensure that the males encounter the females and enable them to lay enough eggs every year to effect survival after allowing for fatalities.

The result of three visits to the Scilly Islands, in the course of which I hunted on twenty-six islands of differing sizes, may help to illustrate this. The extremes were represented by the extensive islands of St. Mary's and Tresco with their sheltered valleys and trees, to small bare rocky pinnacles hardly deserving the title of island on which no plants grew. I found six species of *Lycosa* in the Scillies, all of which can be presumed to live on the large islands although the amount of attention I gave to these two islands only revealed five. As I passed from the large to the intermediate-sized islands with less shelter, *L. tarsalis* promptly disappeared. She was followed by *L. proxima* either on the same account or possibly because marshy ground particularly favoured by this species was lacking. By the time I reached small islets bearing some fairly luxuriant grass or other plants and having areas, may be, of a cricket ground, the three species to survive were *L. nigriceps*, *L. monticola* and *L. pullata* — *but never more than two* on any one of them. The five islands coming in this category all had *L. nigriceps*, but her companion on Great Arthur, Great Ganilly and Menawethan was *L. monticola* whereas on Great and Little Innisvouls it was *L. pullata*. Here they were nearing extinction because there were no *Lycosae* at all on eleven still smaller islets bare of luxuriant vegetation, but Mouls and Hanjague were the only two which had no plants or birds' nests to provide shelter or food for spiders of any family. Here in the Scillies I think it likely that we are watching competition for food and space between three species of *Lycosa* all capable of tolerating the climatic conditions they provide.

The little dark *Lycosa pullata* have a way of turning up in most places and I have watched them whilst lying idly on the pebbles piled up by the sea at Cooden Beach. Here I have noticed that in spring they are all busily engaged in their search for flies, that in early May the males and then the females cast their skins and divide their attention between courtship and food-supply, that towards the end of the month eggs contained in a bluish or brownish sac are attached to most females' spinnerets, and by about the middle of June the young have hatched and are clinging to their mother's back. It is during the first two weeks in June that the males suddenly vanish from senile decay or exhaustion and not, I feel sure, as a result of female attack.

What, I wondered, does this *Lycosa* do when the sea exceeds its usual limits and covers her hunting-ground? Does she nestle amongst the pebbles and manage by some means to subsist till the tide goes down once more? Surely the pounding of the waves on the pebbles would grind the fragile body to pieces. My chance came one May morning when there was an exceptionally high tide and the answer could not have been simpler. As the tide rises the *Lycosa* retreats. When a wave washes further up the shore than its forerunners and overtakes a *Lycosa*, she lies quite still and floats on the surface until the wave is spent and the water runs back to the sea. On these occasions she makes no movement until a pebble is touched, when she takes her opportunity and climbs on to it. There she pauses, as the water drains away from round her pedestal, and then runs back to safety amongst the dry stones.

An interesting point was that she always ran in the right direction. How does she know which way to run? Fifty times I put spiders where the sea caught them up, and every single time they ran in the right direction after they had come to rest on a stone. On a few occasions they started in a wrong direction, but in each case curved their course until it was directly away from the sea. With great care I turned round the stone on which they were resting on the chance of confusing their sense of direction, but this made no difference. They could not have taken their bearings from the sun, for this was obscured by clouds, and they could scarcely have been retracing their tracks by scent or other means, as they had floated there like a cork on the top of the water; nor could it be by the direction in which the water was draining back to the sea, for in all cases it had sunk well below the level of the stones before the homeward journey was made, and the turning of the stone on which they stood made no difference.

Perhaps they had some hazy view of the sea for the sight of Lycosids is second only to the Salticids amongst spiders, and they can see moving objects at a distance of several feet. A screen was placed between the spider and the sea, and the stone on which one alighted was slightly turned. Still the spider ran in the right direction. Next I dug a big crater with gently sloping sides amongst the beach pebbles, and set free spiders one after another into it. Those that alighted on a side always ran upwards from that point directly away from the centre of the crater. Those that were placed right in the centre took a north, south, east or west course quite indiscriminately.

The most obvious explanation is not always the first to occur to one, and in this case they always run away from the sea because the beach happens to slope upwards from it. All collectors of spiders must have

noticed how those placed under a glass tube will always attempt to run
up it; how ground-living spiders liberated in a box of large dimensions,
and provided with soil to make them feel 'at home', will always start
by running across the level ground and attempting to climb up the
sides, whether they be glass, wood or cardboard; how spiders dislodged
by lifting heather or other vegetation growing on a bank will attempt
to escape *up* the bank. Now we have started along this train of thought,
why do *these* spiders run upwards? It may satisfy us to find that the
shore *Lycosa* runs up the beach — it seems to be common-sense,— but
why does a spider pursued by man run up a bank when it might escape
at twice the speed by fleeing in the opposite direction? The answer
to this is that spiders have not got common-sense and that their actions
are governed by rules of procedure. I would suggest that water —
floods more particularly than the sea — destroys a great number of
spiders, that those spiders which run up slopes or vegetation stand a
greater chance of survival, and that ultimately this instinct to run up-
hill when in danger has arisen through natural selection; being blind
rigid instinct, the spider responds to it whether the pursuer be water,
man, or other menace.

Lycosa pullata is no specialist on sea-shores; but what about *L.
purbeckensis* which lives habitually amongst the hardy halophytic plants
on salt-marshes and mud-flats? These areas are often covered by a foot
or more of water which flows so rapidly over their flat surfaces that no
spider could run before it or, if it were carried on the surface of the
advancing water, could be back where it started after the ebb an hour
or two later, as I know to be the case.

On a morning in April when a specially high tide was expected I
stood in a salt marsh at Wootton Creek in the Isle of Wight and here
is an extract from the paper describing what I saw as the water crept
up my legs (Bristowe, 1923).

"The day was sunny and a lot of the spiders were running about,
but, as the tide rose, they retreated to the higher portions of the
plants. Presently I saw one which I had been watching touch the
water several times, like a bather feeling the temperature with his toe
before taking the plunge, and then it deliberately walked down the
stem of the plant beneath the surface, taking with it a bubble of air,
caught by means of its hairy body. I watched several others, and the
same thing occurred, and this is, therefore, how they survive the high
tide. I was puzzled at first by seeing that they dived long before

they were forced to by the submergence of their plant, but this was explained by an individual that got dislodged, for it could not dive without the help of something firm to hold on to, and soon the tip of a leaf swaying in the current was not sufficient aid. Although they can run over the surface, they are far more comfortable beneath it, especially in rough weather; so the wisdom of their submerging whilst something firm remains to cling to becomes clear.

On dull days I found the spiders did not even trouble to move for the tide, but simply remained where they were at the roots of the plants, and allowed the water to creep over them. So, when the day is dull they spend a longer period submerged; but experiments showed me that they need have no fear of being drowned. I made several individuals walk down plants placed in sea-water in jars, and then added more water, so that the plants were completely covered and the spiders unable to reach the surface, and on the average I found their one bubble of air would last them as long as ten hours."

The rising of the tide to higher levels than usual is similar in effect to inland floods — but I found the water in January at Wicken Fen much colder than in April at Wootton when I decided to make the comparison ! Here again the spiders climb up plants, where they may be able to remain until the waters abate, or else escape if they are small by letting out streamers of silk which waft them to safety — but this would only be likely if the sun were shining. I saw one or two Lycosids on the surface of the flood water running until they found a plant to climb, but what was more interesting was to see a few below the surface with a bubble of air acting just like *Lycosa purbeckensis*.

And what of the normal life of *Lycosa rubrofasciata*, *L. proxima* and *L. prativaga* in the fen ? I have seen all three run down plants under the water when they were disturbed, and also the bulkier *Trochosa terricola*. Their ability to collect air automatically round their hairy bodies makes a visit below the water of little significance to them or to Lycosids of the genus *Pirata* of whose similar excursions I shall be speaking presently.

Not many of the other Lycosids are likely to be confused in the field with a *Lycosa* but one notable exception is *Xerolycosa nemoralis* which has, I am sure, often been overlooked in open woodland spaces in southern England where she is found alongside *Lycosa lugubris* whom she much resembles. Both have a broad whitish band on the cephalothorax with black shoulders and some obscure dark bars on their abdomens. The white band is more distinct and the abdomen faintly roseate in *Xerolycosa* with almost a bluish grey bloom as well. When I found her in Ashdown Forest in 1921 she was only known from the woods near Little Common but, having made her acquaintance, I have since found her commonly in dozens of woods stretching across Kent, Sussex and Surrey into Berkshire and Hampshire. Her only relation, *X. miniata,* has a grey body with black markings which make her an inconspicuous inhabitant of our coastal sandhills.

Larger and more powerfully built than the *Lycosae* are our four species of *Tarentula* of which the largest, *T. fabrilis,* is almost a small replica of her notorious relation in Italy with a black belly which is displayed when she rears up on her hind legs in an attitude of menace. She reaches up to 16 mm. in length and has a grey abdomen with a black dagger marking and several black cross bars. She lives in a burrow and is only known from high ground on Bloxworth Heath where unfortunately she is in danger of extinction owing to the ploughing and planting of trees that is in progress there.*The other three species are relatively common and range between 8 to 12 mm. but none of them have the black belly. *T. barpipes* lives on heaths whereas *T. pulverulenta* and *T. cuneata* thrive mostly on downs and open ground where the grass is short. There is something about mountain conditions which breeds a larger race of *T. pulverulenta* above 2,000 ft. (see Plate XVII, p. 176).

Our five species of *Trochosa* are more lethargic and have relatively heavier bodies and shorter legs. They are brown spiders with sleek bodies bearing a dagger stripe passing halfway down the abdomen. They live under stones or amongst heather and other vegetation during the day but seem to prowl in search of food after dark.

Trochosa terricola is the commonest heath species and she has a terrible enemy, a Hunting Wasp called *Anoplius fuscus,* which searches her out as food for her larvae. I often used to see this wasp dragging a *Trochosa* across the sandy paths at Oxshott by the base of one of her legs and watch a burrow being dug for her reception with an egg attached to the lower surface of her abdomen before it was filled in again; but it was a long time before I was able to watch an encounter between these two formidable creatures. Did the spider never come out best? The black and red wasp runs busily over the ground with dark fluttering wings and curled vibrating antennae. They meet and the wasp springs back and then leaps forward again. Things happen very quickly but what seems to happen is that the wasp seizes the spider by a leg and curls its abdomen round under the spider to sting her

*Since reported on Hankley Common, Surrey.

two or three times. During the momentary struggle before the spider collapses I do not believe that the spider even attempts to use her chelicerae. She behaves as though she knows her time has come and that it is hopeless to resist (see fig. 32, p. 69).

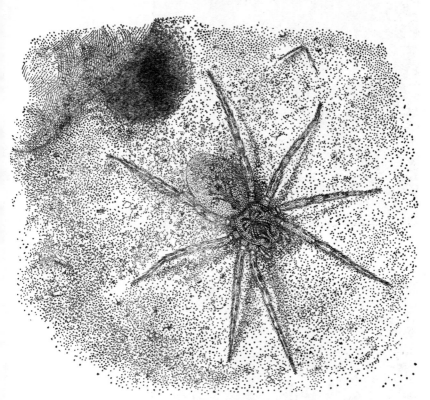

FIG. 82. *Arctosa cinerea* (16 mm.) of river beds

I intervened to collect thirty of the spiders after they had been stung and found that all of them were so effectively paralysed that they could only move the tips of their legs very feebly. Tenderly I placed them in damp cotton wool but only in one case was my attempt to nurse them back to health successful. Fourteen were still alive after four weeks so it will be seen that the wasp larva is efficiently provided with fresh and defenceless food.

Passing to another genus, we have four species of *Arctosa* of which

a. Sitting at her burrow
mouth

b. Seizing the silk rim
to haul it like a curtain
across the entrance

Fig. 83. *Arctosa perita*
(8 mm.)

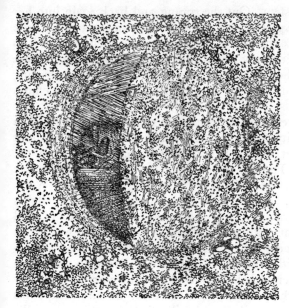

c. Turning to complete the closure with zig-zag sweeps of her spinnerets

FIG. 83. *Arctosa perita* (8 mm.)

only the handsome *A. perita* is at all common. To find *A. alpigena,* for instance, you would have to climb to 3,000 ft. on Cairntoul; and to collect the huge *A. cinerea* a search would be necessary amongst the sand and stones of river beds in northern Britain where she builds a burrow and only emerges on hunting sorties (see fig. 82). Her length of 17 mm. makes her one of our finest spiders but her sombre shades of brown make her dull by comparison with the lesser *A. perita* of our sandhills and heaths. *A. perita* has legs attractively decorated with dark rings and her white body, generously suffused with pale red and light yellow, is ornamented with black markings which make her very difficult to see as she lies flat on the sand. This beautiful *Arctosa* spends most of her time inside lined burrows which she excavates in the sand and from which she pounces on passing insects.

Tracing the geography of the burrow is no easy matter but in some situations it is possible to blow away the loose sand at the top and see that it is shaped like a T or a Y with the top stroke or strokes only perhaps half an inch and the stem often two inches or more in length. One branch is a blind alley; the other is closed in bad weather, but open in fine with the watcher at its threshold.

My first endeavour was to see how *Arctosa* would respond to the teasing of a fine grass stem. Out she sprang and back again into her doorway. Then, as the grass continued to squirm in front of her, she suddenly seized the silk rim of the doorway in her chelicerae and, to my amazement, drew it firmly across three-quarters of the hole like a curtain. In a second she had reversed her position and with sweeping zig-zag strokes of her outstretched spinnerets had closed the last chinks (see fig. 83a, b, c).

With portcullis lowered on the approach of an enemy and with a cloak of near-invisibility for protection when wandering abroad, it might be thought that *Arctosa* would be reasonably free from the attention of enemies. Perhaps this is true, but there is one terrible enemy whose speciality she is. This is the small grey Hunting Wasp, *Pompilus plumbeus* Fabr., which can be seen rushing across bare patches of sand, zig-zagging here and there, and flying to new patches of sand when vegetated boundaries are encountered. Often has this wasp been found carrying *Arctosa* across the sandy spaces after stinging her; sometimes the paralysed spider has been seen buried alive with an egg on her abdomen; but never had the means of her discovery or defeat by a wasp, often smaller than herself, been revealed. So an attempt was made to trail a wasp as it rushed with vibrating antennae across the sand dunes at Trebetherick. Would it 'put up' a spider and then give chase? Or would it come face to face with such a formidable adversary in the narrow confines of the spider's own dimly lit burrow and emerge victorious without mortal wound herself? These were some of the questions I hoped to answer.

The wasp and I covered perhaps twenty yards, the wasp in a headlong rush with rapidly vibrating antennae and I less comfortably on my hands and knees. Suddenly it stopped and rapidly began scratching at the sand with its mandibles and front legs. There was nothing to show me why it had selected this exact spot to dig but the reason was soon apparent. Circling and scraping like an excited terrier at a rabbit hole it suddenly bit through the wall of a closed *Arctosa* burrow and vanished within. Simultaneously out popped an *Arctosa* like a Jack-in-the-box from the other fork of the burrow. Away ran the spider in a more prolonged sprint than I had ever seen her make before and out came the wasp just one second too late.

After circling the burrow with flailing antennae its onward journey continued. During the next hour the same wasp found two more closed burrows but in both cases the spiders escaped as before — one very narrowly by running up the stem of a marram grass. Although this

PLATE XVII. Wolf spiders. *Top: Lycosa paludicola* (9 mm.) weaving a sheet, laying eggs, covering them and spinning the seam whilst rotating the sac. *Centre: Tarentula fabrilis* (16 mm.), one of our rarest and finest spiders. *Bottom left: Trochosa ruricola* (13 mm.) with round egg-sac. *Bottom right: Pirata piratica* (7 mm.) with white narrow-seamed round egg-sac and *Lycosa amentata* (8 mm.) with wide-seamed blue lens-shaped egg-sac.

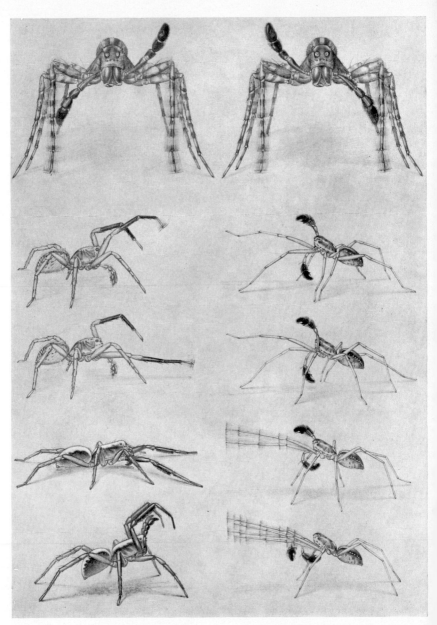

PLATE XVIII. Male Wolf Spiders in courting attitudes. *Top: Lycosa amentata* (7 mm.) *Centre left: Trochosa terricola* (12 mm.) *Bottom left: Tarentula barbipes* (12 mm.) *Right: Lycosa nigriceps* (6 mm.)

was the wasp's unlucky day I had learned three things. The first, that the wasp could detect the presence of a closed burrow on a sunless day by means of the chemotactic sense located in its antennae. The second, that the closed fork of the spider's burrow was an important means of exit in an emergency. And the third, that she behaved as though she had some inborn fear of the wasp which caused her to panic in its presence and to offer no resistance to its trespass. The frantic rush from the burrow and the climbing of a grass stem by a spider which never leaves the ground provided some evidence which persuaded me to make another test.

An *Arctosa* was put in a narrow glass tube of a diameter similar to that of her burrow. A *Pompilus* was then transferred to the same tube. Surely the spider would leap at the wasp and destroy it ? No, at the first touch of the vibrating antennae a forward lunge by the spider was checked and she lay still with her legs crossed and entwined round her cephalothorax in a completely unnatural pose whilst the wasp curled its abdomen round to inflict a sting beneath her in the region of her sternum. Thus a paralysis caused by what I can only describe as fear was replaced by a paralysis caused by poison.

We have seen the value of the second fork in the spider's burrow and of the closed entrance to give her time to escape, but whether she manages to close it after seeing a wasp is at present unknown. It is clear that the wasp hunts mainly by 'scent' but when close to a hole its eyes also help; so it is a question of eyesight and speed which will determine whether the spider which is sitting at the threshold has any chance of escape.

When the entrance is closed the spider seems just to have time to bite her way out of the other fork, but there is no escape when the entrance is open. In rushes the wasp without the slightest hesitation and emerges a minute or two later dragging a paralysed spider by a leg. The mode of her downfall has been illustrated by the experiment in a glass tube and experiments on other spiders have led me to the conclusion that the spider's 'fear' is brought on by a combination of the wasp's warning 'scent' and warning movements conveyed to the spider through her chemotactic sense and her eyes or tactile senses respectively.

After hauling the spider out into the open the wasp grips her by the pedicel and carries her aloft for a short distance before putting her down to scratch a shallow pit. The spider is put in this and then rapidly covered over with sand. This is only a temporary grave whilst it digs

WS—N

the proper burrow, but the advantage of this becomes clear as it chases away no less than three watchful wasps of another kind (*Ceropales maculata*) which have taken to laying their eggs on the prey of other wasps when their backs are turned.

Now it circles round the temporary pit as though to get its bearings and then hurries away a yard or more to dig the burrow. When this is finished in five minutes or more it bustles straight back to the temporary pit, uncovers the spider, carries her to the burrow and deposits her just outside in order to carry out a final inspection. When the wasp reappears it hauls the spider down by a hind leg, lays an egg on her abdomen and all that remains for it to do is to fill in the burrow once more by scratching in the sides.

The genus *Pirata* contains five species of velvety brown spiders varying in length from 4 to 10 mm. which are associated with marshes. Typically they have white bands down the sides of the cephalothorax and a few tiny white spots in two rows down the abdomen. The two smallest species (*P. latitans* and *P. uliginosus*) are not restricted to marshes but at the other extreme the largest species, *P. piscatorius,* is almost invariably found beside standing water. She has interested me ever since I first found that she built a vertical tube in Sphagnum moss (Bristowe, 1922). The upper end is usually covered and has an open doorway from which she darts at passing insects. The lower end leads down to the water and if she is disturbed she runs down a stem under the surface with air encrusting her legs as well as ensheathing her body (see fig. 84, p. 180).

The other two species are widespread and very common but *P. piraticus* is more generally distributed in Scotland than *P. hygrophilus* and extends to Orkney.

As I have mentioned all the genera except one in this brief outline of the family, I ought not to neglect the solitary *Aulonia albimana* which is known only from one tiny heather-floored quarry near Dunster where I first found her in 1936 and again in 1938. There she throve in abundance, but not one step outside it ! She roughly resembles a small *Pirata* at first sight but a white palpal patella distinguishes her from other Lycosids.

By spider standards the Lycosidae have good sight; and it is fascinating to watch the droll antics of a male when he is courting a female. In most of the *Lycosa* males the black palps are conspicuous objects and it is these which play the principal part in courtship poses, their semaphore signalling sometimes being supplemented by leg movements and vibrations of the abdomen. Three instances will illustrate the procedure typical of the genus together with some of the variations.

In *Lycosa amentata* the male stands high on his legs, stretches his palps out sideways and then raises one at an angle of 45° while the other is lowered at a similar angle. Standing in this position of display, he makes his palps and front pair of legs quiver violently and sometimes his abdomen as well. Now the palps are withdrawn and again stretched out in the same manner with their positions reversed — one raised, the other lowered. Repeating these movements over and over again, he advances step by step towards the female, pausing occasionally to lift the front pair of legs slightly off the ground and vibrate them at great speed. Her response to these advances may be attack or retreat to begin with but in time they have their effect and she shows her readiness to accept him by vibrating her own front legs (see Plate XVIII, p. 177).

If this display is like seeing a series of separate photographs thrown as lantern slides on to a screen, the movements of the courting *L, nigriceps* male is carried out more in the tempo of an early film in a sequence of small rapid flickers. In this species the black palpal tarsi are specially large and conspicuous and these are rotated jerkily, roughly in the way one's feet rotate when bicycling with one moving up and forward while the other is travelling back and down. Whilst this continues one front leg is raised and stretched forward, but this leg is changed each time he takes a step towards the female. When he can touch her with his outstretched leg the other is also raised and both are vibrated violently. If she does not retreat or drive him away, his second pair of legs are also raised and vibrated as he begins to climb over her head (see Plate XVIII, p. 177).

A variation on both these themes is found in *L. lugubris*. When the male is close to a female he raises himself high on his legs and stretches his first pair out sideways in roughly a horizontal direction. Posing in this manner he suddenly moves his black palp vertically upwards in a series of little jerky motions. Then, after a brief pause, he raises the other and poses with both palps raised. Suddenly he lowers both palps to their normal position to the accompaniment of a gentle up and down movement of the outstretched front legs. This sequence may be repeated several times and then he sidles rapidly round the female, touching her with his vibrating front legs.

Aulonia albimana has a distinguishing mark of a different sort — a white patella on an otherwise black palp — and it is interesting to see how he features this in his display. After approaching the female with

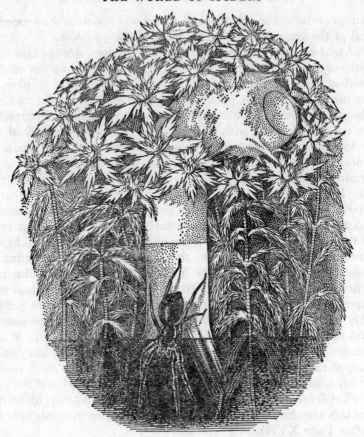

Fig. 84. *Pirata piscatorius* (10 mm.) in her tube amongst sphagnum leading down into the water

trembling legs he stands quite still in front of her with his first pair of legs raised so that the black femurs are upright and the yellow remaining segments are sloping upwards and forwards. In this pose he is raised high on his other legs. Now he stretches one trembling palp vertically downwards in a way which exposes the white ring round his palp to her view. After a short pause he returns this palp to its normal position, stretches the other downwards and continues alternating them in this way until he can move forward to touch her.

In the genus *Trochosa* it is the legs which are distinctively black from tibia to tarsus; so we should not be surprised to find that here it is the legs rather than the palps which are employed to advertise his identity and stimulate the female to accept his advances. The male of *Trochosa ruricola* raises one front leg steeply with the metatarsus and tarsus bent crookedly downwards and outwards. These segments quiver and shake all the time as though he were waving his hand to her. Then he slowly lowers the leg and stretches it out in front of him with the metatarsus and tarsus still gently waving in a fashion which reminds me of the sinuous arm movements of a ballet dancer. Now it is the turn of the other leg and the cycle is completed, though it may have to be repeated over and over again to the accompaniment of palpal vibrations and occasional abdominal pulsations before she sometimes makes a poor imitation of his leg movements, like a pupil trying to imitate her ballet teacher's example.

The behaviour of the *Trochosa terricola* male is on similar lines. He usually starts by raising both his front legs in the shape of an inverted U with the femur vertical, the tibia and patella horizontal and the metatarsus and tarsus bent vertically downwards (see Plate XVIII, p. 177). After posing in this position for a short time, one leg is raised steeply to the position taken up by *T. ruricola* and then lowered.

Again in the genus *Tarentula* we find that the male's front legs are a conspicuous feature; only here it is the femur to the tibia which are black whilst the metatarsus and tarsus are pale in colour. The tibiae are thickened in *T. barbipes* and positively bulbous in *T. cuneata*. In both cases the legs are displayed; but in different ways and not in the *Trochosa* manner. In both *T. pulverulenta* and *T. cuneata* the male moves his palps up and down, at first slowly and then more rapidly. Then his

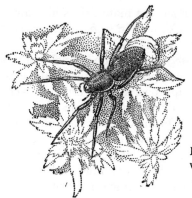

Fig. 85. *Pirata piraticus* (7 mm.) with eggs

abdomen pulsates. Finally he walks about in front of the female with jerky steps, pulsating body and palps, and with his front legs bunched up in front of him. The abdominal pulsations are of such vigour as to make a distinct tapping noise as it hits the ground.

This courtship gives an impression of cringing which is far removed from the elegant prancing of the male *Tarentula barbipes*. He starts by pawing the ground with his front legs in the manner of a horse, and then rears himself in the air with palps stretched upwards and front pair of legs raised in a bent position with the metatarsus and tarsus lowered. A jerk follows which raises the legs still higher and then they are lowered trembling to the ground. Now he takes a step towards her, perhaps two or three, and then up he rears again. Over and over again he rears as he circles round her. now advancing and now re-

FIG. 86.   *Lycosa lugubris* (6 mm.).   Male in courting attitude

treating, until eventually his particularly fierce mate drives him away no longer and his extended front legs take part in some brief sparring before he is finally accepted (see Plate XVIII, p. 177).

The males of our two species of *Xerolycosa* have no special features to display and their courtships mainly comprise vibrations of the legs, palps and abdomens, with *X. miniata* approaching the cringing technique of *Tarentula pulverulenta*. The reactions of the female *X. miniata* were, however, unique in one respect. On the one occasion on which I have seen them mate she imitated his behaviour with vibrating legs drawn in but with the difference that her chelicerae were wide open. For a time they stood facing one another in this manner and then, as he began to move forward, she closed her chelicerae on one of his front and legs drew him gently towards her. This marked the culmination of long-sustained courtship and illustrates its effectiveness in stimulating the female.

In *Arctosa perita* we come on to what I regard as a different style of courtship. He, too, has no specialised decorations for use in courtship, and as his approach to her seems usually to be in the evening when she is at home inside her silk-lined burrow, his technique seems to be adapted less for visual effect than for the conveyance of vibrations. He quivers his abdomen as he approaches her burrow and vibrates it very rapidly on arrival there after drawing in his legs. As his excitement mounts, he alternates abdominal pulsations with a single violent jerk of the entire body — say six pulsations and then the jerk. If the female is not sitting in her entrance, she soon appears. With waving legs he tries to touch her and when she is ready for him she responds in the same way.

Once the female Lycosid's preying instincts have been subdued by the stimulation of his courtship, the male climbs over her head with vibrating legs and leans over one side to insert a palp, changing to the other side in order to insert the second palp. The chief variations in the procedure are in the number of times each palp is used and the time that mating lasts. At one extreme we have both *Tarentula barbipes* and *Xerolycosa miniata* completing the act in half a minute, but with the difference that the *Tarentula* uses each palp two or three times whereas a complete mating seems to comprise the application of one palp only in *Xerolycosa*. I have only watched this mating once, and further courtship soon followed the male's departure, but similar behaviour is also shared by *Pirata piraticus*, according to U. Gerhardt, and by a few spiders in other families.

At the other extreme we have some species of *Lycosa*, including *L. pullata*, where the female often runs about for hours with the male on her back. When she is moving he is lying on her cephalothorax facing in the opposite direction with his head pressed down between her abdomen and cephalothorax. Mating takes places during the intervals when she is quiet but, even so, it is a long process lasting well over an hour, during which both palps are inserted many times. The male *Trochosa* does not suffer these interruptions but his mating also lasts an hour or more and each palp is used three to five times.

A *Lycosa* usually lays her eggs during the night and for the description of *L. paludicola* which follows I am indebted to my observant artist. She starts by weaving a circular disc. This is shaped by rotating her body whilst her spinnerets sweep sideways and her palps maintain touch with the circumference at the opposing edge. Standing over the disc with arched body she lets the eggs flow out in a liquid mass and then, without changing position astride the disc, circles round raising and lowering her abdomen to produce a first covering of soft silk. When this task is completed she sweeps her abdomen from side to side as she continues to circle round and this action provides a layer of tough silk. Now she bites round the circumference of the lenticular sac to sever the anchor threads and pulls it free, a bit at a time. As each bit is freed, she does some 'over-sewing' at the seam where the original disc connects with the cover she has added to it. When the entire egg-sac is freed of attachments and is over-sewn, she holds it in her chelicerae, palps and third pair of legs and rotates it in such a way that the seam is covered by fine strands of silk drawn over it from her spinnerets by the rotating egg-sac (see Plate XVII, p. 176).

When they are completed the *Lycosa* egg-sacs are white but within a few hours they have changed to a yellowish-brown or blue colour and P. Bonnet has shown that this is brought about by dipping them in water or by the humidity in the air. In most genera the egg-sacs are round and the seam is less distinct than in *Lycosa,* but the remarkable thing is that they remain white in *Aulonia* and *Pirata,* which is all the more surprising in the latter genus, considering its marshy surroundings.

Since the Lycosids all carry their egg-sacs attached to their spinnerets, it must be thought that a coloured sac, toning in with the ground, must afford some protection against enemies such as birds, so it is significant that *Pirata,* with her conspicuous white sac, lives chiefly under cover of herbage.

The maternal 'devotion' of the Wolf Spiders to their egg-sacs and young has attracted much interest and admiration. Burrowing forms which do not normally expose themselves and their egg-sacs to the open air bring their eggs to the surface on fine days as though to sun them, the semi-aquatic forms keep their egg-sacs moist by dipping them in water, the mothers give space and air to the hatching spiders by partially unravelling the outer walls of the egg-sac and finally they carry their babies on their backs for about a week until they can fend for themselves. Naturalists have also been impressed by their fierce defence of their egg-sacs and by the memory they seem to display when re-attaching them to their spinnerets after they have been separated for several days (see Plate XIX, p. 192).

These are wonderful features in their lives which are none the less

Fig. 87. *Lycosa* with an empty snail shell instead of her egg-sac

remarkable even if we ultimately conclude that the mother's behaviour is not influenced by feelings of devotion or by memory in the human sense. If a mother's egg-sac is removed we find she will adopt the egg-sac of another species and even pellets of paper, cotton or bread regardless of colour, weight or texture. I have found that she will also fasten a small empty snail-shell or rabbit dropping to her spinnerets to make good the loss of her eggs !

With his customary thoroughness and skill P. Bonnet (1947) has analysed all the evidence available from the literature and added much from personal observation. This analysis leads him to the conclusion that the spiders have an instinctive urge to carry a roughly rounded object attached to the spinnerets after egg-laying and that this object can be of variable colour, texture, weight, smell, size and shape just as I had found. He believes they show no powers of memory but only an instinct whose urge is fulfilled with the aid of her tactile senses. He fully supports T. Savory's (1936) interesting discovery that the urge is greatest just after a spider has laid her eggs and that this steadily abates as her ovaries swell in readiness for laying a fresh batch, a discovery which accounts for certain differences in behaviour noticed by experimenters.

Mistakes of the kind I have mentioned, caused by accidents or the experiments of inquisitive human beings, must be rare and the Wolf Spider's way of life with its rules of behaviour is often as effective as ours although she has no reasoning powers. It would be nice to end on this note but as a naturalist I am bound to notice how often the wonderful protective devices achieved by evolution are countered by evolutionary developments on the enemy's side. No ichneumon has been seen creeping up behind a *Lycosa* to pierce her egg-sac with its ovipositor yet *Gelis fasciatus* Fab. has been bred from the eggs of *Lycosa pullata* and *Pezomachus micrurus* Forst. from those of *L. amentata.*

THE PISAURIDAE

Pisaura mirabilis is the smallest and commonest of our three large Pisaurids. She reaches up to 15 mm. and her lanky slimbodied form is a common sight amongst heather and low herbs in open spaces anywhere from the South of England to the North of Scotland. Predominant colours range from light grey to rich brown with a pale narrow band down the centre of the carapace and an abdominal pattern bordered by wavy lines, faint or distinct, which draw closer together at the hind extremity.

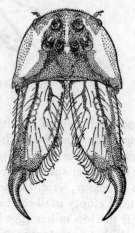

Pisaura has no settled home. She runs among the plants or sits sunning herself on a leaf in a characteristic pose with the two front pairs of legs close together and stretched stiffly outwards at an angle of 30°. She

FIG. 88. *Pisaura* face

favours sheltered positions, even if these are narrow like grassy road verges protected from winds by walls, and her distribution on islands is sharply determined by this factor. Thus she is abundant on those islands in the Scilly group which provides her with the shelter of trees and walls and absent from the remainder. She inhabits Ramsey and Bardsey but does not survive on nearby Skokholm or Skomer.

The final moult takes place in May and this is when a fascinating and unique courtship takes place. The male's taste-by-touch or chemotactic sense warns him of the presence of a female in the vicinity when he crosses her tracks or touches the drag-line thread she has trailed in the course of her rambles. This can be proved by putting him in a box from which a female has been removed as this provides him with the initial stimulus to start his courtship.

The first phase includes the catching of a fly. There is nothing remarkable in this, but he departs entirely from his usual procedure when he stands over it on tip-toes with his abdomen lowered almost vertically and rotates his abdomen feverishly round the insect trailing threads which encircle it. The sexual spell under which he has fallen is so strong even before he has seen the female that he does not now tarry to eat the fly but with excited jerky steps he walks about searching for her with the fly-parcel in his chelicerae. When he finds her he adopts a grotesque pose in front of her (see Plate XX, p. 193). His body is tilted vertically downwards with the spinnerets resting on the ground whilst the first pair of legs are raised with the femurs touching above his head, the patella and tibia raised in an outward direction and the metetarsi and tarsi lowered. In this position the fly-parcel is between him and her with his palps stretched upwards and outwards on either side of it.

What will happen next? If the female is prepared to mate with him she begins to move towards him and, as she advances, he leans further and further backwards with the fly raised upwards. Then, as she reaches upwards to take hold of it in her chelicerae, he smoothly readjusts his position and swivels round until his head is underneath her sternum. Now her chelicerae are firmly embedded in the fly, he is facing in the opposite direction in an inverted, or nearly inverted position under her sternum or a little to one side.

Mating may last well over an hour during which time she sucks the fly whilst he inserts each palp once or twice. At each change of palp he pauses to bite the fly for a short time himself, which may be nothing more than a symbol of renewed courtship, and again when mating is completed.

Variations in the normal procedure add spice to the story and a male who has been put in a female's enclosure with no fly to offer her has been eaten himself. But perhaps we ought not to feel too sorry for him because on other occasions I have watched him cheat by wrapping up the empty carcase of a fly to give her or even run away with the wedding gift at the end of the mating ceremony!

During the first half of July the female may be seen trundling along with a huge light-coloured round egg-sac under her sternum which is attached to her spinnerets by threads and is held in her chelicerae. At about the time the eggs are beginning to hatch, she loosens the outer covering and attaches it to a blade of grass. Then she weaves a tent over it on the outside of which she stands on guard, (see Plate VIII, p. 93). The young emerge in late June or early July, after moulting once inside the egg-sac. Now they cluster together in a ball inside their tent for a few days before moulting for a second time and dispersing.

The nursery tents make the spiders easy to see and show how common they are in some sheltered places. I have counted sixty nurseries in a hundred yards of narrow grass verge along a Hertford-shire lane, thirty-six amongst a low bramble hedge twenty-seven yards in length on St. Agnes in the Scilly Islands and nine clustered in one square yard on Tresco.

In Britain I believe that each female normally lays two batches of eggs.

Dolomedes fimbriatus is our largest and grandest spider. She normally reaches 18 mm. and I once had a special pet who measured 22 mm. She may not be quite as long as a *Segestria florentina* or nearly as long-legged as a House Spider (*Tegenaria*) but she is more thick-set and powerful in appearance. Her rich dark chocolate brown colour with

FIG. 89. *Pisaura mirabilis* (14 mm.) carrying her egg-sac

two white or yellow stripes extending all the way from her head to her spinnerets gives her a handsome appearance, and I always get a thrill when I find her.

Dolomedes could be called the Swamp Spider, if an English name were needed, and this would be far more appropriate than the name 'Raft Spider' by which she has been known for a century owing to one error in the literature which has been blindly copied ever since. The story was that she floated down streams on leaves tied together with silk. In truth she lives in swamps and dykes where the water is usually still and she can be seen sitting on the growing leaf of some water plant with her front legs resting on the surface of the water (see Plate XXI, p. 196).

Watch her and in time you may see her dart across the water to capture an insect which she has seen close at hand or whose struggles in the water have set up ripples which pass along its surface like the vibrations of an insect along a thread. When she makes a sortie like this an anchor thread is attached to the leaf to which she will return laden or empty handed according to her success.

Should she be disturbed by an enemy or a would-be collector, she will run down the plant stem below the water with air encasing her legs as well as her body and remain there for a few minutes until the danger is past.

This splendid spider has a wide but local distribution. I associate her with small pools of standing water in Southern England, but I have been sent one by Mr. Christie from as far north as Sutherland and she is common in New Forest swamps amongst other places.

May and June seem to be the principal months for courtship. The smaller male is cautious in his approach. As he moves slowly forward towards the female he probably conveys distinctive vibrations along the plant or water surface by waggling his sinuous front pair of legs up and down out of step with one another. The legs quiver as they are waggled and at short intervals he pauses in his advance. Slowly he creeps forward until he can touch her with his quivering legs and, although there is no ceremony with a fly in the *Pisaura* fashion, I have noticed that he is less likely to be repulsed if she happens to be eating a fly at the time.

Large dogs sometimes have a very powerful downward stroke with their front legs and a similar action is noticeable in *Dolomedes* which can have the effect of beating an insect firmly down in the water. This is an action which an agile male is able to dodge and although courtship may be a prolonged affair the mating itself is exceptionally short. A palp is inserted, the bulb expands and collapses once, the other palp is inserted, the bulb again expands once and the male leaves her all in the space of a few seconds. Now he retires and before long he spins a few threads in the form of a vertical ribbon on which he deposits a drop of sperm for the recharging of his palps.

In the inconvenient fashion of most spiders, *Dolomedes* usually lays her eggs in the early hours of the morning and P. Bonnet has given an excellent description on which I cannot improve. After spanning a small space between plants with a few haphazard threads, she hangs down from these and weaves a small thick white platform by twisting round in a series of circles which is later converted into a small cup tilted upside down at an angle. With her abdomen poised immediately below this cup a mass of eggs floating in a glutinous fluid is pressed into the cup and a ribbon of white silk is drawn underneath it. Further ribbons are distributed across the cup until the egg-mass is completely covered in. Now she cuts the threads which suspend the resulting egg-sac and hangs suspended by her hind pair of legs, holding it with her other three pairs. At this stage it is uneven in shape but before long it becomes circular through her turning it round and pressing it with her palps, her legs and the tip of her abdomen as she coats it with still more silk. It has lost its snow-white appearance and later it changes to a light brown colour in the air. From start to finish the task of egg-laying and sac-construction may have taken her more than two hours.

FIG. 90. *Dolomedes fimbriatus* (20 mm.) carrying her egg-sac

For the next two or three weeks the mother walks about with her bulky egg-sacs attached by threads to her spinnerets and held firmly in her chelicerae. Sometimes she can be seen dipping the egg-sac into the water and that this is no accidental occurrence is clear from the fact that Bonnet has found the eggs do not hatch unless they are kept damp in this way.

Shortly before they hatch the mother attaches the egg-sac to a plant usually six inches to two feet above the ground and spins some threads over and round it in the form of a small tent much like that of *Pisaura*. She sits on guard on the outer walls of the tent.

When the egg-sac is suspended it looks baggy, due to the mother having unravelled the outer silk threads which had formerly constricted the more capacious inner covering and had allowed no room for the expansion which occurs when the young are hatching. The young make their own way out of the egg-sac and stay together in a round cluster for three or four days. At the end of this time they have their second moult and disperse.

By rearing *Dolomedes* from their eggs Bonnet's careful investigations have shown that three or even four egg-sacs may be made by a female in the course of the summer months and that the number of eggs tend to become fewer in each successive laying. In captivity one individual with four egg-sacs laid 753, 792, 532 and 215 eggs respectively, making a total of 2,292. Another which had three batches laid 785, 774 and 136, making a total of 1,695. A third which only had two batches laid 772 and 479, making a total of 1,251. In Britain I believe two egg-sacs is the usual number.

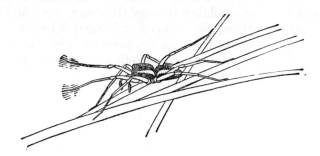

FIG. 91.   Male *Dolomedes* courting (12 mm.)

He has established that ten moults are usual for the female and nine for the male but that certain factors can influence the exact number, (see p. 64).

The normal time taken to reach maturity is eleven or twelve months, but whereas some have their final moult in late spring others do so three months later owing in most cases to their having hatched from a later batch of eggs in the previous year. Once they become adult the females usually live for another three or five months, whereas the male's expectation of life is less.

Dolomedes hibernates in an immature state and merely hides away amongst damp vegetation with legs drawn in close to the body. In this position she stays without food until the warmth of spring returns and then we see her again standing beside her swamp pools.

When Mons. Bonnet made his exhaustive researches he found specimens of a closely allied species, *D. plantarius,* in John Blackwall's collection, but, as these were unlabelled and Blackwall received many collections from other countries, this discovery did not provide proof of its presence in Britain. Proof has now been provided by E. Duffey who collected specimens of *D. plantarius* in East Anglia during 1956.

This new species is almost identical in size and appearance with *D. fimbriatus.* The cephalothorax is slightly wider in relation to its length and the pale bands on the cephalothorax tend to be narrower but it is only the sexual organs which make identification certain. It will take some time to determine the extent of the distribution of this fine species in Britain.

Before parting from the Wolf Spiders I should like briefly to outline the conclusions I reached many years ago as to the functions of visual displays in these families and the functions of tactile forms of courtship used by males in web-building families (Bristowe, 1926 and 1941). They have arisen, I think, by a process of Natural Selection to avoid the more powerful females mistaking the males for prey. The courtship also serves the necessary function of stimulating the females.

PLATE XIX. *Lycosa* carrying her young.

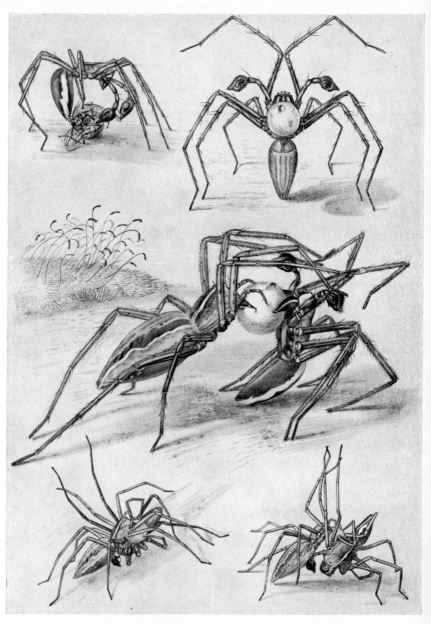

PLATE XX. *Pisaura mirabilis* male (12 mm.) wraps a fly, presents it to and is accepted by the female.

CHAPTER 16

THE AGELENIDAE

'CHARLES and me want to frighten you with the spider again', wrote Princess Anne when five years old to Miss Ulrica Forbes, the artist. In a postscript was added, 'You must be more frightened for me with the spider next time,' which showed that although the spider was a sham one, Miss Forbes was required to pretend she was frightened. Many people do not have to simulate fear when they see a long-legged House Spider (*Tegenaria*) in possession of the bath or running over the floor of the sitting room, and Sax Rohmer, the novelist, once wrote to the Daily Express saying that he had overcome his horror by eating one. I have eaten a House Spider without having

FIG. 92. *Tegenaria* face

the same success. The situation in which I found myself was this: an invitation to play cards after a good dinner; no money in my pockets; a specimen of *T. domestica* walking across the drawing-room carpet. And the consequences? A bet to eat the spider and the amount of my winnings increased at cards by 1100% by the end of the evening. Conclusions: that spiders are lucky but that a horror of House Spiders cannot be cured by eating one !

My interest in spiders is only a spare time hobby so I never expect to make a detailed study of House Spiders for whom I have no affection. Nevertheless I can record with feelings of pride that I was once brave enough to offer myself to the London School of Tropical Medicine as a 'guinea pig' when I tried to persuade them to investigate the widespread belief which used to exist in days when malaria was rampant in Britain that the swallowing of a *Tegenaria* was the best cure.
WS—O

I offered to swallow them and be tested for results. My offer was refused.

There are three common domestic species of House Spider, *Tegenaria domestica*, *T. atrica* and *T. parietina*. The sexual organs provide a sure guide to identification, but with experience they can easily be distinguished when adult by their size, general appearance and markings. Also by their webs and egg-sacs.

Tegenaria domestica reaches a body length of 10 mm. and is the smallest and lightest in colour of the three. Her sheet-web becomes thicker and whiter, owing to its greater opaqueness than those of the other two species, and the diameter of the entrance to the tubular retreat is relatively smaller even after taking her size into account. Her dirty white egg-sac hangs by a few threads from a nearby ledge. This species is almost worldwide in distribution and is so closely associated with man's buildings everywhere that I have heard it suggested she is now completely reliant on man for survival. I have found her in houses from the Scilly Islands to the Shetlands and from Norfolk to the western islands fringing the Irish coast, but I have also found her away from human habitations in the entrances to dry caves and in hollow trees.

Tegenaria atrica can reach about 18 mm. in length and the dark broken bars on her abdomen are usually darker and more clearly defined than in *T. domestica* (see Plate XXIII, p. 204). Her sheet-web is usually of a lighter and more transparent appearance than those of the other two species whilst the diameter of the retreat is greater both actually and in relation to her size. Her egg-sacs are fastened flat against a wall beside her web and partly camouflaged with debris. Although extremely common in houses and sheds from the Scilly Islands northwards, she is scarce in the North of England and Southern Scotland. The remarkable thing about *T. atrica's* distribution is that in Ireland her place is taken by an allied species, *T. larva*. Sim. and, whereas she has only been found in Ireland once, *T. larva* has only been recorded from three places in England. *T. atrica* is much less restricted to houses than the other two species and is common in banks, walls, and even amongst marram grass on sandhills or in the open country amongst heather and other plants in the South West of England. At certain seasons, and particularly in autumn with the approach of cold weather, she makes her way into houses from the outside by way of the overflow pipes from bathrooms or other inlets.

Thirdly we come to *Tegenaria parietina,* often nicknamed the Cardinal Spider from the legend that those living at Hampton Court used to terrify Cardinal Wolsey. The body length can equal that of *T. atrica*

but the legs are much longer and more furry. The chelicerae are a
shade narrower and the abdomen higher with a band down the centre
which often has a light reddish-brown tinge. Her sheet-web covers a
bigger area than that of *T. atrica* if space allows and the entrance to
her retreat is a little smaller despite her longer legs. Her white egg-sac
is built into her retreat. She is restricted to buildings in Southern
England with Nottingham and Staffordshire the northernmost records
where she is very scarce. Strangely enough she has not been found in
Cornwall, Devon or Somerset and she appears to be absent from Wales
whilst there are only two records from Ireland (Dublin and Wicklow).
Like the other two species she is another, and the most disturbing, of
the night prowlers in houses.

Leaving the fireside for the mossy banks along shady lanes and paths
of England and Wales (but not of Scotland, or, more strangely, Ireland)
we are likely to notice some small deeply sagging hammock-shaped
webs. These clearly belong to a *Tegenaria*, but they have a faintly bluish
tinge and a relatively small retreat entrance which helps to distinguish
them from those of the larger *T. atrica* which inhabit the same banks.
These webs belong to *T. silvestris*. She has a body pattern something
like *T. parietina* but as she only reaches 7 mm. in length there is no
likelihood of confusion.

Two other species — *T. pagana* which resembles *T. domestica*, and
T. agrestis Walck which is like *T. atrica* — have been recorded once
only from Dublin and from Wilverley Plain, Hampshire respectively.
Dislike of the *Tegenariae* may have led to their being overlooked elsewhere.

A *Tegenaria* cannot deliver a painful bite. Its unpopularity arises
from its leg span, its rapid movements and general creepyness. The
genus can certainly provide our champion sprinters and I have found
that an adult *T. atrica* female can cover a distance equivalent to 330
times her body length in 10 seconds. If this formula remained true for
a hypothetical man-length spider, this monster could give our fastest
runners a start of 8.5 seconds and still catch them just as they had
covered a distance of a hundred yards !

Brigadier Rayner has given me the interesting piece of information
that spider races used to be staged at Ashcombe Tower, Dawlish,
towards the end of the 18th century. Odds were laid on competing
spiders which were released simultaneously on to a hot plate lying in
the middle of a large table and the first to reach the edge of the table
was the winner. I have little doubt that *T. atrica* was in much demand,

but, although details of many exciting contests for high stakes have been preserved at Ashcombe Tower, it is tantalising to learn that these are temporarily inaccessible.

I have timed the speed of a number of spiders with a stop-watch, and reached the interesting conclusions (1) that, with increasing bulk, athletic stamina is impaired and (2) that the faster a spider can run the sooner she becomes tired. Statistics would show that in these respects man and spider are alike. Provided a full-grown *Tegenaria* is impelled with the end of a pencil to run at top speed without any pause whatever, she collapses in a state of prostration in less than 20 seconds, whereas some relatively slow-moving small spiders with body lengths of 2.5 mm. are still well embarked on a marathon after three quarters of an hour when I myself am exhausted by my part in the proceedings.

In one large spider, *Micrommata,* where the heart beats can be counted through the abdominal wall, I find that her beats have increased from 54 to 240 per minute by the time exhaustion sets in and that about three-quarters of an hour has to elapse before they return to normal. This suggests that the breathing apparatus becomes less adequate for sustained effort as the bulk of a spider increases. The explanation for this lies no doubt in the relative rates of increase in volume, area and length. Thus whereas the body length of a tropical giant (*Theraphosa* or *Lasiodora*) may be 120 times that of the smallest known spider (*Orchestina, Mysmena* or *Theotima*), the surface area is about 14,400 and the volume 1,728,000 times as great. This increase in volume tests the circulatory system and provides a principal reason why spiders in nature could never attain the size that novelists or old-time explorers would have us believe.

In those same mossy banks shared by *T. atrica* and *T. silvestris,* a neat round entrance to a tunnel surrounded by a collar of white silk may be noticed (see Plate III, p. 80). This will belong to one of our two species of *Amaurobius.* Here surely we have a clue as to how the Agelenid type of sheet web arose without in any way implying a direct descent via *Amaurobius.* The stages could have been a hunting spider which excavated a hole in the ground where it stayed on guard when the eggs were laid, a burrow like that of *Amaurobius* where the drag-lines accumulated in time into a white collar, and finally the extension of the collar asymmetrically into a sheet like that of a *Tegenaria.*

In woods or on rocky hill slopes away from roadside banks the burrows of *Amaurobius* extend under stones and logs and it is here that the exact nature of her subterranean tube can best be seen. It broadens out,

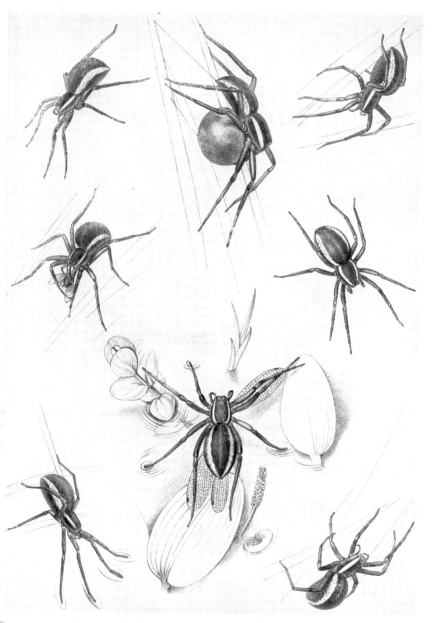

PLATE XXI. *Dolomedes fimbriatus* (20 mm.) sits majestically on plants beside water, sometimes with legs on the surface to detect vibrations.

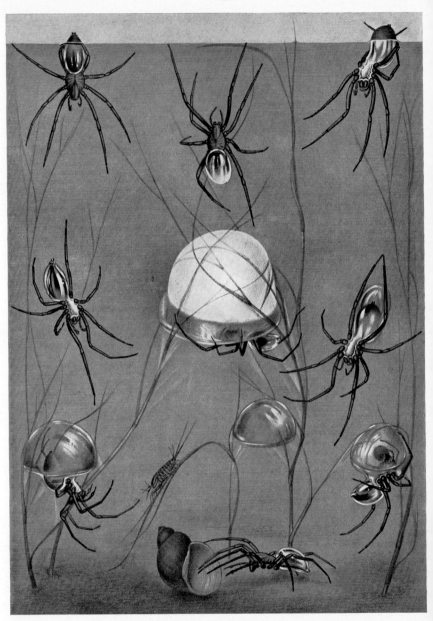

PLATE XXII. The Water Spider (13 mm.) fetches air from the surface with which to stock her diving bell in the upper part of which her egg-sac is placed. When winter comes the males often seal themselves in an empty snail shell with a bubble of air.

Fig. 93. The young of *Amaurobius terrestris* eating their dead mother

sometimes bifurcates and is walled with loose silk. It may be six inches or more in length.

The range of our two species, *A. terrestris* and *A. atropos,* overlaps in the southern counties but I personally associate the latter more with the mountains of England and Wales where I have found her at the summits of hills ranging from Dunkery Beacon to Brecon Beacons, Cader Idris, Snowdonia, Helvellyn and Scafell Pikes. Here she is abundant under stones and yet strangely enough neither species has been found in Ireland and they are practically unknown in Scotland. The distribution of these and other Agelenid species to which I have referred is a puzzle which should stimulate enquiry.

It is rare to see *Amaurobius* standing in the threshold of her burrow in daylight but a torch will show her in this position soon after nightfall. If the silk collar is gently tickled with a fine piece of grass, the spider will rush out to bite it and will sometimes pursue it beyond the edge of the collar. When this happens she appears to be temporarily lost and she has to meander about for a time before finding her way home. Her principal food comprises crawling insects like beetles, woodlice or earwigs and her main harvest is made at night.

Mating takes place in spring or early summer. This lasts two or three hours during which each palp is inserted once (though sometimes each palp may be inserted a second or third time for brief periods). The eggs are laid early in June and these are contained in a circular disc-shaped sac in the spider's tube. When the eggs hatch, the young share their mother's prey for a prolonged period and in fact stay at home until they have reached a more advanced stage of growth than those of any other British spider. They too come to the entrance and may make captures of small insects on their own account, so their threads mingle with those spun by their mother to make the silk collar dense white and more conspicuous in late September than it was earlier in the season.

Autumn and early winter brings us to a critical stage in their domestic history. Sometimes the response to the gentle tickling of the threads with a fine grass will be to attract not the bulky half inch form of the mother but one or more of her babies which now look as though they were a quarter grown or even more. What has happened to their mother? She has produced young which she has guarded, fed and housed for four months and her life span has reached its close. With the arrival of the winter frosts she becomes sluggish, she dies, and her final service to her family is to provide them with her own body as food.

I cannot assert that this is the invariable custom, but I saw it happen in one case and G. H. Locket has confirmed my experience in another case (fig. 93, p. 197).

Following this tragedy it is usual for a few of the young to remain together in their mother's home through the winter and then scatter when warmer weather returns in February or March.

The large sheet-webs of *Agelena labyrinthica* are often conspicuous in July and August spread amongst gorse, heather and grass with a funnel, leading away from the side or centre, at the entrance to which she is usually lurking. She is a handsome spider which reaches 12 mm. in length. The general effect is one of greyness but her abdomen is prettily and clearly marked with a paler longitudinal band bordered by transverse bars of darker colour.

A sheet-web, such as that made by an Agelenid, unequipped with gummy threads is not so lacking in subtlety as might at first be thought. The surface above the main sheet is really a maze of trip-wires and one of the mysteries is how the spider herself darts across them at lightning speed whilst the insect staggers along like a man knee deep in snow. No doubt the tarsal claws, the long hairs with which the tarsi are provided and the angle of the tarsus when running all play some part. We should notice also that the edges slope upwards and that in the case of *Agelena* the sheet is surmounted by many scaffolding threads which arrest the jumps or flights of insects and causes them to fall down on to the sheet.

The vibrations of a tuning fork do not attract the attention of an Agelenid in the way they do when a tuning fork touches the threads of an Argiopid or Dictynid spider. D. A. Parry has pointed out to me that the Agelenid responds chiefly to the gentle dragging or pulling of the threads comprising what I have called the trip-wire layer and these are just the kind of signals transmitted to the spider by an insect as it stumbles across the surface.

An *Agelena* darts rapidly towards a struggling insect and delivers a series of sharp bites which weaken and eventually kill it. Then she picks it up and carries it back to her retreat. This procedure is also followed by *Tegenaria* where, on occasions, I have seen the spider run under the web to spin extra threads below an insect which is struggling to pierce and drop through the sheet. On the homeward journey the spider shows no hesitation in moving straight back to the funnel whether she is running towards it or dragging backwards a heavy insect. This apparent sense of direction is explained by M. Holzapfel (1933) as being nothing more than the spider following the line of greatest tension with the aid of her sensitive tactile senses.

Agelena always seems to have plenty of food derived from the hopping and flying insects which fall on to her sheet and she grows rapidly to her full stature of 12 mm. by July when mating takes place. The lanky male taps the web with his palps as he approaches her and, if she is in a receptive mood, she draws in her legs and remains still. Now we see something which is characteristic of the Agelenidae — a certain amount of manhandling by the male. He seizes her by the femur of a leg and hauls her about until he has found a place and position in which mating is to take place. This may be just in the entrance of the funnel or near the edge of the sheet.

In August the female forsakes her web to lay her eggs and enclose them in a large and very elaborate chamber slung amongst the nearby vegetation. Within the dense white walls of this bulky chamber there is a labyrinth of passages which have earned the spider her name of *labyrinthica*. Here she remains with her eggs and young until she dies.

If I were to provide a distribution map for *Textrix denticulata* it would show that this spider is known to live in nearly every county of England, Scotland, Wales and Ireland, but in my experience she flourishes most near the sea. In contrast to *Agelena*, which avoids small islands, *Textrix* abounds on all the small exposed ones from the Scillies to the Shetlands. Here her small fleecy hammock-web is slung in rock crevices and under stones.

She reaches 7 mm. in length and her long spinnerets combined with her bright markings give her a distinctive appearance. A wide reddish-brown dentate band edged with grey covers most of the upper side of the abdomen which is flanked with black mottling.

May is the month for courtship. The male vibrates the web by drawing in his legs with a jerk and, after repeating this for a time, the female bunches her legs and awaits his approach. He touches her and then seizes a leg in his chelicerae and drags her to a suitable part of the web where he places her on her side. Facing in the opposite direction and standing transversely over her with gently vibrating body, he inserts one of his palps. The bulb swells and collapses regularly every eight seconds and after each collapse the palp is removed, jerked and reinserted. Copulation lasts about half an hour during which each palp may be applied three times.

About three quarters of an hour after a male had left a female I saw him spinning threads and occasionally interrupting his work to chew his palps. The spinning of a tiny platform across one of the angles at the junction of five threads was finished in about ten minutes and he then jerked his body up and down against this until a small drop of sperm appeared. Now he reached each palp round the web alternately about thirteen times so that the sperm drop was absorbed through the web from its lower surface. The absorption process lasted about thirteen minutes.

Besides such giants as *Tegenaria*, the family includes a number of pygmies like *Hahnia, Cryphoeca, Antistea,* and *Tuberta,* some of which reach less than 2 mm. in length. These are mostly to be found in marshy ground or amongst damp vegetation. Then there is *Tetrilus arietinus* which lives in ants' nests and the somewhat larger mouse grey *Cicurina cicur* which may be found in damp cellars in covered drains or wells and other humid retreats. All these smaller Agelenids are awaiting somebody to take an interest in them.

Finally, there is the one and only *Argyroneta*, the famous Water Spider. Many years have gone by since as a schoolboy I first watched this jewel amongst spiders glittering like quicksilver as she swam below the surface of the water enswathed in air. Earlier in the day I had felt surprise at finding a dry spider with a brown cephalothorax and a dark velvety abdomen striding out of the sodden weeds I had dredged from a pond, but now I was enraptured by the transformation into an object of such beauty with her abdomen and sternum encased in gleaming armour as she swam under the water in my aquarium.

Here under the water she spends her life breathing the air she fetches from the surface. Here amongst the water plants she builds her home, stocks it with air, catches her prey, mates, lays eggs and finally dies.

Although *Argyroneta* may be the only spider in the world which can swim freely under water without holding on to plant stems and which stocks a diving bell with air in which to live her life, there is little evidence of structural adaptation. It might be suggested that the tufts of hair, especially those on the hind legs, are unusually luxuriant even for an Agelenid, or that the forward migration of the tracheal spiracle had made breathing more easy for a spider with her habits, but these are comparatively minor modifications. More important though less conspicuous are glandular changes which may have occurred. It is essential for her to remain dry and she is often to be seen rubbing the tarsi of her hind legs over her spinnerets before rubbing her legs together or passing the tarsi over her abdomen. Despite rapid oscillation of the spinnerets during this process there is no sign of silk so it must be supposed that some fluid is emitted which has waterproofing properties.

Let us start following her life from the moment she touches the water in an aquarium. Head downwards she dives below the surface using her bent hind legs as paddles thrusting upwards against the surface film. Poised belly uppermost and with vigorous leg movements similar to those of walking, she swims downwards until she comes in contact with water weeds to which she clings before continuing her exploration.

Her first bubble of air can last several hours if she does not absorb oxygen too rapidly by active movement and provided the oxygen content of the water is high or near saturation point. But she is not descended from a race of nomads like the Wolf Spiders and needs a home, and her method of stocking it with air is easy to watch but difficult to follow in every detail. Although my experience tallies with that of other writers in most respects there will be certain details in my description which have not been mentioned before.

She starts by weaving a little curved platform of silk amongst the plants to which it is anchored. Then she climbs up the plants or swims upwards until her front legs touch the surface film. Now she turns round head downwards with the abdomen directed vertically upwards. The tip must at least connect with the surface layer and it may be projected a short distance above it. The tufted femurs of the fourth pair of legs are bent upwards and slightly outwards alongside the abdomen whilst the tarsi are crossed over the dorsal side of the abdomen near its tip to form a frame. The crossed tarsi project into the air. In the light of what happens later it is important to notice that the third pair of legs are drawn in so as to allow their tips to rest against the tibiae or metatarsi of the fourth pair.

At this stage a downward flip of the body would cloak it with air as it did when she was first released into the aquarium but this would not provide her with enough air to supply both the diving bell and her own immediate requirements on return journeys to the surface. On these occasions the air-collecting technique is different and well worth careful study.

Several things now happen simultaneously during the few crowded seconds I am trying to describe. The abdomen is jerked downwards, and at the same time pivoted so that the ventral surface is downwards, whilst the hind pair of legs are snapped backwards over the tip of the abdomen and stretched out behind with a slight inward curvature so as almost to encompass the elongated bubble which now strains upwards beyond her abdomen. Thus, with a sudden jerk of body and legs an outsize bubble is entrapped and held. An interesting feature which has escaped previous notice is that the backward snap of the hind legs from their crossed position is accomplished with the help of a violent upward kick by the third pair of legs whose tarsi were pressed against the tibiae or metatarsi of the fourth pair.

The large bubble is held by the hind pair of legs as the spider swims or walks down plants to the diving bell with the other three pairs. Directly she reaches it she enters head uppermost with the result that the bubble, which was trailing behind whilst she was swimming down-wards, passes forward. Part of it becomes detached immediately and rises to the top of the silken tent before she turns head downwards to release still more of the air from the abdominal tip, sometimes by stroking it off with her hind tarsi. A short time is now normally devoted to strengthening and extending the silken dome, and sometimes to toilet operations, before returning to the surface for more air. When *Argyroneta* is filling a new diving bell she seldom pauses long and may make six or more journeys in rapid succession but her task is not usually completed in one series. Although the final shape of her home is variable it usually resembles a short wide-based thimble (see Plate XXII, p. 197).

Once the diving bell is completed the oxygen it contains may be gradually absorbed by the water or replenished by oxygen in the water according to whether the oxygen content of the water is low or near to saturation point. Apart from this, however, the carbon dioxide is slowly absorbed by the water and fresh supplies of air are brought from the surface and mixed with the gases which remain, so the spider can continue permanently to live and breathe in its under-water home.

E. Nielsen (1932) has seen water spiders releasing the stale air through a hole bitten in the top of the thimble and then filling it with fresh air after mending the hole, but I think this was an accidental or unusual occurrence.

Argyroneta is widespread in the lakes, ponds and dykes of temperate Europe and Asia. In Britain she extends from the Isle of Wight to Perth amongst such plants as *Elodea, Lemna* and Water Ranunculus. When she moves amongst the weeds she trails a thread behind her, just like most terrestrial spiders, so in the course of time a lot of threads diverge from the diving bell. Although these will signal the vibrations of an insect in the vicinity, they are not employed as a snare. Nielsen has suggested that an *Argyroneta* finds her way back to her home by means of a trailed thread even when she has swum to the surface, but, as her leg movements do not suggest this, I tried passing a long needle between her and the diving bell in a fresh jar where there was no confusion of accumulated threads without encountering any thread. This suggests that she has some sense of direction although she may be assisted by the threads diverging to the diving bell when she approaches it.

The Water Spider is a hunter. During the day she sits in her diving bell with her front legs protruding into the water beneath it. Out she pounces on any water insect which approaches, envelops it in her legs and draws it firmly into her open chelicerae. She is sensitive to vibrations and will even be attracted by the struggles of a terrestrial insect on the surface. At night she goes on excursions and swims belly-uppermost to the bottom where her flailing front legs may stir into motion some small crustaceans or insect larvae. The large adult spiders of half an inch or more can catch and kill tadpoles but after chewing them for a time they usually discard them.

Owing to the external interchange of digestive and half-digested fluids which marks the spider's method of feeding, *Argyroneta* cannot feed in the water so she takes all her prey back to her home. If no home has been built she will climb out of the water to eat her victim on the leaf or stem of a plant.

When a change of skin becomes imminent Nielsen says that she closes her diving bell with silk. A change of skin is a delicate operation which leaves her helpless for several hours, so this closing of her cell is an interesting protective measure. In captivity I have more than once seen them climb out of the water to change their skins in the air and I have thought of this as the usual procedure.

A male which has reached maturity after his final moult stocks his palps with sperm in his home and then goes in search of a female. Although the largest British spider I have ever seen was a monstrous female *Argyroneta* from Kent with a body length of 28 mm., the females are often smaller than the males and usually range between 9 to 13 mm., compared with 9 to 12 mm., for the males. The frequent reversal of the usual relative sizes of the sexes not only makes him a bold courtier but may also lead to a longer association between them than is common amongst spiders.

When he first finds an adult female he tries to gain immediate acceptance after no more elaborate courtship than is represented by an interplay of legs and caresses. When she is not prepared to accept

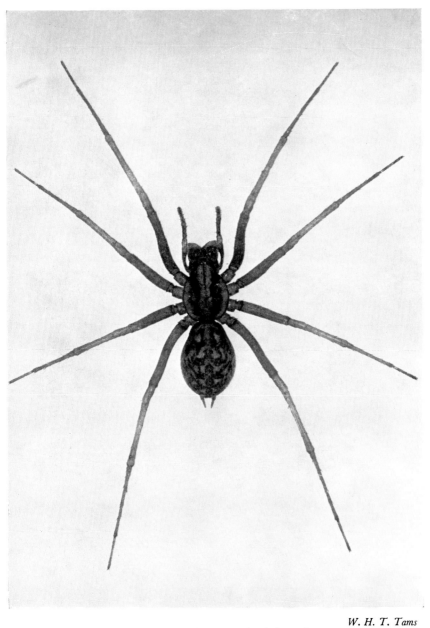

W. H. T. Tams

PLATE XXIII. *Tegenaria atrica* (16 mm.)

a. Cyclosa conica
(6 mm.)
(*W. H. T. Tams*)

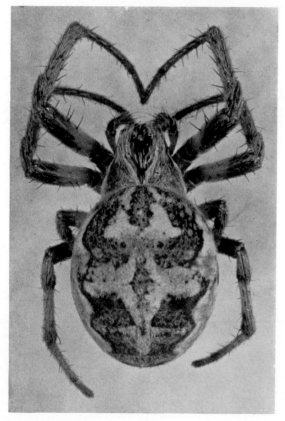

b. Araneus cornutus (9 mm.)
(*W. H. T. Tams*)

PLATE XXIV

him she displays her unwillingness by a series of abdominal jerks and lunges which eventually cause him to retreat.

The mating, which is often repeated, takes place in her home. They face in opposite directions, sternum to sternum, with the female underneath or pressed against the side of the diving bell. They separate in less than a minute, sometimes after only one of his palps has been inserted, but he often remains in her home for long periods during which further mating takes place. Her jerks and lunges will again be a sign for him to leave and then he may search for another female or take possession of the diving bell of an immature spider whom he ejects.

Adults of both sexes can be found throughout the year and mating starts in the spring. In my experience in the South of England the first batch of eggs is laid in the second half of May with another to follow during the first half of July and sometimes a third towards the close of the summer. Fifty to a hundred eggs are usually laid at a time which are enclosed in a dense white egg-sac that completely fills the upper half of the diving bell. A thick partition separates them from the lower half in which she continues to live. Here she remains on guard with the edges drawn in to narrow the entrance against marauders, but always on the alert for passing prey.

Eggs laid in captivity have hatched in three to four weeks and the young spiders then begin biting their way out. According to Nielsen they bite their way round the thick partition. They may stay within the diving bell for two to four weeks longer during which they undergo their second moult, before leaving to set up homes for themselves. Thus from this first batch the young may be found leaving their mother's homes during the second half of June or early in July and from the second batch in mid-August. At such times the aquarium is brightened by the appearance of quantities of tiny spiders in glistening air bubbles moving hither and thither. These are the tiny air-clad babies meeting and darting apart again, building tiny diving bells of their own or standing lightly poised below the surface film. At this stage a lot of them will climb out of the water and float away into the air on threads and in this manner some of them will colonise fresh pools of water though many will perish.

If the pond dries up the Water Spiders can survive for quite a long time in closed cells, but the only occasions on which they voluntarily leave the water are at this early stage in their lives and when they moult, or catch prey before they have built an established home, or when their bodies have got wet and need drying. In nature it is not

uncommon for elderly males to air the damp patches which develop
on the upper surface of their bodies. The same thing will be seen when
specimens we have collected have got wet in the damp weeds or water
in which we carried them home. If these cannot climb above the
surface they will drown.

In this sub-aquatic environment *Argyroneta* has tapped a plentiful
food supply not available to other spiders and has also escaped the
usual enemies, but she finds plenty of fresh ones at her varying stages
of growth. Thus there are numerous insects which will attack them as
they themselves swim in search of food. Beetles and beetle larvae,
dragonfly larvae, *Ranatra* and Water Boatmen will all eat Water Spiders
of suitable size. So, of course, will frogs and fish. Nevertheless *Argyroneta* is usually abundant in any pond she has colonised and I am afraid
the large spiders often eat their smaller brethren.

At the approach of winter the Water Spiders at all stages of growth
descend from their homes near the surface to greater depths where they
build new diving bells of stouter texture which are eventually converted
into closed cells. Here they stay throughout the winter in a state of
immobility from which only warmer weather awakens them. While in
this state of hibernation the one large air bubble can last them from
November until February. Sometimes empty snail shells (*Limnaea* and
Planorbis) at the bottom of the pond are converted into winter retreats
by the males who line them with silk, fill them with air and then seal
themselves inside until warmer weather returns.

Before leaving these interesting spiders we can pause to speculate
on the stages by which their ancestors may have adopted a sub-aquatic
life. The first thing to realise is that there is nothing remarkable in the
capture of air when they submerge themselves. Although such more or
less hairless spiders as *Steatoda, Theridion* and *Pholcus* are in difficulties
almost at once when forced below the surface, others with hairy bodies
like *Tegenaria* and *Herpyllus* are automatically cloaked with air. Fling
them on the surface and they will drown. Force them under and they
will cling to the water plants or move amongst them for as long as their
air supply lasts provided they are totally submerged and they are unable to reach the surface. None the worse for their experience I have
removed such spiders after several hours spent under the water.

Pass now from house spiders like *Tegenaria* and *Herpyllus* to species
which live beside water. Here we find several which invade the frontiers
of the aquatic community or which survive immersion when it is forced
on them by nature.

On the Malayan reefs close to Singapore I have watched *Desis martensi* L. K. and *Diplocanthopoda marina* Abr. sealing themselves into rock crevices with waterproof silk as the tide rises and emerging at low tide to feed. Several of our British species survive occasional floods in their closed silk cells under stones in similar fashion without coming into contact with the water, whilst *Lycosa purbeckensis* goes further in climbing down plant stems, as the tide rises over the salt marshes, bearing a bubble of air which lasts until the waters recede. Then again such swamp-living spiders as *Dolomedes* and *Pirata* also make temporary underwater excursions down the stems of plants, but here it is a protective device to which they resort when they are disturbed.

I do not picture *Argyroneta* having acquired her present habits through a series of hunting ancestors which gradually spent more and more time below the water. The key to *Argyroneta's* origin is linked with the diving bell without which no underwater eating can take place and we must remember that *Argyroneta* comes of a family which spins webs and tubes.

If a fairly dense curved tube is submerged it will entrap air so the rising waters will not immediately drown the spider, and we have seen that *Argyroneta* can survive long periods when she remains inactive in cool conditions. Her ancestors which lived in swampy situations where their retreats were subject to frequent submergence could have survived without vacating their homes. They could, moreover, walk about freely with a bubble of air (cf. *Tegenaria*) and would no doubt react to a moving insect in just the same way as on land, returning to their retreat with it in their chelicerae. A journey to the surface without finding dry land would automatically renew the air supply when they moved below it again. Although many spiders would perish, others survived and adapted their habits, I suggest, to those we have described for *Argyroneta*. Is it not possible that *Argyroneta's* ancestors colonised the subaquatic environment after the Ice Age, when the melting ice caused floods, and formed many ponds and lakes in low-lying areas ? Her lack of substantial structural adaptation suggests a comparatively modern history.

CHAPTER 17

THE THERIDIIDAE & NESTICIDAE

Comb-Footed Spiders

In the Theridiidae we have forty-eight species ranging in body-length from 1 mm. (*Theonoe minutissima*) to 7 mm. (*Theridion tepidariorum*). They live in scaffolding webs of various designs and gain their name of Comb-footed Spiders from the presence of a row of stout, curved, serrated bristles on the tarsi of their fourth pair of legs which play an important part in drawing viscous silk from the spinnerets and flinging it over their prey.

Although a number of characters should make it easy to distinguish a Theridiid from related families, the collector should be warned not to rely implicitly on any one character. Divergencies from what are re-

FIG. 94. *Theridion* face

garded as typical structural features partially bridge the gap between this family and the Nesticidae, Argiopidae and Linyphiidae. This can be illustrated in the following way before going on to describe their behaviour where similar linkages will become apparent.

The typical *Theridion* has a prettily marked globular abdomen which looks too large for her cephalothorax, and short slender legs; she usually has small untoothed chelicerae and her serrated tarsal combs are easy to see. *Enoplognatha thoracica*, on the other hand, differs from *Theridion* in all these respects and draws near to Linyphiid design (see Plate XXVIII, p. 221). The abdomen of *Enoplognatha* is not globular and it is of a dark or even blackish colour without any pattern; the chelicerae are of normal size and bear several teeth on the basal segment, whilst the serrations on the tarsal combs are absent or difficult to

PLATE 3. *Dysdera crocata* (10 mm.)

distinguish. *Enoplognatha* is nevertheless a Theridiid as can be seen by the sexual organs and other characters of the family.

The criss-cross scaffolding webs built by most Theridiidae follow more precise and at the same time more varied designs than casual observation suggests. The central part of the snare is usually more richly served with a trellis-work of threads than the outer area. Sometimes this trellis-work takes the form of six-sided meshes and sometimes it resembles a loosely knitted openwork platform. Some of the threads are studded with drops of gum along at least part of their length and the distribution of these viscous threads varies according to whether they are designed to catch flying or crawling insects.

Some species like *Theridion sisyphium* and *T. pictum* sling their snares well above the ground in spaces amongst the foliage of shrubs. These builders of aerial snares depend on flying insects for food and it is the central trellis-work which is studded with gum.

Many others attach their snares to the ground or to walls, like *Theridion saxatile* and *Steatoda bipunctata,* and here it is crawling insects which form the principal prey. These terrestrial snares have a number of long straight vertical or lateral anchor lines which have drops of gum arranged along their length for a short distance from their points of attachment. They are very tightly stretched and each is easily torn from its moorings by the struggles of a crawling insect which is then lifted from the ground by the contraction of the elastic thread. Where this thread is a vertical one the spider now hauls it up 'hand over hand' until the insect is just within reach when she turns round with her spinnerets towards the insect and flings gummy threads over it with her fourth pair of legs operating alternately.

Unlike the Argiopidae and Linyphiidae the prey is not bitten until it has been wrapped in silk and a further difference from Argiopid behaviour is to be found in the Theridiid practice of casting threads over its victim, instead of revolving it round and round in the band of silk from their spinnerets. The first bites of the enswathed insect are like gentle caresses from which the Theridiid draws back quickly at the first sign of a rebuke. They are directed at the legs and the poison takes rapid effect. If the insect is a hard-coated weevil, we can watch the delicate precision with which her small fangs find the chinks in its armour — where many another spider would fail completely.

One special feature of Theridiid feeding habits is their readiness to accept ants rejected by so many other spiders and it would seem likely that ants represent the staple diet of some species including *Dipoena*.

WS—P

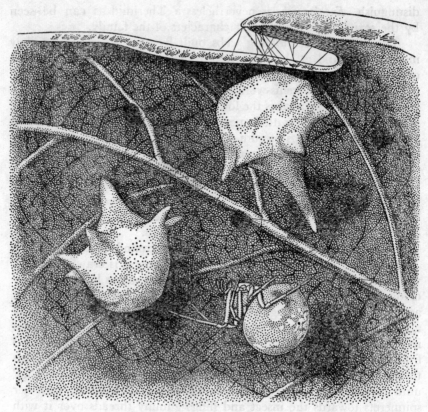

FIG. 95.   *Theridion pallens* (1·75 mm.) with two egg-sacs below an oak leaf

Owing to their having no cheliceral teeth the prey's body fluid is sucked through the small punctures made by the fangs and the insect is not mashed into an unrecognisable pellet as is done by the Argiopidae and Linyphiidae.

Sight enters into their lives only to a limited extent and, whilst they wait for the vibrations of an insect to signal their presence, they may be situated in a variety of places. *Theridion tepidariorum* hangs at least some of her time in the centre of her web with her legs closely folded back against her globular body. This is also the pose and position of *T. lunatum* but I have noticed that she readily adopts for concealment any stray leaf which happens to fall into her web. Several species, including *T. sisyphium*, build a small conical tent whose upper surface is camouflaged with vegetable debris or the remnants of insects whilst *T. saxatile* constructs in her web a much more elaborate retreat of great size coated with sand grains or vegetable fragments fetched from the ground (see Plate XXV, p. 212). Others may sit under a twig or leaf adjoining the web (*T. ovatum*) or take shelter in a neighbouring crevice (*Steatoda bipunctata*).

June is the commonest month for reaching maturity and for the males to go off in search of female webs. Having found one, the male serenades her with a variety of vibrations conveyed along the threads, which are set up by trembling legs and palps or pulsations of the abdomen. The pulsations of the abdomen are of particular significance because in this family jerks of the abdomen cause small teeth at its base to scrape against files at the rear end of the cephalothorax which produces distinctive vibrations along the threads.

It is interesting to find that in the genus *Steatoda* (and in related genera *Teutana, Lithyphantes* etc.) the male adopts the Argiopid practice of weaving a special mating thread on to which he entices the female before copulation takes place.

During copulation both spiders usually hang downwards with their ventral surfaces facing one another in such a manner that the axis of his body may lie at approximately 90° to that of the female. This position is similar to that adopted by many Linyphiids but is not so close or firm an embrace as is typical of the Argiopidae.

One palp is inserted at a time and the bulb swells and collapses once during each insertion, but there are at least four courses that mating may take. In *Theridion ovatum* each palp is inserted several times, in *Steatoda bipunctata* each palp is inserted once, and in *T. tepidariorum* and *T. lunatum* the complete act is accomplished by the single insertion of one palp only for a few minutes. In complete contrast to this a number of Theridions including *T. sisyphium* resemble the Linyphiidae in having a long series of insertions interrupted for brief spells whilst the male withdraws to recharge his palps with sperm.

This outline of the mating procedure found in the family is enough to show not only a general resemblance to that of the Argiopidae and Linyphiidae but also the adoption of specialised Argiopid procedures by some Theridiids and of specialised Linyphiid procedures by others, thereby confirming the close linkage of the three families. Similar linkages will be found when we come to the other related families (Nesticidae, Mimetidae and Tetragnathidae).

The egg-sacs are usually, though not invariably, round and without any sign of a join owing to their being rotated whilst the outer layer of silk is spun. They may be suspended in their mother's web (*Theridion tepidariorum*), plastered in a corner or crevice near the web and covered with gummy threads which are of protective value (*Steatoda*), stored in their mother's open tent (*Theridion sisyphium*), enclosed in a cell with their mother under the ground (*Enoplognatha schaufussi*), or in a curled leaf (*Theridion ovatum*), contained in an extensive cylindrical chamber formed by building walls of silk upwards and downwards between rock faces in the mother's web (*Theridion neglectum*) or even carried round attached by threads to their mother's spinnerets (*Theridion bimaculatum*). The white egg-sacs of the tiny pale *T. pallens* which are slung in their mother's web underneath an oak leaf are knobbly in shape and larger than the spider herself (see fig. 95, p. 210).

One of the commonest species in our gardens throughout Britain, as well as in hedgerows and heaths on holly and gorse, is *Theridion sisyphium*. Black bars and stripes on a background of rust red and white, with flanks and a central surface of light brown, make her one of our prettiest little spiders. She reaches her full stature of 4 mm. in late May or early June and her quite extensive scaffolding web with its conical tent in which she lives is of the aerial type designed to catch flying insects. The central meshes are studded with drops of gum and down she comes to do battle with any insect, regardless of size, which becomes entangled in them. Despite their small chelicerae and unathletic appearance, spiders of the genus *Theridion* are giant-killers and show what by human standards would be described as immense courage.

Some years ago I threw a sandhopper on the sheet web of a fully grown *Agelena labyrinthica* with the object of seeing if she would accept this crustacean. Its struggles attracted the attention of a *T. sisyphium* some of whose outlying threads were connected to the underside of the sheet. Whilst *Agelena* was biting the sandhopper, *Theridion* bit a small hole in the sheet and hurled gummy strands over the struggling crustacean whose strength withstood the first efforts of the *Agelena* to tug it free. Both spiders now bit the sandhopper simultaneously and then *Theridion* began trying to haul it through the hole she had cut. A tug-of-war ensued between the powerfully built 12 mm. *Agelena* and the slim-legged globular pygmy of 4 mm. When *Agelena* had failed to make any headway, she shook the web violently and followed this by launching an attack on the intruder. Retreating half-way through the hole in the web, *Theridion* kept her at bay by hurling viscid threads at

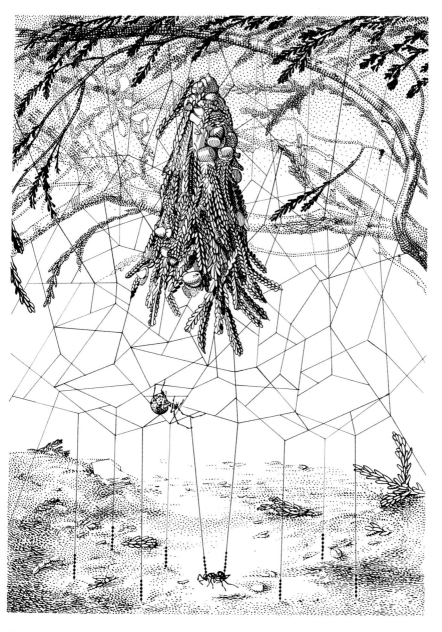

PLATE XXV. *Theridion saxatile* (3.5 mm.) builds a huge tent slung in a snare designed to catch crawling insects.

PLATE XXVI. *Episinus angulatus* (4 mm.) in her simple web.

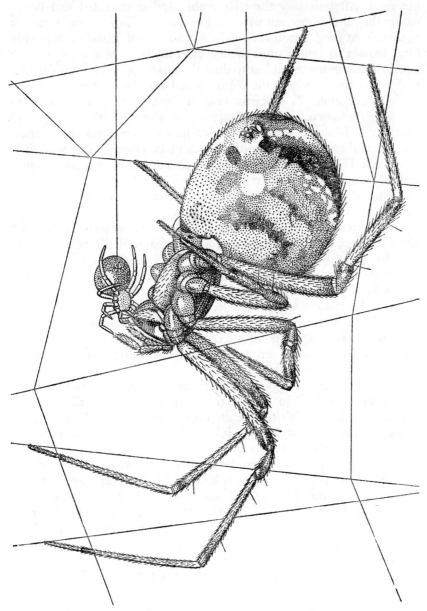

FIG. 96. *Theridion sisyphium* (4 mm.) feeding a baby from her mouth

her rival. After shaking the web again, *Agelena* retreated and began eating the sandhopper but within a few seconds *Theridion* had returned to their joint prey. Again and again *Agelena* chased *Theridion* away only for *Theridion* to return until finally, after the lapse of a quarter of an hour, *Agelena* managed at last to drag the sandhopper free and to retire within her tunnel where the *Theridion* did not follow her.

When a male *T. sisyphium* finds a female's web he walks with vibrating abdomen, feeling and tapping the threads with his palps and front legs. If she is ready to receive him she responds in a similar manner and he approaches until they can touch one another with their front legs. This interplay of legs may not reduce her to a state of submission at once so he retreats and returns several times, perhaps, before she hangs down at a steep angle whilst he tries to insert a palp. This is usually not successful at the first attempt.

After each palp has been inserted for 5 to 10 seconds, he retires a short distance and rapidly weaves a small band of silk which is held taut by the third pair of legs. When this is completed he taps his abdomen against it and deposits a drop of sperm on its lower side into which he dips his palpal emboli several times in quick succession.

Now he returns to the female, who has been vibrating the web meanwhile without changing her position, and again inserts each palp once before retiring to build a fresh sperm web in order to recharge his palps. I have seen a series of seven acts of mating and seven sperm inductions before he left her.

The first batch of eggs may be laid as early as the middle of June. These are contained in a circular sac of greenish-blue silk which is stored in their mother's tent in the upper part of the web. The young hatch during the first half of July and remain a few weeks before scattering in order to set up homes for themselves.

During this period the mother's maternal instincts are highly remarkable and unique so far as is known[*]. On a sunny day soon after emerging from the tent in which they hatched from their egg-sac the mother can be seen hanging downwards with the babies jostling each other to get near her mouth from which a drop of fluid is oozing. Here two or three of them at a time will have their first meal from their mother's mouth. Surely this delightful scene should be set against the sinister reputation that spiders possess (see Plate XXVIII, p. 221 and fig. 96).

Mouth-feeding continues for several days and then the young begin sharing her meals. I have seen the mother and perhaps thirty babies

[*]Noted first by G. H. Locket in 1926.

all feeding at once on a large fly. That this is not just an apathetic failure on her part to drive them away is shown by her departure from normal practice when she has captured the fly. Usually she bites the insect in one or two places and sucks its body fluid through these punctures, but when she has young whose chelicerae might be too feeble to pierce an insect's chitin she passes over its body biting it freely in many places. The agitation of the threads caused by a struggling insect summons the young to approach and, as they get bigger, they can be seen contributing to an insect's capture by flinging silk at it before sharing in the meal.

Most greenhouses are inhabited by our largest *Theridion, T. tepidariorum,* which must have reached us from some warmer country, but she is now so worldwide in distribution that her original homeland is uncertain. She reaches about 7 mm. and her globular abdomen has a number of dark bars and spots on a biscuit-coloured background (see Plate XXVII, p. 220).

Like other Theridions she is undaunted by the size of an opponent and I still remember with what mounting horror and interest I watched her overcome a full-grown House-spider (*Tegenaria atrica*) which I had thrown into her web although this was more than forty years ago. Whenever she drew near, *Tegenaria* lunged fiercely towards her with open fangs from which one bite would have been fatal, yet, somehow, leg after leg was enswathed in silk and then paralyzed with a bite from *Theridion's* small chelicerae.

The courtship and mating position is much like that of other Theridions but the mating is remarkable for its brevity. It is completed with the insertion of one palp for 5 to 10 seconds and it is known from P. Bonnet's breeding experiments (1935) that this is enough to enable her to lay several batches of fertile eggs during ensuing months.

Although 250 eggs may be about the average number in a single batch for *T. tepidariorum,* the number may be nearly double or much less and under exceptionally favourable conditions fresh batches may be laid at such short intervals as a week.

Egg-laying takes place at night and the egg-sac is completed in about eighty minutes. She starts by building a small silk cone beneath which the bundle of eggs is pressed and fastened with a few threads drawn from her spinnerets by her fourth pair of legs. White silk is then spun round the eggs followed by an outer covering of light yellowish silk which changes to a chocolate brown colour later. When she is spinning this outer envelope she revolves the incomplete egg-sac, first one way and then the other. The finished egg-sacs are pear-shaped and these are hung in their mother's web. I have never seen more than seven, but one of Bonnet's captive specimens kept in ideal conditions with plenty of food laid 3,800 eggs distributed between fourteen egg-sacs ! This helps to illustrate the contribution that spiders can make to restore the balance of nature after a season of superabundant insect life.

Eggs hatch in about two weeks but the young spiders do not emerge until a week later after undergoing their first moult inside the egg-sac. In contrast to the young of *T. sisyphium* those of the present species disperse soon after emerging and start building their own little webs.

Under favourable conditions the period from egg to adult may be only three months during which time there are usually seven moults, although sometimes only six are needed by a male. As is usual amongst spiders the natural life of the male is shorter than that of the female and whereas most females will die as autumn approaches some survive the winter.

Theridion ovatum is perhaps our commonest Theridiid. She ranges from the Shetlands to the Scilly Isles amongst shrubs and low herbage where she spins her small inconspicuous web. So common is she that we can scarcely fail to find her if we sweep with a net in meadows amongst nettles, ragwort, grass and umbelliferous plants or beat the lower foliage of brambles over an umbrella. The search is easier still in July and August by which time she has enclosed herself in a curled leaf with her round blue egg-sac. Although bramble leaves are most commonly used, I have found her curling those of nettles, umbellifers, hazel, convolvulus, elm, maple, ash, beech, willow, oak, may and even gorse or grasses.

Theridion ovatum has three main colour forms. In one the abdomen is light cream or white, in the second there are two narrow bright red stripes passing down the upper sides of the abdomen and in the third the whole upper portion of the abdomen is bright red. Such cases of genetic polymorphism are interesting, since we know that sharply distinct forms can only co-exist in a population when there is a selective balance of advantages and disadvantages between them (P. M. Sheppard), yet in this case my observation of the spiders does not make this clear to me. I have made an extensive count of adult females in thirteen counties of England, Wales and Eire. I found percentages of my counts in different places varied from 51 to 87 for whites, from 10 to 44 for stripes and from 0 to 12 for reds, but as extensive collecting in seemingly identical situations in a single area provided still greater variations in counts made during the morning and afternoon of the same day, I came to the conclusion that these were unrelated to climate. My up to date count totals 4,225 specimens and the proportions are shown below:

WHITE		STRIPE		RED	
No.	%	No.	%	No.	%
2714	64.24	1316	31.15	195	4.61

In spite of her delicate appearance *T. ovatum* is an intrepid warrior. If an insect which comes to visit a flower happens to touch one of the gummy threads stretched beside it, the spider emerges from beneath the flower head and flings viscid threads over the insect regardless of its size. I have watched numerous battles in which the 5 mm. spider was victorious over flies many times her own bulk such as *Calliphora vomitaria* or *Eristalis tenax* and even small bees like *Halictus cylindricus*.

Sometimes a commotion in an adjoining web belonging to another spider attracts her attention and she then invades her neighbour's web by way of the connecting threads. Other species will do likewise and whilst two females of *Theridion pictum* were sparring over a struggling insect I watched an invading *T. ovatum* quietly run off with it !

Poaching of this sort is quite common and I have seen one sitting in the webs of a *Linyphia* on several occasions eating a fly with the less belligerent owner cowering, as it were, below her web or else completely absent. Poaching can lead to darker deeds and I once saw a *T. ovatum* eating a *T. sisyphium* in the latter's web.

Mating lasts about fifteen minutes in this species during which time each palp may be inserted alternately fifty or sixty times for periods of 5 to 12 seconds without any pause to recharge the palps with sperm. The bulb swells and collapses once during each insertion and the palp is chewed by the chelicerae after it is extracted.

In this species sperm induction takes place soon after the male has left the female and I have seen the process completed within seventeen minutes of their parting. He spins a few threads which he holds taut with his third pair of legs in the form of a small band. Hanging under this in an inverted position he heaves up and down a few times and then presses his abdomen against the little platform. A small drop of sperm appears on the lower surface which he absorbs through the web by reaching round to the upper surface of the platform with his palps.

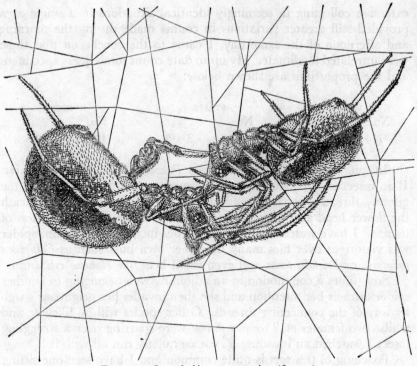

FIG. 97.   *Steatoda bipunctata* mating (6 mm.)

Each palp is inserted about thirteen times before the sperm has all been absorbed.

The mating takes place in late June or July soon after the spiders reach maturity and it is in July and August that the females curl the bramble leaves and enclose themselves in a loose silk cell in which they remain on guard over their blue spherical egg-sac. Often she will be found looking very emaciated in her self-made prison in October and frequently she dies at her post. It is not rare to see a neat hole drilled in the curled leaf by a bird to whom she and sometimes her eggs have fallen victims, but if she is the only victim the eggs are often eaten by an earwig once their mother is no longer there to protect them.

Steatoda bipunctata is a short-legged spider with a shiny abdomen suffused with paler brown markings. She may reach nearly 7 mm. in length. Her principal home is in webs spun beside windows in out-houses, attics and unswept rooms, but she extends into cellars and is

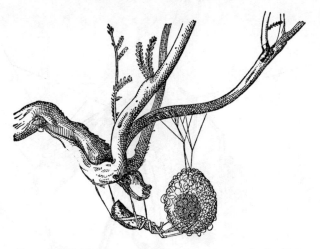

FIG. 98. *Episinus* (4 mm.) with her egg-sac under heather

found less commonly away from human habitations in hollow trees and on the trunks of trees with loose bark beneath which she can find a crevice in which to sit until an insect is caught in her snare. The shining waxy appearance of her abdomen provides a clue, I suspect, to her success in the arid conditions of a house or attic. She loses body moisture relatively slowly and I have found she can survive for months in a dry box or corked tube without water.

The male has large palpal organs which are waved up and down as he walks. He starts serenading the female as early as March by walking about in her web in a jerky manner and twitching his abdomen up and down. If she is in a receptive mood she will respond with a series of plucking movements which lead him to her, but he must first walk backwards and forwards spinning his special mating bridge before mating begins. If she retires to her tubular retreat, he will repeatedly follow her inside with vibrating legs and then come out again until at last he succeeds in enticing her to follow him on to the mating bridge. Here she hangs down slightly and he lunges at her with one palp until at last it is inserted (see fig. 97, p. 218). The normal practice would appear to be for him to insert each palp once for a considerable period, which may be an hour or two, with an interval in between during which he chews his palps and returns to her with renewed stridulatory movements of the abdomen. Both sexes may open their chelicerae during

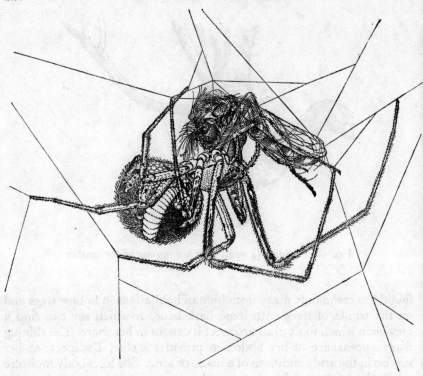

FIG. 99.   *Theridion tinctum* (3 mm.) eating a mosquito whilst herself being slowly eaten by the larva of an ichneumon, *Zatypota percontaria* Mull. (var. *gracilis* Holmg.)

the courtship but in common with other members of the family, the females show little hostility and indeed give much encouragement to their suitors.

The egg-sac is plastered up against the wall or bark adjoining the web and covered over with viscous threads. It contains about 100 to 150 pinkish brown eggs.

Spiders of the genus *Episinus* are so different from other members of the family in general appearance that there is no risk of failure to identify them provided their Theridiid characters have been recognised. The legs and abdomen are both long. The abdomen is rather flattened above. It is narrow in front and widening gradually to the posterior end where it is broad and abruptly truncated with a small conical prominence at each upper corner. The colour of the abdomen is dark

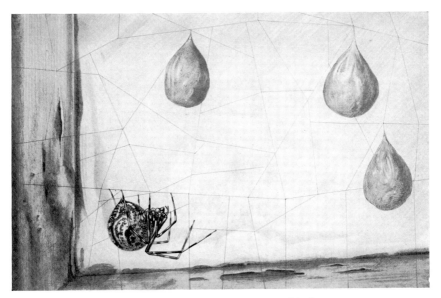

a. Theridion tepidariorum (7 mm.) in her snare with three egg-sacs.

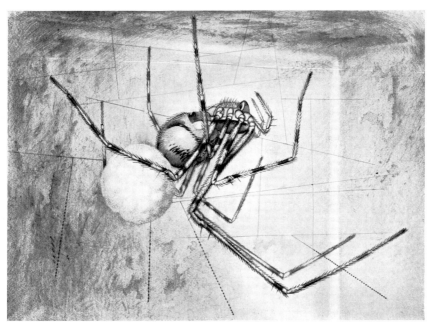

b. Nesticus cellulanus (6 mm.) in her snare with egg-sac attached to her spinnerets.

PLATE XXVII

a. Theridion sisyphium (4 mm.) hanging below her tent whilst feeding young from her mouth.

b. Enoplognatha thoracica (3 mm.) with four egg-sacs under a log.

PLATE XXVIII

yellow-brown with darker markings forming a pattern inside an irregular dark line passing round the margin of its upper surface.

The two species of *Episinus* are very similar in size and appearance so the sexual organs provide the only completely reliable character. Nevertheless *E. truncatus* usually has a dark cephalothorax with no pattern and uniformly dark femurs and tibiae on the first two pairs of legs. Both reach about 4.5 mm. and are to be found close to the ground amongst heather or grass. The webs are difficult to see and extremely simple in design. They are roughly in the form of an H. The spider hangs by her hind pair of legs from the ends of the cross-thread, with a thread also attached to it from her spinnerets. Her front legs are stretched downwards at an angle to hold the two nearly parallel threads which are attached to the ground. For a short distance above their point of attachment to the ground, these threads are gummy to entrap crawling insects like ants (Holm, 1938). The spiders will readily make these snares even in the confined space of a wide glass tube and it must be said that an *Episinus* will also attack and wrap an insect which happens to touch one of the upper threads (see Plate XXVI, p. 213).

Mating takes place in June and the male inserts a palp after no marked preliminary courtship. Each palp is inserted once for about two or three minutes and then they part (Locket, 1927).

The egg-sac is rounded or slightly pear-shaped and suspended by a few threads from a heather twig or from the lower side of a loose stone. Twenty five to fifty light brown eggs can be seen through their white silk covering outside which there is a layer of loosely spun coarse threads (see fig. 98, p. 219).

Spiders of many families can be found, especially in the spring and early summer, with a white larva attached to the upper side of their abdomens. This larva has hatched from an egg laid by a Pimpline ichneumon which first temporarily paralyzes the spider with its sting in order to do this. Like the old man of the sea, it cannot be dislodged

FIG. 100.   *Theridion bimaculatum* (3 mm.) with her huge bundle of eggs attached to her spinnerets

and for weeks the spider feeds as usual whilst the larva grows and finally kills her (see fig. 99, p. 220).

THE NESTICIDAE

The species included in this family have sometimes been attached to the Argiopidae and at other times to the Theridiidae. Their relationship to the Theridiidae is obvious both from a study of their structure and their habits but there are also divergencies which justify their status as a separate family. The male palp is one example (see fig. 3, p. 24).

Most of the foreign species live in caves or other shady situations and this applies to ours. *Nesticus cellulanus* is widespread in Britain and Europe and has recently established herself in the United States. *Eidmanella pallidus*, on the other hand, is common in the United States and has recently been found in Britain by A. F. Millidge under boulders in the Lake District and by A. M. Wild under flower pots in hothouses at Kew.

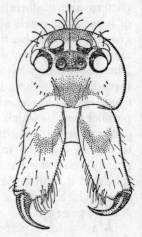

FIG. 101. *Nesticus* face

I have found *Nesticus* in caves, mines, cellars, drains, sewers and in thick vegetation amongst boulders in woods. Keeping her alive in captivity soon discloses her need for damp conditions and that as long as these are provided she can remain healthy in daylight although she seeks the shady side of her prison. Those which live in permanent darkness are paler than others collected from places where there is light.

Nesticus reaches a length of 6 mm. Her abdomen is globular and inclined to be shiny with markings of variable distinctness. Normally a light brown band passes down the centre flanked by paired grey patches. She need not be confused with *Eidmanella* which does not exceed 4 mm. and is of a uniform grey colour.

Nesticus spins webs very similar to those of the Theridiidae (*Steatoda* etc.). This takes the form of a loose platform beneath which straight or forked threads stretch down vertically or at an angle to the walls or floor. If fine powder is blown over these threads, it will be seen that there are short zones extending from their points of attachment to the wall which are studded with globules of gum. These entrap the crawling insects on which she mainly depends for food as in the case of several Theridiids. When we watch her in action we find that she resembles the Theridiidae and differs from the Argiopidae in her method of wrapping an insect. After casting threads over her victim with her hind legs she bites it several times, runs up and down from the insect to the web platform weaving a strong 'rope' and then hauls the trussed insect up behind her after biting it free from the gummy attachments. On arrival below the platform she turns round and casts more threads over it with her hind pair of legs in Theridiid style without twisting the insect round in the manner of an Argiopid.

When a courting male enters a female's web, he jerks it with alternate forward motions of his front legs and she responds with a similar 'code'. No hostility is shown by a receptive female and she assists him in the insertion of one of his palps. Gerhardt (1927) tells us that there are four to six insertions of each palp during which the bulb swells and collapses. They part after about five to ten minutes and he retires to a corner where he builds a small triangular web for sperm induction. The emboli are inserted alternately into the sperm drop for about seven minutes before the induction is completed.

Mature spiders can be found at most seasons and I have seen the females with their round white or pale yellow egg-sacs from June until late August during which season they probably lay three batches of eggs. The egg-sacs are carried by the females of *Nesticus* and *Eidmanella* attached to the spinnerets by a short length of thread (see Plate XXVII, p. 220).

CHAPTER 18

THE MIMETIDAE
Pirate Spiders

Our three species are small-moving hunchbacks varying from 4 to 6 mm. in length with globular abdomens prettily ornamented in black, red, yellow and white markings. The abdominal humps comprise a pair of tiny inconspicuous tubercles in the two commoner species, *Ero furcata* and *E. cambridgei,* but in *E. tuberculata* there are four of which one pair on the highest part of the abdomen are large and directed outwards.

All three are found amongst grass and heather but I have not found *E. tuberculata* further North than Cambridge and Flatford Mill whereas the others extend into Scotland.

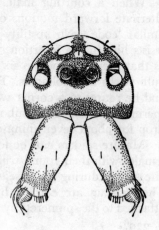

Fig. 102. *Ero* face

These pretty little spiders set me the same problem as *Scytodes*. How did these slow-moving spiders which seemed to spend their time hanging from a few criss-cross threads catch their prey? Several females of *Ero furcata* were collected one May and housed in glass-topped boxes where they were soon hanging from an occasional thread with legs drawn in and every appearance of sleep. The introduction of spring-tails, homopterous bugs, beetles, flies and micro-lepidoptera from the grass clumps in which I had found the spiders excited no notice. After negative results lasting for three days, I introduced a young Theridiid spider of about the same size which I had collected in the grass tufts. This was *Theridion ovatum* which is accustomed to catching insects considerably larger than itself by flinging gummy threads over them, so I awaited results with fear for the safety of my *Ero*. The *Theridion*

a. *Araneus marmoreus pyramidatus* (10 mm.)

b. *Meta segmentata* (8 mm.)

c. *Araneus alsine* (9 mm.)

d. *Argiope bruennichi* (14 mm.)

a. *and* b. by *Walter Murray*
c. *and* d. by *John Sankey*

PLATE 4

began climbing along *Ero's* threads and spinning fresh ones herself. A movement by *Ero* took place at once but it was so stealthy as to be scarcely noticeable. The long spiny front legs were gently unfurled until they were stretching downwards and forwards whilst the body was smoothly pivoted in the direction of *Theridion's* movements. Presently the *Theridion's* wanderings brought her to *Ero* who reached out towards her. Suddenly *Ero* drew the *Theridion* closer with her front legs whilst jerking her body forward to seize the femur of a front leg in her chelicerae. The attack was so rapid and unexpected that one might have thought a fraction of a second would elapse before the *Theridion* delivered a counter-attack, or tried to tear its leg free, but I was certainly unprepared for what did happen. In this I was reminded of the conversation opened by Inspector Gregory with Sherlock Homes in 'Silver Blaze':

"Is there any other point to which you would wish to draw my attention?"

"To the curious incident of the dog in the night-time!"

"The dog did nothing in the night-time."

"That was the curious incident," remarked Sherlock Holmes.

Here, too, the curious incident was that the *Theridion* did nothing. The faintest tremors passed down her legs and then all was still. The *Theridion* had been killed almost instantaneously by what must be a singularly strong poison.

An hour later the two spiders were sitting in exactly the same position and at the end of three hours the *Theridion* had the appearance of being sucked nearly dry whilst *Ero's* only movement had been to transfer her chelicerae to another leg.

In the same manner fell a series of other species of *Theridion* and of Linyphiid. Occasionally, and usually when the opponent was slightly bulkier than *Ero* herself, a leg was seized by the tibia and the spider was able to break away with the loss of a leg before the poison had time to spread.

Although the poison acts so rapidly when the femur of a leg is bitten I have noticed that the effect of a bite in the abdomen is quite different. A Linyphiid which had lain still for perhaps half a minute after being seized by the abdomen suddenly began to struggle violently. The *Ero* released her grip, bit a leg instead and the Linyphiid died almost instantaneously.

Wishing to see how *Ero* launched an attack in natural surroundings, I put one at the edge of a web built by *Theridion pictum*. *Ero* moved

WS—Q

along one of the threads with a stealth so cat-like that the *Theridion's* attention was not attracted. Presently she paused, bit away a few threads to provide a clear space in front of her and hung down in characteristic attitude with legs drawn in. Later on, as evening approached, she began gently jerking the web. Down bustled the plump little *Theridion* to her doom.

Our three species all specialise on other spiders and the likelihood that all the Mimetidae have acquired this strange piratical habit is supported by the knowledge that American relatives in the genus *Mimetus* invade the webs of other spiders.

Even the fiercest of pirates may be gentle in their home life and although *Ero* has no real home life she is not rough with her male. He approaches her beating a lively tattoo with alternated palps on the threads from which she is hanging and then proceeds to walk to and fro strengthening a special thread he has spun on to which he coaxes her with strong rhythmic swinging motions. Here she hangs down with her legs loosely bent and he glides towards her with one palp stretched out in front of him. His legs quiver as he inserts a palp and then, almost as soon as mating has started, he retreats about half an inch along his thread. There has just been time in a single second for the bulb to swell and collapse once. Now he moves forward again to insert the other outstretched palp for a similar period to the accompaniment of vibrating legs and that completes what is probably the shortest mating of any British spider.

He begins chewing his palps an hour or two later and then he constructs a Y-shaped frame, the upper angle of which is filled in with threads. Now he deposits a drop of sperm on the upper surface and retires to the lower surface where he reaches round with his palps in turn and dips his emboli into the drop.

At different times the species grouped in this family have been attached to the Linyphiidae and the Theridiidae so it is of some interest to link the mating habits with the spiders of these and other Argiopoid families. The special mating thread is shared with the Argiopidae and some Theridiidae, whilst the change of position during sperm induction, followed by direct insertion of the embolus into the drop, is foreign to these families but shared with some Linyphiid genera. (*Labulla, Linyphia, Tapinopa, Lepthyphantes*). The act of mating, with its insertion of each palp once and its short duration, relates it more closely to some of the Theridiids and Argiopids than to the Linyphiidae.

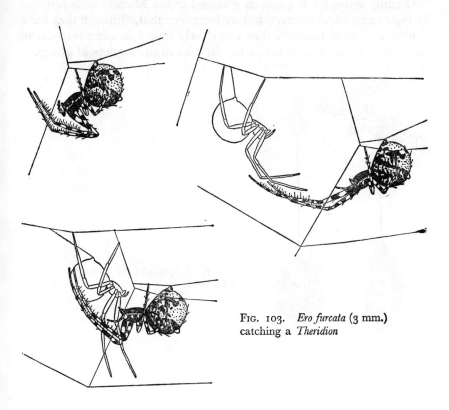

FIG. 103. *Ero furcata* (3 mm.) catching a *Theridion*

The females probably lay about three batches of eight or nine eggs during the summer months which are enclosed in translucent white silk through which they can be seen loosely clustered together. The white covering is enclosed in a trellis-work of gold wiry threads, and a long thick strand of gold silk attached to the apex of the egg-sac suspends it from a plant stem. The egg-sacs of *Ero furcata* and *E. cambridgei* are pear-shaped or nearly circular. These are easily distinguished from the fat cigar-shaped egg-sacs of *E. tuberculata*.

The long suspending thread has a protective value and the mother takes no further interest in her egg-sac once it is completed. Abandonment of the eggs is more in keeping with Linyphiid practice than with that of the Theridiidae where many of the mothers guard their eggs.

Family status for the spiders grouped in the Mimetidae is justified by their anatomical features, but we have seen that, although they have unique biological features, they are closely linked in some respects to one and in others to another of the families in the Argiopoid group.

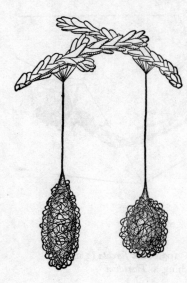

Fig. 104.   Egg-sacs of *Ero tuberculata* and *E. furcata*

CHAPTER 19

THE ARGIOPIDAE
Orb Web Builders

MOST people know the Garden or Diadem Spider (*Araneus diadematus*) whose white cross made her an object of veneration in the Middle Ages and whose portrait has appeared in more books than any other spider, sitting head downwards in the centre of her exquisite orb web. True to her name of Garden Spider I have found her not only in the garden of Buckingham Palace but even in my former roof-garden of fifteen square feet perched high above the street at Holland Park. Yet she is no narrow specialist on gardens for I have found her far from human habitation on heathland, in woods and on cliff faces ranging from the Scillies to the Shetland Islands (see Plate II, p. 65).

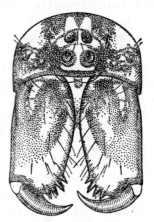

FIG. 105. *Araneus* face

When full-grown in August, after her eighth moult, the female may attain a length of 12 mm. and in this month the smaller male, who has only needed six moults, may be seen travelling in search of a female or courting her. Her first suitor may be fortunate in subduing her instinct to bite and enshroud an intruder like himself, but as the season proceeds each new mate — and none remain for more than one mating — finds it increasingly difficult to do this. The courtship can be a tedious affair to watch and one fraught with risk, which fortunately he is adept at dodging. Stealthily he advances tweaking her web only to be met by a fierce onslaught. Down he swings far out of range in an instant on a thread he had anchored some distance behind him, like a trapeze artist at a circus who decides at the last moment not to entrust himself to the partner who is waiting to grasp him. Over and over again he may have to repeat this stratagem but each time he climbs up and starts all over again with patient persistence.

In common with all other members of the Argiopidae- except *Argiope* herself, he seems to make his task more difficult by spinning a special mating thread on which he has to entice her by tugs and jerks. At last he succeeds in this design and she signals her submission by hanging motionless downwards. Now he bounds forward and jabs at her epigyne with one palp. When finally the palp is inserted after several fruitless attempts, he also hangs down and grasps her firmly with his legs. The palpal bulb remains inflated for about a quarter of a minute and then he withdraws and retires. Further courtship is necessary before he can insert the other palp and after he has succeeded in doing this he leaves her in order to re-charge his palps on a small triangular web before going in search of another female. The insertion of each palp once is not uncommon in this family but in some species two or more insertions are normal. (*A. cornutus, A. sclopetarius, A. redii, Mangora*, etc.).

In September or October the Garden Spider leaves her web to lay her yellow eggs under loose bark or on some surface close at hand. The number varies according to her size but a batch of three to eight hundred is not unusual. In this family they are firmly cemented together in one solid mass. This she provides with a dense cover of coarse yellow silk on to which she attaches a few loose splinters or other convenient detritus with her chelicerae before spinning a further cover of coarse threads which are firmly anchored to the surrounding surface. Her time is drawing to a close and she sits, emaciated, beside her egg-sac during her remaining weeks of life.

Winter is at hand and we see nothing of the babies until, perhaps, a warm sunny day in May when they cluster together in a neat round ball which quickly disintegrates into its component parts in response to any disturbance. These little spiderlings are yellow with a dark patch on the abdomen. They have moulted once in the egg-sac and are not yet ready to weave their snares or feed. One more moult and they go their various ways to set up homes of their own, but I believe the remainder of the summer is too short a period for them to complete their growth and that they will only be ready to lay their eggs when two years have elapsed since their mother did the same.

If we examine the web of a large Garden Spider we will notice that the 'centre' or hub comprises some meshed threads surrounded by a narrow spiral, circling round about six or seven times, which is known as the strengthening spiral. Outside this there is a small space called the free zone before the main spirals begin. These are laid across twenty-five to thirty-five radial threads connected with the hub and stretching outwards to stout threads forming an outer frame. All the threads are dry except for the main or viscid spirals which are studded with gum to catch the legs and bodies of insects. Some departure from concentricity is usually shown by the presence of twenty to thirty spiral threads above the hub compared with twenty-five to forty below it. I must emphasise, however, that figures of this kind vary considerably according to the situation of the web, the weather and the age of the spider. As autumn approaches the spider tends to spin fewer radial and spiral threads.

When the Garden Spider is not sitting head downwards in the centre of her web, her whereabouts can usually be traced by a stout signal thread passing from the hub to some nook amongst neighbouring leaves which she has shaped with a few stout threads. Here she sits holding the signal thread along which she rapidly lowers herself to the hub in response to the movements of an entangled insect. With eight legs outspread at the hub she can rapidly detect the direction of the vibrations and run along the appropriate radius to bite her victim. Having done this she starts on the enshrouding process which so many people have watched with mixed feelings, of admiration when the insect is a wasp and of sorrow when it is a defenceless butterfly. Rotating the insect with her third pair of legs she rapidly winds it up in a wide band of silk drawn from the spinnerets with her hind legs. Presently she pauses to bite the trussed insect again and then carries it to the hub, where she may stay to have her meal, or else travel onwards to her retreat by way of the signal thread.

Although *Meta segmentata* and *Tetragnatha* will sometimes fall vertically on a thread from their inclined webs to seize a passing fly, the Garden Spider shows little sign of dependence on her eyesight and seems to be under no handicap in the capture of her prey when I cover her eyes with paraffin wax. Nor do her eyes warn her to beware of insects decked in black and red or black and yellow colours. The full-grown Garden Spider is not intimidated by a yellow and black wasp (*Vespa*) but it is interesting to watch what happens to her and her relations when the warning is not of a sting but of an unpleasant flavour. Black and red Cinnabar and Burnet moths may be rejected after one touch when rejection is due to the taste-by-touch or chemotactic sense. More often they are bitten and tasted before rejection. Sometimes they are bitten and wrapped somewhat slowly, as though the spider has not got her heart in the job, then bitten again and finally cut out of the web and dropped below.

Many invertebrates, including Sciarid flies and most of the black or black and orange-legged Linyphiid spiders, are distasteful, and perhaps *Meta segmentata* rejects more of these after the first touch than any other Argiopid. *Zygiella* is another with a sensitive palate and on dozens of occasions I have watched her travelling unsteadily to a neighbouring surface on which to wipe away fluid oozing from her mouth after biting *Sciara thomae* or a black and orange Linyphiid.

Naturally the Argiopidae have some enemies like birds and hunting wasps which attack them in their webs, and in Brazil I have even watched Asilid flies (*Plesiomma fuliginosa*) reversing the usual role by seizing an *Araneus*, but for the most part the spiders have little trouble with entangled insects of suitable size, however formidable their armaments may be. Two of the commoner exceptions are *Halictus* bees and Reduviid bugs of the genus *Nabis*. The flexible abdomen of a *Halictus* will bend round to inflict a paralyzing sting whose effects last long enough for the bee to struggle to freedom. The *Nabis* will often manage to snap off one or more legs of an *Araneus* about its own size and to escape whilst the spider is nursing her wounds.

It is often wondered how an Argiopid spider can move so rapidly in her own snare and avoid sticking to her own viscid spirals. Like other web-builders she has a third unpaired tarsal claw shaped like a hook and in this family it is associated with a number of stiff serrated bristles which help to direct the threads into the hook. This is then twisted at an angle to provide a firm grip. Her legs do not stick to her own threads because of a coating of oil, but if we dip her legs in ether she does so at once.

The more closely we examine one of these webs the more inclined we are to use superlatives in describing its delicate beauty, its triumph of engineering artistry, its economy of design and its ingenuity (see Plate XXIX, p. 240). If intelligence were used during her nightly task of building one with fresh gum and new threads, it would have to be of a very high order, so it is of special interest to learn how she sets about her task and whether her result is achieved by reasoning power or blind automation.

'The spinning of an orb-web', says T. H. Savory (1952), 'is a spectacle to be watched and watched and watched'. He is right. For my part I have been lazy enough only to watch, so I have to depend for some details largely on others like R. W. G. Hingston, H. Wiehle, H. Peters and A. Tilquin, whose careful observations in other countries have been usefully summarised in Savory's book on 'The Spider's Web'. There are, of course, variations in the procedure, not all of which are yet fully understood, but, confining ourselves to generalised outlines, we can recognise a number of constructional phases.

1. *The Bridge Line.* The starting point is a bridge line from which the web will be suspended. This line can be laid in more than one way. An *Araneus umbraticus,* for instance, whose web I have completely destroyed, emerges from a crevice in the eaves of my house soon after nightfall and walks along the edge of one of the tiles trailing an anchored thread before fastening it a few inches further on. This is not a method which *A. diadematus* could use for bridging the small stream in my garden and here I have lain in wait to see her standing with abdomen raised to the wind squeezing out a thread which is wafted across the space until it comes to rest on a plant the other side. Now she turns round to face her bridge line which she tugs, as though to test its security, before making a crossing herself. Her journey is stranger than that of any circus tight-rope walker because this first thread may be only a temporary bridge which she breaks and rolls up in front of her as she walks along it whilst the real bridge line is trailed behind her. In other words *A. diadematus* is suspended in mid-air between the temporary and permanent bridge lines.

A third method which I have seen adopted by *Meta segmentata* is for the spider to drop a short distance on a thick thread whilst from another pair of spinnerets a fine thread is wafted outwards or upwards in air currents until it finds an anchorage. Then she swarms up her rope and attends to the temporary gossamer bridge as before.

Perhaps all three methods of bridge-building may be employed by a single species in differing circumstances but only when the first method is used does the spider determine the direction in which her web will be slung. If I destroy the web of my *A. diadematus* day after day, I soon discover that bridging the stream is a fortuitous occurrence which takes place only when the air-currents happen to waft the thread in that particular direction.

The bridge-line is the first foundation and the spider usually strengthens it by passing to and fro with additional threads which coalesce with it.

2. *The First Fork.* Having watched my *A. umbraticus* lay down and pass to and fro along the bridge line, I saw her drop from a central point to the twig of a rose bush three feet below it and fasten a tightly stretched thread. Shining my torch up this vertical thread I found it was not attached to the bridge line at a single point but by a fork which joined it near each end. This mysterious result was explained at my next night's vigil after again destroying the entire web. When she had made her bridge-line she trailed another and separate thread which drooped just below it and was attached to the bridge-line at its ends. It was from this second sagging horizontal line that she had descended on a vertical thread. By pulling this taut the line had been pulled downwards at its centre to form two sides of a triangle whose third side was completed by the horizontal bridge-line.

The spider had dropped from a point on the horizontal line near its centre and it is worth while pausing to find an explanation for the selection of this central point because the consequences have an important effect on the design of the web. Spiders are extremely sensitive to the tension of their threads and Savory has, I think rightly, suggested that it is the central point of the thread where she will encounter the symmetry of forces which provides the stimulus for her to drop. The importance of the result lies in the fact that the apex of this inverted triangle becomes the centre of the finished web — the hub — whilst the two sides and the single thread passing downwards from the apex become the first three radii (the primary radii).

3. *The Frame.* There are variations at every stage in web construction but in my story I will restrict myself to what appear to be the basic principles of construction (see fig. 106, p. 235).

Concentrating on the upper segment within the triangle, she walks up one of the radii from the hub (H) dragging a thread which is fastened at a point F intermediate between the hub and the bridge-line. Reversing her direction she attaches a new thread F_1 to the one she has just spun which she carries down to the hub and up the other primary radius to F_2 where it is hauled tight and fastened. F_2 is now a frame thread whilst F_1 H becomes a secondary radius from the frame to the hub.

In the simplest web-skeleton the frame would be a triangle if she now repeats the same manoeuvre in the other two segments, and so it may be, but more commonly the frame is a polygon as a result of extra frame threads being spun during stage 2 or 3.

4. *The Radial Threads.* A few primary and secondary radii have

been laid down in stages 2 and 3 but by the time the tertiary radii have all been spun in stage 4 there may be one to four dozen according to the custom of the species. The radii are not laid down in any special order. The spider stretches her front legs out laterally when she is at the hub and any wide space between radii will provide the stimulus to move in that direction. Out she runs along a radius trailing a thread until the frame is reached. Here she moves along the frame thread for a fixed number of steps and then fastens the thread and moves back to the centre along this new radius, sometimes reinforcing it as she goes.

With repetitions of this process the empty spaces are filled and we are left with a number of threads radiating out from the centre with a remarkably consistent angle between each.

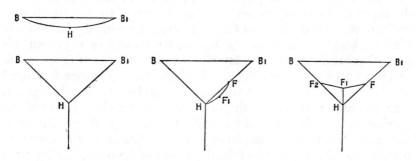

FIG. 106.   The start of an orb web

5. *The Strengthening Spirals.* The centre of the orb began as the point from which three threads diverged. Since then it has become a rough platform due to the radial threads not all being attached to the central point exactly and to some lateral connecting threads having been laid down as she swivelled round to reverse her direction. Now she stands on this platform, feels the radii with her hind legs and, with head inwards, revolves. Each radius is touched with her spinnerets and after a few turns a close set spiral has been spun. These are known as the strengthening spirals.

6. *The Temporary Spirals.* Now she moves outwards and starts weaving a fresh set of spirals, leaving a small space between the end of the strengthening spirals and the beginning of this new set. She walks across the radii on a curved path, trailing a thread which is fastened to each radius in turn. When she is just completing the first circuit, those legs directed towards the hub touch the thread laid down

on the first circuit and she moves outwards with the result that the thread she is trailing does not take the form of a closed circle or series of circles but of one continuous spiral. As she works her way further and further from the centre the distance between the radii she is crossing naturally gets greater and she has to use the spiral of her previous circuit not only as a point of measurement but also as a bridge to cross from radius to radius.

When a certain distance is reached between the radii she stops before the frame threads are reached.

7. *The Viscid Spirals.* Now she pauses for a short time and then turns, back on her tracks and begins spiralling *inwards* towards the centre, using a different kind of silk which, for the first time, is coated with gum. The temporary spiral acts as a bridge and support and is destroyed in the course of her rounds. The new thread is attached to one radius, carried across to the next, stretched with the help of one hind leg and then fastened. C. Warburton showed in 1890 that this stretching breaks up the thin layer of gum into a series of drops which under a microscope gives the viscid spirals the appearance of a bead necklace. Once one circuit has been made, all further threads are fixed after measuring with a leg the distance from the viscid spiral of the previous circuit. Round and round she travels at speed until she nears the centre, where she stops, leaving a space known as the free zone between the viscid spirals and the dry spirals of the strengthening zone.

These are the main operations in the construction of the orb snare but there are still important details to attend to before her masterpiece is complete, like tidying up her hub, building her retreat and adding embellishments, like signatures, which are peculiar to each species.

Having outlined the spider's mode of construction, we now turn to the problem of deciding whether her actions are governed by instinct or intelligence.

"It would be very difficult", wrote Dale Collins, "to write a novel with the worm as hero and to get within his walls of pink skin to learn what passed there." Although we are within the walls of our own pink skins we have not even succeeded in learning all that goes on in our brains and nervous systems, but, apart from that, it would be difficult to write a readable book about human beings if we attempted to analyse their behaviour at every step and to employ the specialised language of 'tropisms', 'taxis', 'reflexes', 'drives', 'kineses' etc. My failure to analyse or resort to these terms as I go along may have led me into the trap of seeming to impute human reactions or motives to spiders, so

I should now like to provide a corrective by explaining fairly briefly what I really think about the instincts and reasoning powers of spiders.

Many spiders abandon their eggs or die before they hatch so we are safe in assuming that they receive no parental instruction. If we take the Garden Spider as an example, the young hatch, scatter and build their first webs without any instruction from their already dead mother, so we can hardly suppose that either the act or the technique is the result of individual learning. Each is immediately capable of spinning an orb web as perfect and as complicated as that of its mother, so here again we can scarcely credit them with individual thought involving intelligence. The webs may not be quite identical with those of their mother and, indeed, they may be more nearly perfect than hers. In some species they are more symmetrical and less specialised, thereby indicating the inheritance of their design from some far distant ancestor. The specialised missing segment of the adult *Zygiella's* web, for instance, is not missing in the baby's early webs whilst the young *Pachygnatha* reverts to the orb web habit abandoned completely by the adults.

Without education the Argiopid spiders gain highest marks for the perfection of their orb webs, but we must still ask ourselves whether these are to any extent the product of a calculating brain which estimates areas, angles, geometrical curves and tensions, or the result of some unswerving inborn laws of procedure which the spiders blindly carry out in total ignorance of purpose.

H. Fabre and R. W. G. Hingston were amongst the earlier seekers for evidence of reasoning on the part of French and Indian Argiopid spiders respectively, and I have since used British spiders to check some of their experiments. My search, like theirs, was in vain and, although my results have not been quite so clear-cut, two examples from watching *Araneus umbraticus* can be mentioned.

The temporary spirals which bridge the radii serve two important purposes. They brace the elastic radii which would otherwise sway awkwardly out of position under the weight of the spider and they enable her to cross easily from one radius to the next as she rapidly circles the web laying down the gummy spirals. If we gently remove these temporary spirals with a pair of scissors without disturbing her, will she spin fresh ones or will she struggle on against the serious difficulties we have created for her ? The answer is that she is totally incapable of adjusting herself to this unusual state of affairs. Instead of spinning fresh temporary spirals in a minute or two before starting to lay down the viscid spirals, she may walk all the way along a sagging radius to the hub before meeting a bridge and then she travels back again to the circumference along the next radius, trailing far too long a thread to span the short distance between the two. Round she circles on her set task, laboriously laying down long lengths of gummy spirals, none of which are stretched tight enough to brace the web. On and on she circles leaving a loose series of spirals which flap and coalesce in the slightest breeze or even under their own weight. The result is a disastrous and useless caricature.

Bearing in mind the manner in which *Araneus* measures the distance from the last spiral with her front legs before attaching the next one to a radius, we may wonder what she will do if we cut away one or several spirals over a small section where they bridge, say, three or four radii. If we are hoping for a glimmer of intelligent improvisation we shall be disappointed. Having stretched in vain for a spiral at the usual distance she will travel outwards as far as is necessary and then measure her new points of attachment from there. Symmetry has vanished and perfection has been lost as easily as that.

Introduce difficulties and the spider seems to be incapable of overcoming them, so what can we think but that the spider has a wonderful inborn mechanical rhythm carrying her blindly through a series of operations in a fixed and unalterable order.

The nightly rhythm has been set in motion in response to a weather condition like the fall of darkness (a tropism), but once that rhythm has been interfered with the whole chain of actions is disturbed because the spider can only continue where she left off. She cannot go back to repair an earlier link in the series of operations.

Fabre once wrote: "Neither weavers or spinners know how to repair their work. These wonderful manufacturers of silk-stuffs lack the least glimmer of that sacred lamp, reason, which enables the stupidest of darning women to mend the heel of an old stocking." But let me try to balance this with a compensating paragraph from Hingston's writing: "Instinct, without question, is the dominating force that controls the wonderful activities of spiders. This force is innate and automatic. It is born with the creature as part of its nature. The animal possesses no choice with respect to it, but must obey its imperious demands. It is a force of amazing perfection and performs acts of such precision that they sometimes seem to surpass intelligence."

If we pursue the behaviour of an *Araneus* after the web is completed, we encounter another series of instinctive actions set in motion by the vibrations of an entangled fly. Here again there is a fixed order with each link in the chain giving rise to the next. H. Peters (1933) has made an analysis along the following lines in Germany:

1. Movement towards the insect. Here the spider's response is set in motion through her tactile sense by vibrations and a change in the tension of the web.
2. The long bite. In response to the continued vibrations of an insect the spider bites it.
3. Wrapping. In response to biting and touching the insect with her palps and legs, the insect is wrapped in silk. Here I think that perhaps three senses are involved, the chemotactic sense and those of touch and taste.
4. The short bite. Here Peters suggests that the stimulus is a tactile one received from the silk threads with which the insect is now enswathed.
5. Carrying the insect. The insect is then transported to the spider's retreat, the stimulus being perhaps one of taste.

Variations in habit, for which we should search in our quest for the glimmerings of intelligence, are noticeable in the way in which a large insect is attached to the spider's spinnerets for transport to the retreat whilst a small insect is carried more simply in the chelicerae and palps. Peters has shown by accurate measurements that weight is the determining factor, a discovery that does not necessarily eliminate intelligence — at least I hope not because if my own luggage is beyond a certain weight I seek the help of a porter.

It is of interest to mention in the course of our search for exceptions to the immutability of chain instincts that Peters found he could break into the middle of the series I have outlined above. An *Araneus* will seize a struggling insect from a pair of forceps and bite it (stage 2). A freshly killed fly which is touched gently against her palps will be wrapped without biting (stage 3). A wrapped fly submitted in the same way is bitten (stage 4) and carried home.

Several instances have been recorded of Argiopid spiders 'cleverly' weighting the downwardly directed frame threads with small pebbles. I once came on an instance myself and was duly impressed until I had destroyed the web and satisfied myself that this was a chance occurrence and not the individual spider's custom. I concluded that frame threads had been fastened to small pebbles on the ground which were lifted later by tensions set up in other parts of the web perhaps after a period of days or weeks when the frame threads had lost some of their elasticity.

Although the general web design of each Argiopid species is remarkably constant she can make adjustments to suit the area within which it has to be spun. Our small vivid green *Araneus cucurbitinus*, for instance, can spin a small horizontal web in the hollow of a lilac leaf in which I have seen as few as one spiral on one side and six on the other, or she can spin a much larger vertical web on a yew hedge where I have counted seventeen spirals above and twenty-three below (see Plate XXXI, p. 256).

Many of us lose some of our reasoning faculties when we get very old and it is noticeable that Argiopid spiders often lose some of their instinctive skill at web-building with the approach of death. Webs tend to become smaller with fewer radii and spirals. Sometimes they are untidy and defective. In extreme cases I have found webs of *Zygiella x-notata* with gummy radii and no spirals.

I have often wondered if spiders posseseed a sense of direction involving memory. Normally they find their way back to their retreats with the utmost ease but sometimes they are guided by a trailed or specially spun thread. *Zygiella*, for instance, has a thread direct from her retreat to the hub. Having enticed several of them to the centre, I have cut this signal thread with scissors and, after a pause, they have invariably run rapidly up one of the two adjacent radii and then along the horizontal frame threads to their retreat. On rare occasions the signal thread is horizontal or even directed downwards which shows that it is not merely a question of the spider running upwards.

Nevertheless, evidence of this kind has to be treated with caution. M. Holzapfel (1933) of Bern neatly showed that *Agelena* finds her way home on her sheet web by following the line of greatest tension. This postulates no more than a delicate sense of touch and a finely developed muscular sense.

Are there no signs of any memory at all?

When an insect enters the web of an *Araneus diadematus* whilst she is engaged eating another insect of reasonable proportions, she leaves her meal to wrap up the new intruder. Having done this she leaves it where it is and goes back to her meal. Does this imply memory? Or, an hour later perhaps, when the meal is completed and she then returns to the second insect? Here I make no suggestion that a sense of direction is involved because the spider can locate a motionless object by the effect of its weight on the thread tensions (and sometimes

PLATE XXIX. Web of *Araneus diadematus*.

E. A. Robins

PLATE XXX. *Argiope bruennichi* (14 mm.) a recent addition to our fauna.

the direction is confirmed by the spider tugging at the threads before moving straight to it).

When Bonnet (1947) was daily feeding a large number of captive *Dolomedes* they accepted flies held in his forceps. Before long he found that the spiders came to associate the raising of the lid of the jar with the presentation of a fly and moved forward in readiness. Bonnet suggested that this provided an example of memory employed by spiders. Savory (1949), however, claims it as 'an excellent example of conditioned reflexes'. By this he means that the spider's pounce, originally a response to the buzzing of a fly, was conditioned to the opening of the jar.

Anything which starts by appearing to be memory similar to our own seems capable of being explained away in some other manner, but if we accept Savory's interpretation we should still notice that something parallel with learning can develop under the rigid regime of reflexes, tropisms and instinctive behaviour since a conditioned reflex is in a sense equivalent to a simple form of memory.

Although spiders speak no language they can transmit and seem able to distinguish certain signals. Like their other skills these are in-born without any need for learning during their own lifetimes. One example is provided by violent jerks of the legs and bodies both in web-building and hunting spiders in situations where they are on the defensive and will attack if the menace does not pass. An *Araneus diadematus* introduced into another spider's web will usually retire in response to violent jerks of the web by the rightful owner. These defensive jerks are brought about by a flexion of the leg muscles in automatic response to various types of stimuli which a human being would group together under the heading of menace. Related to this reflex action would be many others of a similar nature including the rapid vibration of the entire web until she herself becomes an indistinct blur. This defensive action may be set up in response to rough contact with her web or even our passage close to her web coming within her faulty range of vision.

Menace or disturbance of a severe nature will sometimes cause spiders to 'feign death' and, by so doing, to become less conspicuous. Two good examples of this cataleptic reflex are provided by *Araneus umbraticus* and *Floronia bucculenta*. Both drop like stones from their webs on the ends of threads and lie on the ground with legs all tucked in for a period of minutes before climbing back. These spiders are not in a complete state of catalepsis although it may be quite difficult to rouse

WS—R

the *Araneus* into activity. The *Araneus* is dark brown or black and she is hard to see on the ground. The *Floronia* is whitish and would be conspicuous but for the fact that she instantaneously takes on a brownish colour through the muscular contraction of the white-pigmented cells (see p. 264).

Courtship has also produced its signals to the female by the less powerful male. Stimulus through the male's chemotactic senses on coming in contact with a female's web causes him to respond by gently vibrating his legs and body. This transmits vibrations along the threads to the female and it is interesting to find that these vibrations yield a response through the female's tactile senses different from that of a struggling insect's vibrations. His vibrations stimulate the female's sexual instincts. Those of the struggling insects set in train her preying mechanism, the response to the rapid vibrations of a buzzing fly being more intense than to the more laboured twisting of a caterpillar.

These selected examples of spider behaviour may have helped to clear our thoughts and to correct the naturally anthropomorphic angle from which we start to view them. The time has now come to attempt a reconstruction of events and to pronounce a verdict. I find myself singularly ill-equipped to tackle a task like this in a field which extends into so many branches of science outside my own sphere of knowledge and is yet at the same time so specialised, and I approach the task with the utmost humility.

In the beginning the behaviour of plants and animals was influenced no doubt by simple reflex actions and automatic tropistic responses to physical conditions. Later, by the process of natural selection, these developed into series of adaptive behaviours which were inherited and filed, as it were, in the central nervous system for automatic release in response to the right environmental situations or stimuli. Here, in this world of twilight, there was no reasoning mind at work and this did not appear until hundreds of millions of years later — until after, perhaps, the animal kingdom had diverged into two great branches comprising the vertebrate and invertebrate forms.

If we think in terms of two separate and diverging branches of evolution and believe that intelligence involving conscious reasoning did not arise in the vertebrate branch until after the split, we are left with a choice between the conclusion that it developed independently in the invertebrate branch or else, as I believe, that it has never developed there at all.

Reluctantly I favour the view that spiders are incapable of conscious reasoning. Although in some measure they are capable of profiting by experience. I believe they live in a different psychological world where evolution has provided them with an amazing array of automatic rules of behaviour to cope effectively, and indeed brilliantly, with all the usual sets of circumstances they are likely to encounter in the course of their lives. The solutions to problems with which they are confronted are often similar to those which a reasoning mind would provide and this is what makes it so difficult to accept easily that spiders have no intelligence whatever in the sense that we use that word. Yet that is my conclusion although I do not reject the probability that they possess a limited ability to learn or at least something equivalent in its effect to learning.

The miracle of an orb web in an unreasoning world may seem difficult to explain, but I can suggest in outline some of the steps in its evolution. (Bristowe, 1930, 1941).

The first use to which silk was put by spiders was as a protective covering for the eggs. The eggs were delicate morsels for other invertebrates so the species in which the mother remained on guard or concealed them effectively was more likely to survive than one which neglected them. In many cases the spider hid the eggs and herself in some hole in the ground or in a closed silk cell. In other cases she sat beside the egg-sac which was suspended amongst vegetation. In my view these two alternative habits gave rise to two different lines of snare-development. In both cases I suggest that the egg-sac was the hub, as it were, round which the early snares arose.

The early spiders were hunters, but once eggs were laid they settled down to guard them. Anchor threads, or threads which the spider had trailed on brief excursions, gave warning of approaching insects and in time became a permanent feature which was an advantage in the capture of insects.

Some ground-living cell-builders have remained cell-builders (*Clubiona*). Others lined holes in the ground or extended these holes or cells into tubes either with an open entrance or with a hinged trapdoor. Threads sometimes radiated outwards which represented either an extension of the tube lining to hold the rim in place or else stray drag-line threads. In any event they would tend to be arranged evenly round the tube entrance like those of *Segestria* (see Plate IX, p. 112). In others the tube lining extended into a circular collar round the entrance, as in *Amaurobius*, where the collar's development by means of accumulated drag-lines is noticeable as the summer progresses (see

Plate IIIb, p. 80). The asymmetrical extension of the collar into a flat sheet like that we know in the Agelenidae and in foreign Lycosidae and Dipluridae shows that this line of development has occurred several times in different families. In these spiders the hub is the tubular retreat and it should be specially noticed that the eggs are stored in this, (never in the sheet itself), and that the spiders move in an erect position on the upper surface of the sheet.

Turn now to the spiders which hunted on plants and slung their egg-sacs amongst the vegetation. Supporting threads together with accidental drag-lines acted as a warning of approaching prey or enemies. By degrees additional threads around the egg-sacs formed a snare not unlike that of a *Theridion* in superficial appearance. The spider's movements amongst this scaffolding with a drag-line trailed behind her could form a rough platform in course of time not unlike that independently arrived at by some Theridiids, Pholcids and Linyphiids. In contrast to the other line of development it should be noticed that here the hub is in the centre of the web with the spider living at that point, unless she has made a retreat as a secondary protective adaptation, that the egg-sacs are often placed in the centre of the web in their original situation and that the spiders move in an inverted position, even where a dense sheet has developed.

Some foreign Argiopidae live in the centre of their webs and place their egg-sacs there. Some build horizontal sheets in which the meshes are evenly spun instead of being haphazard as in the Linyphiidae. In broad terms, therefore, a likely reconstruction of developments starts from threads radiating outwards from an egg-sac which were subsequently crossed by others coated with gum. These had to be renewed daily in order to fulfil their purpose and a snare in which they were evenly spaced would clearly be more advantageous than one in which clusters of threads and wide gaps were present.

I have said much about the Garden Spider (*Araneus diadematus*) and only mentioned other orb-weavers in passing, so it is time to speak about some of them.

The abdomen of *Araneus diadematus* is much broader in front than behind and the shoulders sometimes bear the suspicion of a prominence on each side which is strongly developed into a large tubercle on each shoulder of three of our species. The only common one is *A. gibbosus* which lives amongst the foliage of trees. *A. angulatus* is found more rarely in similar situations whilst the very rare *A. bituberculatus* lives on heather at Burnham Beeches.

There are only two species whose markings could lead to confusion with the Garden Spider. These are *A. quadratus* and *A. marmoreus*. Seen from above *A. quadratus* is so round that she has no angular shoulders and the most conspicuous markings are four large white spots forming a quadrangle whilst the sinuous dark bands tapering backwards to the spinnerets are less noticeable in this species than in *A. diadematus*. *A. quadratus* often attains 15 mm. or more in length and is certainly our heaviest as well as one of our most handsome spiders. She can be pale greenish yellow, rust red or dark brown and I have found that one which is pale greenish yellow will change to a dark brown shade in the course of a few days if confined in a dry box. A large specimen will lay more than nine hundred eggs which weigh twice as much as she does after this operation is completed. This I have claimed as a record in child-birth. She lives chiefly on heather, herbs or brambles and differs from *A. diadematus* in constructing a strong silk tent as a retreat.

Araneus marmoreus has markings resembling those of *A. quadratus* but her shape approaches that of *A. diadematus* more closely. From both she can be distinguished by a narrow dark line down the centre of the cephalothorax. This species builds her web amongst herbs in damp swampy situations and sits under a curled leaf lined with silk.

The really remarkable thing about this widespread Continental species is that until a few years ago no one had found it in Britain, although the *pyramidatus* form is not uncommon and has been recorded for hundreds of years. We now know that *A. marmoreus* lives here as well, but I have found only four specimens whilst seeing one hundred and sixty *A. marmoreus pyramidatus* at Ardingly, Sussex. The handsome *pyramidatus* form is so different in appearance that she looks like a distinct species with her pale yellow body, ornamented with an area of dark brown in the rear half tapering backwards to the spinnerets (see Plate 4, p. 224).

A much commoner species in the rushes and rank herbage in marshy ground is *A. cornutus* (see Plate XXIV, p. 206). She has a series of wide broken brown bars on an ivory background and lies concealed in a silk cell built in the head of a plant. Once when I disturbed one, I saw her drop on a thread into the water below and then deliberately climb down a plant stem under the surface. Here she remained for fully a minute before climbing back, hand over hand, up her thread.

The larger and darker *Araneus sclopetarius* with white lines faintly outlining a leaf pattern also lives near water but is specially common on bridges crossing rivers, or on fences alongside them. She reaches up to 14 mm. in length and her tendency to flatness of body is reminiscent of the still flatter and darker *A. umbraticus* of our garden outhouses and fences.

The five species I have just mentioned are all found at Flatford Mill and I was put on my mettle by Miss Jennifer Walker when visiting the naturalists' Field Centre there. After telling her it was true I had eaten toasted 'bird-eating' spiders in Siam, where they were relished by the Laos, she invited me to sample a fat *Araneus*. After I had declined, she shamed me by trying one herself. By the end of the afternoon we had sampled five species of spider, including *Agelena*, and we both agreed that *Araneus quadratus*, with a slightly nutty flavour, was the best.

In the two families Argiopidae and Tetragnathidae we have more than forty builders of orb-webs and yet, if size, position, and season are used to reinforce differences in design, I can be tolerably sure of identifying the adults of most species by their webs without seeing the spiders themselves.

Looking closely at that orb web spun across one corner of the window frame a missing segment will be noticed with a stout signal thread passing up the centre from the hub to a tubular retreat, from the backdoor of which the owner can back to safety in case of need. This little spider with the grey leaf pattern on her back is *Zygiella x-notata*. This design is peculiar to our three species of *Zygiella* and if a web like this is seen on shrubs far distant from houses it belongs to *Z. atrica*, or one built by an adult in woods in early or middle summer may be the rare *Z. stroemi*. Sometimes the missing segment is bridged by spirals — usually in late summer or when the signal thread slants at a greater angle than usual from the vertical — but even in these cases the webs are easy to distinguish. There is something about the ovally stretched hub, the thick signal threads and the arrangement of the spirals in the lower part of the web which make them unmistakable.

An orb web will often be seen on sheds or on trees with loose bark in which there are many more spirals above the hub than below it. There is no signal thread and no clue as to the whereabouts of the owner. This belongs to *Araneus umbraticus* whose dark brown or almost black flattened body is well adapted to squeeze into narrow crevices. When she is young she will readily respond to an insect's struggles, but as she grows older she becomes progressively more shy of daylight and refuses to emerge until after dark. This change in habit may be cor-related with a change in food supply. The adult's web is extremely elastic and strong and is fully capable of holding a large night-flying moth. Within an hour of nightfall, the spider is building a new web ready for the night harvest on which she chiefly depends.

By way of contrast, we have species like *Zilla diodea* and *Mangora acalypha*, who spend all their days at the centre of almost perfectly concentric webs spun on heather clumps. In these webs there may be about eleven strengthening spirals, between forty and fifty radii, and about thirty-five closely spaced spirals above and below the hub.

This is a larger number of strengthening spirals and radii than in other species except for the funny little hunch-backed *Cyclosa conica* (see Plate XXIV, p. 205) who spins her webs on shrubs and adds a distinctive band of silk above and below the hub known as the stabilimentum. The remnants of feasts and small vegetable fragments spun into the stabilimentum give it a dark appearance like a narrow twig whose two halves appear to be almost joined when she sits inconspicuously between them with her legs drawn in.

Araneus adiantus is another who sits at the centre of her concentric web amongst heather or grass, but she has fewer strengthening spirals and radii and she usually covers her hub with a fine platform of white silk. In her web the free zone separating the two types of spiral is indistinct, but this is not the case in *A. redii* which is the only other *Araneus* to spin this white platform, sometimes at the hub and at others on an adjoining heather shoot.

Hubs with a circular open space at the centre belong either to *Tetragantha* or *Meta*. The web of a *Tetragnatha* is more open in design, constructed of finer threads and mainly restricted to marshy ground. Although no precise mathematical formula is reliable, it may be mentioned for comparison with *Zilla* and *Mangora* that a *Meta* web usually has only three strengthening spirals and may have only seven to twenty viscid spirals above with twelve to thirty below the hub. The web is often inclined with a signal thread passing to her station under a leaf.

I believe the rare *Araneus alsine* may also have an open hub. This glorious shining orange red spider adorned with a multitude of light spots builds a web of a stronger texture, almost at ground level, and in the shade of rank weeds growing on damp wasteland (see Plate 4, p. 224). She also differs from *Meta* in usually having five strengthening spirals and in building a retreat consisting of a silk lining to a curled leaf.

Roughly speaking it could be said that the small species reach

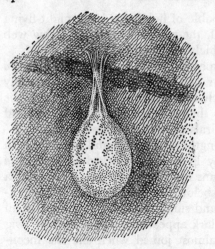

Fig. 107.   Egg-sac of *Meta menardi*

maturity in early summer and the large bulky ones in late summer, but *Meta segmentata* is remarkable in doing both. The spring generation is known as *M. segmentata mengei* on account of small structural differences. The female reaches only 5 mm. compared with up to 8 mm. in the autumn brood.

Meta segmentata is a slimmer and longer-legged spider than the typical *Araneus*, with variable colouring and pattern (see Plate 4, p. 224). She may be as pale as marble or else tinted with yellow or reddish brown. She is undoubtedly our commonest Argiopid from the Orkneys to the Scillies and pitches her inclined web almost everywhere on bushes and low plants. In shadier situations under overhanging banks or in the corners of damp outhouses her place is taken by the darker and larger *M. merianae*. Moving into the deeper gloom of cellars and caves, we meet with the shinier-bodied 13 mm. *M. menardi* (see Plate XXXI, p. 256), whose large pear-shaped white egg-sacs are suspended from the roof on a narrow silken stalk. In recent years a fourth species, *M. bourneti*, has been found in damp culverts and tunnels which can only be distinguished from *M. menardi* under a microscope by the wider epigyne of the female and the shape of the male's palpal paracymbium.

The mating habits of *Meta segmentata* deserve description, both on account of their departure from what is normal in the family and for their great interest.

In April or May and again in September a male will be found lurking motionless in the outskirts of every female's web. She is probably sitting in the centre, but you can watch him for hours without seeing either of them stir. The signal for courtship to begin is given, strangely enough, by a third party, an insect, blundering into the web. The female drops down to it, bites it and begins wrapping it in silk whilst the male is approaching in more leisurely fashion. A chain of events which lead to mating has now begun.

Gently shaking the web and jerking his abdomen slightly he advances with the fly separating him from her. When he is within reach, he tickles her with outstretched front legs. They spar and she retreats. Here it may be as well to mention that he is nearly as large as she is and that his spiny front legs are both longer and stronger than hers. He begins to follow her and then turns back to the insect as though the object of his advance from the outset was to rob the female of her prey. In reality he may wrap some threads round it and he may share a meal with her if he has been engaged in the long fruitless courtship of an unwilling female, but normally the fly is being used for courtship purposes only. Presently she returns to her meal and he gives way, only to return almost immediately in order to walk over her with vibrating legs whilst trailing a thread to a radius beyond her. Along this thread he crosses and recrosses, strengthening what proves later to be the mating thread on to which he is going to entice her.

After he has crossed over her several times, I have often seen him pause beside her and gently begin to wrap her in fine silk. At first I wondered if this was a reversal of the *Argiope* practice, where the female wraps the male in silk during mating with sinister intent, or comparable with the male *Xysticus* who fastens the female to the ground with silk before mating with her, but neither proved to be the case. Before long she always stirs herself into action and tears herself free, so we are left to conclude that this futile wrapping of the female represents the lurking remnants of his preying instincts now dominated by his sexual instincts. Nevertheless the action may serve some purpose in stimulating the female.

When the mating thread is completed he entices her on to it with vibrations and here he taps her with waving front legs. She hangs at first in a nearly horizontal position and then he advances still vibrating the thread and chewing his palps. Her position prevents the sudden bound forward which is so typical of Argiopid males in their attempt to insert a palp, so he advances smoothly with a palp extended as in *Ero* and if his first attempt at insertion fails he turns round and then returns for another trial.

At the moment of contact, the male's chelicerae are open and these are pressed against the female's sternum. It is very difficult to see exactly what happens but I believe that they fasten on to the coxa of one of her hind legs. The male's pressure on the female from above forces her abdomen downwards to the inclined or nearly vertical position typical of the family, with his own body almost parallel and with his head downward like hers. He clasps her less tightly during copulation than is customary in this family, and with only the first two pair of legs. In about three minutes he extracts his palp and leaves her without the haste necessary for survival in many Argiopid species. The insertion of a single palp undoubtedly represents a complete act of copulation for one day, but the failure so far to observe sperm induction suggests that he mates with the same or another female on the following day with the other palp before they are recharged with sperm.

The female *Meta* always seems to be placid in her relations with the male and each female has a cavalier in attendance for several weeks. Attention has been called to this unusual constancy and it was only my suspicious mind which led to the discovery that this constancy is more apparent than real. I chose ten webs and marked the males who were in attendance. Four days later I returned and found that only one of the original males was in the same web whilst the others were scattered amongst neighbouring webs. How, then, can we avoid being suspicious of the single exceptional male's behaviour during those four days ? Had he too paid visits to other webs ?

One male in each web is the rule and if a second one appears on the scene the suitors engage in savage combat ending in death or else a hasty retreat for one of them. This surely must be a factor in this species leading to the survival of the larger males and it is certainly a fact that the males of *Meta segmentata* are larger, relative to the female's size, than those of any other Argiopid species. Indeed a large male is larger than a small female. On some occasions I have seen courtship taking place over the dead body of a vanquished rival.

The establishment in England of a continental species is a matter of interest but when it is a large and handsome addition to our fauna its appearance becomes an exciting event. *Argiope bruennichi* was first noticed by Mrs. Morrison Bell on wasteland near her home at South-bourne, Hants, in 1940 where a thriving colony still survives. Within five years other colonies had been discovered at nearby Iford, at Park-stone and at Allbrook. The history of its arrival would not be complete without mentioning that a single specimen had been found near Rye in 1922 but this, I feel sure, was a stray immigrant and I strongly suspect that we owe the establishment of the species to Mrs. M. J. Marples who brought specimens from southern Europe and released egg-sacs in her Hampshire garden when she had finished studying them a few years before Mrs. Bell's discovery in 1940.

Argiope has a shining silvery cephalothorax and a yellowish abdomen with conspicuous black bars across it. She may reach up to 15 mm. whereas her mate is an inconspicuous light brown dwarf of only 4 mm. (see Plates 4 and XXX, pp. 224 and 241).

The orb webs are not unlike those of the Garden Spider but they are embellished with two striking silvery zig-zag bands, one above and the other below the hub. This signature is present in all foreign spiders of the genus *Argiope* and naturalists have disagreed as to its function. Having seen elaborations of the same technique adopted by many Argiopids in the tropics, I am fully satisfied that the spider in the centre of her web is made less conspicuous by these designs and that they are protective in function.

The female spins her web amongst grass or low herbage and here the diminutive male searches for her after reaching maturity in July. With quivering legs he approaches her and if she is prepared to accept him she remains more or less passive and makes no attempt to repulse him. Indeed she may encourage him by a slight rhythmic swinging of her body and later by pressing her body away from the web so that he can creep under her. Here, with the heads of both spiders directed downwards and with their ventral surfaces facing one another, he chews his palps and then inserts one of them. Directly he has succeeded in doing this he firmly embraces her with all his legs and she slowly draws silk from her spinnerets with her hind pair of legs and wraps it round him. Whilst she is engaged on this sinister task, the palpal bulb has remained expanded for about 10 seconds before the embolus is extracted with a twisting motion. The insertion of the second palp for a similar period completes the copulation and he then attempts to make a hasty retreat despite the retarding threads with which he is bound. Life or death depends on his frenzied struggles at this moment. In my experience, as well as in that of U. Gerhardt (1924) in Germany, a fresh male usually escapes with the loss of one or more legs, but his second mating seals his fate.

This brutal behaviour on the part of our newest immigrant may seem less terrible when we learn from Gerhardt (1933) that the male of an allied species from the eastern Mediterranean, *A. lobata,* dies a natural death immediately after or sometimes even during his second act of copulation.

Features peculiar to *Argiope* lie in the absence of attack by the female during the courtship, the absence of a special mating thread and the wrapping of the male during the process of mating. The egg-sac is also of quite different construction. First she spins a bundle of soft silk flanked with smooth silk which soon turns brown. Then she presses her abdomen against the lower surface, extrudes the egg-mass and lowers her body to hold it in position with white silk threads drawn across it. In the third stage she covers the eggs with a mass of soft flocculent brown silk covered in with a smooth papery layer of white silk which rapidly turns brown. This massive jug-shaped egg-sac is slung amongst the grass close to her web (Bonnet, 1925).

The last species I shall mention is a remarkable globose spider, only 2 mm. in length, called *Theridiosoma gemmosum*. Both her structure and habits place her on the very fringe of the family. She is silvery in colour and lives in swampy ground where she builds a trap snare near the ground. Wiehle (1931) has shown that although a meshed hub and strengthening spirals are present at one stage in the construction, these are bitten out before the web is completed. The snare ultimately resembles a half opened umbrella with a thread leading from the ferrule to a point of attachment, on which the spider sits facing away from the web. This thread is stretched very tight and is released with a jerk when a fly is entangled. Thus in some respects her device is similar to that of *Hyptiotes* but she does not have to rebuild her snare after each capture.

THE TETRAGNATHIDAE

This is a small family comprising three genera and nine species of spiders which probably diverged long ago from the main Argiopid stock at a time when the latter's structure was much simpler than it is today.

The Tetragnathids all have simple sexual organs without any epigyne in the female, very large chelicerae and other structural features in common, but there are such marked differences in the general appearance and habits of *Tetragnatha* and *Pachygnatha* that it is easiest to speak of each genus in turn.

Spiders of the genus *Tetragnatha* have long slim tapering bodies with long fine legs except for the third pair which are useful in holding the narrow stem of a plant whilst the spider and her other legs are stretched along it without projecting to either side. Most of the species are light in colour, sometimes tinged with silver or green and with a delicate tracery of darker lines and veinings, so their shape and colour combined make them very inconspicuous when stretched along a grass stem. Even when they hang in this linear position from the centre of their webs they can look more like a fragment of dry grass than a living spider. A slight disturbance causes them to draw in their legs still more tightly, and a more severe one to drop to the ground.

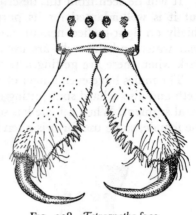

FIG. 108. *Tetragnatha* face

One is inclined to associate *Tetragnatha* with reeds and rushes near water but not all the species are so dependent on damp surroundings as the two largest and commonest, which are *T. extensa* and *T. montana*. These have bodies up to 11 mm. in length. Both mature in June or a little earlier and it really needs a microscopic examination of their cheliceral teeth to be sure of their identity, although pointers to *T. montana* include her tendency to be slightly darker, to drift a little further away from the immediate vicinity of marshy ground and to show less tolerance of exposure to wind. She is not found on our small islands, for instance, whereas *T. extensa* is a usual inhabitant from the Scillies to the Orkneys.

Tetragnatha pinicola and *T. obtusa* have less affinity for water and usually spin their webs in trees or bushes. *T. nigrita* is much darker in colour and may be almost black. In contrast to these species the closely related *Eugnatha striata* is usually a pale yellow with hardly any markings and one usually has to wade or row out to reeds actually growing in water to find her.

Both *Tetragnatha* and *Eugnatha* build orb webs of unusually fine silk whilst other features which help to distinguish them are the wide spacing of the spirals and the centre which is open like a ring with two strengthening spirals outside it. The free zone between these and the gummy spirals is wide and it is usual to find about sixteen radii with fifteen spirals above the hub and eighteen below it. The web is often inclined at an angle or even horizontal.

It will be seen from this description that the web is a flimsy affair but it is well-adapted for its purpose. *Tetragnatha* depends for food chiefly on light-bodied nematocerous or gnat-like flies which abound near water and the webs are usually spun in the evening before it is dark when these are getting active.

The males have even longer chelicerae than the females with larger teeth and also a hard spur jutting outwards from the outer apex of the basal segment. When a male has some special feature not possessed by the female, some use for it is often found during the mating procedure

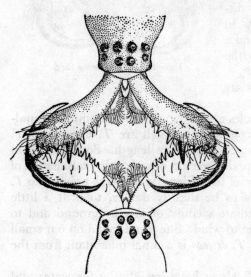

FIG. 109. Male *Tetragnatha* wedging the female's fangs open with a special tooth-like process

and the *Tetragnatha* male is no exception. There is no noticeable courtship in this genus but as they approach one another both open their chelicerae wide. The front legs touch and the male's are pressed outwards against the female's until the legs of both are strangely directed out to the side at an angle of 90° to their bodies. Now their chelicerae are touching and, with a thrill, it can be seen that the spurs wedge hers wide open in such a way that she cannot use them to bite him, whilst a large tooth on the inner border is pressed against the basal segment of her chelicerae and his long fangs complete the hold by curling round outside hers. This hold is maintained throughout the mating. From what may be a horizontal ventral side uppermost position they now drop on threads until they are both hanging vertically and belly to belly with her abdomen contorted in a curve so that it touches his. From this position the male inserts his palps alternately for about a quarter of an hour and then rapidly disengages himself and drops to the ground on a thread.

The females fasten their egg-sacs to blades of grass or to reeds near their web and they are of a distinctive appearance with green tufts on a whitish background in *T. montana,* green tufts on greyish silk in *T. obtusa* and simply an uneven sponge-like covering of grey silk in *T. extensa.* E. Nielsen gives a description of the way in which they are made and also says that in the rarer *Eugnatha,* whose egg-sacs I have never seen, the sac is covered with a smooth dark green layer of silk. (E. Nielsen, 1932).

The remaining genus of *Pachygnatha* has three species with oval abdomens. *P. clercki* is the largest (6 mm.) and *P. degeeri* the smallest (3 mm.). Both are widespread and common at ground level amongst grass and other vegetation, with *P. clercki* seeming to need slightly damper conditions than *P. degeeri.* The upper part of their abdomen is fairly evenly mottled except for a paler band down the centre. The mottling is olive brown in *P. clercki,* with the lighter band yellowish in the male, whilst the cephalothorax is light brown. The markings on *P. degeeri* are darker and the carapace is often black.

I always 'knew' both from the literature and from my own general observation that *Pachygnatha* had abandoned web-building to become a hunter but I began to wonder if this were really true when night-collecting had taught me that they left the ground to climb up amongst the foliage of low plants after dark. Was it possible that they built some kind of transient snare at night which they left when daylight returned ? I collected a number of specimens and found they trailed threads as they climbed but beyond this I could trace no threads whatever. Starting from the conception of *Pachygnatha* having abandoned web-building and the idea that very young specimens might have retained the habit, J. Balogh has now made the interesting discovery that the very young spiders do build small orb webs.

There is no courtship in this genus and here, as in *Tetragnatha,* the male's large chelicerae serve the useful purposes of warding off danger and of holding the female during the mating. In *P. degeeri* the male seizes her chelicerae in his own and holds them closed. His legs all embrace her and she is drawn into a position where she is, as it were, sitting on the upper surface of her abdomen on the ground with her cephalothorax bent steeply upwards at an angle of 90° to the abdomen. His own body is poised straight upwards, his chelicerae holds hers and their abdominal tips are close together, so in effect their bodies are arranged in the form of a triangle; this is not unlike the *Tetragnatha* position except for their being erect instead of hanging. Directly the brief struggle and interplay of legs is over the male inserts a palp. Mating lasts twenty to thirty minutes during which time each palp may be used two or three times.

In *Pachygnatha clercki* the same position is adopted and the bulb swells and collapses rapidly during a much longer period of about two hours in the course of which each palp is only inserted once. The most interesting difference is in the exact nature of the grip secured by the male's chelicerae with which he imprisons her wide open fangs. There is a large tooth on the inner border of his basal segment which wedges her fangs open and then by nearly closing his own strangely kinked fangs hers are securely 'hand-cuffed'.

Thus the holding of the female's chelicerae is typical of the males in this family but they have devised three different methods of doing so.

ADDENDUM

A series of papers by H. M. Peters and P. N. Witt in Germany is opening the door to clearer understanding of the unhesitating route pursued by the orb-webbed spiders in the course of completing their webs. Some of the known design can be explained, for instance, by assuming that the spider travels in whatever direction is the least effort and only turns aside from this under the influence of local stimuli. Part of the most congenial route is the shortest distance from radius to radius when spinning the spiral threads and this course provides a logarithmic spiral. Yet the completed web does not show everywhere the same proportions as the web under construction owing, for instance, to the shifting weight of the spider on the horizontal radii causing some distortion of the angles. Some of Witt's recent work, and that of other investigators in Germany, including D. Wolff and U. Hempel, is important in demonstrating that the different functions playing a part in the construction of the viscid spiral can be eliminated when the spider is spinning under the influence of a variety of neurotropic substances.

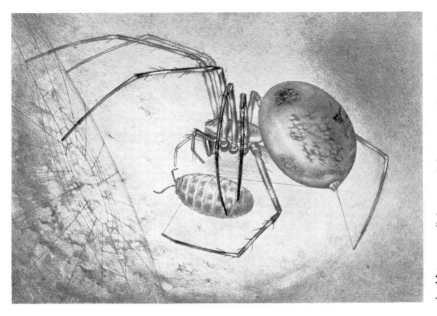

b. Meta menardi (13 mm.) in a cave, hanging from her web to wrap a woodlouse.

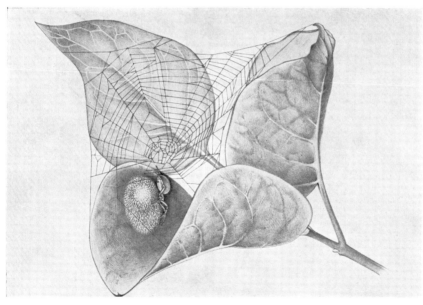

a. The green *Araneus cucurbitinus* (5 mm.) with her egg-sac and orb-web in a confined space between lilac leaves.

Plate xxxi

a. Drapetisca socialis (4 mm.) on a beech trunk.

b. Erigone arctica (2.5 mm.) with two egg-sacs under a stone on the sea-shore.

PLATE XXXII

CHAPTER 20

THE LINYPHIIDAE

Money Spiders

MOST of our two hundred and fifty species have shiny black abdomens with an average body length of 2.5 mm. They are often difficult to identify even with a microscope, so lazy folk, like most lepidopterists, might be tempted conveniently to neglect these dwarfs. It stands to the credit of a series of British workers that their structural features have been closely studied and that the task of identification has recently been eased by the excellent researches of Dr. A. F. Millidge (Locket and Millidge, 1951–53).

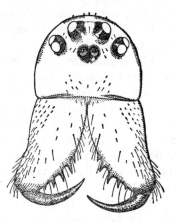

FIG. 110. *Linyphia* face

The Linyphiidae are often reminders of approaching winter. In autumn and early winter they hang beneath dew-covered hammock webs of exquisite delicacy that glisten in every hedge and even amongst the close-cut grass of a garden lawn where at other times they would pass unnoticed. It is also in autumn and early winter that fine days stir their multitude into restless activity, leaving a matted sheet of inter-crossing drag-lines to cloak the fields with a mantle which shimmers in the evening sunlight like a silver sea. It is at such times that we gain some inkling of their vast numbers which exceed by far the total population of all other spiders. They are the dominant spiders in Britain and in all temperate and arctic regions of the northern hemisphere.

The seasonal wandering, I think, has a physiological explanation and is caused by a feeling of unease due to the effect of radiant heat at ground level on these small spiders in seasons when they are physically acclimatised to the cooler conditions of autumn and winter. The urge is to climb upwards and away from this micro-climate at and near to ground level. They leave their webs and for the time being courtship and feeding is banished by this over-riding impulse to climb upwards. Having reached the top of some pinnacle, which may be a plant, a railing or a wall, they behave much like a spider engaged in bridge-building prior to weaving her snare. They stand on 'tip-toes' facing the wind and squeeze silk from their spinnerets which is taken hold of by the air currents and drawn outwards until it becomes anchored to a nearby mooring. In the conditions which cause the mass migrations, however, the prevalent air currents will be upwards and the pull of her kite is soon strong enough to lift the spider into the air. Away she is wafted into the distance.

This explanation seems to meet with general favour without having to resort to some of the earlier explanations as to why or how these wingless creatures embark on flight (Duffey, 1956). Some early obsersers used to think they swam in the air with vigorous motions of their eight legs, others that air-sacs in their bodies helped to lift them in the manner of a balloon, whilst an anonymous genius, signing himself 'S.S', anticipated jet propulsion in 1868 by suggesting that the motive force was provided by the violent emission of a current of air from their bodies !

Although young spiders of several families mingle in a spirit of truce with the Linyphiidae during the gossamer season, more than 80% of the emigrants are Linyphiidae. Predominant amongst these are *Erigone dentipalpis*, *E. atra*, *Bathyphantes gracilis*, *Meioneta rurestris*, *Lepthyphantes tenuis*, *Areoncus humilis*, *Oedothorax fuscus*, *Savignia frontata* and *Dicymbium nigrum*. Although they usually live so unobtrusively under cover of grass, these can be regarded as the most abundant species in Britain. They certainly made up a high proportion of the spider population in an undisturbed field of Cock's Foot Grass (*Dactylis glomerata*) near Bexhill when I found that the density of Linyphiidae varied from about 400,000 to 800,000 per acre from February to June and increased to over 1,000,000 from August to December. The highest density I encountered was about 1,665,000 Linyphiidae in October when the total spider population per acre was not far short of two and a quarter million (Bristowe, 1939 and 1941, p. xii).

The progress of the flights has been traced to some extent after we lose sight of them in the air. Some Linyphiids have been found in swallows' stomachs for instance. Others have been caught in nets rigged from wireless masts, kites, the masts of ships over a hundred miles from land in the North Sea and from aeroplanes. Some American Linyphiids have been caught in aeroplanes flying over the United States up to an altitude of 14,000 feet, but the bulk of the evidence suggests that the principal density of the spider parachutists lies below a few hundred feet. Nevertheless we have to get used to the idea of an extensive floating population of spiders, insects and plant spores in the air above us and the importance of this as a factor in dispersal must be reckoned with.

To illustrate this, let me take two experiences of my own on such widely separated islands as Jan Mayen in the arctic and Krakatau on the equator between Java and Sumatra. Jan Mayen is a tiny volcanic island of oceanic origin with three or four hundred miles of sea separating it from Greenland and Iceland. The spider fauna is limited to four Linyphiid species — *Hilaira frigida, Collinsia holmgreni, Erigone tirolensis* and *Meioneta nigripes*. They are all found in Britain inhabiting, as it were, tiny islands in the air represented by scattered mountain tips above 3,000 feet, and elsewhere they are found on mountains in Europe and have a circum-polar distribution in the arctic at low levels. In other words they are to be found in widely scattered areas where climatic conditions suit them. To cross three or four hundred miles of arctic ocean must surely be a test of any but the most hardy aeronauts, but these species have succeeded at some time in reaching Jan Mayen by this means.

The story of Krakatau is well-known. It was the scene of the greatest volcanic eruption in man's history when two-thirds of one island were blown away and the fauna and flora completely blotted out in August 1883. Nine months later a visitor wrote that 'Notwithstanding all my searches, I was not able to observe any symptoms of animal life. I only discovered one microscopic spider — only one ! Not even a blade of grass appeared until more than a year had elapsed'. By the time I visited these islands forty-eight years later they were all covered in jungle and inhabited by over ninety species of spider ! Eight of these were Linyphiids (which is a high proportion for the tropics) and none of the families which are incapable of aerial distribution were represented except by one domestic Scytodid and two Pholcids which were found only in the huts imported for occasional observation by the Dutch volcano experts. Apart from a small island ten miles away the nearest land from which aeronauts would have had to set forth was twenty-five miles away.

The special object of my expedition was to land on a new island less than six months old which had just been erupted by a submarine volcano whose gentler activities were still in progress at one end. It looked unpromising enough as we rowed the three miles which separated it from the other islands and sprang ashore on to its bare expanse of black ash, cinders and pumice, yet Collembola and a winged Anthicid beetle were soon found in abundance as well as an occasional Cosmopterygid moth, a mosquito and two queen ants. Before I left the island my hopes were satisfied by the discovery of three spiders — a Lycosid, a Ctenid and a Linyphiid (Bristowe, 1931, Reimoser, 1934).

Jan Mayen and Krakatau provide valuable evidence of the power of spiders and insects to cross the sea by air and to establish themselves where climatic conditions are suitable. Indeed we can now play havoc with much of the former evidence advanced in support of land-bridges which were sometimes imagined to explain the distribution of spiders and other invertebrates.

Our species of Linyphiidae range in body length from barely 1 mm. (*Saloca diceros* and *Glyphesis cottonae*) to 6 mm. (*Linyphia triangularis* and *L. montana*) and the small size of the majority conceals from us the grotesque heads of many of the males in the sub-family Erigoninae. Eyes situated at the top of the strange lobes and turrets might suggest aids to vision if the spiders were not known to be extremely short-sighted so the explanation must be sought elsewhere. Less than 20% of the Linyphiidae have well-marked abdominal patterns and it may be useful to know that these all belong to genera in the sub-family Linyphiinae: *Linyphia, Tapinopa, Labulla, Stemonyphantes, Lepthyphantes, Bathyphantes, Bolyphantes, Floronia, Drapetisca, Poeciloneta,* and *Taranucnus*. A more general feature distinguishing the two sub-families is the presence of a palpal claw in most female Linyphiinae but, as there are exceptions to this, the most reliable character is provided by the armature of the legs. There is one dorsal spine on the fourth tibia of the Erigoninae and none on any of the metatarsi, whereas in the Linyphiinae the fourth tibia has two dorsal spines, except in a few species where there is one on this tibia and one short spine on the metatarsi of the first and second pairs of legs.

Apart from the tiny black (*Erigone, Meioneta* etc.,) or slim striped (*Lepthyphantes, Bathyphantes*) Money Spiders which run over us when we are sitting out of doors, the most noticeable species is *Linyphia triangularis*

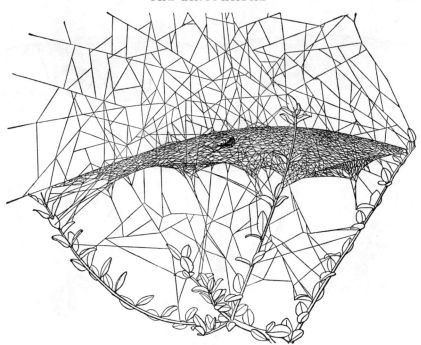

Fig. 111.   *Linyphia triangularis* (6 mm.) stands below her slightly domed sheet

because she builds her delicate sheet web in nearly every garden shrub
with stiff foliage. She is also common in hedges, gorse bushes and tall
grass. Scaffolding threads above and below the sheet hold it in position
and arch the centre slightly above the level of the edges. In the rare
Scottish *L. marginata* the effect is much more pronounced and the shape
is like that of the dome of St. Paul's, but in all other species the sheet is
flat or else sags like a hammock. *L. triangularis* builds no retreat and
she stands in an inverted position on the underside of her sheet ready
to dart at any insect which falls on to it. Although the scaffolding
threads below the sheet often appear to be quite dense, comparatively
few impede her movements because the relatively few threads which
are attached to the lower surface of the sheet connect with what is
sometimes almost a second platform of horizontal threads below the
main sheet.

    None of the threads are sticky and attempts to feed her with active
flies are usually doomed to failure, so it may be wondered how she

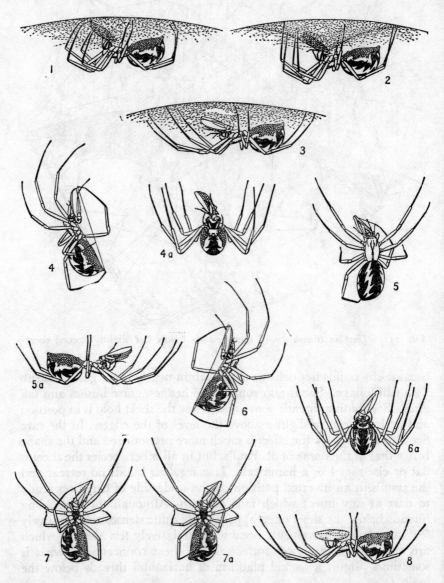

FIG. 112. *Linyphia triangularis* (6 mm.) wrapping an insect. She wraps, turns through 90° and wraps again. This is usually repeated until turned through a complete circle.

succeeds in getting enough food. Her diet mostly comprises small and clumsy fliers or hoppers like Jassids or Cercopids which hit the upper scaffolding, or stopping-threads, and fall on to the sheet. If an insect clings to, or climbs up, one of these threads she shakes the web violently and, if this does not dislodge it, she runs round the edge of the sheet or tears a hole and gives chase.

When an insect has fallen on to the sheet some distance from the *Linyphia*, and she has not reached it in one dash before it lies still, she sits patiently waiting for it to renew its struggles, but sometimes she will tug the web which often leads the insect to betray its position. The sheet is not of course really a smooth surface on which to run and the insect, wallowing in trip threads, is soon overtaken and bitten through the web from below. If it is of some size a series of peck-like bites are delivered on the run, and if it tries to wriggle through the flimsy sheet the *Linyphia* may run hastily round in circles below it to strengthen the sheet with fresh threads. Presently the wounded and weakened insect is held firmly in the spider's chelicerae and after a pause *Linyphia* exerts an upward pressure with her legs whilst pulling the insect downwards through the sheet. Still holding it in her chelicerae and palps, she drags it a short distance away from the torn web and then begins to wrap it up in silk unless it is very small. There is a marked ritual about this.

The sheet is touched with the spinnerets and then, with lowered abdomen, the hind legs alternately draw out and direct threads over the insect. After each hind leg has been used two or three times, the *Linyphia* again touches the lower surface of the sheet with her spinnerets, pivots through an angle of about 90° and repeats the process. The compass is then boxed by two similar turns through 90° accompanied by further wrapping. The meal can now start (see fig. 112).

Should a second insect fall into the web whilst the meal is in progress, the *Linyphia* leaves the first one hanging from the sheet whilst she attends to the newcomer. She usually returns to the first insect after trussing the second or even a third one, thereby suggesting for our consideration the existence of memory.

Linyphia montana builds in the same holly or gorse and hedgerow shrubs as *L. triangularis*, but her sheet is easily distinguished because it sags into a hammock with the lower scaffolding threads tugging it down at the points of attachment into little pinnacles. She differs also in living concealed under a leaf or piece of bark at one edge of the sheet from which she emerges in response to an insect's struggles. When the insect has been seized she may continue to suck its juices for some time before pulling it through the sheet and carrying it to her retreat without wrapping it.

The web designs of different species vary considerably. A sheet may be woven across a hoof impression, a flower-pot or a space in the foliage of a shrub and attached by its edges without any scaffolding threads to support it.

Floronia, which approaches *L. triangularis* in size, draws her extensive horizontal sheet tightly across shady spaces in bramble bushes and sits beneath it. She has a high dumpy abdomen and the dorsal surface gives a general impression of being white with brown venations except for a few small black spots or bars near the tip. It was whilst studying this spider's habits that I made an exciting discovery. When she was disturbed she dropped to the ground and lay still. In that instant her general body colour had changed to a dingy brown hue which made her very difficult to see. This instantaneous colour change was a unique and unrecorded occurrence amongst spiders and almost unknown amongst invertebrates. Under a microscope I saw that the white pattern was made up of numbers of pigmented intestinal guanin cells separated by narrow or wider lines where the body fluid provided a brown effect. After shaking the spider in a glass tube I found that the white areas contracted almost to pin-points and exposed much more of the brown body fluid which gave the spider its earthy hue. Gradually the white cells regained their normal areas over a period of several minutes (see fig. 113).

During a visit to Australia in 1957, Mr. N. L. Roberts drew my attention to a similar occurrence in an Argiopid (*Phonognatha wagneri*).

Other species which span open spaces without scaffolding threads include *Labulla thoracica* and *Stemonyphantes lineatus*. Both these are amongst the larger species of the family. They mostly live at ground level and are especially associated in my mind with the spaces between the root buttresses of trees and the entrance to rabbit holes respectively. Both emerge from retreats only when an insect's struggles attract their attention. *Tapinopa longidens* is a small species, which bridges cavities under stones or heather, and has a small web, unlike that of any other spider, which glistens as though a snail had covered it with its slime.

All the species whose webs I have mentioned so far belong to the sub-family Linyphiinae but small sheet webs are also typical of the Erigoninae. I have never detected any gummy threads in the Linyphiine snares (although E. Nielsen (1932) says that these are included in the dome and stopping threads of *Linyphia marginata*) but I believe that *Erigone* and some of the other Erigoninae may employ viscid strands like the Theridiidae.

Although sheet webs are typical of the family, there must be many cases where the confined spaces in which they live would not allow

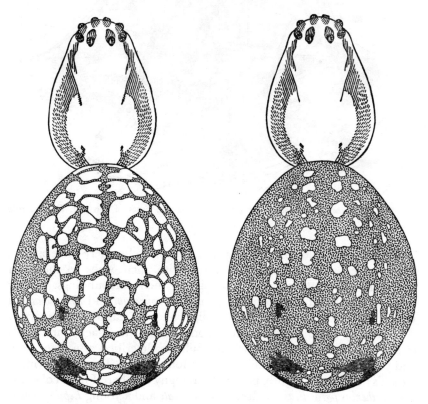

Fig. 113. The instantaneous colour change of *Floronia bucculenta* (5 mm.) when she is disturbed and drops to the ground

them to be identified as such and where the snares comprise little more than a few criss-cross threads, or threads passing in and out around close-packed pebbles or vegetation. Certain Linyphiid species, for instance, abound amongst the drenched pebbles and clinker of sewage beds. More than two thirds of the numerous specimens sent to me from

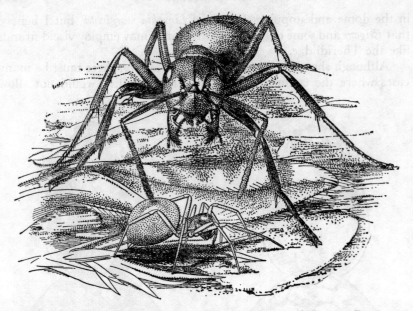

FIG. 114. *Thyreosthenius biovatus* (2 mm.) lives in the nests of the ant, *Formica rufa*

these situations comprise *Lessertia dentichelis,* but elsewhere these spiders festoon the walls of some coal mines with their webs so they can obviously adapt their spinning habits to their surroundings. Other common species in filter beds are *Porrhomma convexum* and *Erigone arctica* which are typical elsewhere in coal mines and the seashore respectively.

Similarly there could be little room amongst the packed materials of a bird's nest for anything which could be described as a sheet web. and yet many small Linyphids are to be found there. The twigs forming a rook's nest are less tightly packed than many and here I have collected *Thyreosthenius parasiticus, Lophocarenum nemorale* and a young *Lepthyphantes,* whilst in the glutinous evil smelling nests of cormorants and shags on their spray-drenched rocks I have found *Halorates reprobus* to be an habitual inhabitant.

I believe that all these species do build little sheet webs when space permits, but we may suppose the three Linyphiids which have adopted life in ants' nests as a speciality have abandoned web-making entirely in the ant galleries and merely pounce on the little flies and Collembola which I have found them eating. *Thyreosthenius biovatus* is common in the nests of *Formica rufa* and *F. pratensis*. *Evansia merens* is a northern species mostly associated with *Formica fusca* whilst the rare *Acartauchenius scurrilis* lives with the tiny *Tetramorium caespitum* in the South of England. Here in this sheltered home these small spiders live their strange lives and lay their eggs without being molested by their fierce hosts. Usually they seem to avoid too intimate a contact with the ants but, when contact is unavoidable, they appear to agitate their front legs, which may mean that they have learned the language 'spoken' by the ants with their antennae.

One species which undoubtedly has abandoned all web-building is *Drapetisca socialis*. This beautiful little species with her grey mottled body and annulated legs sits motionless with legs outstretched on the trunks of various kinds of trees, especially beech and conifers, where she is almost invisible until she is made to move. During the day she is always still and I have never yet seen her eating anything until after nightfall when she presumably wakens into activity (see Plate XXXII, p. 257).

The Linyphiidae have their full share of specialists and there are few habitats to whose conditions none have adapted themselves. *Porrhomma campbelli* and *Lepthyphantes insignis* thrive in moles' nests; *Porrhomma convexum* and *P. egeria* in caves and mines; and sixteen species, of which I have mentioned four in speaking about Jan Mayen, are more or less restricted to the higher slopes of our mountains. Many are found only in marshland and five of these are unknown outside the Cambridge-shire fens—*Entelecara omissa*, *Maro sublestus*, *Centromerus incultus*, *Glyphesis servulus* and *Maso gallica*. Then there are the spiders of the sea-shore and *Trichoncus affinis* which nestles amongst the shingle at Dungeness.

More than one species of *Erigone* commonly makes its home at high tide mark in the fringe of decaying seaweed distributed along the shore, and here these black shiny-bodied little spiders will often be found in profusion alongside sandhoppers, springtails, flies, beetles and mites. One of these species, *Erigone arctica*, is the dominant spider in these situations on Loch Fyne (see Plate XXXII, p. 257). Here she spins her slender web across small cavities both in the seaweed and amongst pebbles lower down the shore where the sea must often cover her at high tide. The mystery of her survival tempted me to make a few experiments.

Ten specimens were gently placed on stones surrounded by water in wide basins. The sun was shining and they ran rapidly over the stones, and also quite freely over the surface of the surrounding water. If, however, they did not encounter dry land after travelling an inch or two, they usually returned to their starting point on a stone by the same route with the help of an anchor thread they had trailed before making their sorties. Sometimes they became bolder or were set in motion by an eddy of wind and skimmed over the surface to the edge of the bowls with their abdomens raised and acting as sails. This method of progression across the water sometimes takes them hundreds of yards out to sea as I know from past observation when sailing off the Scottish coast on calm days. When they 'sail' in this way, they merely stand on the water raised high on their legs, and let the gentle breezes carry them scudding over the surface.

Although this was interesting it had only shown their ability to move over the water without being drowned, so I pushed them one by one under the water on the leaves of a Silverweed which grows just above the seaweed fringe, in order to see what would happen when they were submerged. The leaves and stones were totally covered with sea-water so as to prevent the spiders walking to the surface and I was now surprised to see them running actively over the stones, apparently just as much at ease under the water as they had been above it, although there was no sign of any air bubble round their smooth bodies. Soon they ran under the stones and were lost to sight.

After waiting an hour and a quarter I anxiously turned over the stones and found the spiders were all in perfect health although they had spun no silk cells or retired to any pocket of air which might have been entrapped under the stones. Repetition made it abundantly clear that this *Erigone* can survive under water for longer than the period of submergence by a high tide, so the assumption must be that they simply remain clinging to their webs or to the underside of a stone and take no notice of the rising tide. It is also clear from repeated observation that they carry no air supply other than that stored in their book-lungs and tracheae. So long as they do not consume oxygen too rapidly by unnecessary movement these small spiders can subsist for two hours or more on this supply.

It is interesting to note that the egg-sacs of *Erigone* are also well-designed to withstand immersion. In appearance they are nipple-shaped and covered with a waterproof papery layer of silk which may be pinkish or yellow-tinged. One female may lay four or five of these and plaster them firmly to the underside of a stone close to her web. They resemble the egg-sacs of the *Gnaphosid* genus, *Zelotes*, but they are, of course, much smaller.

Early in August the male of our common garden and woodland Linyphia, *L. triangularis,* appears as if by magic in every female's web and for weeks they live peacefully together. He is slimmer than the female but he is longer and has abnormally large chelicerae so one is tempted to wonder if marital peace is associated in any way with his ability to protect himself! Differences between the sexes have so often proved to have a functional purpose that I tried in vain to find one for the large chelicerae. His courtship was marked by pulsations of the abdomen, jerky steps, leg vibrations and tweakings of the web as in most members of the family, but no use was made of the chelicerae. Appendages tend to be longer in males than in females and it is noticeable that the male chelicerae in this species are relatively longer in large than in small specimens, so the abnormality seems to be merely one of allometric growth.

The mating position is usually similar to that adopted in the Theridiidae with the female hanging head downwards at an angle and the male also head downwards, and in the same plane but nearly horizontal, with his two pairs of front legs lightly holding her. The general rule for the family is for mating to be interrupted at intervals for him to recharge his palps with sperm as in some of the Theridiidae, so it is a long affair which sometimes lasts up to two or three hours. Not uncommonly the sperm web is spun across a hole he has bitten in her sheet and comprises a tiny platform of triangular shape spun across the angle where two threads meet. These threads are held by the third pair of legs as he alternately reaches his palps round to the upper surface to absorb the sperm drop through the web. Of course there are departures from this general procedure and I can bring out some of the variations by comparing what I have seen in three of the small Money Spider species, the first of which belongs to the Linyphiinae and the other two to the Erigoninae.

In *Meioneta saxatilis* the male changed his palps rapidly after one expansion and collapse of the bulb, pausing to chew each palp after its extraction before inserting the other. Each insertion lasted only three or four seconds in the early phases but later this rate slowed down to nine seconds. Mating lasted two hours and was divided into five phases separated by periods of about three minutes when he left her to refill his palps with sperm. On each occasion he tickled her with his legs before leaving her and she remained motionless during his absence. The same sperm web is never used twice either by this or any other spider.

A small point worth mentioning in connection with the courting of *Gongylidium rufipes* is that the female bares her fangs during courtship although she does not snap at him. The significance of this action may be more apparent when I outline the procedure in the next Erigonine species. The male *Gongylidium* inserts his palp for very brief spells but in contrast to *Meioneta* the palp is chewed and usually inserted a second time before being changed for the other. In this species the mating lasted nearly three hours and was divided into eight phases by the intervals for sperm induction. It took him up to two minutes to re-charge his palps from a small web spun in the form of a ribbon by sideways movements of the body, but intervals between the phases varied from two and a half minutes to about half an hour which may not be typical.

My third example, *Hypomma bituberculatum*, is much the most inter-esting. The male's head has two large lobes side by side with lateral grooves at their bases and I had long been hoping to find some expla-nation or useful function for the lobes, turrets and grooves with which so many Erigonine males are equipped. *Hypomma* seems to have re-vealed the main solution to this mystery but confirmation with other species is needed.

The male advanced with quivering abdomen and with palps moving up and down in a manner which brought his stridulatory apparatus into action. At first she retreated as he approached. Then she turned on him with fangs bared but, unlike the *Gongylidium* female, she lunged at him. His behaviour was extraordinary. He drew in his legs and made no attempt to escape or to defend himself. Her chelicerae closed on his head lobes with the fangs resting in their lateral grooves and there they remained whilst he inserted a palp. (Fig. 116).

After one expansion of the bulb the palps were changed and after each had been inserted twice he sat quite still and she loosened her hold. After a pause of a few seconds he incited her once more by vibrating his body and twitching his abdomen until she seized him by the head again. There were six such sessions in a quarter of an hour before he moved away to re-charge his palps. Unexpectedly he changed his position to stand above the sperm web to deposit and absorb the sperm. Then, after courting her afresh and having his head seized, five sessions similar to those I have described above took place before he again left her after seven minutes to replenish his palps with sperm.

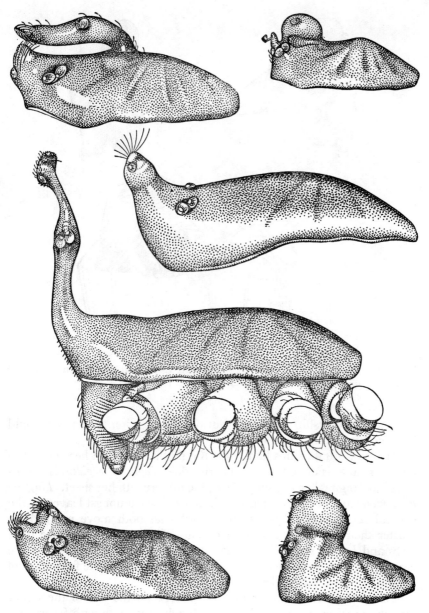

FIG. 115. The strange heads of Erigonine males: *Tigellinus furcillatus, Wideria antica, Savignia frontata, Walckenaera acuminata, Diplocephalus* and *Peponocranium*

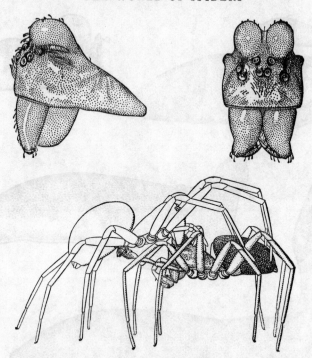

Fɪɢ. 116. *Hypomma bituberculatum* (3 mm.). The turret and grooves on the male's head are gripped by the female during mating

Further courtship took place but on this occasion the female would have nothing more to do with him.

It is not usual in this family for the mother to sit on her eggs or to guard them as is done by most Theridiidae. *Tapinopa longidens* is exceptional in slinging her pot-shaped egg-sac underneath her sheet. *Linyphia triangularis* moves downwards to spin her egg-sac amongst leaves on the ground, *Lepthyphantes leprosus* and *L. nebulosus* both move upwards to plaster their egg-sacs on bark or on the ceiling of a shed above their webs and *Labulla* secures hers under loose bark. Once the egg-sacs are completed they leave them and this is connected with the frequency of egg-laying by small spiders.

As usual there is some relationship between the size of the spider and the number of eggs laid in each batch, but those with fewer eggs in each batch seem to lay more batches. *Linyphia triangularis* may lay up to fifty eggs but the number is in single figures amongst the smallest species. This is partly due to the egg-diameter and the length of the freshly hatched spider being a larger fraction of their mother's length in small than in large spiders. In *Erigone arctica*, for instance, I found that the freshly emerged spider was no less than one third of its mother's body length. A natural effect of this is that small spiders need fewer moults than large ones before attaining the size reached at maturity, and in the Linyphiidae I believe this varies from four down to three moults.

I have shown that the Linyphiidae are the dominant spiders in Britain, both in numbers of species and in population, and this is primarily due to climatic considerations coupled with a plentiful supply of small insects on which to feed. Being small they naturally have a host of potential enemies so I was intensely interested to discover that most of the species with black or dark abdomens are distasteful to predaceous invertebrates although they are eaten by birds and toads. I have seen a centipede drop *Erigonidium* and *Pocadicnemis* after biting them and then rub its mouth energetically from side to side on the ground whilst the spiders escaped. I have also seen fifteen species refused by other spiders — often thrown out of their webs by web-builders and sometimes causing the spiders to wipe their mouths on a leaf. However I must not claim too much for this partial immunity from enemies because our little black-bodied *Erigones* are exceptions to this general rule and they must rank amongst our most abundant spiders.

CHAPTER 21

ON COLLECTING SPIDERS

A DVICE on how to collect spiders is usually dull and uninspiring. It has followed a more or less uniform pattern ever since those who collected them were just 'bottlers' and 'county-listers' so it is now largely outmoded. The advice in a dozen books or articles amounts to little more than to beat bushes into an umbrella, to sweep vegetation with a stout net, to shake moss and dead leaves over a newspaper, to search diligently at the roots of vegetation and generally to leave no stone unturned. Passing on to the captured spiders, we are advised to kill them in 40 to 50% alcohol and later to transfer the specimens to tubes full of 70% alcohol which should be closed with cotton-wool and inverted in wide-necked glass-stoppered bottles filled with alcohol. No tube in the collection should contain more than one species and the serious collector should keep specimens from different localities in separate tubes with labels in each tube written in Indian ink or in pencil.

I dispute none of this and yet it has become of little more use to many collectors than instructions on deep sea dredging would be to a trout fisherman. It is certainly not suited to all requirements and makes no attempt to capture the fun or excitement. It gives no encourage-ment to the imaginative planning or ingenuity necessary to the success-ful ecologist or to the broader approach found even amongst the oft-despised timbromaniacs, or philatelists as they are now called, many of whom extend their collecting to items of postal history. The fact is that techniques and apparatus for collecting will vary widely according to the objective.

What is the collector's objective? Let us suppose that he intends the spider fauna of an extensive area. Here the long term distant and its completion so remote as to lose dynamic split up into a series of short term objectives. Strangely experience in another field of endeavour will illustrate this need. On the running track I used to find it difficult to concentrate on a finishing post round a bend only 220 yards away but easy, over the same distance, to put my entire enthusiasm and concentrated effort into reaching a hurdle 20 yards in front of me, and then the next, and the next, until the tape was close in front of me. If a sprinter were to read and heed these remarks, I feel sure he could beat his own best time over, say, 220 yards by fixing clearly defined landmarks at short intervals along the track and then concentrating on reaching each in turn.

In like manner I advocate the splitting of all long term collecting objectives into a series of short term targets, in such a way that every day's hunting can be provided with a special zest and often represent the completion of a small piece of research on its own.

Many people set out to make a comprehensive collection of species in a large area. It will eventually be necessary to investigate the widest range of environments that imagination can provide, so why not plan to concentrate on each in turn instead of rambling hither and thither? Suppose a thorough search has been made in a cave. Surely this will give a special interest to learning whether any or all of the same species inhabit either damp or dry cellars and to explaining the differences.

Darkness combined with humidity and freedom from temperature extremes can also occur in hollow trees and this is a situation that the Cave Spider, *Meta menardi*, has colonised in Richmond Park. Darkness may also be encountered in sheds or attics and from these one can pass on to list the inhabitants of houses where light and more arid conditions prevail but where extremes of climate will be avoided. And, finally, what about hot-houses where both temperature and light are vastly different but where humidity is usually high? Even here the light can be eliminated by living under a flower pot and the American cave or subterranean *Eidmanella pallidus* has recently been found at Kew, with the Lake District as the only other recorded British locality where it lives in cavities under stones.

Other subterranean habitats like mines, sewers, crypts, culverts and moles' nests can also be explored and each enquiry represents a separate bit of research which will provide some fresh species and stimulate thought in finding reasons for differences or similarities. To what extent are the differences due to temperature, humidity, light intensity, food supply, shelter from wind and means of dispersal?

Let me give another example of the same approach to collecting. Random search in, say, an oak wood may give good results, but how much more interesting these results will be if the search is made according to some imaginative plan much of which can be improvised and varied in the light of what is seen after arrival there. The micro-climate of a rook's nest in the upper branches is as different from that of a moorhen's nest beside a pond in the same wood as a wind-swept hillside is from a marsh, so the spider population in birds' nests will provide an intriguing subject for enquiry. The spider population of a single oak tree in May and again in July would be illuminating. Linyphiidae would be found amongst the dead leaves at its base, others including *Labulla* in the space between the root buttresses, others on the bark or under it. Advancing to the branches and twigs, fresh species like *Clubiona brevipes*, *Anyphaena* and *Ballus* might be caught, whilst under the leaves themselves *Theridion pallens* may be nestling with her strange egg-sacs.

Turn from the oak tree to the other foliage and see how the haul from this tree compares with the population on hazel, yew, elder or bracken. It can be just as interesting to find nothing at all on, say, some bracken or bluebell plants as to find a lot. Why is there nothing except a stray *Meta* or *Linyphia* ?

Since spiders are found almost everywhere in Britain from the sea-weed cast ashore at high tide mark, or the deepest coal mine, to the summit of our highest mountains, there is an amazing variety of situations to explore because many species are 'fussy' as to their requirements which is another way of saying that there are specialists at sea level and at high altitudes, on sand-hills and on chalk downs, in marshes and in ants' nests, etc.

The attitude of mind favouring a series of short term objectives will not only make collecting more interesting but it will certainly increase the value of the collector's work provided careful notes are kept and the task is approached in a spirit of speculation and research. Indeed it will be one of those rare cases where the parts are greater than the whole ! By the whole I mean the compilation of a list of spiders inhabiting a wide area like a county in the manner of so many people in the past.

It should go without saying that each short term objective requires thoroughness of search whether it can be completed in a matter of hours or days. This can be illustrated by assuming a thousand specimens of some small spider lurking amongst the grass clumps in an acre field whose population is being examined. If these spiders are evenly distributed, a leisurely search in forty clumps might be expected to produce just one specimen. It follows from this that a tired or impatient person is a bad collector and that his chances of success would be improved if he carried a ground-sheet on which to sit whilst he concentrated on one small piece of ground at a time.

Our greatest spider collector, the Rev. O. Pickard-Cambridge, used to complain as he got older that he was losing 'the eye of faith and the finger of instinct' and when Dr. A. R. Jackson reached the late fifties he half-seriously attributed the growing elusiveness of spiders to some spirit which wished him ill. Is it my imagination that the special spiders I could always count on finding when I wanted them are beginning to get rarer ? The answer lies, of course, in adapting one's methods, like a tennis player who is no longer young, and learning to employ less vigour but more cunning. Impatience and a growing frustration at not finding *Attulus saltator* on the sandhills at Sandwich where it used to abound, led to the ventilation of my grievance during our picnic lunch. My twelve year old daughter soon pointed one out to me from the ground-sheet on which we were sitting. This was followed by the discovery of others as we sat peacefully having our lunch recovering from the strenuous search which had gone before. Movement will cause many spiders to 'freeze' or to hide if impatience makes us move too quickly or prevents our waiting until they reappear and this was the mistake I had been making.

In order to get the best view of Lycosids and Thomisids when walking, it pays to move very slowly and smoothly with eyes directed to the ground about six feet ahead. If it is the spiders' snares which are to disclose their owner's presence, the collector's movements should be in a direction towards the sun, preferably in the evening when the sun is low or else when they are garnished with dew in the early morning.

A knowledge of the habits of each species and of the exact habitats in which they thrive is a great saver of time and energy. *Oonops pulcher* is a spider which people cannot find when they want it. If this is wanted in a hurry, try searching the trunks of Plane trees in London with a torch at night, if you have courage, or else peel off the bark with a screw-driver if nobody is watching ! I first learned of their abundance in London through gaining permission to search the gardens of Buckingham Palace some years ago and in this oasis I found twenty-six species in an hour or two despite the limitations placed on me by an attentive gardener. *Oonops* was particularly plentiful.

Examples could be multiplied; but there is still the problem to face of the time and energy expended in searching for the right place to search in a neighbourhood which is new to you. Maps will help but local knowledge gleaned from a local naturalist is far more important. Where is there a wide expanse of undulating heathland undisturbed by the Forestry Commissioners and unstifled by bracken? Are there any extensive marshes harbouring a variety of plant associations and where there are pools or ditches which do not dry up in summer? Are there any places which botanists or entomologists associate with rare plants or insects, for experience has shown that in such places there will be rare spiders as well. One has only to think of the New Forest, Bloxworth Heath, Box Hill and Wicken Fen to realise the importance of this as a clue.

It is the ambition of most collectors to find a species new to science or to the country. New species are awaiting discovery in Britain — but where? In his search for such a prize the collector may make discoveries far more important than the mere addition of a species to the British list and if it does appear it is likely so do so as an exciting surprise when least expected. Who would dream of searching deliberately for a species new to science amongst the larders of a Malayan hunting wasp and yet one was sent to me some years ago? Or, more fantastic still, in the stomachs of frogs and toads in America, Africa and the Canary Islands? Or picked up in nets when floating in the air by aeroplanes in the U.S.A.? Species new to science have been described from all these situations and some people might think it equally unexpected to learn that three species which I had added to the British list — *Oonops domesticus, Euophrys lanigera,* and *Physocyclus simoni* were subsequently found to have been living freely but unrecognised in the British Museum (Natural History)! May I be forgiven for disclosing this secret.

My own most dramatic discoveries of species new to Britain were of dozens of *Aulonia* disporting themselves around me in a tiny disused quarry near Dunster where I was eating a sandwich lunch, and of *Physocyclus* lit up by the narrow beam of a torch in a cellar at Bury St. Edmunds. These are further instances of the unexpected.

There are many other occasions when the discovery can only be made at home under the microscope. The expert can get careless about collecting or examining common species he feels sure he can identify at sight, like *Ciniflo ferox, Sitticus pubescens* or *Dysdera,* but can we really be quite certain that we have not got lurking in our collections some of the closely allied continental species? Several discoveries of this kind have been made in recent years, the latest of these being the recognition by G. H. Locket that our common *Theridon melanurum* (=*denticu-latum*) has concealed the identity of a second species *T. neglectum.*

The chances of collecting a new species can, of course, be improved by knowledge, skilful collecting and ingenious planning. I have already advised the careful search of areas harbouring rare plants and insects, but beyond this there are neglected deep caverns where eyeless pre-glacial forms might thrill us by their discovery, and neglected districts like Hereford and East Anglia. Even since I drafted this chapter two new species have been found in East Anglia. Then there are ideas to be followed up based on what Continental experience might lead us to expect in Britain. The Faeroes have got *Lycosa eiseni* Thor., *Trichopterna globipes* L. K., *Erigone psychrophila* Thor., and *Bolyphantes index* Thor. Do they also inhabit Shetland? My brief visit there was marred by almost continuous rain so I cannot be at all sure. There are the seven species mentioned in the appendix which inhabit the Channel Islands for which an eye should be kept open. After all *Araneus triguttatus, Prosopotheca corniculans* and other species were known in those islands before we found them in Britain. One more example is the Lycosid, *Tricca lutetiana* Sim., which is known in Holland, Belgium, Germany and France and which is not unlikely to inhabit ground with thick vegetation and bushes on the land side of sand dunes on our eastern coast.

Returning now to the apparatus mentioned at the beginning of the chapter — the umbrella, the sweeping net and the newspaper — these are undoubtedly needed on many occasions. For special purposes each collector is likely to devise his own tools. A screw-driver is helpful for stripping bark, a trowel when digging for *Atypus,* a water net for *Argyro-neta,* bags for collecting birds' nests, a torch for night work and even a tuning fork as a luxury to tempt *Ciniflo* to emerge quickly from her retreat! A sieve is favoured by some people, a funnel by others and a flotation tank by others for separating small spiders from heather or dense vegetation. Jars buried with rims level with the ground have been used as traps and also gummy bands round tree trunks. For personal comfort, I recommend gumboots for work in marshy ground and a small ground-sheet on which to squat when sifting grass. Last, and most important of all, a plentiful supply of corked glass tubes are recommended some of which should contain alcohol for killing speci-mens not being taken home alive for observation.

The collector is advised not to pick up spiders in his fingers — this is to save them, not him, from injury. Some collectors use suction tubes leading into a bottle for small specimens, but personally I rely on coaxing the spiders into an empty tube. Sometimes they can be guided to walk into a horizontal tube, but if it is placed vertically over them they soon try to climb upwards and their capture can be completed either with a thumb or a piece of stiff paper.

When keeping spiders alive at home it should be known that they die more often from lack of water than from shortage of food. Although most house spiders can live for months without water, those kinds which spend their lives in marshes may be dead before they reach home unless they are accompanied by a little damp moss.

When spiders die they soon shrink, shrivel, and lose their colour and other distinguishing marks, so they must be prevented from getting dry. This is why they are kept permanently in alcohol and whenever specimens are removed with forceps for examination under a microscope, they should still stand beneath alcohol in a shallow dish and propped in the right position by small pellets of paper, cottonwool or some other substance. This is not nearly so easy as it sounds. Dissecting needles should be used for arranging the legs or moving them when they obscure the view. Powerful illumination from above suitably directed on the spider is essential for microscope work.

If I have made the task of collecting sound too diffuse or elaborate, let me draw to a close by emphasising that there are occasions when no visible equipment is necessary. If, however, you are a timid mortal this is when you should beware of danger from your fellow men. Fresh in mind is my plotting of the area in London, bounded by Horseferry Road, Grosvenor Place, Piccadilly, St. James's Street, Whitehall and Millbank, within which the easily identifiable silk tubes of the large *Segestria florentina* are to be found. Places of special triumph included Westminster Abbey, Buckingham Palace, St. James's Palace and 10 Downing Street, but what risks I ran as I idled along the byeways of Piccadilly, or examined the walls of palaces and the Prime Minister's garden wall, or even dared without success to find the spider in the ramparts of Scotland Yard. A butterfly net would have attracted attention but it would have served as a passport. I could not forget that I was once arrested in the Louvre for taking a small bottle of alcohol out of my pocket to collect a *Meioneta rurestris* dangling from the brim of my hat. Or that on another occasion whilst watching *Araneus alsine* and *A. marmoreus pyramidatus* in a marshy valley on the Wakehurst Estate, near Ardingly, I was threatened with dog and brandished stick by an angry gamekeeper. This was indeed an amazing coincidence because my ancestor, John de Burstow, had been prevented from hunting larger quarry over the same area by William de Wakehurst, Forester to Sir Peter de Sabaudia, exactly 700 years earlier; In 1252 the Sheriff gave his ruling:

"It is commanded to him Peter, that he allows John to use the aforesaid chace as he and his predecessors were accustomed to use it from ancient times."

In my case the incident ended happily by Sir Henry Price giving me permission to chase spiders anywhere on his land.

APPENDIX

Spiders Recorded from England, Wales, Ireland and Scotland
up to 1958 *

MANY names, and some familiar to us, have unfortunately been changed since my list of species was published in 1939/41. Tiresome though this is, it was in a good cause. The International Commission of Zoological Nomenclature had steadfastly refused to recognise the validity of names given to spiders before the appearance of the tenth edition of Linnaeus' 'Systema Naturae' in 1758 until Mons. Pierre Bonnet organised world opinion in favour of accepting those bestowed on spiders by C. A. Clerck one year earlier in 1757. Justice has now been done to Clerck. Victory inspired Bonnet to write a forty-six page epic in verse in 1948 describing the laws of nomenclature.

I follow B. J. Kaston (1946) in adopting the generic name *Ctenium* in place of *Robertus* and H. Wiehle in substituting *Theridion melanurum* Hahn for *T. denticulatum* Walck. (see Locket and Millidge, *Ann. Mag. Nat. Hist.*, 12, X, 1957). Rightly perhaps., but too late for my decision or incorporation in this book, it is now advocated that *Theridion* should be replaced by *Theridium* and that *T. ovatum* should be transferred to the genus *Enoplognatha*.

In the lists which follow I recognise 584* species and 10 sub-species without counting 7 further species which inhabit the Channel Islands: *Zodarium italicum* Can., *Zelotes civicus* Sim., *Heliophanus aeneus* Hahn, *H. tribulosus* Sim., *Pellenes nigrociliatus* Sim., *Tarentula albofasciata* Brul., and *Tegenaria picta* Sim.

I follow custom established by others, but time and study is likely to show that some closely related species are really a species with a subspecies, whilst some subspecies should be reduced in status to forms (varieties). For example, I count *Araneus marmoreus pyramidatus* as a form and not a subspecies.

Normally subspecies have developed small structural differences after long geographical isolation, but they will still be capable of mating with the parent stock and producing fertile eggs. G. H. Locket has reared young from mixed marriages of *Lycosa pullata* with *L. prativaga* without yet establishing that the offspring are fertile but it is not unlikely that *L. prativaga* should be regarded as a subspecies of *L. pullata*.

Isolation can also come about through seasonal separation as in the case of *Meta segmentata* where one brood mates in April and another in

*See Addendum, p. xiv, for 21 additions to this total. Also for some changes in nomenclature.

September. Here small structural differences justify the spring brood being recognised as a subspecies, *M. segmentata mengei.*

In the table which follows I show the numbers of species in each family together with their known occurrence in England, Wales, Ireland and Scotland. They are allotted to twenty-four families at present though I am coming to the view that *Theridiosoma* deserves a family to itself and that neither *Zora* nor *Agroeca* fit comfortably into the family Clubionidae.

Order ARANEAE

	Total	England	Wales	Ireland	Scotland
MYGALOMORPHAE					
Atypidae	1	1	1	1	0
ARANEOMORPHAE					
Eresidae	1	1	0	0	0
Dictynidae	16	15	10	6	6
Uloboridae	2	2	0	1	0
Oonopidae	5	5	2	2	2
Dysderidae	6	6	4	4	3
Scytodidae	1	1	0	0	0
Pholcidae	2	2	1	1	1
Gnaphosidae	27	25	12	9	14
Clubionidae	38	36	25	20	22
Anyphaenidae	1	1	1	1	1
Sparassidae	1	1	1	1	0
Thomisidae	37	37	24	17	16
Salticidae	33	33	12	13	13
Oxyopidae	1	1	0	0	0
Lycosidae	37	36	26	20	23
Pisauridae	3	3	2	2	2
Agelenidae	22	22	14	13	12
Mimetidae	3	3	2	2	2
Theridiidae	48	46	21	28	24
Nesticidae	2	2	1	1	1
Tetragnathidae	9	9	7	9	6
Argiopidae	38	38	22	19	20
Linyphiidae	250	237	146	148	169
Total:	584	562	334	318	337

If we included the ten sub-species, we could add to these totals 9 for England, 2 for Wales, 5 for Ireland and 4 for Scotland.

England has, of course, been searched more intensively than the other three countries but climate and proximity to the Continent undoubtedly provides England with a richer fauna. Two English counties, Hampshire and Dorset, are known to have more than four hundred species and several others more than three hundred, including Yorkshire, Staffordshire, Northumberland, Sussex and Surrey.

In the list which follows the letters E, W, I and S indicate their known occurrence in England, Wales, Ireland and Scotland respectively.

Family ATYPIDAE
Atypus affinis Eichw.   E, W, I.

Family ERESIDAE
Eresus niger (Pet.)   E.

Family DICTYNIDAE
Ciniflo fenestralis (Stroem)   E, W, I, S.
C. similis Bl.   E, W, I, S.
C. ferox (Walck.)   E, W, I, S.
Dictyna arundinacea (Linn.)   E, W, I, S.
D. pusilla Thor.   E, W, S.
D. major Menge   S.
D. uncinata Thor.   E, W, I.
D. latens (Fab.)   E, W, I.
D. puella Sim.   E.
D. flavescens (Walck.)   E.
D. viridissima (Walck.)   E.
Lathys humilis (Bl.)   E, W.
L. stigmatisata (Menge)   E.
Argenna subnigra   E, W.
   (O.P.-Camb.)
Protadia patula (Sim.)   E, W.
Altella lucida (Sim.)   E.

Family ULOBORIDAE
Uloborus walckenaerius Latr.   E.
Hyptiotes paradoxus (C.L.K.)   E, I.

Family OONOPIDAE
Oonops pulcher Templ.   E, W, I, S.
O. domesticus de Dalm.   E, W, S.
Ischnothyreus velox Jacks.   E.
Triaeris stenaspis Sim.   E, I.
Diblemma donisthorpei   E.
   (O.P.-Camb.)

Family DYSDERIDAE
Dysdera erythrina (Walck.)   E, W, I.
D. crocata C.L.K.   E, W, I, S.
Harpactea hombergi (Scop.)   E, W, I, S.
Segestria senoculata (Linn.)   E, W, I, S.
S. bavarica C.L.K.   E.
S. florentina (Rossi)   E.

Family SCYTODIDAE
Scytodes thoracica Latr.   E.

Family PHOLCIDAE
Pholcus phalangioides (Fuess.)   E, W, I, S.
Physocyclus simoni Berl.   E.

Family GNAPHOSIDAE
Drassodes lapidosus (Walck.)   E, W, I, S.
   D. lapidosus macer (Thor.)   E, W.
   D. lapidosus cupreus (Bl.)   E, I, S.
D. pubescens (Thor.)   E, W, S.
D. signifer (C.L.K.)   E, W, I, S.
D. dalmatensis (L.Koch)   E.
D. silvestris (Bl.)   E, W, S.
D. minor (O.P.-Camb.)   E.
D. sorenseni (Strand)   S.
Herpyllus blackwalli (Thor.)   E, W, I, S.
Phaeocedus braccatus   E.
   (L. Koch)
Zelotes pedestris (C.L.K.)   E.
Z. lutetianus (L. Koch)   E, I, S.
Z. pusillus (C.L.K.)   E, W, I, S.
Z. rusticus (L. Koch)   E.
Z. praeficus (L. Koch)   E.
Z. electus (C.L.K.)   E, W, S.
Z. latreillei (Sim.)   E, W, I, S.
Z. apricorum (L. Koch)   E, W, I, S.

APPENDIX 285

Z. serotinus (L. Koch) E, W, I, S.
Z. petrensis (C.L.K.) E.
Gnaphosa lugubris (C.L.K.) E.
G. occidentalis Sim. E.
G. leporina (L. Koch) E, S.
Micaria pulicaria (Sund.) E, W, I, S.
M. scintillans (O.P.-Camb.) E.
M. alpina L. Koch W.
M. subopaca Westr. E.
M. silesiaca L. Koch E.

Family CLUBIONIDAE
Clubiona corticalis (Walck.) E, W.
C. reclusa O.P.-Camb. E, W, I, S.
C. subsultans Thor. S.
C. stagnatilis Kulcz. E, W, I, S.
C. rosserae Locket E.
C. norvegica Strand E.
C. coerulescens L. Koch E, S.
C. pallidula (Clerck) E, W, I, S.
C. phragmitis C.L.K. E, W, I, S.
C. terrestris Westr. E, W, I, S.
C. neglecta O.P.-Camb. E, W, I, S.
C. lutescens Westr. E, W, I, S.
C. compta C.L.K. E, W, I, S.
C. brevipes Bl. E, W, I, S.
C. trivialis C.L.K. E, W, I, S.
C. juvenis Sim. I.
C. genevensis L. Koch W, E.
C. diversa O.P.-Camb. E, W, I, S.
C. subtilis L. Koch E, W, S.
Cheiracanthium erraticum (Walck.) E, W, I, S.
C. pennyi O.P.-Camb. E.
C. virescens (Sund.) E, W, I, S.
Agroeca brunnea (Bl.) E, W, S.
A. proxima (O.P.-Camb.) E, W, I. S.
A. inopina O.P.-Camb. E, W.
A. lusatica (L. Koch) E.
A. cuprea Menge E.
Agraecina striata (Kulcz.) E.
Scotina celans (Bl.) E, W, I.
S. gracilipes (Bl.) E, W, I, S.
S. palliardi (L. Koch) E.
Liocranum rupicola (Walck.) E, W. I.
Zora spinimana (Sund.) E, W, I, S.
Z. armillata Sim. E.
Z. nemoralis (Bl.) E, W, S.

Z. silvestris Kulcz. E
Phrurolithus festivus (C.L.K.) E, W, I, S.
P. minimus C.L.K. E.

Family ANYPHAENIDAE
Anyphaena accentuata (Walck.) E, W, I, S.

Family SPARASSIDAE
Micrommata virescens (Clerck) E, W, I.

Family THOMISIDAE
Thomisus onustus Walck. E.
Diaea dorsata (Fabr.) E, W.
Misumena vatia (Clerck) E, W, I.
Pistius truncatus (Pallas) E.
Xysticus cristatus (Clerck) E, W, I, S.
X. audax (Schrank) E, W, I, S.
X. kochi Thor. E, W, S.
X. erraticus (Bl.) E, W, I, S.
X. lanio C.L.K. E, I, W, S.
X. ulmi (Hahn) E, I, S. W.
X. bifasciatus C.L.K. E, W, S.
X. luctator L. Koch E.
X. sabulosus (Hahn) E, I, S.
X. luctuosus (Bl.) E, W, S.
X. acerbus Thor. E, W.
X. robustus (Hahn) E.
Oxyptila blackwalli Sim. E.
O. scabricula (Westr.) E, W.
O. nigrita (Thor.) E.
O. sanctuaria (O.P.-Camb.) E, W, I.
O. praticola (C.L.K.) E, W, I.
O. trux (Bl.) E, W, I, S.
O. simplex (O.P.-Camb.) E, S, W.
O. atomaria (Panz.) E, W, I, S.
O. brevipes (Hahn) E, W, I.
Philodromus dispar Walck. E, W, I.
P. aureolus (Clerck) E, W, I, S.
P. aureolus caespiticolis Walck. E, W, I, S.
P. collinus C.L.K. E.
P. fallax Sund. E, W.
P. histrio (Latr.) E, S, W
P. emarginatus (Schr.) E, I, S.
P. rufus Walck. E.
P. margaritatus (Clerck) E.
Thanatus striatus C.L.K. E.
T. formicinus (Clerck) E.

286 APPENDIX

Tibellus maritimus (Menge) E, W, I.
T. oblongus (Walck.) E, W, I, S.

Family SALTICIDAE
Salticus scenicus (Clerck) E, W, I, S.
S. cingulatus (Panz.) E, W, I, S.
S. zebraneus (C.L.K.) E.
Heliophanus cupreus (Walck.) E, W, I, S.
H. flavipes C.L.K. E, W, I, S.
H. expers (O.P.-Camb.) E.
Marpissa muscosa (Clerck) E.
M. pomatia (Walck.) E.
Bianor aenescens (Simon) E.
Hyctia nivoyi (Lucas) E, W, I.
Ballus depressus (Walck.) E.
Neon reticulatus (Bl.) E, W, I, S.
N. valentulus Falc. E.
Euophrys frontalis (Walck.) E, W, I, S.
E. molesta O.P.-Camb. E.
E. petrensis C.L.K. E, I, S.
E. erratica (Walck.) E, W, I, S.
E. aequipes (O.P.-Camb.) E, S.
E. lanigera (Simon) E.
E. browningi Mill & Lock. E.
Sitticus pubescens (Fabr.) E, W, I.
S. caricis (Westr.) E.
S. floricola (C.L.K.) E, I.
S. rupicola (C.L.K.) E.
Attulus saltator (Sim.) E, W.
Evarcha falcata (Clerck) E, W, I, S.
E. arcuata (Clerck) E, S.
Aelurillus v-insignitus (Clerck) E, S.
Phlegra fasciata (Hahn) E.
Synageles venator (Lucas) E, W.
Myrmarachne formicaria E.
(Degeer)
Hasarius adansoni (Aud.) E, I, S.
Pellenes tripunctatus (Walck.) E.

Family OXYOPIDAE
Oxyopes heterophthalmus Latr. E.

Family LYCOSIDAE
Lycosa arenicola O.P.-Camb. E, W, I.
L. agricola Thor. E, W, I, S.
L. agrestis Westr. E.
L. purbeckensis E, W, I, S.
(F.O. P.-Camb.)

L. monticola (Clerck) E, W, I, S.
L. tarsalis Thor. E, W, I, S.
L. tarsalis herbigrada Bl. E, I, S.
L. pullata (Clerck) E, W, I, S.
L. prativaga L. Koch E, W, I, S.
L. amentata (Clerck) E, W, I, S.
L. nigriceps Thor. E, W, I, S.
L. lugubris (Walck.) E, W, I, S.
L. hortensis Thor. E, S.
L. proxima C.L.K. E, W.
L. trailli O.P.-Camb. E, W, S.
L. paludicola (Clerck) E.
L. rubrofasciata (Ohl.) E.
Xerolycosa nemoralis (Westr.) E.
X. miniata (C.L.K.) E, W, S.
Tarentula pulverulenta E, W, I, S.
(Clerck)
T. cuneata (Clerck) E.
T. barbipes (Sund.) E, W, S.
T. fabrilis (Clerck) E.
Trochosa ruricola (Degeer) E, W, I, S.
T. robusta (Simon) E.
T. terricola Thor. E, W, I, S.
T. spinipalpis E, W.
(F.O. P.-Camb.)
T. fulvolineata (Luc.) E.
Arctosa perita (Latr.) E, W, I, S.
A. leopardus (Sund.) E, W, I, S.
A. cinerea (Fabr.) E, W, I, S.
A. alpigena (Dol.) S.
Pirata piraticus (Clerck) E, W, I, S.
P. hygrophilus Thor. E, W, I, S.
P. latitans (Bl.) E, W, I, S.
P. piscatorius (Clerck) E, I, S, W.
P. uliginosus (Thor.) E, W.
Aulonia albimana (Walck.) E.

Family PISAURIDAE
Pisaura mirabilis (Clerck) E, W, I, S.
Dolomedes fimbriatus (Clerck) E, I, S, W.
D. plantarius (Clerck) E.

Family AGELENIDAE
Argyroneta aquatica (Clerck) E, W, I, S.
Agelena labyrinthica (Clerck) E, W, I.
Textrix denticulata (Oliv.) E, W, I, S.
Tegenaria atrica C.L.K. E, W, I, S.
T. larva Simon E, I.

T. parietina (Fourc.)	E, I.	*T. aulicum* C.L.K.	E, I.
T. agrestis (Walck.)	E.	*T. lunatum* (Clerck)	E, I.
T. domestica (Clerck)	E, W, I, S.	*T. saxatile* C.L.K.	E.I.
T. pagana (C.L.K.)	E, I.	*T. tepidariorum* C.L.K.	E, W, I, S.
T. silvestris L. Koch	E, W.	*T. tepidariorum simulans*	E.
Amaurobius atropos (Walck.)	E, W, S.	Thor.	
A. terrestris (Wid.)	E, S.	*T. sisyphium* (Clerck)	E, W, I, S.
Cicurina cicur (Fabr.)	E.	*T. impressum* L. Koch	E, W, S.
Cryphoeca silvicola (C.L.K.)	E, W, I, S.	*T. pictum* (Walck.)	E, S.
Tetrilus arietinus Thor.	E.	*T. simile* C.L.K.	E, I, S.
T. arietinus macrophthalmus	E, W.	*T. varians* Hahn	E, W, I, S.
Kulcz.		*T. melanurum* Hahn	E, W, I, S.
Tuberta moerens	E.	*T. neglectum* Wiehle	E.
(O.P.-Camb.)		*T. familiare* O.P.-Camb.	E.
Antistea elegans (Bl.)	E, W, I, S.	*T. blackwalli* O.P.-Camb.	E, I.
Hahnia montana (Bl.)	E, W, I, S.	*T. tinctum* (Walck.)	E, W, I.
H. candida Simon	E, S.	*T. ovatum* (Clerck)	E, W, I, S.
H. nava (Bl.)	E, W, I, S.	*T. instabile* O.P.-Camb.	E, I.
H. helveola Simon	E, W, I, S.	*T. bellicosum* Simon	E, W, S.
H. pusilla C.L.K.	E, W.	*T. bimaculatum* (Linn.)	E, W, I, S.
		T. pallens Bl.	E, W, I, S.
Family MIMETIDAE		*Enoplognatha thoracica* (Hahn)	E, W, I, S.
Ero cambridgei Kulcz.	E, I, S, W.	*E. schaufussi* (L. Koch)	E.
E. furcata (Vill.)	E, W, I, S.	*E. mandibularis nigrocincta*	F.
E. tuberculata (Degeer)	E.	Sim.	
		Ctenium lividus (Bl.)	E, W, I, S.
Family THERIDIIDAE		*C. arundineti* (O.P.-Camb.)	E, W, I, S.
Episinus angulatus (Bl.)	E, W, I, S.	*C. neglectus* (O.P.-Camb.)	E, W, I, S.
E. truncatus Latr.	E, I.	*C. scoticus* Jackson	S.
E. maculipes Cav.	E.	*C. insignis* O.P.-Camb.	E.
Euryopis flavomaculata	E, I, S.	*Pholcomma gibbum* (Westr.)	E, W, I, S.
(C.L.K.)		*Theonoe minutissima*	E, W, I, S.
Dipoena erythropus (Simon)	E.	(O.P.-Camb.)	
D. prona (Menge)	E.		
D. inornata (O.P.-Camb.)	E, I, W.	Family NESTICIDAE	
D. tristis (Hahn)	E, I.	*Nesticus cellulanus* (Clerck)	E, W, I, S.
D. coracina (C.L.K.)	E.	*Eidmanella pallidus* Emerton	E.
D. melanogaster (C.L K.)	E.		
D. torva (Thor.)	S.	Family TETRAGNATHIDAE	
Crustulina guttata (Wider)	E, W, S.	*Tetragnatha extensa* (Linn.)	E, W, I, S.
C. sticta (O.P.-Camb.)	E.	*T. pinicola* L. Koch	E, W, I, S.
Asagena phalerata (Panz.)	E, W, S.	*T. montana* Simon	E, W, I, S.
Lithyphantes albomaculatus	E.	*T. obtusa* C.L.K.	E, I, W.
(Degeer)		*T. nigrita* Lendl	E, I.
Steatoda bipunctata (Linn.)	E, W, I, S.	*Eugnatha striata* (L. Koch)	E, I.
Teutana grossa (C.L.K.)	E, I.	*Pachygnatha clercki* Sund.	E, W, I, S.
Theridion vittatum C.L.K.	E, I.	*P. listeri* Sund.	E, W, I, S.
T. pulchellum (Walck.)	E.	*P. degeeri* Sund.	E, W, I, S.

Family ARGIOPIDAE

Meta segmentata (Clerck)	E, W, I, S.
M. segmentata mengei (Bl.)	E, W, I, S.
M. merianae (Scop.)	E, W, I, S.
M. menardi (Latr.)	E, W, I, S.
M. bourneti Simon	E.
Araneus bituberculatus (Walck.)	E.
A. gibbosus (Walck.)	E, W, I.
A. angulatus Clerck.	E.
A. diadematus Clerck	E, W, I, S.
A. quadratus Clerck	E, W, I, S.
A. marmoreus Clerck	E.
A. marmoreus pyramidatus Clerck	E, W, S.
A. alsine (Walck.)	E, W.
A. cornutus Clerck	E, W, I, S.
A. sclopetarius Clerck	E, W.
A. patagiatus Clerck	E, W, I, S.
A. ceropegius (Walck.)	E.
A. umbraticus Clerck	E, W, I, S.
A. redii (Scop.)	E, W, I, S.
A. adiantus (Walck.)	E, W, I.
A. sturmi (Hahn)	E, W, S.
A. triguttatus (Fabr.)	E, S.
A. cucurbitinus Clerck	E, W, I, S.
A. cucurbitinus opisthographus Kulcz.	E.
A. inconspicuus (Simon)	E.
A. alpicus (L. Koch)	E.
A. displicatus westringi (Thor.)	E.
Zilla diodia (Walck.)	E.
Singa albovittata (Westr.)	E.
S. pygmaea (Sund.)	E, I, S, W.
S. sanguinea C.L.K.	E, I.
S. heri (Hahn)	E.
S. hamata (Clerck)	E, S.
Cercidia prominens (Westr.)	E, W, S.
Zygiella x-notata (Clerck)	E, W, I, S.
Z. atrica (C.L.K.)	E, W, I, S.
Z. stroemi (Thor.)	E, S.
Mangora acalypha (Walck.)	E, W, I.
Cyclosa conica (Pall.)	E, W, I, S.
Argiope bruennichi (Scop.)	E.
Theridiosoma gemmosum (L. Koch)	E, I.

Family LINYPHIIDAE

Ceratinella brevipes (Westr.)	E, W, I, S.
C. brevis (Wid.)	E, W, I, S.
C. scabrosa (O.P.-Camb.)	E, I.
Walckeaenra acuminata Bl.	E, W, I, S.
Wideria antica (Wid.)	E, W, I, S.
W. cucullata (C.L.K.)	E, W, I, S.
W. nodosa (O.P.-Camb.)	E, I, S.
W. melanocephala (O.P.-Camb.)	E, W, I.
W. capito (Westr.)	E, W, S.
W. fugax (O.P.-Camb.)	E.
W. polita (Sim.)	E.
Trachynella nudipalpis (Westr.)	E, W, I, S.
T. obtusa (Bl.)	E, S.
Prosopotheca monoceros (Wid.)	E, W, S.
P. corniculans (O.P.-Camb.)	E.
P. incisa (O.P.-Camb.)	E, W.
Tigellinus furcillatus (Menge)	E.
Cornicularia unicornis (O.P.-Camb.)	E, W, I.
C. kochi (O.P.-Camb.)	E, W.
C. karpinskii (O.P.-Camb.)	E, W, S.
C. cuspidata (Bl.)	E, W, I, S.
C. vigilax (Bl.)	E, W, I, S.
Dicymbium nigrum (Bl.)	E, W, I, S.
D. tibiale (Bl.)	E, W, I, S.
Entelecara acuminata (Wid.)	E, W.
E. congenera (O P.-Cambr.)	E.
E. erythropus (Westr.)	E, W, I, S.
E. flavipes (Bl.)	E, S.
E. omissa O.P.-Cambr.	E.
E. errata O.P.-Cambr.	E, W.
Moebelia penicillata (Westr.)	E, I, S.
Erigonidium graminicola (Sund.)	E, W, I, S.
Gnathonarium dentatum (Wid.)	E, W, I, S.
Tmeticus affinis (Bl.)	E, W.
Gongylidium rufipes (Sund.)	E, W, I, S.
Dismodicus bifrons (Bl.)	E, W, I, S.
D. elevatus (C.L.K.)	S.
Hypomma bituberculatum (Wid.)	E, W, I, S.
H. fulvum Bose.	E.
H. cornutum (Bl.)	E, W, I, S.
Metopobactrus prominulus (O.P.-Camb.)	E, W, I, S.
Hybocoptus decollatus (Sim.)	E.

Praestigia duffeyi Mill.	E.
Baryphyma pratensis (Bl.)	E.
Gonatium rubens (Bl.)	E, W, I, S.
G. rubellum (Bl.)	E, W, I, S.
G. corallipes (Cambr.)	E.
Minyrioloides trifons (O.P.-Camb.)	E, I, S.
Maso sundevalli (Westr.)	E, W, I, S.
M. gallica Sim.	E.
Peponocranium ludicrum (O.P.-Camb.)	E, W, I, S.
Pocadicnemis pumila (Bl.)	E, W, I, S.
Hypselistes jacksoni (O.P.-Camb.)	E, W.
H. florens (O.P.-Camb.)	E.
Oedothorax gibbosus (Bl.)	E, W, I, S.
Oe. tuberosus (Bl.)	E, W, I, S.
Oe. fuscus (Bl.)	E, W, I, S.
Oe. agrestis (Bl.)	E, W, I, S.
Oe. retusus (Westr.)	E, W, I, S.
Oe. apicatus (Bl.)	E, W, I, S.
Trichopterna thorelli (Westr.)	E, I, S.
T. blackwalli O.P.-Camb.	E, I, S.
T. mengei (Sim.)	E, I, S, W.
Lophocarenum parallelum (Wid.)	E, W, I, S.
L. nemorale (Bl.)	E, W, I, S.
L. stramineum (Menge)	E.
L. elongatum (Wid.)	S.
L. radicicola (L. Koch)	E.
Silometopus elegans (O.P.-Camb.)	E, W, I, S.
S. curtus (Sim.)	E, I, S.
S. ambiguus (O.P.-Camb.)	E, S.
S. interjectus (O.P.-Camb.)	E, I, S.
S. incurvatus (O. P.-Camb.)	E, S.
Mecopisthes pusillus (Menge)	E.
Cnephalocotes obscurus (Bl.)	E, W, I, S.
Acartauchenius scurrilis (O.P.-Camb.)	E.
Trichoncus saxicola (O.P.-Camb.)	E, I.
T. affinis Kulcz.	E.
Styloctetor romanus (O.P.-Camb.)	E, W.
Anacotyle stativa (Sim.)	E, I.
Evansia merens O.P.-Camb.	E, W, I, S.
Tiso vagans (Bl.)	E, W, I, S.

WS—U

T. aestivus (L. Koch)	W, S.
Troxochrus scabriculus (Westr.)	E, W, I, S.
T. cirrifrons (O.P.-Camb.)	E, W, I.
Minyriolus pusillus (Wid.)	E, W, I, S.
Tapinocyba praecox (O.P.-Camb.)	E, I, W.
T. pallens (O.P.-Camb.)	E, W, S.
T. insecta (L. Koch)	E, I.
T. mitis (O.P.-Camb.)	E.
T. antepenultima (O.P.-Camb.)	E.
Aulacocyba subitanea (O.P.-Camb.)	E, W, S.
Perimones britteni (Jacks.)	E, S.
Thyreosthenius parasiticus (Westr.)	E, I, S.
T. biovatus (O.P.-Camb.)	E, S.
Monocephalus fuscipes (Bl.)	E, W, I, S.
M. castaneipes (Sim.)	E, W, I, S.
Lophomma punctatum (Bl.)	E, W, I, S.
Mioxena blanda (Sim.)	E.
Saloca diceros (O.P.-Camb.)	E.
Jacksonella falconeri (Jacks.)	E, S.
Gongylidiellum vivum (O.P.-Camb.)	E, W, I, S.
G. latebricola (O.P.-Camb.)	E, S.
G. murcidum Sim.	E, S.
G. calcariferum Sim.	E.
Micrargus herbigradus (Bl.)	E, W, S.
M. subaequalis (Westr.)	E, W, I, S.
M. laudatus (O.P.-Camb .)	E, W.
Notioscopus sarcinatus (O.P.-Camb.)	E.
Glyphesis cottonae (La Touche)	E.
G. servulus Sim.	E.
Erigonella hiemalis (Bl.)	E, W, I, S.
E. ignobilis (O.P.-Camb.)	E, W, I.
Savignia frontata (Bl.)	E, W, I, S.
Diplocephalus cristatus (Bl.)	E, W, I, S.
D. permixtus (O.P.-Camb.)	E, W, I, S.
D. latifrons (O.P.-Camb.)	E, W, I, S.
D. adjacens O.P.-Camb.	E.
D. jacksoni O.P.-Camb.	E.
D. picinus (Bl.)	E, W, I, S.
D. protuberans (O.P.-Camb.)	E.
Araeoncus humilis (Bl.)	E, W, I, S.

A. crassiceps (Westr.)   E, I, S.
Panamomops sulcifrons (Wid.)   E.
Lessertia dentichelis (Sim.)   E, W, I, S.
Asthenargus paganus (Sim.)   E, I, W, S.
Caledonia evansi O.P.-   E, S.
   Camb.
Typhocrestus digitatus   E, W, I, S.
   (O.P.-Camb.)
Collinsia distincta (Sim.)   E.
C. holmgreni (Thor.)   S.
Scotargus inerrans   E, S.
   (O.P.-Camb.)
Diplocentria bidentata   E, I, S.
   (Emert.)
Erigone dentipalpis (Wid.)   E, W, I, S.
E. atra (Bl.)   E, W, I, S.
E. promiscua (O.P.-Camb.)   E, W, I, S.
E. arctica (White)   E, I, S.
E. longipalpis (Sund.)   E, W, I, S.
E. tirolensis L. Koch   S.
E. capra Sim.   I.
E. welchi Jacks.   I.
E. vagans Aud.   E.
Rhaebothorax morulus   E, W, I, S.
   (O.P.-Camb.)
Eboria fausta (O.P.-Camb.)   E, W, S.
E. caliginosa Falc.   E, S.
Donacochara speciosa (Thor.)   E, I.
Leptorhoptrum robustum   E, W, I, S.
   (Westr.)
Drepanotylus uncatus   E, W, I, S.
   (O.P.-Camb.)
Phaulothrix hardyi (Bl.)   E, I, S.
Hilaira excisa (O.P.-Camb.)   E, W, I, S.
H. frigida (Thor.)   E, W, I, S.
H. nubigena Hull   E.
H. pervicax Hull   E, S.
Halorates reprobus   E, W, I, S.
   (O.P.-Camb.)
Ostearius melanopygius   E, W.
   (O.P.-Camb.)
Hillhousia misera   E, W, S.
   (O.P.-Camb.)
Porrhomma pygmaeum (Bl.)   E, I, S, W.
P. convexum (Westr.)   E, I, S.
P. rosenhaueri (L. Koch)   I.
P. pallidum Jacks   E, I, S, W.
P. campbelli F.O.P.-Camb.   E, W, I.

P. microphthalmum   E, S.
   (O.P.-Camb.)
P. errans (Bl.)   E, I.
P. egeria Sim.   E, I, S.
P. oblitum (O.P.-Camb.)   E.
P. montanum Jacks.   E, W, S.
Syedrula innotabilis   E, I, S.
   (O.P.-Camb.)
S. gracilis (Menge)   E.
Agyneta subtilis (O.P.-   E, W, I, S.
   Camb.)
A. conigera (O.P.-Camb.)   E, W, I, S.
A. decora (O.P.-Camb.)   E, I, S.
A. cauta (O.P.-Camb.)   E, W.
A. ramosa Jacks.   E, W.
Meioneta rurestris (C.L.K.)   E, W, I, S.
Meioneta mollis (O.P.-Camb.)   E, W.
M. saxatilis (Bl.)   E, W, I, S.
M. beata (O.P.-Camb.)   E, S.
M. gulosa (L. Koch)   E, W, S.
M. nigripes (Sim.)   S.
Microneta viaria (Bl.)   E, W, I, S.
Maro minutus O.P.-Camb.   E, W.
M. sublestus Falc.   E.
Centromerus sylvaticus (Bl.)   E, W, I, S.
C. expertus (O.P.-Camb.)   E, W, I, S.
C. prudens (O.P.-Camb.)   E, W, I, S.
C. arcanus (O.P.-Camb.)   E, W, I, S.
C. laevitarsis (Sim.)   E.
C. capucinus (Sim.)   E
C. dilutus (O.P.-Camb.)   E, W, I. S.
C. incilium (L. Koch)   E, S.
C. incultus Falc.   E.
C. subacutus (O.P.-Camb.)   E.
C. serratus (O.P.-Camb.)   E.
C. jacksoni Denis   E.
C. persimilis (O.P.-Camb.)   E.
Centromerita bicolor (Bl.)   E, W, I, S.
C. concinna (Thor.)   E, W, I, S.
Sintula cornigera (Bl.)   E, S.
Oreonetides abnormis (Bl.)   E, W, I, S.
O. firmus (O.P.-Camb.)   E, I, S, W.
O. vaginatus (Thor.)   E, W, I, S.
Macrargus rufus (Wid.)   E, W, I, S.
   M. rufus carpenteri   E, S.
     (O.P.-Camb.)
Bathyphantes dorsalis (Wid.)   E, W, I, S.
B. concolor (Wid.)   E, W, I, S.

B. approximatus	E, W, I, S.	*L. tenuis* (Bl.)	E, W, I, S.
(O.P.-Camb.)		*L. zimmermanni* Bertk.	E, W, I, S.
B. pullatus (O.P.-Camb.)	E, W, I, S.	*L. cristatus* (Menge)	E, W, I, S.
B. gracilis (Bl.)	E, W, I, S.	*L. mengei* Kulcz.	E, W, I, S.
B. parvulus (Westr.)	E.	*L. flavipes* (Bl.)	E, W, I, S.
B. nigrinus (Westr.)	E, W, I, S.	*L. tenebricola* (Wid.)	E, W, S.
B. setiger F.O.P.-Camb.	E, I.	*L. ericaeus* (Bl.)	E, W, I, S.
Poeciloneta globosa (Wid.)	E, W, I, S.	*L. pallidus* (O.P.-Camb.)	E, W, I, S.
Drapetisca socialis (Sund.)	E, W, I, S.	*L. pinicola* Sim.	E, W, S.
Tapinopa longidens (Wid.)	E, W, I, S.	*L. insignis* O.P.-Camb.	E.
Floronia bucculenta (Clerck)	E, W, I.	*L. angulatus* (O.P.-Camb.)	E, S.
Taranucnus setosus	E.	*L. audax* Sor.	S.
(O.P.-Camb.)		*L. carri* Jacks.	E.
Labulla thoracica (Wid.)	E, W, I.	*L. expunctus* (O.P.-Camb.)	S.
Stemonyphantes lineatus (Linn.)	E, W, I, S.	*Helophora insignis* (Bl.)	E, W, I, S.
Bolyphantes luteolus (Bl.)	E, W, I, S.	*Linyphia triangularis* (Clerck)	E, W, I, S.
B. luteolus subnigripes	I.	*L. montana* (Clerck)	E, W, I, S.
(O.P.-Camb.)		*L. clathrata* Sund.	E, W, I, S.
B. alticeps (Sund.)	E, W, S.	*L. peltata* Wid.	E, W, I, S.
Lepthyphantes nebulosus	E, W, I, S.	*L. pusilla* Sund.	E, W, I, S.
(Sund.)		*L. hortensis* Sund.	E, W, I, S.
L. leprosus (Ohl.)	E, W, I, S.	*L. impigra* O.P.-Camb.	E, I.
L. minutus (Bl.)	E, W, I, S.	*L. furtiva* O.P.-Camb.	E.
L. alacris (Bl.)	E, W, I, S.	*L. marginata* C.L.K.	S.
L. whymperi F.O.P.-Cambr.	E, W, I, S.	*Mengea scopigera* (Grube)	E, W, I, S.
L. obscurus (Bl.)	E, W, I, S.	*M. warburtoni* (O.P.-Camb.)	E, I.

See Addendum, p. xiv, for 21 additions, up to 1968.

BIBLIOGRAPHY

A complete list of spider literature up to 1939 will be found in P. Bonnet's *Bibliographia Araneorum*, Vol. 1., 1945.

BALOGH, J. (1934). Vorläufige Mitellung uber radnetzbauende Pachygnathen. *Folia zool. hydrobiol.* 6 (1).

BERLAND, L. and FAGE, L. (1926–37). Posthumous revision of E. Simon's Les Arachnides de France, 6 (pts 2–5). Paris.

BLACKWALL, J. (1861–64). A History of the Spiders of Great Britain and Ireland. London.

BONNET, P. (1925). Sur la ponte des oeufs chez Argiope bruennichi. *Bull. Soc. ent. Fr.*

— (1927). Etude et considérations sur la fécondité chez les Araneides. *Mem. Soc. zool. Fr.*, 28 (3).

— (1930). La mue, l'autotomie et la régénération chez les Araignées avec une étude des Dolomedes d'Europe. *Thèse Fac. sci. Toulouse*, 44.

— (1935). La longévité chez les Araignées. *Bull. Soc. ent. Fr.*, 40 (19).

— (1935). Theridion tepidariorum C.L.K., Araignée cosmopolite: répartition, cycle vital, moeurs. *Bull. Soc. hist. nat. Toulouse*, 68.

— (1937). Elevage de Physocyclus simoni. *Bull. Soc. hist. nat. Toulouse*, 71 (4).

— (1947). L'Instinct maternel des Araignées. *Bull. Soc. d'Hist. Nat. Toulouse*, 81.

BRISTOWE, W. S. (1922). Spiders Found in the Neighbourhood of Oxshott. *Proc. S. Lond. Ent. Nat. Hist. Soc.*

— (1923). A British Semi-Marine Spider. *Ann. Mag. Nat. Hist.* (9) 12.

— (1925). Fauna of the Arctic Island of Jan Mayen and its probable Origin. *Ann. Mag. Nat. Hist.* (9) 15.

— (1926). The Mating Habits of British Thomisid and Sparassid Spiders. *Ann. Mag. Nat. Hist.* (9) 18.

— and G. H. LOCKET. (1926). The Courtship of British Lycosid Spiders and its probable significance. *Proc. Zool. Soc. Lond.*

— (1929). The Spiders of the Scilly Islands. *Proc. Zool. Soc. Lond.*

— (1929). The Mating Habits of Spiders, with special reference to the Problems surrounding Sex Dimorphism. *Proc. Zool. Soc. Lond.*

— (1930). A Supplementary Note on the Mating Habit of Spiders. *Proc. Zool. Soc. Lond.*

(1931). The Mating Habits of Spiders: a Second Supplement. *Proc. Zool. Soc. Lond.*

(1933). The Liphistiid Spiders. With an Appendix on their Internal Anatomy by J. Millot. *Proc. Zool. Soc. Lond.*

(1938). The Classification of Spiders. *Proc. Zool. Soc. Lond.* (B) 108 (2).

(1939–41). The Comity of Spiders. 2 vols. *Ray Society,* London.

(1945). Spider Superstitions and Folklore. *Trans. Connecticut Acad. Arts and Sciences.* 36.

(1947). Spiders. King Penguin Books. Harmondsworth.

(1948). Notes on the Structure and Systematic Position of Oonopid Spiders. *Proc. Zool. Soc. Lond.,* 118.

(1954). The Chelicerae of Spiders. *Endeavour.* 13.

CLOUDSLEY-THOMPSON, J. L. (1957). Nocturnal Ecology and Water-Relations of the British Cribellate Spiders of the genus *Ciniflo. J. Linn. Soc. Zool.,* XLIII, 43.

DUFFEY, E. (1956). Aerial Dispersal in a known Spider Population. *J. Anim. Ecol.* 25.

ENOCK, F. (1885). The Life-History of *Atypus piceus. Trans. Ent. Soc. Lond.*

(1892). Additional Notes and Observations on the Life-History of *Atypus piceus. Trans. Ent. Soc. Lond.*

FABRE, J. H. (1912). The Life of the Spider. (Translated by A. Teixeira de Mattos).

FORBES, Ulrica. (1956). Sunday Express, Aug. 12.

GABRITSCHEVSKY, E. (1927). Experiments on Colour Changes and Regeneration in the Crab Spider, *Misumena vatia. Journ. Exper. Zool. Philad,* 47.

GERHARDT, U. (1924). Weitere studien über die Biologie der Spinnen. *Arch. Naturges.,* 90a.

(1926). Weitere Untersuchungen zur Biologie der Spinnen. *Z. Morph. Ökol. Tiere,* 6.

(1927). Neue biologische Untersuchungen an einkeimischen und auslandischen Spinnen. *Z. Morph. Ökol. Tiere,* 8.

(1928). Biologische Studien an griechischen, carsischen und deutschen Spinnen. *Z. Morph. Ökol. Tiere.* 10.

(1929). Zur vergleichenden Sexualbiologie primitiver spinnen. *Z. Morph. Ökol. Tiere.* 14.

(1930). Biologische Untersuchungen an südfranzosischen spinnen. *Z. Morph. Ökol. Tiere,* 19.

(1933). Neue Untersuchangen zur Sexualbiologie der Spinnen. *Z. Morph. Ökol. Tiere.* 27.

GERTSCH, W. J. (1949). American Spiders. New York.

GORVETT, H. (1956). Tegumental Glands and Terrestrial Life in Woodlice. *Proc. Zool. Soc. Lond.* 126 (2).

HARM, M. (1931). Beiträge zur Kenntnis des Baues, der Funktion und der

Entwicklung des akzessorischen Kopulationsorgans von Segestria bavarica C. L. Koch. *Z. Morph. Ökol. Tiere,* 22 (4).

HINGSTON, R. W. G. (1920). A Naturalist in Himalaya. London.

(1928). Problems of Instinct and Intelligence. London.

HIRST, A. S. (1923). On some Arachnid remains from the Old Red Sandstone. *Ann. Mag. Nat. Hist.* (9) 12.

HOLM, A. (1938). Beitrage zur Biologie der Theridiiden. *Festchrift E. Strand,* 5.

HOLZAPFEL, M. (1933). Die Bedeutung der Netzstarrheit fur die Orientierung der Trichterspinne Agelena labyrinthica. *Rev. suisse Zool.* 40.

HOOKE, R. (1665). Micrographia. Royal Society, London.

KASTON, B. J. (1948). Spiders of Connecticut. *State Geological and Nat. Hist. Survey. Bull.* 70.

KIRBY, W. (1835). History, Habits and Instincts of Animals. *Bridgewater Treatise,* 7.

LOCKET, G. H. (1926). Mating Habits of some Web-Spinning Spiders. *Proc. Zool. Soc.* (4).

LOCKET, G. H. and MILLIDGE, A. F. (1951–53). British Spiders, 2 vols. *Ray Society,* London.

MARPLES, M. J. and B. J. (1937). Note on the Spiders Hyptiotes paradoxus and Cyclosa conica. *Proc. Zool. Soc.* (A) 107.

MILLOT, J. (1949). Araneae and other Orders in 'Traité de Zoologie'. Paris.

MILLOT, J. (1929). Sur la glande cephalothoracique d'une Araignée (*Scytodes thoracica* Latr.) *C.R.Acad. sci.,* 189.

MONTEROSSO, B. (1928). Note araneologiche sur la biologia degli Scitodidi e la ghiandola glutinifera di essi. *Arch. Zool. Ital.,* 12 (1).

NIELSEN E. (1932). The Biology of Spiders. Vol. 1 in English summarising Vol. 2 in Danish. Copenhagen.

NORGAARD, E. (1941). On the Biology of Eresus niger Pet. *Ent. Medd.,* 22 (2).

OPIE, I. and P. (1951). The Oxford Dictionary of Nursery Rhymes. Oxford.

PALMGREN, P. (1936). Experimentelle Untersuchungen über die Function der Trichobothrien bei Tegenaria derhami Scop. *Act. Zool. Fenn.,* 19.

PETERS, H. (1933). Weitere Untersuchungen uber die Fanghandlung der Kreuzspinne. *Z. vergl. Physiol.* 19.

(1933). Kleine Beiträge zur Biologie der Kreuzspinne. *Z. Morph. Ökol. Tiere.* 26.

PETCH, R. (1948). A Revised List of British Entomogenous Fungi. *Trans. Brit. Mycol. Soc.,* 31.

PETRUNKEVITCH, A. (1942). A Study of Amber Spiders. *Trans. Connect. Acad. Arts Sci.,* 34.

(1949). A Study of Palaeozoic Arachnida. *Trans. Connect. Acad. Arts Sci.,* 37.

(1950). Baltic Amber Spiders in the Museum of Comparative Zoology. *Bull. Mus. Comp. Zool. Harvard*, 103.

PICKARD-CAMBRIDGE, O. (1879–81). The Spiders of Dorset.

POWER, H. (1664). Experimental Philosophy. London.

POWER, M. E. (1945). Sir Christopher Wren and the Micrographia. *Trans. Connect. Acad. Arts Sci.*, 36.

RAW, F. (1957). Origin of Chelicerates. *J. Palaeont.*, 31.

REIMOSER, E. (1934). The Spiders of Krakatau. *Proc. Zool. Soc. Lond.*

SAVORY, T. (1928). The Biology of Spiders. London.

(1935). The Arachnida. London.

(1936). Mechanistic Biology and Animal Behaviour. London.

(1952). The Spider's Web. London.

SCHNEIDER, A. (1892). *Tabl. zool.* 2.

SHEPPARD, P. M. (1958). Natural Selection and Heredity (Chap. 4).

SPRAT, T. (1667). History of the Royal Society, for the improving of natural knowledge. London.

S.S. (1868). The Gossamer. *Science Gossip.*

TILQUIN, A. (1942). La Toile geometrique des Araignées, Paris.

WARBURTON, C. (1890). The Spinning Apparatus of Geometric Spiders. *Quart. J. Micr. Sci.*, 31.

(1912). Spiders. Cambridge.

WIEHLE, H. (1927). Beiträge zur Kenntnis des Radnetzbaues der Epeiriden, Tetragnathiden und Uloboriden. *Z. Morph. Ökol. Tiere*, 8.

(1931). Neue Beiträge zur Kenntnis des Fanggewebes der Spinnen aus den Familien Argiopidae, Uloboridae und Theridiidae. *Z. Morph. Ökol. Tiere*, 22.

WITT, P. N. (1949). Verschiedene Wirkung von Coffein und Pervitin auf den Netzbau der Spinne. *Helv. Phys. Acta* 7, p. 65.

(1952). Ein einfaches prinzip zur deutung einiger proportionen im spinnennetz. *Behaviour*, Vol. 4, pp. 172–189.

WOLFF, D. and HEMPEL, U. (1951). Versuche über die Beeinflussung des Netzbaues von Zilla x-natata durch Pervitin, Scopolamin und Strychnin. *Zschr. f. vergl. Physiol.* 33, p. 497.

YOSHIKURA, M. (1954). Embryological Studies on the Liphistiid Spider, *Heptathela kimurai*. *Kumamoto J. Sci.*, B (3).

INDEX

Illustrations are in bold type and these are listed first. Where a subject is dealt with, like mating habits, under each of the 24 families in their respective chapters, the pages are not all indexed though examples may be provided.